Strange
Doorways
PAUL BEARDSLEY
Neosome
Productions

Strange Doorways

by

Paul Beardsley

Strange Doorways

This version first published in the UK in 2024

by Neosome Ltd.

ISBN HB: 9781739349318

10 9 8 7 6 5 4 3 2 1

Contents

Prologue

Guildford, October 1994

One evening after a demanding day at my new job I fell asleep in front of the TV and dreamed a vivid dream. I was back in my room at the University of Surrey. It was the start of a new academic year, and my suitcase was lying open on the bed, waiting for me to unpack it. The room was much as I remembered, except for the addition of a second window which they must have put in during the summer.

They had left the original window alone. It was the typical sash type. I had to lean over my desk to slide it up or down, and whenever I did it creaked loudly. I was on the ground floor so I had to latch it shut if I went out. It gave me a good view of a well-used path that crossed the campus; I was often distracted from my studies when certain students passed by.

But it was the new window that demanded my attention, because it made no sense. They had put it high up in one of the interior walls, the one my room shared with the stairwell, so that it overlooked my bed. It was plate glass, about three feet across and two feet high.

For several moments I just stared in disbelief. What in God's name were they thinking? Anyone going up or down the stairs would have a clear view of the inside of my room! This had to be some mistake. I went out into the hall and partway up the stairs to check. No, there was no mistake - the window really was located just above the half-landing, and I could look down at the open suitcase on my bed.

This was my room, my haven, my secure place for the past year.

I hadn't even been consulted.

I willed myself to calmness. I was making too much of it. Site Services were always making arbitrary decisions, such as not turning on the central heating until a predetermined date, regardless of the actual temperature. The window was just one more example, and the remedy was really quite straightforward: I had merely to remember to keep the curtains closed. So I drew them closed.

It was only when I returned to my room that it occurred to me that the curtains were on the stairwell side of the window.

*

I was woken by the phone ringing, but it stopped before I was out of my armchair. My mother had answered it on the upstairs extension, I guessed; she was doing the household finances in the study. It was an autumnal evening, and rain was lashing against the windows. I listened keenly, hoping the phone call was for me, hoping my mother would call down the stairs to tell me it was Sarah.

The rain was actually rather pleasant to listen to, although I doubted Sarah would have agreed. She had been sent on a team-building exercise earlier in the week; she hadn't known what it entailed, but suspected it involved being outdoors. I imagined her in a phone box in some dark and remote place, soaked to the skin and miserable as she pushed coins into the slot.

When half a minute had passed without my mother calling me, it was clear that it was not Sarah. I sat back down, picked up the copy of *Auto Trader* that had slipped off my lap onto the floor, and resumed my search for an affordable car. But my mind wasn't really on it. I was distracted by the dream. University had been a great time in my life, but it had finished three months ago. I had moved on. I had a job at Guildford Borough Council, which is where I met Sarah, and was now thinking about moving out of my parents' house - depending, largely, on how serious things were getting. Since meeting her, I had hardly thought about my life as a student.

Fully five minutes after the phone had first rung, I heard my mother calling down the stairs. "Phi-lip!" She said something else I couldn't make out so I went out into the hall.

"What did you say?"

"I said Dawn's on the phone. And she's dying to see you."

"*Dawn*? Seriously? What the hell is *she* phoning me for?"

Dawn had been in the year below me at university. We had been "an item," as she liked to put it, throughout most of my final year. But surely she didn't think we were *still* an item? Not waiting for an answer, I picked up the extension in the hall.

"Hello?"

Dawn greeted me with gushing enthusiasm. She was calling from one of the pay phones on the university campus, having just got back about an hour ago. I imagined her soaked by the rain in her short run across the open space, strands of hair stuck to her face, her makeup running, a large drip hanging under her nose. I contrasted this image with my earlier one of Sarah; she looked *good* in the rain. Dawn could not speak for long, because she had used up most of her change talking to my mother. Once she had explained all this she asked, "So when am I going to see you?"

I had no idea what to say to this. We had never formally split up, but there had been an unspoken agreement – at least that's how I had taken it. I thought back to the last day of my final term – a recent enough memory at the time, but one which now plays in my mind like an old cine film: my fellow students (looking amusingly young now) clearing out rooms, gathering on the campus, waiting with bags and cases while parents arrived in their cars to take them home. The farewells, the hugs, in some cases the tears, and the exchange of addresses and promises to keep in touch. That was when Dawn had asked me if I would be coming to stay at the farmhouse over the summer, as I had over the Easter break and the Christmas break before that.

She hadn't seemed unduly disappointed when I told her I was too busy. She knew I was starting a job at the Council; I explained that I wanted to get myself properly established before I started taking my annual leave. And that seemed to be an end to it. I contacted her a couple of weeks after that and sent her an invitation to my graduation ceremony (which she couldn't make), but as the weeks went by and our communication dwindled to nothing, I assumed she was as content as I was to let things quietly fade away. By then I had met Sarah Compton in the Housing Department.

"Philip?" Dawn's voice was insistent, and whiney. "Are you still there?"

"Sorry, I was thinking. I'm a bit busy tomorrow evening."

"What about Thursday then? It's Disco Night in the Union Bar!"

I winced. "I'd... I'd *really* rather not, Dawn."

"You'd rather not what, Philip?" She had already switched to her *I hope you're not going to upset me* tone.

I could have told her there and then that we had long ago stopped being "an item." But perhaps she realised. Perhaps she just wanted to meet up for old times' sake. And if she *didn't* realise... Well, it was only right and proper that I put her straight. Not on the phone, certainly not when her money was going to run out in the next few seconds. So I quickly suggested we meet for dinner at 7.30 on Friday evening at the *Indian Cottage.* It was a place I frequently visited, with friends, family, and, most recently, Sarah Compton.

"Friday, 7.30," Dawn repeated.

"Yes."

"You *will* be there?"

"I'll be there."

"You promise?"

"Of course I do."

And then her money ran out.

*

Sarah phoned me later that evening, not from a remote phone box as it turned out, but from a warm room in a convention hotel. She was having a good time, she said, apart from missing me, and apart from having to avoid the attentions of Creepy Martin from Accounts. In the past she had made it clear that she had no objections to me meeting up with old university friends, so I told her about my planned dinner with Dawn. I did not mention that Dawn and I had slept together for most of my final year, but, given that I had no intention of sleeping with Dawn ever again, I did not think it was that important. Even so, there was an element of guilt; I was at that age when absolute disclosure is considered a prerequisite of a meaningful relationship. And the more I thought about it, the more uncertain I felt. Towards the end, my relationship with Dawn had been nothing more than habit and convenience – at least that's how I saw it. But what if Dawn had seen it as something more?

After some consideration I decided I was taking the matter far too seriously. It was hardly of Earth-shattering importance, and whatever was going through Dawn's mind right now, it would all be sorted out in three days' time. In the meantime, I told myself, I was not going to lose any sleep over it.

As it turned out, I was quite wrong about that.

*

Everyone knows about insomnia dreams. Everyone who's ever lain awake watching the digital clock on the bedside table as the glowing display marks the diminishing number of hours left for sleep: 3am, 4am, 5am. The dawn chorus begins, there's the intermittent electric hum of a milk float as the milkman does his round, and through the gap in the curtains the sky begins to lighten. That is when the tiredness really kicks in. It is the beginning of a demanding new day, and you do not know how you are going to cope because you have not slept *at all*.

And yet you know that simply cannot be true. Because if you did not sleep *at all*, how is it that you can remember dreaming?

*

That night, I found myself lying awake and thinking about that absurd window. Had it really been there all along and I'd somehow failed to notice it? Was that even possible? Did other students – and one or two lecturers I could think of – open the curtains and look in on Dawn and me as we had sex, watching the sad progression from love's athletic passion to drunken fumbling and mechanical misplaced duty? Or was it a dream metaphor for an all-seeing God? It was fruitless to speculate, but that didn't stop me.

I remember one insomnia dream from that night. It was a memory-dream from very early childhood. I was in a butcher's shop with my grandfather, and we were queuing at the counter. I was too small to see over the counter, but the door under the flap was open, and through it I could see an interior door that had also been left open and which led to a hallway. This hallway intrigued me, because it looked similar to the one in our house.

There was wallpaper on the walls, a table with a tall vase and a telephone on it, and stairs. And yet it was in a butcher's! Intrigued by the realisation that the shop was part of someone's home, I walked under the counter flap and made for the interior door to get a closer look. But before I reached it I was stopped by a large man in an apron. He said, "These doorways are not meant for you, son."

I was a wreck the next morning. I missed my usual train, and got into work twelve minutes late. Fortunately Amanda, my line manager, was away on the same team-building exercise as Sarah, and she had not given me much to get on with. Still, the day dragged unbearably while I sat stiffly at my desk, drinking vending machine coffee and trying not to nod off. On the train home I set my watch alarm, afraid I might fall asleep and miss my stop. I thought about the dream, and the peculiar phrase the butcher had used. I was certain I was remembering the actual wording I had heard as a child: *These doorways are not meant for you.*

I didn't want a repeat of Tuesday night, so that evening I did some exercises, drank hot milk, and found some tranquilisers in the medicine cabinet in the bathroom – well past their expiry date, as it happened. I watched *Panorama* on the little TV on the chest of drawers in my bedroom and patiently waited for sleep to find me. Sleep never came looking.

At 3am I paced around the house, trying to be quiet so as not to awaken my parents. Rain was battering against the windows again; otherwise I might have gone out for a walk. There was no place I wanted to go, I just wanted to get away from my unsleeping self. On inspiration I dug out a copy of my final year dissertation and sat at the large oak table in the kitchen to read it. I had once joked that it was a guaranteed cure for insomnia; now was the time to put that claim to the test.

It was A4 in size, with a red cover, and big black letters which read *England: A History of Myth and the Myth of History: An Investigation by Philip A. Hamilton.* The pomposity of the title was deliberate – an attempt at irony – but looking at it now I could see how it just didn't work. I had used two colons and three different fonts for no reason other than that I could. Opening it up, I saw that I had used even more fonts on the contents page. What was I thinking? What the *hell* was I thinking? Sitting under the strip light, I leafed through the pages and found myself astonished and dismayed by what I had written. The opportunities I had missed to say something truly insightful! I'd hardly understood myth at all, and my concept of history was nebulous and shallow. Why hadn't I seen this four months ago before I submitted it for marking? Why was I seeing it *now*?

This time, my insomnia dreams were fleeting, disconnected things. Nothing really stood out except for a brief scene in which I was overcome with sorrow as I wandered alone through a field in the direction of a ruined abbey. It was early morning; a dew-drenched spider's web in one of the abbey windows caught the rising sun. I was being followed, but not in a threatening way.

Whenever I turned around my pursuer was nowhere to be seen but as soon as I faced forward again the pursuit resumed. It might have been a once-loved dog from my childhood, old now and neglected, willing to forgive me for abandoning it if only we could be together again for its last days. I walked determinedly on.

In reality I had never owned a dog.

Thursday's was the third and final sleepless night. I lay in bed dwelling on the mistakes I had made. Going to a university less than half an hour's train journey from home had seemed like a good idea because it meant I was far away enough to be independent, while at the same time I could take my laundry home at the weekends and take friends home to enjoy my mother's excellent cooking. But now it all seemed stupid. Getting into a heavy relationship with someone in the year below me, someone who would still be in the area for a year after I'd moved on, stupid. Failing to make a clean break with her. Stupid! Failing to sort it out when she phoned on Tuesday, thus depriving myself of three nights of sleep. *Stupid!* Further stupid thoughts arose as if in a conscious effort to keep sleep away. What if she brought her brothers along? No she wouldn't, she absolutely wouldn't. But what if they came along anyway, just in case?

Dawn had two older brothers called William and Benjamin. She called them Bill and Ben; I did not. The first time I saw them I thought they looked like nightclub bouncers; as it turned out, they did occasionally moonlight at the Nocturne Club near Chichester, but by day they were builders. When I stayed at the farm house they never made eye contact with me, and rarely addressed me directly, or by name. Conversations with them typically began and ended with a peremptory, "You're wanted in the dining room," "Mother wants to know how long you're staying," or "Our sister doesn't like you doing that." At the end of my last visit William had driven me back to the train station in Chichester; that had been the most interminable fifteen minutes of my life.

They weren't going to be at the restaurant. William would never eat Indian food; even given an English option, he wouldn't be able to tolerate the smell. Or the fact that the staff had a different skin colour to his own.

This time I dreamed I was in a vast graveyard that seemed to extend in every direction I could see. Not that I could see very far; the sunlight was so bright I could barely open my eyes. I was walking towards a sarcophagus adorned with a larger-than-life stone angel. A human figure sat on the flat slab beside it, and as my eyes finally began to adjust I recognised Dawn's features. Her raven-black hair reached below her shoulders, and she was slimmer than I remembered. Not slim; *thin* – bordering on anorexic. When she saw me she jumped off the sarcophagus. "You came!" she cried, and ran into my arms. I hugged her tightly, unwilling ever to let her go. I was overcome with emotion once again, and so was she.

Friday was hell. I was so tired I could taste it: a metallic taste at the back of my tongue. When I got home I ran myself a bath. The water was painfully hot and I hadn't left enough room to add cold water so I had to let some go down the plug hole. My parents didn't approve of wasting hot water. It took me twenty minutes of adjustment and acclimatisation before it was bearable. Once in, I found myself dozing off. Sleep had found me at last.

It was over all too soon. I was suddenly aware of my mother hammering on the bathroom door, asking me if I realised how late it was. The bath water had gone cold.

I had missed the train so I had to take a taxi. I resented the unnecessary expense. It was gone eight o'clock when I finally arrived at the *Indian Cottage* – half an hour later than promised. In my rush I had forgotten my watch but there was a large clock in the seating area where people usually waited to collect their takeaway meals. Dawn was sitting on a high stool under the clock, waiting for me. The way she sat reminded me of the last of the insomnia dreams; she jumped up, cried, "Philip, you came!" and ran into my arms. By now I had half convinced myself that this meeting really was for old times' sake, so I was a little startled when she kissed me full on the mouth, twice. Dawn was affectionate by nature, I reminded myself, and we *had* been close, but still I felt uneasy.

We were seated at the table by the fish tank. Dawn had her back to it. A waiter brought us drinks and poppadums; Dawn had ordered them before my arrival. She raised her glass – mineral water instead of her usual white wine – and said, “To another year.”

Another year? Surely she wasn’t thinking... On impulse I raised my own glass and said, “Your *final* year.” She might have frowned at my deliberate misinterpretation, but we clinked glasses and sipped our drinks.

“So, how’s it going?” I asked.

“I’m doing fine, Philip. Just fine.”

The waiter returned to take our order. I looked across the table at Dawn as she scrutinised the menu. She was not *quite* the woman in the dream after all. Her raven-black hair had been cropped short since our last meeting, and she had put on weight; her black dress no longer flattered her. When she had finished reading the menu in its entirety, she decided on chicken tikka massala. She always decided on chicken tikka massala. I told the waiter I would have a meat vindaloo. Dawn raised an eyebrow.

“You’ll stink of garlic.”

“Yes, I expect I will.”

She gave me a look, opened her mouth to speak, then said nothing. She poked a hole in the middle of a plain poppadom, clearly expecting it to break into four equal pieces. It did not; they *do* not. Yet still she expected it to happen every time we ate Indian food. I remembered finding it quite charming the first time we'd had Indian together, but quickly came to find it irritating. This time I found it both irritating and *disturbing*, but I could not say why. I was tired, desperately horribly tired, and finding it hard to think. I found myself mesmerised by the blue and yellow tropical fish behind Dawn, and the unending stream of bubbles from the air pump. It was important that I stay focused, that I mention Sarah soon, but it had to come out naturally. I wasn't here to put her down.

She was talking again.

"Do you remember Roger and Cynthia?" she asked as she piled chutney onto a poppadom fragment. I did, vaguely. "They're in my tutor group now. Isn't that great? And before you ask, they're back together too."

"Too"? What did that "too" mean? As well as being in her tutor group, or as well as us? "Listen Dawn, I think we need to be clear..."

She waved a hand dismissively and talked over me. "You know, it was such a *sensible* decision not to meet up over the holiday. You had your job, I had my final year dissertation to think about. Now I'll be the first to admit it, it hasn't been easy, but I don't think it's done *either* of us any harm in the long run."

"What in God's name are you talking about?" I demanded. But she had crammed the piled poppadom fragment into her mouth; she was waving both her hands near her mouth to indicate that she could not speak for the moment.

And then I remembered the first time I had seen her poke a hole in a poppadom. It had been here, in this restaurant, at this very *table*. She had sat with her back to the fish tank that time too. It had been our first evening out. It had been a year ago to the day.

She thought we were celebrating our first anniversary. I rose abruptly, causing our drinks to spill and nearly knocking my chair over. She looked up at me, concerned. She gulped down the laden poppadum fragment and said, "What's the matter, Philip? You look awful!"

"I'm... I'm just tired," I muttered. "I haven't been sleeping. I just need... Look, will you excuse me?"

The *Indian Cottage* was legendary for the distance between the main restaurant and the toilets. I went through a swing door with a circular frosted glass window in it, down a winding flight of wooden steps, through a door and then along a very long corridor. It was carpeted, with pictures on the left hand wall, mostly scenes from the

Arthurian legends for some reason. The corridor dog-legged. I passed an open cupboard filled from floor to ceiling with large bottles of bleach. In the opposite wall there was a decrepit wooden door that I supposed led to steps up to street level – I could see the glow of a street lamp through the grimy glass. There was no sound except the noise of traffic. On impulse I checked the door. I seriously considered using it to make a quick getaway. I would have done it, I really would, and hang the shame and consequences. But it was locked, and not so decrepit that I could have easily kicked it open.

The lighting was poor at the end of the corridor. I went through another swing door into the anteroom, which was in complete darkness. I groped for a light switch, but found none, and assumed the bulb must have gone. I could not remember which side of the anteroom the men's toilets were on and there was not enough light from the corridor for me to see the doors, let alone the signs on them. I reached to the left. My fingers touched wood. Door or panelling? I suspected the latter, but pushed anyway. It swung open on stiff hinges.

Beyond it was another corridor, somewhat narrower than the first, with lights set in the walls rather than the ceiling. I was intrigued, because I did not remember this corridor at all. The glow from the wall lights dimly illuminated the little anteroom; I could see now that the men's toilet was on the right as I had come in, the ladies' straight ahead, and there was a switch in the corner between them. I flicked the switch, and the anteroom light came on. The thing I had pushed open was a hinged panel that took up the whole of the left wall; it had a row of coat hooks along the top as if to complete its disguise.

A curious thing to find, but I had other things on my mind.

In the privacy of the toilet cubicle I thought about the situation I had got myself into. If only I'd told Dawn I was seeing someone else when she'd phoned! All this "doing the right thing" business was adolescent nonsense, and it hadn't done either of us any favours. I was twenty-two, for God's sake. I wasn't a student any more, I wasn't a lovesick *teenager*, I was an adult with a reasonably good job and in a new relationship that looked as if it might be going somewhere.

Whatever Dawn was thinking, it was time to put her straight. And it didn't even need to be a big deal. Whatever she'd been saying in the restaurant, Dawn must have known it was all over; she was clinging on to a dead relationship. Well, one way or another, her clinging would end tonight. I splashed cold water on my face so that I was a bit more awake, and left the toilet.

And yet despite my desire to settle the matter as quickly as possible, I did not head directly back to the restaurant. I was curious about that corridor with the lights in the walls. Hinged panelling clearly qualified as a secret door - one I must have passed on a dozen, two dozen occasions with no inkling it was there. If I hadn't been disoriented and groping in the dark, I would still have been none the wiser.

Did the restaurant owners even know about it?

I would have preferred to investigate it in other circumstances – ones in which I was neither desperately tired nor facing the prospect of an unpleasant scene – but I was not sure I would get another opportunity. The owners might wallpaper over the panelling, or they might provide new customer toilets closer to the actual restaurant and prevent access to these ones. Or – and this was my irrational yet strangely compelling concern – the corridor might not *be* there next time.

I pushed the panelling again. It swung open as before. This time I stepped across the threshold and onto the thin grey carpet. I was through the secret door, inside the hidden corridor. The secret door swung closed behind me. The walls were tiled. Old, small white tiles that were a little grimy to the touch. The light fittings were circular, recessed at around chest height. I passed them at regular intervals as I walked, wondering what I had discovered. Was this a network of underground corridors that criss-crossed Guildford? The main corridor must already have taken me to the far side of the block of shops and houses; perhaps this one led under the road and into another block altogether. Maybe I would find an exit.

Further on, the light fittings became more infrequent. At first I thought they were more widely spaced, but several were no longer lit, or were made dim by their covering of grime and old cobwebs. I nearly hit my head on some low ducting. The corridor turned at right angles to the right. There were steps leading down. I hesitated, feeling I was getting further and further away from the normal world. Then I descended.

The gloom at the bottom of the steps was more oppressive, even though my eyes had had time to adjust. One wall light was covered with so many layers of cobwebs that it was barely visible. I found a pen in my pocket and used it to tear a hole in the layers. As soon as I did this I became aware of tiny scuttling movements along the wall nearby, and I was unnerved by the impression of a group of spiders cooperating to undo the damage I had done in order to cover the light once more. I was about to head back when I noticed a flickering rectangle of light on the wall ahead. Curious, I approached.

There was an open door in the opposite wall, and beyond it, a room. A large colour television balanced on an old dresser was the source of the flickering light, and a hard-faced bald man sat on an old settee watched it as he ate food from a plastic tray. He wasn't aware of me at first, and for a few moments I stood in the doorway, staring in fascination at the TV screen.

It showed a tube station – Earls Court according to the sign – and forty or fifty commuters. Nearly all the commuters, men and women alike, were dressed in what appeared to be Beefeater uniforms. The voice of a newsreader was saying, "...has described as 'baseless' the rumour that slithermen have been sighted within fifteen rem of London Prime. We spoke to passengers on the..." Then the man on the settee noticed me standing in the doorway. He glared at me, leaned over and slammed the door in my face.

Hurriedly I retreated up the stairs and headed back the way I had come. Perhaps my eyes had been dazzled by the TV, because the gloom seemed more oppressive than before, and when I touched one of the walls, the grime seemed thicker. A fresh cobweb broke against my face, and a little further on, another. I shuddered and brushed at my face and hair.

Under the fear and disgust and overwhelming tiredness, my mind was working overtime. What had I seen on that television? Where was it being broadcast from? Because whatever else was going on, I was sure of two things. For one, the news item was not any kind of spoof. For another, whatever it said on that tube station wall, it was not *our* Earls Court.

When I got back to the restaurant, Dawn was in tears. One of the waiters was sitting with her, consoling her; he looked at me coldly as I returned, and left the table to allow our drama to play out. Our food had been served. My rice had gone cold and my meat vindaloo had dried out on the hotplate. I could not believe it; I had been gone ten minutes, fifteen at the very most.

Had I fallen asleep in the toilet cubicle? Had I dreamt about the corridor? I glanced at the big clock in the waiting area and saw that it was gone half past nine. And yet Dawn was still here.

"I thought you'd left me," she said, still sobbing. Then her self-pity swiftly changed to anger, as it so often did. "Where the hell have you been?" I was about to tell her exactly what had happened, exactly what I had seen. She cut me off to spell out what should have been obvious. She was pregnant.

Part 1. Insomnia Dreams

"These doorways are not meant for you."

Chapter 1. It's Not Over

Woking, December 2005

It wasn't until we saw the Martian war machine that I decided the day hadn't been a complete waste of time

Miss Havers and I had slipped out of the teachers' conference early, and were taking a shortcut back to Woking Station, one that a local delegate had recommended. We were laughing about some stupid stuff only we found funny when we emerged from a side street into the town, and that's when we saw it: a malevolent-looking steel tripod about twenty feet high towering over us against the dark sky of a late afternoon in winter. It had a bulbous body, and resembled a giant three-legged harvestman spider pausing in its spindly walk.

Miss Havers froze mid-sentence, grabbed my arm and said, "What in God's name is *that*?"

For one ludicrous moment I was as startled as she was. This was wrong, this didn't belong, not here in the real world. And then the moment passed and I knew exactly what it was. It was a well-known landmark; I'd even seen a news item about it. "It's a Martian war machine for goodness sake," I said in a deliberately condescending tone, "what do you *think* it is?"

"A *what*?"

"A Martian war machine."

"Martian? Come now, Mr Hamilton. They've *been* to Mars. They sent... *rockets* up and they sent back pictures and things. If they'd found any Martians, they... Well, they would have *said*."

"It's from *The War of the Worlds*," I explained with exaggerated patience. She gave me a blank look. "The novel by H.G. Wells," I added. Still she looked blank. "You know – fiction?"

"Ah!" she said, realisation dawning. "You mean that film with Tom Cruise."

I exhaled, exasperated.

“Yes of course. That film with Tom Cruise.”

“So what’s it doing here?”

“It’s art. This is where the Martians originally landed, in the book, so the local council decided to commemorate it by building...” Then the penny dropped. “Hang on a minute. You teach English Literature. How can an English Literature teacher not have heard of H.G. Wells?”

She grinned.

“Hook, line and sinker, Mr Hamilton. Some days you're just too easy.” Still holding my arm she pulled me towards it. “Come on, let’s get some photos.”

“Photos? You brought a camera?”

She narrowed her eyes. “Have you even *looked* at your mobile since you bought it?”

*

On the crowded train back to Portsmouth, Miss Havers showed me how to scroll through the photographs we had taken: the war machine against the dark sky, the war machine reflected in a nearby shop front, a perspective view up one of its legs, a close-up of Miss Havers screaming in terror, another of me screaming in terror, and so on.

“Kirsty's going to love this,” I said.

“What, the fact you've finally joined the twenty-first century and bought yourself a mobile phone?”

“Touché!” It wasn't what I meant, of course, but it was true enough. All her friends' parents had a mobile; most of her *friends* had one. “No, I mean the pictures. She read *War of the Worlds* last year. Won an Advanced Reader sticker for it.”

“Really? She's a very bright girl, your daughter. Is it your weekend with her?”

I nodded. “I'm picking her up when we get back. Assuming my car has passed its MOT, that is. Tomorrow morning I'm taking her to archery club. It's kind of a surprise.”

“*Kind* of a surprise? How can it be kind of a surprise? Surely it either is one or it isn't.”

“Well she's expecting it because I promised to take her as soon as her age was in double figures.”

Miss Havers frowned. “I thought she turned ten last April.”

“Yes, that's what makes it kind of a surprise. You see, I had too much on in April. Too much on in May as well. But she didn't say anything, and eventually I found out she thought double figures meant both digits the same - you know, eleven, twenty-two, thirty-three and so on.”

“And you've let her continue believing that? Mr Hamilton, you are a terrible father!”

“Well obviously I *will* put her right, but in the meantime it's given me a breathing space. Tomorrow she'll think she's getting her surprise four months early rather than eight months late.” I grinned. “That's what I call a win-win situation.”

She gave me a disapproving look over her glasses, the one she usually reserved for making her pupils wither.

“So what have you got planned for the weekend?” I asked. In reply she took out her own mobile and showed me a picture of her new partner - very pretty, fifteen years her junior, and mad on football. “We're going to Fratton Park to watch a bunch of grown men kicking a ball around for an hour. I expect I'll enjoy every second of it.”

“Ninety minutes,” I said.

“What?”

“Football matches last ninety minutes. Not just an hour. It’s kind of a tradition.”

“Oh, sweet Jesus.”

*

Our train pulled in at Portsmouth & Southsea Station a little after five o'clock. We checked the arrival times, and came to the conclusion that the colleagues of ours who had not sneaked out early were more than an hour behind us.

“We’re a pair of truants, Miss Havers,” I said.

“Not that I could possibly approve, Mr Hamilton, but it does add a certain *piquancy* to the start of the weekend, doesn’t it?”

We called in at the garage at the end of my road. To my relief my Fiesta had passed its MOT. I didn't like having to ask Dawn's brothers to bring Kirsty over at the best of times, and this was not the best of times. After dropping Miss Havers off at her house I headed for Singleton to collect my daughter.

*

I recalled the first occasion she came to stay. Kirsty's grandmother had brought her in her specially adapted Land Rover. It was a Friday evening and the weather was foul. I invited Mrs Price in while Kirsty explored her new home-from-home. Mrs Price had had to park some distance from the house, so I helped her into her wheelchair and held an umbrella over her as she wheeled herself along the pavement and up the short path to my front door. We sat at the kitchen table while Kirsty carried her little suitcase up to her new bedroom. Mrs Price and I talked briefly about the house itself, notably how well placed it was for Southsea Grammar, which was less than twenty minutes’ walk away. We talked briefly about my new teaching job that was to begin in September, and how I would spend the intervening time putting my DIY skills to good use. The house needed a lot of work.

It was a companionable few minutes for the most part, during which we talked only of safe and neutral matters, except for one moment when Mrs Price found herself blurting out, “How did it ever get to this stage?" I could think of nothing to say to that; the real mystery was how we had lasted eight years.

After that first time, the arthritis got so bad that Mrs Price could no longer drive. If I didn't collect Kirsty myself, one of Dawn's brothers would bring her over. Never Dawn herself. Benjamin would acknowledge me with a curt nod from the driver's seat when he was on his own. William did not even extend me that courtesy. Sometimes he would sound the horn as soon as Kirsty had disembarked with her suitcase, then drive away as soon as he saw me appear at the front door to let her in.

In fact there was one occasion when William *did* get out of his car to talk to me. It was the last time he'd driven over, three months ago. My next door neighbours, a Jamaican couple, had a daughter, Yasmin, who was Kirsty's age. Yasmin had come out of her house to greet Kirsty on her arrival, and the two children had embraced.

William drew me aside, as if to take me into his confidence, and said, "I don't want any arguments, but she's not to mix with the likes of *that*. You understand me?"

I replied, "Do you have a problem with her because she's black, or because she's deaf?"

William glared at me, said nothing more, and got back into his car, making the tyres screech as he pulled away.

*

I'd be borrowing Yasmin tomorrow for archery club. I often borrowed her. Two months ago we'd gone to Thorpe Park. She and Kirsty had sat in the back of the car in silence, a long silence interspersed with giggles. From time to time I'd look at the pair of them in the rear view mirror, chatting away to each other in British Sign Language.

I smiled at the memory as I came off the A27 at the Chichester roundabout. A song that I didn't like began playing on the radio, so I pushed a slightly stretched Blondie cassette into the player slot instead. Maybe when I could afford a new car I'd get one with a CD player, but until then I pretended the cassette player was my conscious decision to be retro. Kirsty pretended to believe me.

Before long I was on the country road to Singleton. The sky was clear and the stars were bright. I'd missed that since moving to Southsea, and I missed the time when I saw Kirsty every weekend, every day. For eight years, watching her grow had been a continuous process; now it was at discrete fortnightly intervals, and a lot could change in two weeks. She would be starting secondary school next September, and it wouldn't be long before she'd be interested in boys. After that, maybe the alternate weekend visits would become a duty, an imposition on her social life.

But it hadn't happened yet. Perhaps it wouldn't happen, not in any lasting sense at least. Kirsty and I had a bond. Among other things, she loved stories, and I loved telling them. On those occasions that I didn't collect or return her, she would complain that the journeys with Uncle Bill and Uncle Ben were boring because she never got stories out of them.

Last Halloween she had plonked herself on my lap after dinner and demanded a ghost story. I had delivered, and as luck would have it there was an eerie wind outside and an intermittent fault in the lighting which ramped up the atmosphere. At the end she looked me in the eye and said, "Daddy, that one was worthy of Cousin Martin." The highest accolade.

*

At the Price Estate I pulled up on the gravel drive alongside Dawn's Fiat Punto outside the barn conversion that had been my home for eight years. There were no other cars, which was good news: it meant neither of her brothers were home.

The security light came on and harshly illuminated the drive. I got out of my car. No light showed in any of the windows, not on the ground floor nor from either of the two dormers. I rang the bell anyway, but there was no answer. This wasn't unusual; Dawn and

Kirsty spent a lot of time in the main house, on account of Mrs Price's increased dependence. There had been talk of them moving in permanently and putting the barn conversion up for rent.

But something didn't feel right. All the windows were closed, even the small one in the cloakroom that had to be kept open whenever the tumble drier was on – as it invariably was on a Friday evening in winter. I looked at Dawn's car again. It looked more abandoned than parked. Come to think of it, I'd had that same thought last time I was here, a month ago. Had she not driven it in all that time?

After a long wait I rang the bell again. Still no answer. My sense of unease was out of all proportion to its cause. It was obvious that Dawn and Kirsty weren't in. I would find them in the main house with Mrs Price, along with the answers to this little mystery – if a change in the laundry routine and a car parked at an odd angle could even be called that. Still I hesitated, unable to draw my eyes away from the darkness visible through the frosted glass panes of the front door. I had known darkness in the eight years the place had been my home – there had been power cuts, and it was out in the country – but that had been a mere absence of light. This was something else, an altogether more *active* kind of darkness.

If I kept still long enough the security light would go off, my eyes would have time to adjust, and I'd see light leak out through gaps in the curtain if there was any. Or I could simply go in. The thought made me tingle; it would be like trespassing, but worse. I still had my own key – I pulled it out of my pocket, it was on a ring along with my other keys – and as far as I knew the lock hadn't been changed. I glanced over my shoulder in the direction of the main house, for all the world as if I was seriously considering it. Twenty metres away, Mrs Price sat in her wheelchair, watching me from the open front door. Even at that distance I must have looked furtive.

By the time I reached the main house Mrs Price had glided down the hall into the room they called the parlour. It had mismatched furniture and was never well lit. It always reminded me of the waiting room at the dentist's. My heart was now beating rapidly with the certainty that something was very wrong.

"Sit down, Philip," she commanded. I sat down in the gloom.

"What's going on, Mrs Price?"

"Benjamin called me on his mobile. He's in town with Dawn." She hesitated. "They've lost Kirsty."

"*Lost* her? What do you mean, *lost* her?"

"Now calm down, Philip, it's not a big drama, I'm sure she'll turn up soon. If everybody panicked every time their child wandered off for five minutes..."

"Where did they lose her?"

"They were in Chichester. Sit *down*, Philip. Please!"

It was only then that I saw the anxiety in her eyes. I'd got up again; I remained standing for a few moments, then complied. She began to explain. Benjamin and Dawn had picked Kirsty up after school and taken her to see the big school she'd be starting at next year – Chichester High, where I'd taught for five years. Afterwards they happened to bump into Megan Jeffries in the Chichester Gate car park. Megan Jeffries was an immensely popular girl and Kirsty was occasionally "in" with her crowd. Megan was having a birthday party in the Chichester Gate McDonald's, and one of her close friends had dropped out, so she invited Kirsty there and then to join them "to make up the numbers." So Benjamin and Dawn arranged to pick Kirsty up in an hour, and Benjamin phoned his mother to tell her to expect them back a bit later. But when they returned to the fast food restaurant at the appointed time, Kirsty was nowhere to be seen.

"Who was looking after the children?"

"Megan's parents, I would imagine."

I doubted that. Megan's father, maybe, but not both parents. I knew her father from parents' evenings. Roger Jeffries: nervous, insipid, always trying to break the tension that only he felt by making jokes only he laughed at. I had not met his wife, as she had never once attended - she had "more important" things to do, Jeffries would say with air quotes before forcing a chuckle. But ineffectual as he was, he was a father. Surely he couldn't have lost a child in his care in a restaurant?

"It's Whitby all over again," I said. "It's followed her. It's *found* her."

"What are you talking about, Philip? *What* has followed her? You're not making sense!"

"Whitby," I repeated in a whisper. I was shuddering uncontrollably now, acutely aware of how quickly my rationality had evaporated, and how I must have sounded. "Three, no four years ago. She went missing while we were staying at my cousin's. She turned up again eventually, obviously, but... there was *something there.* We didn't see it, none of us adults saw it, but it was definitely there. It tried to touch her. I thought it had got to her when I found her standing under the Whalebone Arch. She was a ghost, she was so pale..." The shuddering grew worse and then suddenly stopped. I was back in control. In my normal voice I said, "How long ago did she go missing?"

She looked at the clock on the mantelpiece. It was getting on for seven. "Half an hour ago, maybe forty minutes."

"You mean you don't know exactly? Why are we even dis*cussing* this? I've got to get over there."

Mrs Price shook her head. "No. They can sort it out. You would not be... welcome."

"Welcome? What's *that* got to do with it? I'm her *father* for God's sake! Look, we've got a special bond, Kirsty and me. I'll find her, like I found her in Whitby."

"Let me speak to Benjamin, see if he's got any news." She wheeled her chair over to the phone. She had to leaf through the address book with her arthritic, nicotine-stained fingers to find his mobile number, then, with equally painful slowness she dialled the number on the rotary dial. She waited a few moments, then grimaced and hung up. "His phone's switched off."

"I need to get over there," I said again.

"No! No, Philip, there's no point. If his phone is switched off it means he's driving. So he'll be on his way back here now."

"If he's on his way back, why didn't he phone to say he found her?"

"I don't know. Maybe the battery is flat, or maybe..." She broke off.

"Maybe what? Maybe he hasn't found her? Why would he be on his way back if he hasn't found her?"

"If he hadn't found her he'd have phoned." Aware of the inconsistency, she added, rather unconvincingly, "I'm sure of it."

"Doesn't Dawn have a mobile?"

"No."

So we waited. Silence filled the prolonged gaps between the loud ticks of the clock on the mantelpiece. The drive from Chichester Gate to the Price estate was twenty minutes, twenty five at most, and if Mrs Price was right they were already on their way. After some minutes Mrs Price asked me if I wanted anything to drink. My throat was parched, but I shook my head. She asked me if I was sure. Instead of answering, I said, "I love her *so much*."

Mrs Price smiled, a sorrowful, warm smile. "I know." She wiped the side of her face as if brushing away a tear; in the dimly lit room I could not be sure. "She feels exactly the same way about you. Despite everything."

I frowned, puzzled by her wording. She did get that I meant Kirsty, didn't she? I was about to respond when I heard the sound of a vehicle pulling up on the gravel drive. I hurried to the front door, Mrs Price following.

Outside, the night air had turned very cold. Dawn and Benjamin were emerging from the latter's black Mercedes. Kirsty was not with them; there was nobody in the back. In the glare of the security light, Dawn's makeup was smeared by her crying. She hurried towards me the way she used to when she wanted me to take her in my arms and tell her everything would be all right. She stopped abruptly, just out of reach, as if belatedly remembering that we didn't do that any more. Benjamin hung back.

"Where's Kirsty?" I demanded.

Dawn said, "Couldn't... find..."

"You couldn't *find* her? Why the hell did you leave Chichester without her?"

"The police said it would be... they would... I didn't feel well, Philip. I had to get... had to get home, had to... home... I..."

There was a screech of tyres and a spray of gravel as a second black Mercedes arrived on the drive. William's. Presumably Benjamin had briefed him and told him to get over here. William got out of his car, glaring at me as if I were an intruder they had caught on their land. He stalked towards me, pausing only when Benjamin put a hand on his arm. They stood behind their sister. Dawn and I faced each other in the freezing air, not close enough to touch. Mrs Price, in her wheelchair, was positioned in the doorway again. I'd married into this family. Kirsty was the only good thing that had resulted from that stupid decision I'd made a decade ago. And now...

"You've lost my daughter." I spoke quietly, unable to summon the anger I should be feeling. Then, with more force, "You've lost my *daughter*!

Dawn was speaking, or trying to.

"I can't, I cah-cah-cah-cah can't..."

And then she collapsed. I hadn't hit her, hadn't been close enough to hit her even if I did that sort of thing, had barely raised a hand in gesture, but her brothers moved in on me anyway. William first. He punched me in the stomach. I doubled up in pain. Benjamin got behind me, pinning my arms to my sides as William delivered a second sickening punch. He followed this with an undercut to my mouth. I spat blood onto his suede jacket.

After that there followed a slap, resoundingly loud. But I didn't feel this, I only heard it, and it was a moment or two before it registered that I was not the recipient. Dazed and surprised, I looked up. Mrs Price had got out of her wheelchair and she had walked. She delivered a second ferocious slap to her son. William turned, about to retaliate, realising his mistake just in time. Benjamin released me.

Mrs Price panted for a moment or two. I think William, Benjamin and I were all caught in the moment: she was standing, she had walked! But this was not some miraculous instance of healing. Far from it, she was in agony. Finally recovering her voice, she said,

"Look to your sister, you worthless, worthless creatures. She is having an epileptic seizure."

And so she was. This was new to me, something that must have started since the divorce. It explained why Benjamin had brought her home rather than remain in Chichester. She lay thrashing on the gravel uttering incoherent sounds, and for a moment I was afraid she would swallow her tongue – I wasn't sure if that was really a thing – but then Benjamin was kneeling beside her, attending to her. William was helping his mother back into her wheelchair. I remained in a crouch, afraid to straighten up and at a complete loss as to what to do. We should have been joining forces to find Kirsty, but it wasn't happening. What sort of people were they? What sort of people were Dawn's brothers? Their niece was missing, their sister was having a fit, and their first priority was to beat up the missing girl's father.

William turned back to me. For a moment I thought he was going to offer to help me up. He said, "Don't think this is over."

I spat blood again but it did not reach him this time. "You stupid savage," I said. "We should be looking for my daughter!"

"Your *daughter*?" He laughed unpleasantly. "*Your* daughter? Get this straight, you little shit. Kirsty is not your daughter. You're *nothing* to her."

He spoke in a low voice, but Benjamin heard. He looked up from where he was putting his rolled-up jacket under Dawn's head as a makeshift pillow.

"Mum's right, you really are a worthless fucking idiot, Bill," he said. "A worthless fucking *idiot*!"

William was stunned by Benjamin's words - whether by his brother's unprecedented anger towards him, or by the validity of the accusation, I could not tell. But were William's words true?

Kirsty was missing. That was what mattered. I could not, *would* not allow a taunt to distract me from this. But what if it were true? *What if it were true?* Dawn was still thrashing about on the gravel and Mrs Price was obviously suffering from her exertions. None of it was my problem. Forcing myself to get up, I staggered to my car. I got the door open, folded myself behind the steering wheel. For a moment my head swam from the pain in my mouth and stomach. It dimly occurred to me that I hadn't been in a fight since Year 8.

William's words, his taunt... that wasn't what was troubling me. It was Benjamin's reaction. Shock that William had let slip something he should never have. Key in ignition. Turn. Started first time. Thank god I'd had it serviced as well as MOTed. The Blondie track "Sunday Girl" came on, the tape so stretched now that Debbie Harry's voice had dropped an octave. In the rear view mirror I looked anew at the family I was no longer any part of. I sprayed gravel as I drove away.

I was never meant to find out.

*

Into the cold, starry night. Hardly anyone else on the road; no fast-approaching Mercedes headlights behind me, despite my looking out for them for the last ten minutes. Either William and Benjamin had taken the other route or they hadn't left the house.

I wasn't Kirsty's father. The thought was a recurring twinge in the back of my mind, as if it felt duty bound to keep reminding me. Maybe it wouldn't mean that much in the long term, maybe it wouldn't make any difference to our relationship. My love for Kirsty did not depend on shared genetic material.

Maybe her uncles still hadn't left the house. Their sister needed attention, their mother needed attention, and they knew I'd make straight for Chichester Gate, so it wasn't urgent that they get themselves there. Maybe Dawn had even told them about what had happened in Whitby four years ago. That last part was a bit of a stretch. But unless they really had taken the other route, I had a head start on them.

But what if I didn't find Kirsty this time? What if our bond was weaker because... because of what I now knew? What if I'd been right and that *thing* really had followed her from Whitby? It's easy to be rational when you haven't been beaten up and your loved ones are all safe.

Chapter 2. Red Riding Hood

Whitby, October 2001

When Kirsty was six, she, Dawn and I went to Whitby for a holiday. We stayed with my cousin Martin and his wife Phoebe. It was the first time we had seen them since the wedding. They were career-driven – he a journalist, she a chef – and had no children of their own. But they took to Kirsty from practically the moment she stepped out of the car. Put simply, they adored her. Martin was a natural born storyteller, and he regaled Kirsty with an ongoing, child-friendly version of *Dracula*. Phoebe spent the first afternoon of our visit teaching her how to bake bread and cakes. Phoebe was normally obsessive about keeping the kitchen clean and tidy, but by the end of that afternoon it was barely identifiable, and she couldn't have cared less.

In the early hours of the following morning, the whole house was awoken by Kirsty's screaming. We found her on the landing, refusing to go back into Martin's study where he'd set up a camp bed for her. She'd seen something that had scared her. It was a spider the size of a large dog.

"You must have been dreaming, Sweetheart," I told her, as gently and as patiently as I could manage in my torn-from-sleep state.

"No, Daddy, I saw it. I saw its shadow on the wall. It's still in my room!"

"It's probably just an ordinary spider," I told her. "It must have crawled over your nightlight.

"It's still in my room!" she repeated.

Martin placed a hand on my shoulder and gravely informed me that he'd underestimated the burden that came with fatherhood.

"In other words," I said, "you aren't above delegating spider duty to a guest."

He smiled. "I am glad we understand one another, Philip. No, seriously, I really *am* glad!"

The three bleary-eyed adults and Kirsty stood in the doorway, watching, as I moved in. The room was bathed in the pink glow of Kirsty's nightlight. I switched on the main light.

A wooden crucifix had been screwed onto the wall in the place where the upright met the crosspiece, but irregularities in the wall's surface meant it wasn't quite flush, and the spider had squeezed into one of the spaces. It wasn't the size of a dog, but it was large. The upright of the crucifix was over an inch wide, and the creature's legs stuck out on either side of it. It was one of those hairless beasts, the sort you find in sheds and garages when they haven't been opened up for months.

The spider was aware of me; it withdrew, the tips of its legs still showing. I looked around for a glass or something to catch it in, but all I could find was an empty yoghurt pot which I didn't for one moment think was big enough for this monster. I looked around for something else. My glance fell on a heavy book. Seeing my glance from her safe position in the doorway, Dawn said, "Don't you *dare* kill it!" I was about to retort; I stopped myself in time. Instead, I took hold of the crucifix, twisted it, and the spider dropped, not quite to the floor. I grabbed hold of its thread with my right hand, moved over to the sash window and wiggled at the latch with my left. The spider was climbing back up its thread – I really should have thought this through and opened the window first. I got the latch loose, and forced the creaking upper half of the window to slide down. The spider had almost reached my hand. I thrust it out through the opening and shook it free – I had the satisfaction of seeing its malevolent form fall past the lower pane – and slammed the window shut again.

The adults in the doorway – and Kirsty – applauded. I bowed. I was the hero of the night. And nobody had the least inkling of how terrified I had been throughout.

*

On the Wednesday evening as we were getting ready for bed, Dawn abruptly announced that she wanted to go home the next day.

"It's Thursday tomorrow," I said, puzzled. "We're staying till Saturday."

"I *know* that was the *plan*," she said in a pained voice, "but I want to go home to*mor*row. We'll stay for breakfast, and then we'll leave."

"Have you heard from work?" Dawn had a part-time job at an estate agent's in Chichester.

"How would I have heard from work? Do you think I bought a mobile all of a sudden? Do you think they just *guessed* the number?"

"I don't know, you might have given them Martin and Phoebe's phone number."

"Why would I *do* that?"

"I don't *know* why you'd do that, Dawn. It's why I'm asking."

"I didn't give them Martin's phone number. They have no idea where I am."

"So what's the matter? Are you feeling unwell?"

"There's nothing wrong with *me*."

"Well why the sudden change? I thought you were getting on well with Martin and Phoebe."

"Oh, *very* well," she said in a tone of whiny sarcasm. The wonderful day was over.

It was Phoebe, she eventually explained. Phoebe, apparently, had been making snide remark after snide remark about her ever since we'd arrived. I was at a loss; I had been present during most of the conversations between the two women, and they had seemed pleasant enough to me. When I said this, Dawn replied, "You always were *so* naïve, Philip. It was endearing to begin with, but now it's just tiresome. And don't tell me you didn't notice the way she was dressed the other night!"

I had no idea what she was talking about. *Which* other night? And then the penny dropped.

"It was the early hours of the morning!" I said, staring at her in utter disbelief. "What did you *expect* her to be wearing? Do you think she planted the spider in Kirsty's room just so that she could parade about in her nightie?"

"I wouldn't put *anything* past that woman."

I gritted my teeth and succeeded in not giving voice to anything I'd regret. This was learned behaviour. Instead I said, "Look, Dawn. We haven't seen Martin and Phoebe for six years, and we're not likely to see them again any time soon. They've taken time off work for us. And Kirsty is loving every minute. So please, don't do this."

Eventually Dawn gave in with poor grace and we settled down. For a long while I lay listening to the storm outside as it whipped branches against the window panes. Was Dawn really jealous of my cousin-in-law? She had no reason to be. Admittedly there was a bit of an attraction between Phoebe and me, an entirely innocent one that I was pretty sure was mutual, but there was no danger of anything ever coming of it. I had made a vow. Not just the marriage vow, but the one I'd made later, when Kirsty was three months old.

It had been the night I turned my life around. I was getting hammered at *The Fox* while unknown to me my baby daughter was being rushed into St Richard's Hospital. Dawn or one of her brothers must have guessed where I was because the phone behind the bar rang while the landlord was serving me. He took the call, then looked me in the eye and said, "Yes, he's here." I moved to take the receiver from him but he did not offer it; he continued to hold it to his ear, occasionally nodding and saying, "I see," in grave tones. Significantly, he reached for the Guinness tap to stop the flow. I strained to hear what was being said but the pub was too noisy. Finally he said, "Yes, I'll let him know," and hung up.

"What the hell is going on?" I demanded.

"Your daughter has bacterial meningitis."

The sickening constriction in my heart and stomach was entirely unexpected. I'd *prayed* for this, or something like it. I'd prayed for Dawn to miscarry, or to die in childbirth. Either of these would have met my requirements. Marrying Dawn had been by far the worst mistake I'd ever made, but if her baby died, there would be no reason for us to stay together. I would be free once more, and maybe, just maybe, there was an outside chance that Sarah and I could pick up where we'd left off. Ask and you shall receive. I had asked, and just this once, it seemed, I had received, albeit a little late.

Too drunk to cycle, I left my bike leaning against the wall of *The Fox* and staggered along the country road, eventually arriving at the Price Estate. The main house was empty. Dawn's mother had left me a note to say where they had taken Kirsty. I was in no fit state to drive to the hospital myself, and did not think my presence would be appreciated anyway. So I went into the guest room of the barn conversion, which was where I had been sleeping for the past few weeks, and prayed. There was a large crucifix on the wall, similar in style to the one in Phoebe and Martin's guest room. I knelt facing it, and offered up my new prayer, with the pious state that can sometimes be found in drunkenness.

"Please God, let Kirsty live."

The act of uttering these words caused me to weep uncontrollably. I wiped my eyes and squeezed them shut. An even more horrifying thought crossed my mind, made manifest in my imagination. Meningitis could lead to amputation. Multiple amputation. *Quadruple* amputation. I shuddered for maybe a full minute. I eventually continued. "Please God, do not let Kirsty bear the brunt of the petty malice and bad feeling that accompanied her birth. Let her live a long and prosperous and happy life, Lord, with two loving parents. Lord, I beg that you forgive my wicked thoughts and my prayers for her death and Dawn's, and grant me the opportunity to change my ways and up my game as a husband and father. For Kirsty's sake I commit myself to this marriage, if it is your will. I promise I will not find fault with Dawn, or wish any longer for things that might have been. Only... only *please* God, don't take Kirsty from me! Please God, *don't take Kirsty from me*!"

And so I went on in this vein, with long intervals of weeping. I must have prayed for more than an hour - certainly long enough for Dawn's family to return from the hospital. I heard a creak on the landing, as if someone had been standing listening and had just shifted their weight as they moved away. I did not turn around to see who it was; instead I raised my eyes to the crucifix. At the sight of it I recoiled in shock.

*

What with the storm outside, the row inside, and my immersion into memories I did not normally choose to revisit, I expected to sleep badly. In fact, when I looked at the clock on the bedside table it was not even midnight, and I had already slept.

I had already dreamed, too. The first part of the dream was a reasonably accurate recollection. I was drinking alone in *The Fox* once again but this time it was some weeks before the night I turned my life around. I'd finished an evening shift at the petrol station at Lavant; cycling home, I'd decided to stop off for a pint or two, more to delay going home than because of a developing alcohol dependence.

The regulars, while not unfriendly, knew me well enough to give me space, but on this occasion an old man with a "knowing" smile approached me at the bar and said, "You do realise what you've taken on with that Price girl?" I retorted that I had little choice in the matter at this late stage, which he seemed to find side-splittingly funny. A somewhat younger man at the bar picked up on what the older man had been saying. "It's the brothers you need to worry about," he confided. "I've worked with Benjamin and he's not so bad once you get to know him. But *William*. I'm telling you, you don't want to get on the wrong side of *him*. He likes to be in charge, if you get what I'm saying, and he always gets what he wants. Even Benjamin won't stand up to him then. Do you understand what I'm saying? Even Benjamin won't stand up to him."

It wasn't anything I hadn't heard before. William's own mother had said similar things. But I couldn't see what it had to do with me. I'd done the right thing, at no small cost. I'd married Dawn when I could have abandoned her, or pressured her into having an abortion. So what was William's problem? Did he think he had to assert his dominance over me? Did he think he had to compete with me for his sister's affection?

Six years on, I still didn't know.

In the dream time had shifted forward again, and it was once more the night Kirsty went into hospital. I was on my knees in the guest room, and someone shifted their weight behind me as I finished my prayer, and I looked up at the crucifix.

What I saw may have been a true recollection, but it occurred to me that my memory of the event may have been overwritten by the occasion of the spider in Martin's study. The crucifix was covered in cobwebs, forming the shape of a kite.

*

We were walking along New Quay Road in the aftermath of the storm. Dawn was a short distance ahead with Martin, and it was apparent from her body language that he had drawn her out of her mood, which had lasted all through to the end of breakfast. Phoebe and I followed some distance behind, and Kirsty, wearing a red jacket that Phoebe had bought her the previous day, flitted between the two mixed couples. She looked like Little Red Riding Hood; it was impossible to lose sight of her.

Two hours earlier she'd come downstairs bleary-eyed, not wanting her Coco Pops, and complaining that she hadn't slept all night because of the storm. Moments later, Martin had breezed into the kitchen, asking who was up for a fossil hunt. Somehow he managed to make it sound like the most exciting prospect in the world, just as he had done the Captain Cook tour yesterday, and the steam train journey the day before. Kirsty could hardly have been more thrilled if he'd promised live dinosaurs. So she had to backpedal and make out she wasn't *that* tired. Phoebe, taking pity on her, poured her a mug of coffee, promised her it would keep her awake, and told her she could have a nap in the afternoon if she still felt tired.

The moment Martin and Phoebe's backs were turned, Dawn flashed me a glare that said, "Do you see *now* how she undermines me?" She followed it with looks that said, "Coffee indeed! She's six years old!" I shook my head once, impatiently. She had a bee in her bonnet about children drinking coffee. To me it was a non-issue.

Now, the state of relative harmony was an unlooked-for bonus. Kirsty was walking between Martin and Dawn, holding hands with the pair of them. Phoebe commented on how like a cosy family the three of them looked.

"Oh yes?" I said. "And where does that leave us?"

"Where do *you* think?" She was smiling as she spoke. She put her hand through my arm. "You could have done a lot worse, you know."

"Well obviously *I* could have done worse. But I don't think you could." I shook my head, grinning. "No. You'd never have put up with me. I'm much too untidy for a start."

"Philip Hamilton! You make me sound like an obsessive-compulsive! In any case, I'm sure you're not as bad as all that."

"You haven't seen my study."

"Well maybe I could have adapted. Or *you* could have, given time and a bit of discipline."

I raised a suggestive eyebrow in response to that last word, and Phoebe burst out laughing. She disengaged her hand to hit me with it. Then she sighed, as if reluctant to abandon the silly fantasy, and in a quiet voice she pointed out, "If it *had* been us, there would have been no Kirsty."

Her momentarily serious tone was so out of keeping with the banter that had existed up till that point that I found myself looking ahead to make sure Kirsty was still with Martin and Dawn. Phoebe and I had lagged behind somewhat, and there were other people walking in the space between the two mixed couples. Without a word we quickened our pace to catch up, only to see Dawn and Martin walking side by side without Kirsty.

She was gone.

*

Everybody was calm and reasonable, and there was no talk of apportioning blame; it was simply a case of both mixed couples thinking she was with the other. Children disappear, it's a fact of life. They are easily distracted, they move quickly, and they fit into spaces too small for adults. Every parent knows the feeling of sickening panic in the pit of the stomach, but usually it doesn't last long.

We called her name repeatedly. Martin had a deep, loud voice that carried. A minute passed, and another. There was no reply, no flash of red jacket.

Phoebe said, "I think we should check the ship."

The replica of Captain Cook's ship, *The Endeavour*, floated in a basin on the River Esk on the other side of New Quay Road. I hurried over to it, my heart beating rapidly. We'd visited the ship the previous day; had Kirsty crossed the road for another look? There were railings at the edge of the basin, but not all the way round. Kirsty wasn't stupid, but she *was* six years old. What if...?

"Phone the emergency services!" I ordered as the others caught up with me. Phoebe and Martin both had mobile phones. I was calling Kirsty's name quite frantically now. I looked over the edge of the basin, afraid to see her bright red jacket in the water.

She was not in the water. She was not on the ship either. She was nowhere.

The police responded promptly. I had a recent photograph of Kirsty in my wallet which I showed to several uniformed officers. Minutes later, they sent out a patrol car with a roof-mounted public address to alert people to look out for a missing girl in a red jacket.

Time passed. I told myself she couldn't have been kidnapped. It was broad daylight, there were too many witnesses, and Kirsty would have screamed blue murder if anybody had tried to force her into a car. It made no sense. Children don't vanish just because one of their parents briefly imagines a life without them. But when you eliminate the impossible, and you're left with *nothing*, you start to wonder if you were too hasty with what you eliminated.

Absurdly, I found myself thinking of spiders. Or perhaps it wasn't so absurd; my mind was simply seeking a different approach. More precisely, it was my fear of spiders that I was thinking about. How the relationship between the size of a spider and the fear it engenders in an arachnophobe is not quite linear. A bird-eater is obviously more frightening than a house spider, but above a certain size the hypothetical creature becomes a real threat, so the fear is no longer irrational – aside, of course, from the irrationality of supposing such a creature to exist – and above a certain size after that the creature ceases to be credible. A trapdoor spider with a body the size of a small dog was, to my mind, more frightening than the giant spiders of B-movies or Shelob in *The Lord of the Rings*.

When this random train of thought had passed I became aware that something had changed. The atmosphere of solidarity had evaporated. If I hadn't been so besotted with my cousin's wife, Dawn told me in a harsh whisper after drawing me aside, I might have taken her advice of the night before. If only we had left that morning as *she* had suggested, she would still have her daughter.

Even the most unfounded accusations can cut, and I was not altogether certain how unfounded this one was. Abruptly I announced that I would find Kirsty on my own. Martin and Phoebe had respected our privacy, although they could not have failed to hear Dawn's words. Now Martin turned to me, nodded wisely and reassuringly, handed me his mobile and said, “Take this with you and ring Phoebe's number when you find her. Trust your instincts. You *will* find her.”

Unsure if I was really following my instincts or simply walking away from Dawn’s accusations, I headed uphill. I worked through my anger as I followed my seemingly random route. I blamed the police for not getting an immediate result. I blamed Dawn for making it about *her* instead of Kirsty, and for saying “my daughter” instead of “our daughter”. I blamed Phoebe for coming out with all that nonsense about me marrying her instead of Dawn, because by doing so she had tempted me into wishing Kirsty into non-existence.

And I had given in to Phoebe’s temptation. Had I broken my covenant with God in doing that? Did I even believe in such things any more? Sure, I took the vow seriously enough, but that didn't mean I thought the terms of the contract were being jealously monitored by a celestial insurance underwriter. I thought again of how the cobwebs had formed on the crucifix six years ago as I prayed for Kirsty's deliverance - and this time I was sure it was an authentic memory. I thought of the spider I had dislodged from the crucifix in Martin’s study. Why did it keep coming back to spiders?

I reached the top of the hill overlooking the bay, close to the famous arch formed from two huge whalebones fixed into the ground, and sat on a nearby bench. I had an uninterrupted view of the path below. On the cliff top on the far side of the river, the remains of Whitby Abbey were framed in the arch. From the coast road, the distant sound of the police PA carried on the sea breeze.

When something goes missing, and you’ve searched all the obvious places, and some of the not-so-obvious places, there comes a point where the physical act of searching becomes a random flailing, and it is far more fruitful to search the mind. It was an approach that often worked for everyday items mislaid in the house, but would it work for a missing person in an unfamiliar town?

I tried picturing Kirsty from the point where we had last seen her – and here things took another unpleasant turn. Not trapdoor spiders this time; this time, in my imagination, she had become the girl in the red coat in Steven Spielberg's otherwise black-and-white *Schindler's List*. The colourful girl who moved with apparent freedom in the Nazi-occupied monochrome world, but ultimately her fate was the same as that of so many others.

Mercifully a burst of electronic music interrupted these morbid thoughts. I recognised "Playground Twist" by Siouxsie and the Banshees; it seemed to be coming from my pocket. Several bemused seconds passed before I realised it was the ringtone of Martin's mobile. My heart leapt: had Kirsty turned up, or did Phoebe have some dreadful news for me? I fumbled with the phone, unsure how to answer it, scared that it would cut out or go into voicemail or whatever it was mobiles did when you didn't answer them straightaway. I found a green button with a picture of a handset, pressed it, said, "Hello?"

It was Martin's editor wanting to speak to him. I patiently explained who I was and why I was borrowing Martin's phone. The editor said, "I'm really sorry to hear that. I wonder, though, could you just tell him..." He proceeded to rattle off a lengthy message. I hung up on him.

I had risen from the bench, and once more had a clear view down the side of the hill. I was about to be drawn back into my morbid thoughts when I was finally struck by the sheer stupidity of it all. The spider was not a symbol of a broken vow or an instrument of God's vengeance. It was just a *spider*. I was arachnophobic but I wasn't stupid; an irrational fear didn't alter the fact that I knew the world was subject to rational laws.

So with a single effort of will I reclaimed my sense of perspective, my reason, my worldview. And it struck me as ironic, even at the time, that Kirsty should reappear at that very moment, for all the world as if my conscious rejection of superstition had brought her back into existence.

She was standing beneath the Whalebone Arch, a bewildered look on her face. I screamed her name, caught her in a crushing embrace. She was in tears; she was saying, "I couldn't find you, I couldn't find you anywhere! Please Daddy, don't leave me again!"

*

I drove us back to Singleton in silence. It was not a comfortable silence. As I drove I tried to make sense of what had happened.

Kirsty had been more tired than we realised; the storm really had kept her awake for almost the whole night. But in her eagerness to go on the promised fossil hunt, she had concealed this as well as she could. The coffee had helped but it was only a temporary measure.

While Phoebe and I were having our chat, somebody on New Quay Road had been waving to attract someone's attention – I was pretty sure I could remember seeing this – and Kirsty had seen the waving arm reflected in the open basement window down the side of the New Angel Hotel. At this point the two mixed couples were quite far apart, and Kirsty must have thought the reflection was Cousin Martin beckoning her, so she turned down the alleyway that ran alongside the hotel. A few moments later she heard Cousin Martin calling her name; his voice sounded as if it was coming from inside the basement. Seeing no doors, she had climbed in through the window.

After that, her account became decidedly vague. The four of us listened intently, along with a female police officer who had accompanied us back to Phoebe and Martin's home. Kirsty had run because someone was chasing her, she explained. Was that why she had climbed in through the window? the officer asked, apparently not satisfied with this. No, he started chasing her *after* she realised she had lost us. She was in a narrow place with cupboards. Most of the cupboards had glass doors; some had jars of jam in them, others had *things* that moved, and some had both. She saw her pursuer when he came slithering down a rope. Had he touched her? No, but he had tried to. He'd grabbed hold of the hood of her jacket. She managed to break free, and then she had run until her legs ached, and she found me standing under the Whalebone Arch.

"But you were gone for nearly two *hours*," I'd said.

The police officer said, "Now Kirsty, this is very important. I want you to describe the man who tried to touch you."

Kirsty shook her head. "He wasn't a man."

Her words chilled me - there was an association in the back of my mind that I couldn't quite recall. Martin and I exchanged glances. Then Phoebe began to laugh uncontrollably. Aware of everyone's stares, she pulled herself together, apologised for her inappropriate reaction, and said, "Kirsty, was he Dracula?"

Kirsty looked at me for reassurance, then at the police officer. "I suppose he must have been." Then her face cracked into a smile.

"He's not real, is he?"

With that, there was a collective sigh of relief. *Obviously* she had wriggled in through the basement window, fallen asleep, and everything after that was a dream. The mystery was solved – and the fact that Kirsty was safe meant it didn't matter unduly that some of the details didn't quite add up.

There was the timing between her wandering off and hearing Martin calling her. There was the police's failure to investigate an open window near the scene of her disappearance. But the thing that really didn't make sense was my failure to see her until she had reached the Whalebone Arch. From my position on the hill I'd had a clear view down the path, I'd been looking out for her, and there hadn't been anything to conceal her as she had come up the path.

Why hadn't I seen her?

Then the answer came to me. It was obvious, it was straightforward, it didn't involve anything supernatural... and yet it raised more questions than it answered. The reason why I hadn't seen her sooner was simply because...

"Perhaps you'll listen to me next time," said Dawn abruptly, breaking into the uncomfortable silence and cutting into my thoughts.

"What? What are you talking about?"

"If we'd gone home when *I* said, none of this would have happened, would it? So perhaps now you'll start listening to me."

"I found her, didn't I?" My voice was harsh. "And then I listened to you. That's why she won't be going on a fossil hunt today. That's why we're going home early. That's why we've just aborted the best holiday we've had in *years*."

She was silent after that. Stubbornly silent. She would remain that way until I'd drawn her out of her silence. That would mean backtracking on everything I had said, regardless of whether or not I was right and however much she needed to hear it. With the return of the silence, I tried to get back to whatever it was I'd been thinking about. But for the life of me I could not remember what it was.

I thought about Martin and Phoebe instead. They would be moving to Edinburgh soon. Before our departure they made us promise we'd visit them once they'd settled in. I promised, knowing it was not going to happen. Not as long as Dawn and I were together. I still had my bargain with God – my rejection of superstition had not quite extended to that, I realised now – but I didn't know how much longer I could keep it up. More than anything, I could not forgive Dawn for putting point-scoring above Kirsty's welfare. I could not forgive her for her look of triumph when she had said, "*If you hadn't been so besotted with your cousin's wife...*"

She hadn't won. Not that it was a competition, but I was the one who found Kirsty. I had trusted my instincts and they had delivered.

The journey home took a further five hours. Mercifully, Kirsty slept for most of it.

Chapter 3. The Stench of Burning Feathers on the Breeze

Chichester, December 2005

Chichester Gate was a recently-opened leisure park. It consisted of a large rectangular parking area with a Premier Travel Inn at its south end; the north end was made up of a paved strip flanked by restaurants, a gym and a multiplex cinema. The administration building of Chichester High School, where I had worked for five years, took up most of the length of the east side. I drove along the access road which swept in from the west, passing between the Cineworld and the McDonald's where Kirsty was last seen.

There were spaces near the McDonald's, but no sign of the black Mercedes, which meant I was probably still ahead of Dawn's brothers. Playing it safe, I parked my Fiesta some distance away so they wouldn't see it when they arrived.

The police presence was evident as I walked back towards the McDonald's. Two squad cars were parked nearby. The sound of a PA from the Terminus Road to the north was muffled by the intervening buildings but I did catch Kirsty's name, mainly because I was listening for it. Nearby an officer was having a conversation with a fat bald man outside the fire door of Frankie & Benny's. They would want to speak to me. But there were things I needed to do first.

The McDonald's restaurant was a small, single-story building with a pitched roof and plate glass windows instead of walls on three sides. Inside were the usual plastic tables and chairs, and several customers, nearly all younger than me, sitting at the tables or ordering food. I was a little surprised to see that it was business as usual. At the counter a tall, spotty youth of about nineteen asked me what he could get me. I ordered a regular black coffee to justify my presence and asked if I could borrow a telephone directory.

He gave me the once-over, taking in my swollen lip, and in an apparent leap of logic or intuition asked, "Are you the father of the missing girls?"

"Girls?" The plural took me by surprise. "How many are involved?"

"Two. There was a copper in here when I started my shift. He was going over the CCTV footage but I don't think he found anything."

"Where is he now?"

He shrugged. "Investigating, I suppose. No point in hanging around here."

"What if the girls turn up here?"

"He said to let them know. Do you want sugar with that?"

"No thank you."

Before taking a seat I checked out the party area, which was currently unoccupied. It was dominated by a big table where Megan and her guests would have sat. There was no possibility that Kirsty was hiding under the table, but I looked anyway. I noticed a small green heart drawn on the table's surface in what I supposed was crayon or marker pen.

I sipped my coffee, trying with limited success to avoid burning my hurt lip. The youth who had served me brought me a local telephone directory. I found Roger Jeffries' number. It took a couple of attempts to ring him – I was not yet familiar with my mobile phone and had forgotten you have to enter the area code even if you're calling from within it – but eventually I got through.

His wife answered. I told her I was Kirsty's father. She had no idea who Kirsty was. I asked if I could speak to her husband. She had no idea where he was. I felt my temper rising, but then she told me she could get me his mobile number if I wanted it. She told me to wait. A full minute later she rattled it off. I wrote it at the top of the directory page with the red biro I used for marking. She hung up without checking that I'd copied it correctly.

I had copied it correctly. Jeffries answered. When I told him I was Kirsty's father, he said, "Oh God, Peter, I'm so sorry, I can't believe it, I really don't know what to say, have you heard anything?"

"My name's Philip, and no I haven't, that's why I'm phoning you."

"If there's anything I can do to help, really, I mean anything at all, I just feel so terrible about all this, I mean if it was my Megan I'd be frantic by now..."

"Where are you?"

"I'm at Chichester Gate, waiting for Kirsty's uncle to get back."

I was slightly surprised by this - if he was here in the restaurant, why hadn't I heard his phone ring? No, he was outside, pacing around in the car park - I could see him through the window. I hadn't seen him when I arrived so he'd probably been in his car then. He wasn't looking in my direction, and I decided he didn't need to know where I was calling from.

"Tell me what happened, please."

He told me. It was a long-winded account, but it amounted to the following: His daughter Megan had invited nine guests, including her best friend Chloe Faulkner, who was staying with them while her parents were away in Derby. Kirsty was a last minute replacement when Ingrid Larssen dropped out. The party had started at about five, with all the guests apart from Kirsty giving Megan presents while the McDonald's staff waited on them. Jeffries had then handed out "freaky" make-up sets that his wife had bought for a Halloween party that got cancelled. These sets contained green lipstick, fake blood and so on.

For the following hour the children had been eating and chatting and laughing and milling around and applying the make-up to each other, and nobody had left the party area except to go to the toilet (always in groups of two or more) or to talk to the staff, although

Jeffries admitted it was impossible to keep an eye on every one of the ten girls for every second of the party, and it was hard to tell them apart once they had applied the make-up.

Then at about six Dawn and Benjamin had arrived with a wrapped present for Kirsty to give to Megan, and that was when they discovered both Kirsty and Chloe were missing. After a short, fruitless search which included all the staff and kitchen areas, Benjamin called the police. They arrived promptly, the police station being a very short distance from Chichester Gate, and instigated a search for the missing children. Dawn gave the police a description, some recent photographs and contact details. Statements were taken from everyone present, and Megan remembered talking to Chloe about five minutes before her disappearance was noticed.

It was while the statements were being taken that Dawn began to get anxious, and Benjamin decided to get her home. She wasn't happy about this, but the police agreed it was probably for the best. A distraught mother having an epileptic fit was a complication they could do without.

"So let me get this straight," I said when he had finished. "Your one job was to look after ten girls, and you managed to lose two of them?"

The comment was unnecessary, and I am now ashamed of the satisfaction it gave me to see him cringe as he paced about in the car park, still unaware that I was watching him.

"I'm really sorry, Pete. I'm really sorry. I'm keeping a look out for them, and if it comes to a search party..."

"I'll let you know," I said, and rang off before he could launch into another lengthy apology.

So, why would Kirsty have left the restaurant? Cineworld were showing *The Chronicles of Narnia*, I'd noticed, but I couldn't imagine her just walking out, even if it had been at the other girl's insistence. Besides, it was the first place the police would have checked. The staff would have noticed two ten-year-old girls wearing

Halloween make-up in December. *Anybody* would have noticed them.

I sipped at my coffee. My instincts weren't delivering, and I had no idea where to go from here. I needed to make my presence known to the police, preferably before Dawn's brothers arrived on the scene.

So, next step was to report to the police station. But my instinct hadn't completely let me down; on my way out I took one last look at the green heart on the party table. It wasn't marker pen or crayon. It was lipstick. Lipstick from one of the Halloween make-up sets.

The Price brothers were arriving as I stepped out into the chill breeze. I was sure they did not see me; they went on to park close to where Jeffries was waiting as I walked quickly across the car park. I exited Chichester Gate via the paved area between the Nuffield Fitness Centre and the administration building of Chichester High. As I came out onto Stockbridge Road, I was aware of the slight but distinctive stench of what I took to be burning feathers.

There was a girl on the other side of the road. She was lit from behind by a streetlamp, but even in silhouette I could see that she was not Kirsty. She appeared to have come out of the municipal building opposite, her head bowed as if she was looking for something she'd dropped. She was heading towards me, walking into the road. The railway gates had just gone down, so there was no traffic on her side. There was a lorry approaching on my side, showing no sign of slowing – I guessed the driver was on his mobile – and the girl was about to walk into its path. From the movement of her shoulders I could see that she was either holding back from or building up to a scream. She released it as I ran out in front of the lorry – the sound of her scream merging with that of the brakes, belatedly applied – and scooped her up and carried her back to the far pavement. It was a terrible scream, an expression of anguish, physical pain and utter bewilderment, and it went on and on and on.

Once safe I hugged her to me, and she hugged me back with her left arm; her right arm she clutched to her chest. “You’re safe, Chloe,” I told her as soothingly as I could manage. “I’m Kirsty’s dad, you’re safe with me, I’ll get you home.” I had found the source of the smell I had taken to be burning feathers; nearly all the golden hair on the right side of her head had been burnt away, and a patch of her scalp the size of a two pence coin was raw – whether by heat or by having her hair tugged out, I could not say. I told her again and again that she was safe, and that I would get her home, and presently her screaming died down to a whimper. As I released her, I got a close look at her face. I almost reeled in shock at what I saw before I realised it was merely Halloween make-up, green lipstick and all, smeared by tears.

I gently pulled her hand away from her chest; she reluctantly allowed me to do this. There was a red burn mark across her wrist, as if she had rested it on a central heating pipe – a pipe apparently hot enough to burn through the sleeve of her party dress.

A fleeting memory of a dirty white jacket, pushed to the back of a wardrobe... Where had *that* thought come from? But it vanished as quickly as it had come. Chloe was not wearing a jacket or a coat. I took off my own jacket, got her left arm into the left sleeve, and draped the right side over her shoulder.

“Was Kirsty with you?” I asked. She shook her head – I couldn’t tell if she meant no or she didn’t know or she simply couldn’t bring herself to speak. “Do you know where she is?” She shook her head again, her eyes vacant and unfocused. I had to bite back my impatience. What had happened to her? What ordeal had she been through? As gently as I could manage, I said, “Chloe, did Kirsty get away?” She shook her head once more, and this time I couldn’t help but interpret it as *No she did not.*

For a moment I stood there, helpless, torn between the natural protective instincts I felt towards Chloe and the bitter thought, *Why couldn’t Kirsty have been the one who got away?*

I had followed my instincts and I had got results. But I'd found the wrong child. Chloe and Kirsty were not best friends. Chloe was a beautiful child. Her injuries would heal and she would grow up to be a beautiful woman. She had a privileged position in Megan Jeffries's clique. Kirsty, meanwhile, was expected to feel grateful when people like Megan invited her to stand in for the absent guest of choice. All of which made it somewhat surprising that it was Kirsty and Chloe who had gone missing together.

Pushing back the sleeve of my jacket, I took Chloe's good hand and led her in the direction of the police station. We walked, painfully slowly, alongside the canal basin. I was afraid to look, afraid to see police divers searching for a body. I looked. There were no police divers. Not yet, anyway.

Inside the police station, the desk sergeant and two other officers were being berated by a heavily-tattooed woman in her mid-thirties. Apparently oblivious to the fact that it was December, she was wearing a top resembling a string vest that didn't quite cover her bulging stomach. I heard her saying, "He's done nothing wrong, it's you lot picking on him!" as I pushed the doors open and led my charge through. A preternatural silence seemed to fall, and all eyes turned towards us as the argument trailed off.

"I have Chloe Faulkner," I announced. "She is injured."

Chapter 4. Room 28

I was walking in the darkness across a field in Hunston, close to the Chichester canal. The air was freezing. There were about a hundred of us spread out in a long line, mostly police officers in high vis, and a handful of civilians who had volunteered to help with the search. We were carrying heavy torches. As a result of a misunderstanding I had been teamed up with my brothers-in-law, but to their credit and mine we were, in fact, working as a team. We came to a barbed wire fence. After Benjamin had crawled through, William held the wire up to enable me to pass, and I followed Benjamin without any fear of William "accidentally" letting the wire spring into my back. Benjamin took my hand to help me get up again. I didn't need his assistance but was grateful for the gesture.

We were through, and ready to resume the search. But William and Benjamin were looking at me strangely. Eventually William said, "Aren't you going to answer that?" and I realised my mobile had been ringing for some time, repeatedly playing the first eight notes of "Forever Autumn". Apart from phoning the mobile myself to test it, I had never received a call on it. I hurriedly searched my jacket pockets, certain it was Kirsty. It was a certainty that flew in the face of logic, because Kirsty didn't even know I had a mobile.

I couldn't find it. I had to find it. If I could find it, I could answer it, and I would hear Kirsty's voice, and know she was okay. How she'd got my number was a mystery for another day - she could have been kidnapped by the man who had sold me the phone for all I knew. It didn't matter, just as long as I could speak to her. I'd patted every pocket before realising it must have fallen out when I'd crawled under the barbed wire.

As I was searching in the grass near the fence it came to me that none of this was happening. It was a dream, a lucid dream, and with that realisation I knew I would awaken shortly. At the same time I saw it, a blue-white glow in the long grass. I grabbed at it, fumbled for the button with the green handset icon, desperate to speak to my daughter before I woke up.

I woke up.

I was in Room 28 of the Premier Inn, lying on the bed in my clothes, not including shoes or jacket. Had my mobile rung in real life? I'd given my number to the police; what if they'd phoned me with news? I got up, switched the light on and went over to my jacket which lay crumpled on the desk chair. There was Hallowe'en make-up smeared on the collar, and a brown stain that was probably Chloe's blood. I found the mobile and fiddled with it until I could get it to display the call register.

Nobody had phoned.

I called reception to ask if anybody had tried to contact me on the hotel phone. Nobody had. Maybe somebody in one of the adjacent rooms had the same ring tone as me. Maybe. It wouldn't have been *that* strange a coincidence.

According to my phone it was exactly four o'clock in the morning. I couldn't believe I had slept at all, let alone slept so soundly. My daughter was out there somewhere and I had been sleeping. I walked into the bathroom, splashed cold water onto my face, then went back to the bed. I sat down on it and set about making sense of things.

First things first: I had to be rational. I was no use to Kirsty or anyone else if I wasn't rational. I needed sleep to function, and if I could get it, so much to the good. It was not as if I could be doing anything else right now.

The search party was probably going ahead much as I'd dreamed it, minus myself and my brothers-in-law. I wasn't happy about my own lack of involvement, but I had to see it from the point of view of the police. In cases like this, close family members were automatically under suspicion, former stepfathers even more so. The police wouldn't be doing their job if they took everything I said at face value.

So how did it look to them? Maybe they saw Kirsty as a bored and restless ten-year-old girl wondering why she has to spend every other weekend with a man who used to be her stepfather but isn't even *that* any more. When Chloe Faulkner suggests they go off somewhere, Kirsty jumps at the chance to disappear before the weekend.

What had happened after that was difficult to account for. I lay back on the bed and stared up at the ceiling of the hotel room, the light still on, trying to imagine. Kirsty had a penchant for hiding under sofas and beds and tables, revealing herself at unexpected moments. I thought of the party table at the McDonald's, and how I had expected her to emerge from under it. Then I thought of the lorry that had almost hit Chloe. An unpleasant idea came into my mind. What if a lorry had stopped outside the fast food restaurant, for deliveries perhaps, and the two girls had concealed themselves under the trailer. Maybe they were stowing away; maybe they were *playing* at stowing away, or maybe Chloe had dared Kirsty to hide there with her before her mother and uncle returned to take her away.

But the lorry driver had returned sooner than expected; he'd left the engine on, and pulled away before the girls had time to get clear. Chloe had caught her hair in the axle, and burned her arm on the exhaust pipe. It wasn't very likely. But it *was* possible. And as long as it was a possibility...

After a brief hesitation I phoned the police station. The desk sergeant who answered sounded familiar; if he was the one I'd spoken to when I'd brought Chloe in, he must have been on duty for over nine hours. I introduced myself as Kirsty's father, then launched into an account of my speculations. He listened patiently. Spoken aloud, my idea didn't sound as ludicrous as I'd feared, but it wasn't really convincing either. It was the sort of explanation Watson might have offered before Sherlock Holmes produced the right one.

"I suppose it's pretty unlikely," I admitted after trailing off at the end.

"It's something to consider," the desk sergeant said with gruff gentleness, then added, as if thinking aloud, "It would explain why there's nothing on the CCTV footage."

I blinked. Was he supposed to tell me that?

"You will let me know if there's any development?"

"Yes, Mr Hamilton, you will be informed."

"I'm staying in the Premier Inn, so that I'm on hand in case... You know."

He patiently fielded some more of my questions until I realised that further prolongation of the call was not achieving anything. After hanging up I willed myself to fall asleep. I wanted to get back into the dream so that I could take the call from Kirsty. Maybe she'd gone to a place where she could only communicate through dreams. No, that was irrational - and thank God I hadn't shared *that* idea with the desk sergeant! But maybe I knew more than I realised, and the ringing phone was my subconscious trying to get through to me.

Unsurprisingly, willing myself to sleep did not result in me falling asleep, and I lay awake for a long time, listening for my phone to ring and wondering where she had gone. I thought about the long interview at the police station. They'd asked me about my injuries; I played down the one-sided fight with Dawn's brothers as I didn't want to risk sidetracking the investigation. Beyond my role as de facto suspect I got the impression that I wasn't really under suspicion. I could account for my whereabouts throughout the day. Miss Havers would vouch for my movements to and from Woking, and the garage mechanics would say what time I collected my car. I hadn't known Kirsty was at a party in Chichester, and even if I had I simply hadn't had time to kidnap her - even leaving aside my lack of motive, given that I was meant to be picking her up anyway.

Nevertheless two police officers had gone with me to the car park. One shone a heavy-duty torch into the boot of my car and found a toolbox and stacks of exercise books that needed marking, but no space to hide an abducted girl. But that excursion had been after my jacket was returned to me, and I caught my last sight of Chloe before she was led to a waiting ambulance. She was still practically catatonic. The makeup had been cleaned off her face but now she looked ghostlike. As they were helping her into the vehicle she stopped in its doorway, turned, and addressing me directly, said,

"They moved like spiders."

It was the only thing she'd said since I found her, and she did not speak again.

*

At some point I must have stopped trying to will myself to sleep because I slept solidly for three hours. I did not dream of finding my phone. Rather, I dreamed that the police continued to interview me in a windowless room with a table, the only lighting an anglepoise lamp that shone in my face. They asked me all the same questions as before, and although they didn't say it in so many words, their insinuations were clear enough: they thought I knew where Kirsty was.

When I awoke it occurred to me that they were right.

Chapter 5. Red Houses

Guildford, April 2003

On Kirsty's eighth birthday we went to see a West End matinee performance of *The Lion King*. It was the first Friday of the Easter holiday. After the performance we set off for Guildford to stay at my parents' house for a few days.

We travelled by train. It was crowded as we left Waterloo Station, so Kirsty sat on my lap. She drew my arms around her waist, pretending they were a seatbelt and my hands were the clasps, and leaned back against me contentedly. I whispered to her, "Do you want a story?"

She nodded vigorously. "Can I have Dick Whittington, because we've just been to London."

"Okay. Do you want the historical version, or the legend?"

She pretended to consider. "The legend," she said after a few moments.

"Hmm, an interesting choice," I said. "Could it be because there's a cat in the legend?"

Kirsty giggled and covered her face with her hands, as if embarrassed that I had seen through her clever ruse so easily. She had always wanted a cat, but her mother was allergic to their fur. I glanced across at Dawn. She was reading *Heat* magazine.

"A story it is then. But you know I'm not as good as Cousin Martin."

"Just do your best, Daddy."

"Very well." And so I began.

But on this occasion I did not get very far. Kirsty was distracted by something she had noticed out of the train window. I looked where she was looking, at a very long row of terrace houses.

"Do people *live* in them?" she asked in amazement.

"Of course they do. Why wouldn't they?"

"They go on for miles!"

"They have dividing walls," I explained. "Just like in a semi-detached house, or a town house."

"But what do they do when the bin men come?"

"They have to carry their dustbins through the house. In through the back door, out through the front door."

She twisted round to look me in the eye to see if I was having her on. Then a thought struck her. "What if there were doors in all the dividers?"

"Do you mean secret doors?"

She nodded. "And you can only open them with skeleton keys. You could walk for miles without ever having to go outside!" After a thoughtful pause she added, "Perhaps when you get to the end, you find a hidden trapdoor with steps leading down into a big cellar. But the cellar isn't just underneath the house, it's also underneath the gap, so you come to some more steps that lead up into the next row."

We discussed the possibilities for much of the rest of the journey. Between us we envisioned a continuous network of buildings stretching the length and breadth of London. Various characters, including Dick Whittington, his cat (who was cousin to the lion king), and several others I had made up in previous stories (mostly based on Kirsty's dolls and cuddly toys), would pop up in unlikely places across the city. Sometimes they scampered across roofs, or sneaked through occupied rooms (unnoticed by the occupants who dozed in their rocking chairs), or picked the locks of cellars, or wriggled along pipes that passed under the road.

Kirsty's birthday was a total success. Even Dawn's manner was amenable, as it generally was when we stayed at my parents' house. They had always liked her, and she liked them.

That night I found myself lying awake in my parents' guest room bed. It was a different kind of insomnia, an almost *restful* form of sleeplessness. For two hours I listened contentedly to the familiar creaking of the floorboards and the groaning of the water pipes. This was my home. It wasn't my bedroom, but I had occasionally slept in this room too when I was a child, so it was close enough.

My mind was unwilling to abandon the fantastical idea that Kirsty and I had been developing on the train. At 2am, realising I wasn't going to get any sleep until I'd got it out of my system, I slipped out of the bed, tiptoed downstairs to the kitchen (avoiding the stair that creaked), switched on the strip light above the wooden table and put a saucepan of milk on the cooker. While it was heating up I went into the dining room to begin a search. I found what I was looking for in the sideboard, and returned to the kitchen, just in time to turn off the burner before the milk boiled over.

My father was a tegestologist – that is to say, a beer mat collector. He had told me two years earlier that he didn't collect them any more, but some of the ones in the sideboard were recent; one advertised a beer festival in the summer. I would rib him about it later, but for now, I had work to do.

I poured myself a mug of hot milk, took it over to the kitchen table and sat down. I had gathered a large pile of square black beer mats, and a smaller pile of red ones. I placed a straight row of eight black mats on the table, their edges touching. The row represented a street of connected houses; the touching edges were the dividing walls. These were ordinary houses; there were no doors in these connecting walls. I made a second row of eight, separate from and parallel to the first, and then a third. These were not three different streets, but rather three versions of the *same* street.

Next I made a fourth parallel row of eight, this time with red mats. These red houses *did* have doors in their dividing walls. If you began in the first red house, you could walk through a succession of communicating doors until you arrived at the last red house.

I drank a few mouthfuls of hot milk and considered. So far, all very straightforward; nothing I had come up with was controversial, except the idea that there could be different versions of the same street. The next part was more of a conceptual leap, however.

I swapped the first black house from the first row with the first red house. I swapped the second black house from the second row with the second red house, and the third black house from the third row with the third red house. So each of the three "normal" versions of the street now had a single red house in a different, contiguous position. But it was *still* possible to walk through the communicating door from the first red house into the second, and then the second into the third.

In other words, the doors in the dividing walls were portals between parallel universes. It was nonsense, of course. I was using beer mats to put a pseudoscientific spin on a fairy tale scenario, an amusing way to spend half an hour while unable to sleep. Now it was time to put the beer mats back in the sideboard and go back to bed and forget all about it.

But I wasn't prepared to do that. I couldn't explain the experience I'd had eight years ago, but that was no reason to pretend it hadn't happened; *that* would have been irrational. There was no question about it: I had stumbled upon a secret door that led to a version of London that had a different Earls Court tube station.

I returned my attention to the beer mats. What would a red house look like from outside? Uninhabited, I supposed, and dilapidated, its gardens overgrown and its windows boarded up. What would it be like living next door to one? Quiet, except when the *travellers* are passing through. Late at night you hear the communicating door opening and closing, and people moving about.

Briefly roused from your sleep, you nudge your partner awake and say, "It sounds like someone has finally moved in!" You even wonder why you hadn't heard a removal van, and why they are moving in at such an unearthly hour. But the next day you see there is no change, the place is still uninhabited; even the weeds that grew right up to the front door remain undisturbed, and you wonder if perhaps you'd only dreamed you'd heard movements in the night, or maybe it was ghosts.

I spent another half hour working out variations and considering possibilities. Just how long could the street be? What if two red houses appeared in different locations of the same version of the street? And what if you *didn't* assume you'd only dreamt that you'd heard movements? Maybe you were a law-abiding citizen, not the sort who normally broke into other people's property, but what if curiosity got the better of you? Perhaps a credit card would get that front door open, or you could jemmy a window and climb in. Once inside, you'd find the communicating door. And this is where it would get weird. Because it would appear to lead back into your own house, even though you knew there was no corresponding connecting door on your own side of the wall. Then the curiosity that had got you into the house in the first place would compel you to open that door, and you would step through it into... what? A house that occupied the same space as your own? A lounge with different furniture, different pictures on the mantelpiece, and a view from the window of a different front garden, but otherwise similar to your own? Or would it be abandoned like the first "red house", only this time you were inside so you could open the front door without having to force it? Could you step out into another England, another world?

It was a little after 3am when I returned to bed. Dawn was sleeping soundly, unaware of my nocturnal wanderings. I lay beside her, not touching, still thinking about dimension-crossing doorways. If that really was what I had found in the Indian restaurant all those years ago, then presumably it was still there.

We would go into Guildford tomorrow (or rather today), I decided. Just Dawn and me. My parents would be delighted to have Kirsty to themselves for a while, and Dawn and I would enjoy exploring our old haunts, something we had not really done since our student days. We would work up an appetite shopping, have lunch in the *Indian Cottage*, go to the cinema or maybe catch a play at the Yvonne Arnaud Theatre.

I was going back. My heart pounded at the thought. *I was going back.*

*

Dawn was shaking me. "Wake up Philip. We're here."

"Just a little longer," I muttered.

"Come on lazy boy! The train's not going to wait. We're in Guildford already!"

I suddenly realised that I wasn't in my parents' guestroom bed now, I had dozed off on the train. Shocked into wakefulness, I hurried for the door before the guard lost his patience. A moment later I was standing dazed on the platform as the train pulled away and Dawn, tutting, said, "What are you *like*?"

"Well here we are!" I said, as if we'd just got off a plane in the Bahamas. Her playful castigation had put me in an excellent humour. "Where would you like to go first?"

"Shopping."

She tried on a succession of dresses in a succession of dress shops. I ostentatiously stifled yawns and assured her her bum did not look big in any of them. She didn't buy anything. She returned the favour when I insisted on visiting the comic shop. "I haven't reverted to my childhood," I assured her. "I just want to find out if Tintin's dog – er, what's his name again?"

"Snowy."

"Ah yes, thank you." I grinned as if I'd won a point by getting her to admit she knew his name. "It's just that Kirsty was wanting to know..."

"Oh no! Don't try and blame it on Kirsty!"

"She wanted to know if he was a talking dog. I mean yes, he talked in the stories, but she wanted to know if he was capable of verbal interaction with the human characters, or if his speech was merely Hergé inferring his state of mind."

"Is that what Kirsty asked you? In those actual words?"

"Don't underestimate her, she's a very articulate young girl!"

I didn't buy anything either.

When lunchtime approached, Dawn declared that we hadn't done enough to work up an appetite, so we headed for Guildford Castle. The path that wound around it was steep, steeper than she remembered, so I took her by the hand and led the way. We meandered past a succession of gardens. When we reached the top we were both panting, and neither in any particular hurry to break contact.

We sat together on a bench, looking at the view. Our shoulders touched. "Ah, Guildford," Dawn said. "We should come back here more often."

"We should," I agreed. I didn't want to say more for fear of breaking the mood, or expressing myself badly. I felt as if our future could still be ahead of us. Not in a wind-back-time sense; it wasn't a wish to undo the last eight years, even if I could have done it without losing Kirsty. Rather, it was the realisation that at thirty I wasn't exactly at the end of my life, and, on reflection, there was quite a lot that I did not regret.

There was no longer a fish tank in the *Indian Cottage*, and I didn't recognise any of the staff. They did a lunchtime menu, so I had a mild curry. Afterwards I ordered a sweet for Dawn and coffees for both of us. Then I feigned a stomach upset.

I raced along the very long corridor to the toilet anteroom. I noticed other changes along the way: the decrepit door through which I had tried to make my escape had since been replaced with a proper fire exit, and the Arthurian pictures on the opposite wall had been removed – faded rectangles showed where they had been. This time there was a light on in the anteroom. As before, the ladies' was opposite the entrance, the gents' to the right. I turned to the panelling on my left.

It was not as I remembered. The row of coat hooks had been removed, and purple flock wallpaper had been pasted over it. It did not look remotely like a doorway. It was a blank wall.

It's never the same when you come back, I thought. The secret lift turns out to be a broom cupboard; the secret passageway is bricked up; the haunted house was demolished, not recently but years before the time you thought you'd visited it. All the evidence that anything remarkable ever happened has gone. I had told Kirsty stories like this at Hallowe'en and at Christmas time; she would sit on my lap, tingling with safe-fear while the candlelight flickered and the wind howled around the converted barn.

But I had come prepared. After checking that nobody was in the gents' (and hoping nobody would come out of the ladies') I took a Stanley knife from my pocket and cut through the flock wallpaper where I remembered the door frame to be. This proved harder and more time-consuming than I expected, but my persistence paid off. I pushed gently. The "wall" gave slightly. I was not mistaken: they might have covered it, but the hidden door was still there! I pushed harder, and with great reluctance the panelling swung open.

My heart pounded. The corridor was still there. It was no longer lit, but I was prepared for that too – I took out a small but powerful torch and shone it into the darkness. The walls of the hidden corridor extended far into the distance. I stepped across the threshold. The floor felt sticky. Behind me I heard the sound of a man coughing; he was in the "ordinary" corridor, the one beyond the anteroom, and I realised he was on his way to the gents'. Hurriedly I pushed the panelling shut behind me. I heard the door to the anteroom open so I switched off my torch in case its light showed where I had cut through the wallpaper. I held my breath.

As my eyes adjusted, I realised the corridor was not in total darkness after all. There was an exceedingly dim glow coming from the walls. I was slightly shocked to realise that the lights in the walls had not been removed or switched off - they had simply been covered! I touched a wall near one of the glows. Its texture made me think of dirty silk. I pressed it. It gave like foam in old furniture. I cut at it with the Stanley knife, made a gash and tore at the stuff to reveal one shining wall light. The coating over it was nearly two inches thick.

I walked further along the corridor, drawn by a combination of disgust and fascination. The floor became less sticky and the coating on the walls became harder. By the time I passed the low ducting the coating was as hard as brick, and indistinguishable from the wall itself.

Past the turn, I came to the downward flight of steps. But the corridor below was filled with the dirty silk stuff, almost to its ceiling; only the top three steps remained uncovered. At that point my disgust overrode my fascination, and it occurred to me then that I might be in danger. I headed back, walking more quickly than before.

The wall light near the entrance was still exposed where I had cut at the coating, but I was aware of movements around the frame of the hinged panelling. In the light from my torch the moving things resembled fat spiders. They fled at my approach but – and this detail really unnerved me – they did not flee far from the frame. They were trying to seal my exit! Frantic now, I hacked at the place where the gap between the door and the frame had been. In truth, the stuff was not yet thick enough to present a real obstacle. Once I'd got a fingertip grip on the edge I pulled the panelling open, dashed through into the anteroom and swung it shut behind me.

There was nobody else in the anteroom, and the gents' was free again. I washed my hands and face and brushed at my clothes. I took my jacket off and shook it to make sure it was clear of the spider-things.

I was calm then. A moment later I was elated. So much for the secret passageways that disappear when you visit them a second time.

This one had tried to do just that – but I had returned too soon for it and I had *caught it in the act*!

I was overjoyed. I wanted to tell Dawn. I had promised myself I would not keep it secret from her if I found it again, and I had. The spider-things had been alerted; in a day or two that panelling would undoubtedly be closed for good, and in a month or two the corridor would be filled in with the solidifying silk-stuff. But it hadn't happened yet.

I hurried back to the restaurant. I had been gone a long time from Dawn's point of view but she was unconcerned. She had joined a couple at another table and was in animated conversation with them. She introduced the man – a former student called Adrian whom Dawn had met during her abruptly curtailed final year at university. His wife's name was Sarah.

She was my Sarah.

I had often thought about her, and I had often imagined us meeting again. But it had never been like this in my imagination. I stared at her, and she stared back, an unreadable expression in her eyes, for all the world as if she didn't know who I was. What was going on here? Was she overcome with anger and bitterness for the way I had abandoned her to marry my ex-girlfriend? Was she wracked with conflicting emotions? *Why was she pretending not to know me?*

But she wasn't pretending. I realised that as soon as I saw the flicker of recognition belatedly appear in her eyes. She let out a cry, "Philip!" and stepped forward to hug me. There was no mystery; it had been more than eight years, and we'd only dated for a few weeks. She hadn't recognised me straight away because I simply hadn't been that important.

I took her in my arms. I held her tightly, and for too long. She was pregnant.

Chapter 6. Red Pull Cord

Chichester, December 2005

There was nothing irrational about what I was planning, I was simply leaving no stone unturned. If what I had in mind proved to be wrong, then no harm done. If, on the other hand, I was right...

The McDonald's was fairly busy. It was a Saturday morning, the first day of the rest of my life. I was having a quarter pounder with cheese and a coffee for breakfast. I had to share a table for four with an elderly couple who barely glanced at me once the "Is this seat taken?" interchange had been concluded. There was a look of distaste on the wife's face. Whether this was at my bruised appearance or at the necessity of having to eat in a fast food restaurant for whatever reason, I could not tell.

I'd managed to get a look at the party table before purchasing my meal. The green lipstick heart had been cleaned off. I noted the positions and directions of the three security cameras; from this I could at least glean where the two girls *hadn't* gone.

There had to be a hidden door somewhere. Unfortunately there wasn't a long corridor in this restaurant; the doors to the toilets were partly offset from the main eating area, but they were visible to some of the tables.

Customers came and went as I lingered over my breakfast. The elderly couple departed, to be replaced by a man stinking of stale cigarette smoke who sat with his son and daughter, apparently twins of about seven. Whenever he spoke to them it was invariably to berate them.

I got up to buy a second coffee and burger and found another table. This one gave me a different view of the restaurant, but I couldn't for the life of me see where They could have hidden a secret door.

It occurred to me that that was kind of the point.

Other things crossed my mind while I ate. Did Kirsty know she wasn't really my daughter? (The thought still stabbed at my heart.) I was certain she did not know. William was stupid enough to have told her, stupid enough to let it slip to her just as he had let it slip to me. He might have backtracked afterwards, told her he was only teasing. But no, it hadn't happened. If it had, I would know about it.

In all conscience, in all honesty, I could not imagine Kirsty wanting to get out of her fortnightly visits. I was not like the father at the table I had just vacated; I didn't stink, and I never swore in her presence, let alone at her. I respected her boundaries and her privacy. I took her to fun places, I told her stories, and I didn't think I ever bored her.

I'd also prayed for her to die. Sure, that had been a very long time ago and I had thoroughly repented of it, but the fact remained. Maybe William had somehow found out about it. (I remembered the creak on the landing behind me when I had prayed to the cobweb-covered crucifix.) Maybe he'd told Kirsty. And she knew well enough without him needing to tell her that I'd broken my marriage vow. Even if she didn't know about the other vow.

This line of thinking was getting me nowhere. On impulse I got up, made my way to the toilet, then mimed getting a vibrated phone call through my trouser pocket. Nobody was paying me any attention anyway, but if someone did happen to look in my direction I thought my interrupted walk would look natural enough. I maintained a generic one-sided conversation, with silences and occasional nods, while I got a closer look at the place where a hidden door ought to be. The doors for Ladies, Gents, Disabled and Staff Only did not leave much space, but it occurred to me that the hidden door didn't have to be full width, or height.

My attention was drawn by a section of wall with three coat hooks. The hinged wooden panelling in Guildford had had similar coat hooks. Casually I made to lean against that part of the wall, affected a stumble and fell a little heavily against it. But this wall proved to be solid.

And suddenly the whole thing felt stupid. Whatever I'd experienced ten years ago, or imagined I'd experienced, it didn't mean my daughter had slipped through a hidden door into a parallel world.

There was nobody in the gents except for one man who was leaving as I entered. I used a urinal, then went over to a basin and splashed cold water over my face. I needed to be wide awake, I needed to be *really* rational.

Then I caught a glimpse of something in the mirror that was so wrong it caused my heartbeat to spike. It didn't belong here, it shouldn't *be* here, but there it was, in here with me. Afraid even to acknowledge what I'd just seen, I turned slowly around to face the thing that was behind me.

I was alone in a completely normal men's room. Nothing was out of place.

The memory of the emotional reaction remained even as I strained to remember what had prompted it. *What had I just seen?*

I was interrupted by the noise of the door slamming open; the man who stank and who swore at his children came in. He did not acknowledge me as he made for one of the stalls.

I lingered for a few moments, aware of the pointlessness of chasing an elusive memory in a public toilet. I went out.

*

There was no point in staying in the hotel any longer. Whatever my dreaming mind was trying to tell me, Kirsty wasn't going to phone me on my mobile. She wouldn't know I was in the hotel. If she did try to phone me, she'd call me on my landline number, so it made sense to get home as soon as possible.

If she did turn up in Chichester, it wasn't that much of a drive from Southsea to come and collect her.

On top of everything else, another night in a hotel was an expense I could ill afford.

Driving home, I suddenly realised what it was that I'd seen in the men's room mirror. It was a red pull cord. Just that, mystery solved. I frowned, bemused. Because I couldn't for the life of me imagine why a red pull cord would have freaked me out.

The thread of a huge dangling spider, perhaps? No, that hadn't been on my mind. No horribly realistic demon doll hanging by the neck either, or anything along those lines. I'd seen a red pull cord that was no more and no less than it appeared to be but it had provoked a strong reaction. Why would it do that?

Maybe that sort of thing is normal when someone loses their child?

Chapter 7. Where Our Prayers Go

The house felt empty on Sunday evenings after Kirsty was gone, or on those weekends when she didn't visit. But that was as nothing compared to the feeling now. She was lost and she might never come again. I hadn't given up hope, but there was no getting away from the possibility that she had been killed.

I picked mail up from the door mat. A red LED winked on the answerphone in the hall. A single message. It was from Dawn telling me that Kirsty was at a party at the McDonald's in Chichester Gate. My heart skipped as hope overrode reason, but reason made a quick comeback and I realised Dawn must have made the call from Benjamin's mobile yesterday afternoon. I couldn't believe everything had been normal less than a day ago. It occurred to me that if Miss Havers and I hadn't slipped out of the conference and caught an earlier train, I would have got this message before heading off to collect Kirsty.

There had been no other calls, neither on the landline nor my mobile. No news really wasn't good news. Baseless speculation thrives in the absence of information.

There was too much that didn't feel right. I found myself thinking about the misdirection used by stage magicians, or by the criminal mastermind in stories by the likes of Agatha Christie. The failure of the CCTV cameras to pick up anything was surely a form of negative evidence, like Sherlock Holmes's dog that didn't bark. The girls all wearing make-up so that Roger Jeffries could not tell them apart - that was beginning to sound a little too convenient.

Had Kirsty even been at the party?

William arriving at the Price Estate within seconds of Benjamin and Dawn. Coincidence? Probably. But the more I thought about it, the more it felt as if they were expecting me to turn up at the McDonald's, and my failure to do so had scuppered their plans, whatever they had been. I recalled how I had stood at the front door of the barn conversion, and how I had sensed (or perhaps imagined) a preternatural darkness inside, and how I had almost been tempted to go in. Had that been my instincts at work? Did they have Kirsty tied up in there?

And was whatever had happened to Chloe Faulkner a necessary part of the misdirection, or merely a ghastly accident?

I ran through some scenarios, action I could take. In one I drove over to Singleton that afternoon, parked in the pub car park and walked boldly through the gates of the Price Estate. In some versions of events my key still fitted the front door lock, while in others I used a crowbar. Either way, I was in before William and Benjamin realised what was happening; before they'd even come out of the main house I got the door to the guest room open, the room I'd slept in during those final days before I moved out, the room from which I had sensed the darkness. Before William and Benjamin had hurried across the gravel drive I removed the gag from my daughter and I held her to me and told her she was safe, and as my brothers-in-law were about to come in through the front door the police arrived, sirens blaring, because I'd called them on my mobile immediately prior to leaving the pub car park.

I wondered if the fact that I wasn't *really* going to enact this scenario was indicative of cowardice, or simply an acknowledgement that deep down I didn't think it was very likely.

There was another, more immediate scenario that I also played out in my mind. In this one I went next door to tell my neighbours David and Esther what had happened to Kirsty. Yasmin, their deaf ten year old daughter and Kirsty's friend, would be aware that something was wrong, otherwise why hadn't I picked her up in the morning to join us for archery club? I would crouch down to her level and enunciate very deliberately so that she could read it from my lips and I would tell her exactly what had happened. Yasmin's eyes would widen in disbelief, David would go to hug her reassuringly, she would break free or else she would turn and beat her fists ineffectually against his chest and I would feel ashamed of myself for thinking the noise she made when she cried made her sound retarded.

This one played out much as I'd imagined.

*

David and Esther were good, kind neighbours. I stayed for a while, aware of Yasmin's sobbing, just audible from the bedroom above. Esther told me she'd known something was wrong because there had been reporters round that morning. They'd asked David where I was when he'd gone out for a newspaper, but they had not hung around for long.

I was often a guest in my neighbours' house, sometimes with Kirsty, sometimes on my own, and once with the Spanish teacher Montse - a short but sweet relationship that might have gone somewhere if she hadn't had family issues that forced her to go back to Spain. These get-togethers typically consisted of a beer (just one - they were strict about alcohol consumption), an easy-going chat, and one of Esther's dangerously hot curries.

The evenings inevitably ended with a prayer. I considered this a small price to pay for their company and hospitality. However, on one occasion I found myself reflecting on how, after the death of both my parents, I had endeavoured to put all forms of superstition and irrationality behind me, and this time that also involved taking the difficult final step of including my religious beliefs.

The timing of their deaths had undoubtedly been a staggering coincidence. They had been hit by a lorry on the Woking Road Roundabout on the very day my divorce from Dawn was finalised, the very day I had broken my covenant with God. But the only way I could get past that, the only way I could function as a rational human being was to accept it as no more than that: a coincidence. God had thus gone the way of precognitive dreams and giant trapdoor spiders. So on one occasion while David was clearing away plates, I casually asked Esther if she'd ever considered the possibility that there was no God. She gave me a long, puzzled look, amused rather than angry or offended, as if I'd asked why it never rains on bank holidays or why plumbers always undercharge. Still looking me in the eye she said, "If there were no God, where would our prayers go?"

That night, I found myself musing on her words. When I drifted off to sleep I dreamt that I was in an immense building with an endless succession of doors and rooms and corridors. All the rooms looked recently abandoned or not yet occupied, with a single exception. A man with his back to me (and unaware of me standing quietly in the doorway) was kneeling in prayer before a crucifix on the wall. He might have *been* me, and the crucifix might have been covered in cobwebs forming the shape of a kite, and the floorboard might have creaked as I shifted my weight.

*

On leaving Esther and David's that afternoon I could hear the phone ringing in my hall. I fumbled with my keys, got the front door open, but it stopped ringing just before I got to it. I dialed 1471 but the caller's number was withheld. It was all I could do to stop myself smashing the handset into the cradle. There were no messages.

I was beginning to sense a pattern.

Angry, I threw myself down on the settee and switched on the TV. I wanted a beer. I'd *had* a beer while I was next door, but I wanted another, and I didn't have any in the house. I'd had a beer, and we'd prayed, Esther insisting, "You've got to have faith. She *will* be found." But I wanted tangible results, and I wanted them now.

The phone rang again. I leapt up, grabbed the phone from the hall and muted the TV. Please be news, please please please be news.

"Hello?"

I recognised the voice of Kerry Marshall, the school secretary. It had come to the school's attention that I was currently undergoing domestic difficulties, and after due consideration it had been decided that the best course of action for all concerned was to allow me compassionate leave until the end of term while these issues were being resolved.

"'Domestic difficulties'?" I exploded. "Is that supposed to be some kind of euphemism? I've lost my *daughter*!" It was never a good idea to get angry with Kerry Marshall - she was petty, vindictive, had a long memory, rumour had it she was sleeping with the head teacher - but I was well past caring. I had the satisfaction of hearing her lost for words. When she resumed speaking it was to repeat what she'd just said in slow, deliberate tones as if I hadn't understood the first time. That was how she always handled disagreement. But my attention had been snatched away by what I was seeing on the muted TV.

There had been a delay of several seconds before I recognised the parlour in the Price Estate. There must have been a lighting crew because for once the room was brightly lit, which was probably the main reason for the delay. That, and the incongruity of seeing a familiar place on TV.

Dawn sat between her brothers on the settee, their mother looking very frail in her wheelchair at one end. Dawn looked terrible, really terrible, her eyes silently begging for anybody who knew anything to come forward. The picture changed to a recent photograph of a very happy-looking Kirsty, then changed back to the Price family. Dawn mouthed silent words, then broke down in silent tears. William took over then, his anger buried under shocked distress.

It didn't occur to me to unmute the TV. The only sound in the room was the wasp-under-an-upturned-glass buzz of Kerry Marshall on the phone. I cancelled the call and watched the appeal to the end.

I would watch it with the sound on when they showed it again later. But for now... For now, the fact that it was general knowledge gave crystal hardness to the reality of it all.

*

I told myself I was going out for fresh air, but if that had been true I wouldn't have taken the car. Waitrose was less than twenty minutes away, less than fifteen if I walked briskly, but I wasn't walking, I was driving. I would have something heavy to carry.

The sky wasn't quite overcast. At the Elm Grove traffic lights I turned right into Grove Road South and passed the school where I worked. High railings formed a barrier between the playground and the pavement. There were brick and glass buildings at the far side, dating back to the 1960s, and on the nearside a white building shaped to look like a castle. Kerry Marshall would be in the castle right now, no doubt typing up a report detailing how I had responded to her phone call.

Maybe I'd have responded better if she'd spoken plainly, or given me the option of taking time off rather than delivering it as a done deal. But she wasn't going to change.

A little further on I turned left into Marmion Road. The first eight notes of "Forever Autumn" played from deep inside my right trouser pocket when I was just sufficiently far from the Waitrose car park to not be able to get my phone out in time. This was getting ridiculous.

As predicted, my phone had stopped ringing by the time I was parked. But then I remembered a thing called call register.

The Waitrose car park is roughly one third multistory, two thirds open ground. I had parked in the multistory part, and the concrete meant I was not getting a signal. Nevertheless, the name of the caller appeared on the display: Miss Havers.

There was a pedestrian exit, a gap in a shoulder-high wooden fence which came out near one end of Stanley Lane. This was a straight, single-track road with a dozen or two garage doors on one side and the full length of the car park fence on the other. About halfway along there was a boy in a yellow raincoat, standing with his back to me. He must have sensed my presence because he turned suddenly. I was reminded of occasions when I stood quietly in the playground or a classroom doorway watching a boy about to grab a fire extinguisher or vault over a bannister or go out of bounds, only to realise (usually from his audience's sudden silence) that there was a teacher behind him. But I was mistaken about this boy. When he turned, I saw he was not in fact a boy, but a man, and not a young man at that. He was five foot two in height, if that, hence my assumption. I was not so sure now if he'd sensed me; I had the distinct impression he had been looking back to check that the coast was clear. If that impression was correct, though, what on earth had he been planning?

He walked away, in no particular hurry. I turned my attention back to my phone, and called Miss Havers's number.

As it rang, a part of me didn't want her to answer. We were friends out of school and out of hours, but to date that had not included outside term time or weekends. The first time I call her on a Saturday, and it's for something like this...I reminded myself that I was returning her call.

She answered. "Mr Hamilton? Oh thank God! Are you okay?"

"You've heard?" I asked.

"I'm not sure. What did you say to Kerry Marshall? I've never known her to... it was all I could do to make out what she was even saying. Has something happened to Kirsty?"

"She's missing," I said. I'd thought seeing the appeal on the muted TV was the final hammer blow of reality, but hearing myself say those words was something else again. "It's been -" I checked my watch; it was a bit after half past two "- less than twenty four hours."

"Oh God! What happened?"

I told her everything. I told her about the fight at the Price Estate, I told her about finding Chloe Faulkner and the police interrogation, I even told her about the dream in the hotel room.

No, I didn't tell her everything. I didn't mention the red pull cord or the secret doors.

I walked as I talked. I came out on Palmerston Road, the main shopping part of Southsea, and continued on past the pedestrianised part until I reached Clarence Parade, the road that separates the town from the common. I stood on the pavement looking out across the common towards the D-Day Museum and Southsea Castle. Beyond was the sea.

I often took Kirsty to the common to see the kites. There were sometimes groups of people flying elaborate and amusing ones such as the top and bottom halves of Homer Simpson. There was only one today, a straightforward kite-shaped kite. It didn't even have a tail. I watched it bob about in the random air currents against the grey sky, and thought once again about the cobwebs on the crucifix in the nursery.

It was getting on for three o'clock, and I was aware of the sounds of a football game about to start at Miss Havers's end. "If you need me, you know how to contact me," she said, raising her voice to be heard. Then, as a final thought before ringing off, she repeated a point she had already made: "Make sure the Family Liaison Officer keeps you informed of developments."

It suddenly occurred to me that nothing had been said about a Family Liaison Officer while I was at the police station in Chichester. It also occurred to me that there was something else I hadn't told Miss Havers: the fact that I wasn't Kirsty's real father.

Was that going to make a difference?

*

Back at Waitrose I bought a box of 24 cans of lager. I wasn't an alcoholic, I didn't have a drink problem, and when Kirsty finally did turn up she wasn't going to find me unshowered, unshaven and drunk. The house would be clean and tidy, and it would feel like home to her, whatever she had come back from.

But I needed a drink now, and this was much cheaper than the pub.

When I got home I drank one straight from the can without waiting for it to chill.

Chapter 8. The Father

They broadcast the appeal again on the early evening news, so I watched it with sound on for the first time. It was the usual tears and "If anybody knows anything, please get in touch," sort of thing.

I wasn't mentioned. That didn't surprise me, though I confess it dismayed me. I wasn't Kirsty's father; I wasn't *anybody's* father, I was simply the ex-partner of Kirsty's mother. But it struck me that the real father wasn't getting a mention either. That was surely significant. Was he out there somewhere, watching the appeal? Would the police have investigated him? Did he even know he had a daughter?

Although Kirsty didn't know I wasn't her real father, she might well have met her real father without being informed of the relationship. Maybe Dawn was still in touch with him; maybe she'd bumped into him in town and introduced him to Kirsty as an old school friend, or a friend of the family, or someone from work. If he lived or worked in Chichester, he might have become a familiar figure to Kirsty. Perhaps he didn't even realise Kirsty was his daughter, or hadn't realised until Dawn had made a slip of the tongue and he'd done the maths. Then, entirely by chance, he'd gone into McDonald's yesterday evening, seen ten girls milling around wearing Hallowe'en makeup, and realised one of them was his daughter. Then, when Roger Jeffries was distracted, he'd called her over. "Hey Kirsty, your mother's in the car park. She wants to speak to you outside." Kirsty would have gone with him, not screaming blue murder because he wasn't a stranger, and not saying goodbye to her friends because she thought she'd be coming straight back, and didn't want to advertise that she was probably about to get a telling off from her mother for some reason. Chloe might have followed Kirsty out of suspicion, or curiosity. Or maybe her disappearance was unrelated.

Perhapses and maybes aside, it was a credible scenario. A man with a clean record abducts a child - on impulse - because he's discovered she's his daughter. (He must have had a clean record, or Dawn would never have let him near Kirsty.) Maybe he'd seen the appeal on TV and realised what a stupid thing he'd done, and right now he was phoning the police to turn himself in.

That didn't quite make sense, because the police would surely have investigated him already. Unless Dawn hadn't told them who the real father was.

I sat back on the sofa and opened another beer. Aloud, I said, "Was it you, Howard? Are you the real father?"

Howard had been a student in Dawn's year at university. He had been studying theatre, and fancied himself as a playwright. He had a terrible skin condition and a chip on his shoulder – justified, he claimed, by years of putting up with people saying, "Can you puss the salt, Howard," or "What time is zit?" whenever they addressed him. Sensing it was far from being over for him, I'd made an effort to... what? Be his friend? Maybe not be a friend exactly, but I at least tried to treat him with decency, and not exclude him when I was part of a group.

On those occasional Friday afternoons when I was planning on going home for the weekend without Dawn, he would sidle up to me and say, "Let me know if your good lady needs satisfying while you're away. I'm happy to oblige." Then there was the Christmas disco when the slow dances started, and Dawn had invited Howard to dance with her. Recognising it for the pity gesture it was, he had declined.

Could Howard have got her pregnant? A slow-dance was one thing, but would he have turned down an offer of pity sex? The idea seemed almost comical, and the only reason I didn't dismiss it out of hand was because I couldn't remember anyone else who had been so blatant about his intentions towards Dawn. But it might not have been like that. Events could have been inadvertently set in motion during one of the weekends when I wasn't around. A summer evening in the union bar, Dawn slightly drunk and naturally affectionate, bestowing kisses on everyone *except* Howard. On her way back to her room, Howard appears in the corridor as if he just happened to be taking a short-cut through her hall of residence at the moment when she's unlocking her door. Howard greeting her as if surprised to see her, then casually mentioning how alienated she made him feel in the bar, making a bit of a joke of it but at the same time making her feel bad for missing him out, so now she feels she has to make it up to him. Draws him into her room, leaving the light off so she doesn't have to look at what she's kissing. What happens next is a misunderstanding, nothing so dramatic as rape. Or perhaps it *is* rape, but Howard can justify it in his own mind. More than that, he can plant doubt in her mind afterwards: "You *invited* me in, then *you* came onto *me* so strong! What was I *supposed* to think?" And as long as the doubt is in her mind, she can't tell anyone because she knows what her brothers would do to him if they found out. I think about how they behaved towards me, and I'd *married* her.

So the matter is quietly forgotten.

And now I needed to know if the child I had brought up and loved with all my heart had really been Howard's daughter all along.

I finished my beer, then called Dawn's number. It rang and rang. It went to answerphone. I hung up, waited a bit, and called again. On the fifth attempt Benjamin answered.

"Can I speak to Dawn please?"

"Who is this?"

"Come on Benjamin, you know my voice."

"You're drunk, Philip. You're slurring."

"Dawn and I are going to have to talk sooner or later - and it's in Kirsty's best interest that it's sooner."

A short pause. Benjamin said, "I'm sorry about... you know."

I could hardly believe it. He was actually *apologising* for his part in the assault. I hadn't expected that at all. I'd played it down when the police asked me about my injuries because I didn't want it to distract from the real issue.

"You weren't the one who hit me," I said. I was trying to sound magnanimous in my forgiveness but the tone came out all wrong.

Another awkward pause. I said, “I honestly didn't know about Dawn's... condition. Is she okay?”

“As well as can be expected, given that she’s just lost her daughter. It's epilepsy.”

“Yes, I sort of gathered it was that. Look, I need to talk to her,” I pressed. “I thought of something. It might be important, might be a clue.”

His voice was deep, authoritative. “Tell me then.”

I shook my head. “No, I need to run it past Dawn first. I’m sorry, I can't explain why, Ben. I will. Just... not yet.”

Another pause. I heard a door opening, and William's distinctive cough. Benjamin said, “Wait a minute.”

There was a muffled conversation between the brothers. I wondered what in God's name had possessed me to address him as Ben. Eventually he came back on the line. “Dawn won't talk to you,” he told me. “I mean, she can't right now. What was it you wanted to say to her?”

I was at a loss. If I ended the conversation now, I would have achieved nothing. I had been on the verge of mentioning the possibility that Howard was Kirsty's father but I'd stopped myself in time. I assumed - rightly or wrongly - that Dawn had not told her brothers who the real father was. Howard hadn't been referred to on the TV appeal, but if I mentioned him now - even just his first name - they would force it out of Dawn: his full name, where he lived at the time, how long he had pestered her before she finally gave in. And it would only have been a matter of time before they found him. Maybe they would find him before the police did.

It flashed across my mind that Kirsty's disappearance had been an elaborate hoax all along, designed to bring the real father's identity to light. But no, that surely wasn’t it.

“We need to pool our resources, Ben,” I said at last. I'd done it again, called him by his diminutive. I pressed on. “One of us might know something, maybe she said something that was trivial or meaningless on its own. You know, like we've both got half the jigsaw each but the picture has to be complete before..." I was talking metaphors with the nightclub bouncer who had held me while his brother me up. "Make a list of Kirsty's friends, places she goes. Any boy she might have mentioned, talked about more than once, maybe blushed if asked about him. Anything like that."

"Dawn told the police everything," Benjamin replied. "We all have. Everything relevant."

"But what if something *seemingly* irrelevant..."

"I'm sorry, Philip." Then, as if conscious of how compassionate he was sounding in William's hearing, he added, "This is a matter for Kirsty's family." That hurt. I was aware of William's voice saying, "Give me the phone!" Then without any preamble he said, "We told the police everything we know. Nobody wants a hanger-on pretending to be Sherlock fucking Holmes."

No apology from William, then. Not that I'd expected one from him. But before he could hang up I said, "Wait! How can you know?"

The question evidently piqued his curiosity sufficiently. "How can I know *what*?"

"How do you actually *know* I'm not Kirsty's father?"

"You've got the wrong blood type."

That was unexpected. Dawn knew my blood type - she had gone with me to donate blood on one occasion - but Kirsty's? "Kirsty's too young to give blood," I said. "How the hell would you know what *her* blood type is?"

"She needed a transfusion. When she was a baby. When she needed her family, because you weren't there for her. You remember that, don't you?"

"Of course I remember," I said bitterly, but he wasn't finished with me.

"I know what you're thinking, *Philip.* You're thinking me and my brother are being unreasonable and not doing everything we can for Kirsty. Well think about this, *Philip.* If you'd made a go of things with Dawn, if you'd given Kirsty a stable background, she might not of run away. But you didn't, and she did. So you had your chance, and look what you did with it. So don't talk to me and my brother about Kirsty's best interest. Get off the phone, and *stay the fuck away from my family.*"

He hung up. I sat there speechless, my knuckles white where I'd been gripping the handset in my impotent rage.

I was still in this state of rage when I finally got a call from the Family Liaison Officer on my land line. I wasn't sure what the role of an FLO was supposed to be; Miss Havers had told me they were there to give support, but I'd read somewhere that they were primarily concerned with gathering evidence. Judging by her matter-of-fact manner, I guessed the latter was closer to the truth. She asked me to confirm a number of personal details - date and place of birth, address of permanent residence and so on - and concluded by asking me my relationship to the missing person.

"Her father," I said.

"According to our records, that is not the case, Mr Hamilton," she said.

"What? How can that be...?" I wondered how many more rugs were going to get pulled out from under me. Wasn't it my name on the birth certificate? Had I even signed it? My memory of that time was blurred, but surely... "At the time of her disappearance, I was legally responsible for her, and had no reason to doubt my paternity," I said. I spoke with deliberate precision now; it occurred to me that if I was still slurring, she was probably picking up on it, and being deliberately precise probably wasn't helping. I added, "I take it from your reference to 'the missing person' that she still hasn't been found?"

"No, Mr Hamilton."

I vented my rage then, berating her and her colleagues for not doing enough. She took it calmly; I wasn't saying anything she hadn't heard a hundred times. She assured me they were going through the CCTV footage from Chichester Gate itself and from the surrounding roads and railways, that there was no possibility that Kirsty's body had been dumped into the canal, and that her friend Chloe would be interviewed as soon as - but not until - she was in a fit state. She further assured me that they were treating this matter with the utmost seriousness, and they would inform me as soon as they had anything to report.

She was convincing enough, but I couldn't quite overcome the feeling that I was somehow irrelevant, just a man who had once had a relationship with Kirsty's mother - I wasn't even her stepfather! - and therefore a box to be ticked, someone who had to be kept in the loop.

"Have you interviewed Kirsty's real father?" I abruptly asked.

"We can't give out that sort of information," she replied.

"Do you even know who he is?"

"Who do *you* think he is, Mr Hamilton?"

"Howard," I said. I struggled to recall his surname; it had been a while. "Marlow," I said at last. I knew he had the same surname as one of Shakespeare's contemporaries, but spelled differently. "M-A-R-L-O-W. Like the playwright, but without the E." I remembered how he'd often claimed his talent was in his genes, although there was no evidence that he was descended from Kit Marlowe.

"Howard Marlow," she repeated. She tried to cover it, but I was sure I detected a note of sudden interest in her voice. Which made me think, had they even asked Dawn who the real father was? Had Dawn evaded the question? Claimed she didn't know? Hinted she'd had a number of one night stands with men she'd met at a pub or a night club?

I gave the FLO all the information I could remember about Howard. I didn't know his address - I'd probably never known it, and in any case it had been over a decade - but they'd be able to track him down. If my assumptions were correct, I might have my daughter back in no time.

If.

"Do you have my mobile number?" I asked. "In case you find her while I'm out."

My mobile number was on their records. She read it out to me.

"You will speak to Howard Marlow, won't you?"

"We'll investigate every lead, Mr Hamilton. In the meantime, will you do something for me?"

"What?"

"Promise me you'll lay off the booze. Look, I may be way off-beam here, but my instincts tell me this isn't the real you. Have an early night and get yourself a good night's sleep."

"I promise," I said, and hung up.

It was a promise more easily given than kept.

Chapter 9. Found

I made myself a pot of tea. I sat huddle in my armchair listening for the phone, the TV quiet in the background, the telephone within easy reach.

Late afternoon turning into evening. The phone did not ring.

Late evening. Night. Eleven o'clock, the time I'd usually be in bed if I had school in the morning, although it was a Saturday night. I had a shower with the door open so I'd be able to hear the phone extension in the bedroom.

I lay in bed on my back staring into darkness. I reminded myself that I was using my instinct. From time to time I would glance to my left at the LED clock, watching the hours pass, willing myself to sleep.

*

When the phone finally rang I was awake and sitting up and holding it to my ear before it had a chance to ring a second time. "Yes?"

"She's been found," said the FLO.

"Really? How is she?"

"She's a bit shaken, but unhurt. The station doctor wanted to keep her in for observation, but she's anxious to see you. An officer will drive her to your house within the hour."

"Thank God. Thank God. Thank God. Thank God."

*

That is not what happened.

The insomnia dreams were back.

The scene that had no basis in reality played itself out over and over again before morning came.

Chapter 10. The Man Without The Birthmark

The morning came cold and bright, a backdrop to a happy ending that had not transpired. Two nights had passed since Kirsty had gone missing. The probability of her being found alive had plummeted. The phone remained silent.

Maybe they hadn't been able to track down Howard Marlow, or he wasn't at home. Or my instincts were wrong, and he had nothing to do with Kirsty's disappearance, and wasn't even her father in the first place.

By mid morning I still hadn't heard anything. I phoned the number the FLO had given me. She wasn't on duty. Instead I was put through to a male officer. I had to explain who I was, which meant going through the whole not-really-Kirsty's-father routine again. It didn't help that I hadn't made a note of the name of the female officer from yesterday.

"Did you find Howard Marlow?" I asked once everything was cleared up.

"We are not exploring that line of enquiry any further," he eventually told me.

*

Howard must have had an alibi. Or he'd left the country, or had died. Or most likely of all, he had never had sex with Dawn. Just because I'd imagined it happening didn't mean it had. In all the time we were married, Dawn had never mentioned Howard. No, that wasn't quite true; he *had* come up in conversation, maybe half a dozen times. On those occasions, if I was the one who brought him up, Dawn would laugh and say, "Ugh, don't remind me!" or something along those lines. The point being, she didn't avoid the subject. I didn't know if that ruled out the possibility of rape, but it did make it seem unlikely.

Was it consensual, then? Something she had done when drunk and regretted the following morning? No, I didn't think so. If it had happened, there was no way Howard would have kept it secret. He would have dropped heavy hints, or "accidentally" let it slip somehow or other, and he would probably have done it in company. And even if he hadn't had his way with my girlfriend, if he so much as *suspected* Dawn of going with someone else he would have let me know about that too – if he couldn't have her to himself, he would at least claim the consolation prize of souring our relationship.

These speculations were getting me nowhere. All the while, Kirsty was out there, lost and in danger. I should be out there looking for her. But where? The police had thoroughly searched Chichester and were widening their search. There really wasn't anything I could do; there was nothing left for me to contribute, apart from sharing my vague sense of wrongness, and a conviction that there was an undefined darkness inside the barn conversion that had been my home for eight years.

I sat by the phone in case Kirsty rang. Hours passed. I tried doing normal things in the hope I could convince myself that by doing so, the world would return to normal, Kirsty would be found, and I would be working again. If life were normal, I would be preparing for next term. Mathematics didn't change much from one year to the next, but there was a new syllabus for History, and I'd been informed of some areas for improvement after my last observation. I'd been advised that I could be more proactive in finding means of "involved" learning.

I tried reading through course notes about Elizabethan England but found my eyes were sliding off the page. I had more success with some illustrated articles in past issues of *History Today* and *BBC History Magazine*, and even made notes towards writing a play about Walsingham in the form of a James Bond parody. For a while I was actually quite productive, but my anxiety kept imposing itself, and the telephone's stubborn refusal to ring was drilling into my nerves.

Tiredness hit me when I got up to get lunch. Somehow I'd forgotten how sleep-deprived I really was. I let myself fall back into my chair and briefly dozed. I was in Elizabethan London, in a tavern. Kit Marlowe was there. I was threatening to stab him with the bread knife if he did not tell me where my daughter was. But the dream was fleeting, without climax or resolution.

*

A little later, when I was fairly sure I was awake and not dreaming, I walked into Southsea to get something to eat. I was sitting on a bench in the pedestrianised area eating a hot pie when I heard the first eight tinny notes of "Forever Autumn" from my jacket pocket. For once I managed to answer my mobile phone before the ring tone stopped.

Miss Havers's voice: "Any news?"

"If there were news you would know about it," I said.

There was a brief silence as she processed the compliment, then asked, "Is the Family Liaison Officer keeping you up to date?"

"Yes, I got a call this morning. There haven't been any developments."

"This *morning*?" she echoed, incredulous. "This is your *daughter* who's missing! They should be updating you *hourly*. At *least*."

I remembered her telling me that she had dated a police officer a few years ago. She knew these things.

"It's not as simple as that," I explained. "It turns out... it turns out she's not my daughter after all."

There was a long, long silence. I felt oddly ashamed. I was aware that somebody was watching me, and listening to my half of the conversation. He was sitting on another bench, next to a raised flower bed. It was the man in the yellow raincoat, the man I had mistaken for a boy when I'd seen him in the road next to the Waitrose car park. I could not have mistaken him for a boy now; he was close enough that I could see the stubble on his chin, and the wrinkles on his forehead and at the corners of his eyes.

"That shouldn't make any difference," Miss Havers eventually said. "To all intents and purposes you *are* her father. Do you know who her real father is?"

"Her biological father? No, no I don't. I thought it was somebody we knew at university but the police seem to have ruled that out."

"It shouldn't matter," Miss Havers insisted. "If he hasn't come forward, and Dawn hasn't said who he is, it makes no difference."

"It feels as if it does," I said.

"What do you mean?"

"It's hard to explain. William told me the very evening she'd gone missing, and it felt... retroactive. As if she'd never been my daughter. As if I'd imagined the last ten years. Not completely, but it's..." I swallowed. "It's as if I accepted it too easily."

"Listen to me, Mr Hamilton. Kirsty is your daughter. Genes mean nothing. You brought her up as your own. Lots of people adopt children, and lots of fathers are not blood relations, and sometimes they don't even know it, but it's not what counts. Love is what counts, and by that reckoning you are one of the best fathers I know."

"You told me once I was a terrible father."

"And you know I only said it because it was so far away from being true that I could joke about it."

It was my turn to process a compliment. When I could speak again I thanked her.

But when we finished our conversation I found myself thinking about the time in Whitby when I had wished my daughter out of existence. This time I was the one who had been wished out of existence.

Thus began a new phase of my outlook. In Whitby I had put aside all superstition, but now I had lost my certainty that the world operated on rational rules. Maybe it didn't operate on rules at all. Or maybe they were rules that I had yet to learn.

The anticipation of learning them filled me with a sense of fear, and a tingling excitement that was not altogether unpleasant. It did not occur to me that I might fail to learn them.

*

That night I met the living dead.

Fully dressed, I had fallen into a restless sleep in front of the television, and awoken to find the cuffs of my jeans wet, as if I had walked through long grass after the rain. I noticed the wet trouser cuffs before I noticed that I was not sitting in my armchair at all, but lying on a bench looking out to sea.

Stiffly I moved to a more upright position. The moon, nearly full, hung over the sea. The waves crashed gently over the shingle on the beach. It must have been this sound, I supposed, that had lulled me off to sleep in the first place - but that didn't make sense because I would not have heard it from the house.

“I'm a somnambulist, then,” I said out loud, mildly surprised and almost amused. “I didn't see *that* coming.”

I was freezing. I got up to move about, clapping my gloved hands together. I was wearing a long coat, and had a woollen hat in one of the pockets, which I put on. I remembered leaving the house. It had been raining, and I had continued to skim through books and articles on the Elizabethan age, the TV ignored in the background, but then the sky had cleared and I'd gone out, hoping to tire myself enough to sleep. I had no idea how long I'd been dozing on the bench.

As I turned, I saw the little man in the yellow raincoat walking away from the bench. These encounters were now too frequent to be coincidental. I made to follow him; I thought about shouting after him, but then I was distracted by a sharp crack, possibly the sound of a vehicle backfiring, and the sight of somebody running across the common, as if in terror. I traced his path backwards, and saw a pair of animated corpses, their pale skins half in shadow from the streetlamps along Serpentine Road at the edge of the common. They moved stiffly yet fluidly, their faces skulls. The woman's skull still sported long white hair which cascaded to her shoulders and (now up close) shone in the moonlight. They had an air of arrogance and confidence and menace. They had seen me and there was no mistaking it, they were heading towards me.

I backed against a tree. The bark was solid through my coat and gloved hands. If this was a dream, it was a vivid and tactile one.

The undead pair halted a short distance away. The dead man spoke. He said, "Mr Hamilton." He had a deep voice, a northern accent. He said something else which I didn't catch, then added, "I hope to God she's okay."

The morbid illusion had been so complete, yet it evaporated the moment he spoke. They were people I knew, people who liked to dress up and get made up and go to Gothic-themed parties. "Good evening Tony." I nodded at the woman. "Mildred." I added, "I don't mind admitting you gave me quite a scare.

Tony laughed, a little embarrassed. "Sorry about that, sometimes we forget we're in character."

Mildred said, "What about the other girl? Chloe? Has she said anything?"

I regarded my companions. They were aiming for Byronic vampires rather than Romero's zombies. Tony's pure white hair, shaved to within a millimetre of his scalp, gave him a Lon Chaney look, enhanced by his whitened face and black eyeliner, and lines drawn from the corners of his mouth to make it appear wider than it was. Mildred looked more like a white-haired Morticia Addams. I knew them better as Mr and Mrs Webster, who dressed rather more conventionally when they attended parents' evening. Their introverted son, Sebastien, silently excelled in my Mathematics classes and equally silently floundered in my History classes. Both parents worked for the Housing Department of Portsmouth City Council. In the evenings Tony wrote short stories for a small-press magazine called *The Velvet Kings*, and Mildred illustrated them. They made a good team, apparently, famous within their niche market. Their *very* niche market.

"I'm sure Chloe knows something," I said. "But she's in no fit state."

"You must be out of your mind with worry."

"I am, Mildred. I really am."

"There's nothing we can say to you that will help. But we can listen. Can't we, Tony?"

Tony readily agreed. I thanked them both.

But for some minutes the three of us walked in silence. It was as comfortable, companionable a silence I could have hoped for in the circumstances. When conversation started up again, we talked at first of mundane things. Tony had received an email at work consisting of a number of very funny jokes, and he had forwarded them to several colleagues. "Two of the jokes were not what you'd call politically correct," he explained. "Unfortunately the head of department saw them."

"What happened?"

"All concerned have to attend a training course in Equal Opportunities and Diversity. Like we can really afford the time right now! The irony is, the 'offensive' jokes weren't even the funny ones - I wouldn't have bothered forwarding it for them."

In turn I told them how Miss Havers and I and two other members of staff had been sent to Woking for a similar event because we had shown "insufficient disapproval" towards a pupil who had made some "edgy" remarks during a school assembly. I mentioned the Martian war machine, and I shared a brief anecdote about a speaker at the conference who insisted we should never say "homosexual" because it means "man sex". Tony chuckled at that. He had a deep-voiced laugh. "Sounds like she's got her Greek and Latin mixed up."

"That's exactly what I told her."

"Really?" He chuckled again. "I bet she didn't like that! What did she say?"

"Well to be fair she looked it up during the break and admitted she'd got it wrong."

Still chuckling, Tony said, "At least you got to see the Martian. I wish our training course was in Woking."

Our aimless walk across the common curved back towards the coast, where we found another bench facing the sea. Glancing back, I saw that the little man in the yellow raincoat had been following us from a distance. I was about to remark but Tony beat me to it. "It's that man again," he said in a low voice, his comment directed at his wife.

"Do you think it *is* him?" Mildred asked.

"There's no mistaking him. That air of determined-dignity-in-the-face-of-adversity. Not to mention the 1970s fashion sense. And that walk! Like he's not used to being out of doors."

"A closet agoraphobe, perhaps?"

Tony chuckled once more for several long moments. "Nice one! I might steal that."

"You usually do."

I cut in as we sat down on the bench. "You've seen him before?"

Tony nodded. Mildred said, "*If* it's him. He kind of made his presence felt when we were in Whitby."

"*Whitby*?"

"We were up there for a Goth festival. It seemed that wherever we went, he was there too, following us."

"Following *you,* Mildred," Tony clarified. In a mock stage-whisper he told me, "I think he had a bit of a crush."

"When was this?" I asked.

"Last year."

Not the occasion when Kirsty went missing, then. Nevertheless...

"Granted, he looks like him," Mildred said. "But the man in Whitby had a birthmark. A port-wine stain I think you call it? Anyway, it covered nearly half his face and the underside of his chin.

But he doesn't have it now. I've seen him up close and there's no birthmark at all."

"It's him," said Tony with certainty.

"How can it be him if he doesn't have the birthmark?" Mildred said. I had the feeling they'd rehearsed this argument before.

"He could have got rid of it."

"How?"

"Laser surgery."

"Really? He doesn't exactly look the sort who could afford that, does he? I didn't think it was available on the National Health."

"Maybe he covered it with makeup."

"He'd put makeup on when he hasn't shaved for at least three days?"

They continued in this vein for a while. I zoned out, my mind racing through possibilities. He was a private detective sent by Dawn's family, thinking I secretly knew Kirsty's whereabouts? Unlikely, but possible; I'd found Chloe, after all. What if he was connected with Kirsty's disappearance? Even more unlikely; he wouldn't want me to see his face, certainly not in front of witnesses. But what about the Whitby connection? Was it even a connection?

Or maybe he wasn't following me at all. He was Mildred's stalker, not mine.

For a moment I'd honestly thought I was on the verge of a breakthrough. But this was all not-quite evidence that didn't quite connect. I was getting nowhere.

"Don't look now, but he's back," Tony said, looking over his shoulder. His words jolted me out of my maudlin state.

"Where?" Mildred asked.

"Right now? Disappearing behind the war memorial, trying very hard to look natural."

"What did you just say?" I said sharply, but he didn't need to repeat it. He'd said, "Don't look now," and although it was a trivial-seeming coincidence, the film *Don't Look Now* had been on the TV before I came out. I hadn't been watching, but I'd looked up when the Donald Sutherland character stood screaming with his drowned daughter in his arms. She had been wearing a red coat.

It was the main reason I had left the house.

"I know why I didn't see her," I said. The Websters picked up on my tone. They fell silent, the man without the birthmark forgotten.

"Kirsty went missing once before. Four years ago, when she was six," I explained. "We were on holiday in Whitby. It was a fraught few hours. We called the police and everything. I eventually found her on my own. But the thing I've never understood is, why didn't I see her straight away?"

"What do you mean?" Mildred asked.

"I was looking down the hillside from the Whalebone Arch. She should have been in plain view long before she got to the top of the hill. But I didn't see her until she was practically in my arms. I've never understood why, but I do now. Or rather, I *remember* why."

Tony and Mildred looked bemused. They exchanged glances. After a lengthy silence Tony said, "Well? Are you going to tell us?"

"She was wearing a red coat when she went missing. With a hood. That's why I didn't see her. I was looking out for a girl in a red coat."

"She lost the coat?" Mildred asked.

I shook my head. "No. She was still wearing it. But... it wasn't red any more." I glanced up, surprised to note that they were still listening, and not just with polite interest, although I would have continued anyway. "It was white. A dirty off-white, with the faintest tinge of pink, like someone had painted over a red wall with multiple coats of white paint but the original red still showed through. There were marks on the hood that made me think of a spider's legs. They were long and jointed, and brown, the colour of mud or... excrement." I didn't feel comfortable saying "shit" to the parents of one of my pupils. "I realised later the marks were made by the dirt on somebody's fingers. They had tried to grab Kirsty. They had got hold of her hood. She got free, but not before..."

"Not before they drained the colour out of the coat, like a vampire draining blood from an animal," Tony finished. He looked at me for confirmation; I nodded.

There was a silence. At length, Tony asked, "What happened to the coat?"

I pictured Kirsty sitting in the back of the car on the way home from Whitby. Was she wearing the pink-tinged dirty white coat then? I couldn't remember. "We got home from Whitby. Kirsty put it in her wardrobe at the end with the clothes she hardly ever wore. She never got it out again. One afternoon, while she was out shopping with her mother and uncle, I took it outside and burnt it."

Mildred said, "And you've only just remembered this now?"

I shook my head. "No, I didn't forget, I just didn't make the connection." Then, unsure if I was wise to do so, I added, "That seems to be the way it works."

It felt immensely satisfying to have solved at least one small mystery. It didn't even matter that it raised more questions than it answered.

*

Later, in the comfort of my bed, I wondered if I would ever sleep again.

When morning came I remembered one insomnia dream. I was following a schoolgirl up the hill in Whitby. I only saw her from behind but I was sure she was my daughter, even though her hair was blonde and she was wearing it in pigtails. She was wearing the coat, and it was white, but it was a clean white with no tinge of pink, and no marks on the hood. I was certain she knew I was following her but she did not turn around. I tried to call to her but I could not. This was not the familiar dream problem of my throat constricting;

for some inexplicable reason I was uncertain about my daughter's *name.*

At length we came to the Whalebone Arch. She paused under it, then began to turn so that she would face me at last. But I was distracted. High above her the bones of the Whalebone Arch met at the apex; as I watched they appeared to soften as if melting, and they began to droop.

I looked down again to see the girl's face, but she had turned away. I had missed my chance.

Chapter 11. Losing Control

Days passed. No clues, no developments, no demands for a ransom. The FLO - the original one - kept in touch with me once or twice a day. My sanity remained in suspension, helped in no small part by phone calls from well-wishing friends and relatives. I wished my parents were still alive. I would even have settled for the moral support of Mrs Price, but it wasn't to be.

The erratic sleep patterns continued, and so did my wanderings. I wanted to speak to the man without the birthmark, but he was no longer the mysterious background figure who kept turning up unlooked for. I went to the pie shop during the day and the common at night, thinking he might revisit these places, but there was no sign of him. Perhaps if Mildred had been with me he would have appeared. Or perhaps he'd moved on.

I kept searching. He had to know *something*. He'd been seen in Whitby, and Kirsty had once gone missing in Whitby. Not much to base hopes on, but it was all I had.

On the Wednesday evening there was a light, near-freezing rain. I walked into the town wearing a raincoat with a high collar, a waterproof hood, and a pair of woollen gloves. From time to time I stopped in shop doorways, partly for shelter when the rain pounded down more heavily, and partly to give him an opportunity to show up.

Just as I was on the point of giving up I thought I saw his yellow coat in the distance turning off Grove Road South into Marmion Road. I hurried to catch up with him but quickly lost track of him. I stopped outside a pub called *The Marmion Tavern*. A poster in the entrance promised live music from a local band called Glee Division. I went in.

I froze in the doorway, dismayed. There was no sign of the man without the birthmark; instead, several of my fellow teachers were sitting around three tables that they had moved together. Miss Havers was among them. Across the room, the band was setting up. My colleagues were evidently here for the gig.

I didn't want to see them. Or rather, I didn't want them to see me. I didn't want to be Banquo's Ghost at their gathering, and I didn't want them to be thinking I was the kind of father who went out to the pub when his daughter was missing. I considered making a discreet exit - after all, the person I was looking for was not here - but Terry, the Religious Studies teacher caught sight of me.

"Philip, over here!" he called.

I hesitated. I made no attempt to do the surprised, "oh I didn't see you" look; I didn't need to.

Miss Havers had risen from her seat. She came over and locked me in a tight embrace. No need to tell her there was no news.

"How are you coping?" she asked after a while.

"I'm... coping." I replied. I added, "I couldn't stay in the house. I couldn't just keep waiting for the phone to ring. There's nowhere I can go, nothing I can do."

"It's okay, it's okay. Don't give up hope. Come and sit with us." Sensing my reluctance she added, "At least for a while." She ended the embrace after a final squeeze and the others shifted to make space for me. I sat, coat still buttoned.

Even after the bizarre experiences that would follow - indeed, I cannot say they have truly come to an end - that evening stands out as one of the most surreal in my life. It was the sheer ordinariness of attending a social event for all the world as if my daughter hadn't disappeared off the face of the Earth, and for all the world as if I wasn't so sleep-deprived that I felt as if I'd passed through some barrier onto the other side of dreaming.

Miss Havers introduced me to Laura, her new partner, a pretty spiky-haired woman in her mid thirties, then went to the bar to get me a drink. I remembered Laura from the phone photo on the way back from Woking.

"She calls you Mr Hamilton?" said Laura quizzically.

“It’s a running joke we’ve got,” I explained. “A teacher thing. Well, we don’t all do it, but she and I always address each other formally, even when it’s an informal occasion.” I smiled and added, “Sensible people call me Phil.”

She reddened. “Oh God. I’m so sorry. You’re the one with the missing daughter.”

“Yes.”

“Oh God, I'm so sorry,” she repeated. “I didn’t make the connection. She's only ever referred to you as Phil. With me, I mean. God, I hope you find her soon.”

I was searching for something to say to reassure her when a deafening burst of electric guitar chords drowned out all conversation in the pub. This was the live music that the poster had threatened; the band was tuning up. The guitarist adjusted an amplifier, and played another chord at a much more reasonable volume. but Laura winced as if in physical pain.

“Glee Division,” Miss Havers explained as she returned with a tray of drinks, redundantly adding, “They’re a Joy Division tribute band.”

Across from me, a woman I didn’t recognise leaned forward and said, “The lead singer used to be at Southsea Grammar. Hayden Young, his name. He got himself expelled in Year 10.”

“Yes, I remember hearing about that,” I said. “It was before my time.”

Terry, seeing my puzzlement, explained, “This is Jane. Supply teacher. She’s covering for you.”

“For History,” Jane clarified. “I wouldn’t have a clue about Maths. But I did teach Hayden, several years ago. Not the loveliest child to teach. Did you know he tried his luck on *The X-Factor*.”

“Really? How did he get on?”

“Not... well.”

“But you came along this evening to give him your support?”

"Oh, I wouldn't miss this for the world!"

Further conversation became impossible as Glee Division launched into their set. They began by murdering "No Love Lost", a song I only recognised because it had a long instrumental intro before Hayden finally burst into song. I glanced over at Miss Havers and Laura. The former looked as if she was determined to enjoy this come what may; the latter was bracing herself for the worst evening in her life. I looked back at Hayden. His attention was on us; when he sang the title lyric, he had an arrogant look that seemed to say, "You lot expelled me, but look where I am *now*!"

I sat back in my chair, my coat still buttoned up. I wasn't going to stay long, but for the moment I felt an odd kind of comfort, the reassurance that the mundane world was carrying on as before, waiting for me to rejoin it. Kirsty *would* return, and the world would welcome me back. I just had to be a little bit patient, and have a little more faith.

The song ended. The teachers around the three tables applauded politely. I don't think anybody else in the pub joined in. Glee Division launched straight into a barely recognisable "Atmosphere"

When they were a few notes into "Transmission" the man without the birthmark came into the pub.

"That's him!" I said, getting up so abruptly I nearly caused drinks to spill. If anybody had even heard me they would have had no idea who I was talking about. I made for the bar, hoping I could get there before he was served. I would casually say, "Let me get that," and pay for his drink - judging by his appearance, I doubted he could afford to turn down many offers like that. Once I had paid he would feel obliged to talk. If he ignored me, or pretended he hadn't been following me, or it turned out he wasn't the man the Websters had seen in Whitby after all... well, I would cross those bridges when I came to them.

Hayden Young had started swinging his arms up in front of his face while he shout-sang the repeated word "dance" with an increasingly manic intensity. The man without the birthmark looked as if he was about to be served; he showed no sign of having seen me, and appeared to have no interest in the band. I sidled over to the bar and positioned myself beside him just as the barman asked him what he wanted. I was about to make my offer to pay when I was distracted by a collective gasp.

Hayden Young was thrashing about on the floor, having an epileptic fit. The collective gasp changed to one of derisory laughter as it became obvious that he was putting it on. I did not join in the laughter. Sickened, I clutched the edge of the bar, thinking of Dawn on the gravel driveway less than a week ago, just before her brothers laid into me. Whatever my feelings for her, she had been my wife for eight years, and what she'd been going through that evening... it had been real, and it wasn't funny.

For several moments I simply couldn't do anything.

The emotional paralysis passed, but I had missed my chance. The man without the birthmark had his wallet out and was paying for his pint of bitter.

Still he showed no sign that he knew I was beside him. I'd lost my conversational opening, but I wasn't about to give up on my one tenuous lead.

He was wearing a threadbare suit under his yellow raincoat. As he put his wallet away the jacket shifted, and I saw the glint of the pistol he was carrying.

I knew then who he was. Not a detective sent by the Price family to investigate me, as I had previously thought. No, they had sent him to kill me.

I fled.

Chapter 12. Forbidden Knowledge

Once outside in the icy rain I wondered if I had made a serious mistake.

I had no idea how hit-men operated. Why *would* I know? I was a teacher, for God's sake. The stories, the films, even the supposedly true accounts were a contradictory mess in my mind. The most likely-seeming scenario was that the killer would follow his intended victim for days in order to identify his routine, then kill him when his guard was down and he was in a lonely place. Even the most callous of killers wouldn't want to be dealing with witnesses. This was an age of mobile phones with video cameras and internet connections.

By fleeing from *The Marmion Tavern* I had thrown away my one advantage. My only hope now was that he hadn't seen me.

The freezing rain got heavier. I walked quickly along Marmion Road, unsure which way to go, wary of drawing attention to myself by running. Should I head for home? No – he'd surely know where I lived. Head for a police station then? Possibly. The nearest one was some distance away, and I'd have to work out a route that didn't leave me too exposed.

I stopped at a covered way at the front of Waitrose. It extended over the pavement, with a row of brick pillars supporting it along the kerb. I positioned myself by one of the pillars so that I could see the door of *The Marmion Tavern* whilst remaining more-or-less concealed.

Now that I was outside in the freezing cold, I began to wonder if I really had seen what I thought I'd seen. Did professional hit-men *really* reveal their guns by accident in crowded pubs? Maybe he was one of those people who keep their mobiles in a shoulder holster to *look* like a gun. If so, I could risk looking very foolish if I involved the police.

I had just finished buttoning up my coat and putting my gloves back on when the door to the pub opened. The man without the birthmark came out. He hadn't had time to finish his drink, so there was no longer any doubt - he really was after me. He looked in the other direction first, so I was able to withdraw behind the pillar.

There were other people about. A tall middle-aged couple passed between my pillar and the doors of the pub, partially blocking my pursuer's view. I made a run for it.

I rounded a corner without being seen. Now that there was no doubt in my mind, I took out my mobile phone. I managed to dial 999 without taking my gloves off. A group of revellers, already drunk, were staggering down the side street towards me as I waited for the emergency operator to answer. Eventually a female voice asked me which service I required. Before she had finished speaking I said, "I'm in Southsea, there's a man with a gun after me." The revellers drew alongside me as I looked for the road name, and a remark one of them had made set them all off laughing. "I'm in Richmond Place," I said through the laughter. "No, I'm serious! I honestly think he's going to kill me!"

The operator asked me to describe my pursuer. I gave details of his height, his clothes, where I had seen his gun – and then, idiotically, I mentioned his birthmark. The operator wanted details: was it a port-wine stain, and what part of the face did it cover? I tried to explain that he didn't have it any more. That was when I glanced back and saw him appear among the revellers.

I ducked into Stanley Lane and hurried along it. This was the road where I had first encountered the man who was now chasing me. On the left it was lined with garage doors for most of its length, and on the right the Waitrose car park. Trying to catch my breath, I hesitated at the gap in the fence that gave access to the car park, but decided against going that way; most of it was open space, and I was pretty sure the exits were locked at this time of night.

I ran on, intent on getting to the end of Stanley Lane, and around the corner into the main town, where there would be witnesses. But with every leaden step I was sure my pursuer would appear behind me long before I reached the end of the road. And even if I got there without him shooting me in the back, that was hardly going to be the end of the chase. There was still a way to go before the High Street, and I was badly out of condition; I'd run hardly any distance and I was already wheezing like a man twice my age.

Thrusting my mobile back into a coat pocket as I ran, I slowed a little to push the door of one of the garages. It did not move. I tried the next one. Same result. Could I climb onto a roof and over the other side? Height was the one advantage I had over my pursuer. Presumably I'd drop down into someone's back garden, or an alleyway or something, and make my escape that way, or even take refuge in a house. I could reach the roof edge easily enough, but could I pull myself up before the man without the birthmark came round the corner and saw me? If only there was a dustbin or pile of boxes or *anything* to give me extra height...

There were no dustbins. There was a bollard in the dropped-kerb pavement directly in front of one of the garage doors a little further along. And despite my sleep-deprived state, the absurdity of the bollard struck me. Its purpose was to restrict the movement of vehicles. In which case, why in God's name would anybody put one right in front of a *garage*?

Closer up, it was obvious that the bollard was not going to assist me in my attempt to climb. But there had to be something special about the garage itself. I turned the handle and pushed the door - it was one of those up-and-over types - and it lifted a couple of feet before hitting the bollard. Space enough to get in. I lay down on the icy pavement and rolled through the gap onto the oily concrete floor, pulling the door shut after me. Facing the door I lay on my side in the darkness for maybe half a minute, willing my panting breaths to be quieter, and not to cut into my lungs so painfully.

After what seemed like an eternity I heard the sound of running footsteps. They passed close by, then receded towards the far end of Stanley Lane. Still I remained as quiet as I could manage. I couldn't be sure those were the gunman's footsteps, or that he wasn't hiding at the end of the road waiting for me to emerge. Or maybe he had found another way into the car park and would be coming out of the gap in the fence any moment.

Sooner or later I would have to move. Sooner or later I did; I rolled away from the door and rose. I must have moved into the range of a motion detector, because a fluorescent light flickered on overhead. The edge of the garage door, I noted, fit quite snugly against the threshold; I hoped the light didn't spill out underneath it.

I turned my attention to the garage itself. It was immediately obvious that there really was something special about it.

There was no car. That was not surprising, of course. There was a wooden door in the right-hand wall, the sort that would normally connect an integral garage to a house. This was not an integral garage, though, so logically the side door should connect to the adjacent garage. I tried it; it was locked.

There were shelves on the wall opposite the side door. On the shelves there were various items typically found in garages: old tins of paint and a plastic container of weed-killer, and beside the shelves an old bicycle without a front wheel, some stacked flower pots and an aluminium step-ladder with a missing rung.

But it was the back wall that really grabbed my attention. Or rather, the absence of a back wall. There was a wooden frame that delineated the place where it should have been. There were rectangular marks in the sides of the frame that were unmistakably left by hinges that had been torn out. There was darkness beyond the absent back wall, but as I approached it I triggered a second motion detector, evidently one more sensitive than the first, and a second fluorescent tube flickered on.

The back of the garage was not open to an alleyway or garden as I had expected, but to a second garage.

My initial impression was that they were simply two garages built back-to-back with the dividing wall removed. If the front entrance to this second garage was accessible from the house side, then it would account for the bollard - the owners wouldn't need rear access to their garages, and probably considered it a security risk. Rather than take the chance of having their cars stolen via the Stanley Lane entrance, they had opted to render the back garage door unusable.

It almost made sense.

I stepped through the frame into the second garage. It was similar to the first: a wooden side door in the right-hand wall, a yard brush and another aluminium step-ladder - one with all its rungs - leaning against the opposite wall, a neatly-stacked pile of cardboard boxes that had once contained a desktop computer.

And then another rectangular opening, and a *third* garage beyond that.

There was no rationalising it. I was inside a corridor of garages, all joined end-to-end where no buildings should have existed.

I thought of the Indian restaurant in Guildford. It was a good hour's drive from Portsmouth, but there had to be a relationship between two impossible spaces, if not a direct connection.

As I walked through the third garage towards the fourth, I found I was remembering. I had seen things like this before, not just in Guildford, but in other places too. There had been a doorway in the petrol station on the road to Midhurst. I'd done night shifts there for three weeks, employed through an agency. I'd seen it every night; I'd once changed the month on the calendar that hung from a mesh over its frosted glass window. It never occurred to me that according to conventional logic it couldn't lead anywhere; seen from outside, the corresponding part of the building was a blank outside wall with some bins next to it.

There was the health centre waiting room in Portsmouth. A door with a sign that I thought said, "Staff Only." But staff never used it.

The fluorescent tube did not come on in the fourth garage. Either it or the motion detector was not working. The one in the fifth did. There was a large puddle in the middle of the floor, and numerous stacks of newspapers tied up with string and resting on the lid of a chest freezer that ran alongside the left wall.

I remembered a second hand bookshop where I had bought a selection of history text books. It too had a door which I misremembered as being marked "Staff only." A subway in

Horsham where I had got into an argument with a busker (my fault; I was being a jerk). He had positioned himself and his open guitar case next to a doorway that appeared at the time to be an inspection panel.

As a teenager I had been called into an office in a supermarket in Guildford, wrongly accused of shoplifting. Actually that one was a false identification; a cupboard with an oddly positioned door, but a mundane cupboard for all that. There were others, however. I couldn't place them all, or grasp their significance right now - and one in particular was lingering evasively at the tip of my mind - but I knew they had to be similar to this. But whatever the broader implications, the immediate one was that I was *safe*. The man without the birthmark couldn't *possibly* follow me in here. Nobody could. I looked at my mobile phone. "No signal." I smiled slightly and nodded; that was how it should be.

A black van mostly filled the sixth garage. It had the hunched design of an animal about to pounce. Its registration number was a T, an H and a backward C, then 44, and an upside-down V.

Had this garage once been open to the world? Perhaps its owner, in some parallel version of Portsmouth, had parked it one evening, then come down the next morning to find not just the vehicle but the entire garage gone. Or perhaps his garage was still there but its entrance led somewhere else. I thought of the time I had mapped out the red houses using my father's beer mats. I suspected that I'd got the right general idea, but had fallen short of the sheer complexity.

I could have squeezed past the black van, but chose instead to lean against the front of it. In this safe place I had time to think; my need for sleep had become much less acute, and my thoughts seemed more lucid than they had been since Kirsty's disappearance. As I rested there, I watched the darkness fall. In the absence of movement, each motion sensor timed out: the light in the first garage went off, and I could no longer see the garage door. For a moment I imagined it vanishing. Not in a way that left this corridor of garages open to Stanley Lane; rather, I imagined another garage beyond the first one, occupying the space that should have been that road, and others beyond it where the Waitrose car park should have been. And so on into the darkness, into infinity.

The light in the second garage went out, and it was as if the darkness was marching towards me. I registered this impression with neither fear nor joy. The third garage went dark. The fourth, which had not been illuminated, remained dark. A short interval later it was the turn of the fifth light to go out, and finally the sixth.

I was in complete darkness in an impossible place. I would remain in darkness as long as I kept still. Even as my eyes adjusted it stayed dark; there was not even an indicator light on the side of the freezer in the fifth garage.

Why did the Price brothers want me dead? (It did not occur to me that anybody else might have sent this hitman after me.) Was it because they didn't like me? Hardly. They'd never liked me, and they'd had eight years to do something about it while I was married to their sister, and a further two after the divorce. So why now, immediately after Kirsty's disappearance? Were the events linked?

Did they think I had something to do with her disappearance?

No, that wasn't likely either. If they really thought I knew something, the last thing they'd want to do was kill me.

What if they believed I knew something? Not about Kirsty's whereabouts, but something I wasn't meant to know? Something about them. Something I didn't *know* I knew - and in my lucid state I was aware that that should have sounded like a contradiction, but it did not. Something obvious that I'd somehow managed to miss, something hidden in plain sight.

I remembered how one Friday after school, Miss Havers and I had argued over whether the expression "hidden in plain sight" was a cliche. We'd been sitting at a table outside Caffe Nero shortly before the summer break, and she'd said it was lazy, and she'd taken a pupil to task for using it in a story. I countered that it exactly described a recognised situation, just as "conspicuous by its absence" did, and there was no point in reinventing the wheel.

It occurred to me that she was probably worried about me. I had left the pub without a word of farewell, and obviously not in a good state. Maybe she'd tried to ring me; if she'd had the least conception of just how unreachable I was right now!

I longed for the normality that I would get back once I found Kirsty alive and well. Miss Havers and I would resume our weekly natter, as she liked to put it, sometimes in a cafe, more often at the pub. We'd talked about anything and everything during those sessions, usually setting each other off laughing uncontrollably. Anything and everything except for the one topic that remained out of bounds. And one day, when she finally did open up on that taboo subject, my response had nearly cost our friendship.

We'd been talking about magic realist novels, and the conversation had turned to the sexuality of some of the authors, including Jeanette Winterson, as I recalled. Then, evidently feeling the time was right, Miss Havers had lowered her voice and finally confided in me that she was in fact a lesbian.

Without thinking I'd replied, "Well duh!"

Her expression frosted. She was quiet for a long time. I tried to change the subject but she wasn't having it. Eventually she demanded to know who had told me. I apologised for the tone, but assured her that nobody had.

"So how did you know?" she persisted coldly.

"I just knew. It was... pronoun avoidance."

"What's *that* supposed to mean?"

"Pronouns. You know, like *I, you, he, she...*"

"I know what a pronoun is, I'm an English teacher."

"Look, you never say 'he' when you're referring to your partner. In fact you only ever say 'my partner' – sometimes two or three times in a sentence." I smiled, but her frostiness persisted. Uncomfortably, I concluded, "It's kind of hard to miss."

I didn't add that I thought everybody knew - which, as it turned out, they did. Soon after that it became an open secret among the staff, and then not a secret at all outside school.

So what other dogs were there that didn't bark in the night time? The Price brothers thought I knew something and they wanted me dead before I could reveal it. *What did I know that I didn't know I knew?*

Standing motionless in the absolute darkness, leaning against the van, it was obvious. I'd ruled out Howard. By extension, I'd also ruled out anybody else from the university. I could safely rule out anybody from the village too. Except for one.

I'd been very drunk the first time I heard it said, and so I might not have remembered, but I'd since heard very similar things said by other people.

" *William likes to be in charge, if you know what I'm saying, and he gets what he wants. Even Benjamin won't stand up to him.*"

I let that sink in. I nodded slowly. It all made sense now. Once William had let slip the lesser secret, they knew it was only a matter of time before I worked out the greater secret. That was why they had to kill me.

And for one infinitesimally but undeniable moment, I wondered, knowing what I knew now, if I still wanted to find Kirsty.

The fleeting thought was interrupted almost before it was fully formed. The door to the first garage was opening. The man without the birthmark had found my hiding place.

Chapter 13. The Slithermen

In the darkness it was easy enough to guess what was happening. The man rolled under the partly-opened up-and-over door, just as I had done, and pulled it shut behind him. Then he stood up, and his movement triggered the motion sensor. The fluorescent tube in the first garage came on, bathing him in a pool of light. He stood for some moments, looking in my general direction, but unless he had some form of infrared vision, I was confident he would not be able to see me. I was fairly certain he hadn't drawn his gun yet.

There was nothing about his body language that gave any indication he was aware of the impossibility of the space he had entered. Unable to make out his facial expression from this distance, it suddenly occurred to me that he was seeing the garage's back wall. To everybody except me, it was an ordinary garage.

He glanced at the floor, perhaps looking for footprints I might have left from oil on my shoes. Then he started walking. Towards me. He strode unhesitatingly through the space where the back wall should have been, demolishing in a step my optimistic theory. The second fluorescent tube came on. He was nearly at the third garage before I'd registered just how much danger I was in. I moved; the light in my garage came on, revealing my position.

Hurriedly I squeezed between the crouching van and the wall. I tried the connecting door. It was locked. In near panic I tried the connecting door in the seventh garage. That was locked too, but the one in the eighth was not. I risked a look back.

The third garage light had come on. The fourth had failed to come on for him as it had failed for me. The fifth had not come on yet, so I guessed he was pausing in the darkness to watch my movements, just in case I had something up my sleeve.

Perhaps he thought I would double-back down the other side of the van, or pounce on him from its roof, or even get its engine started and run him down. But if he thought any of these things, he didn't think them for long. The light in the fifth garage came on.

My only chance was to go through the connecting door, into some parallel Southsea. But he'd know I'd gone that way. Unless...

On impulse I took my mobile out of my pocket and threw it as far as I could into the darkness. Motion detectors in the next three garages responded, and their lights came on. I slipped through the connecting door and closed it softly behind me.

There was no bolt on the other side, and no key in the lock.

I found myself in a carpeted dining room. I was intruding in somebody's house, and my shoes were dirty. My eyes adjusted to the dim light, which I realised was from a streetlamp shining through the kitchen window and through the open serving hatch. There was no sound of any movement in the kitchen.

The dining room was filthy, table and sideboard covered by layers of dust and cobwebs. Six places were set at the large table, china plates, silver cutlery, crystal wine glasses. Hesitating at the doorway to what I supposed was the hall, I wasted precious seconds needlessly trying to identify what was wrong with the room. The items on the table were themselves dirty; not just from dust and cobwebs, but there were also little bits of gristle and smears of old gravy on the plates and cutlery, residues of red wine remaining in the glasses and a lipstick mark on one of the rims. Much as you might expect at the end of a meal, but at each setting everything was placed as at the beginning: dirty plate with dirty forks on the left, dirty knives on the right, dirty glass on its coaster.

The hallway was relatively free of dust and cobwebs, and as dimly lit as the dining room. Light from an upstairs window - probably the same streetlamp as before - shone down the staircase on my left. On my right were three or four closed doors, and at the far end of the hall a large wooden front door. I hurried towards this, anxious to get out of the house as soon as humanly possible. In addition to the threat of the gunman, I was concerned about being caught trespassing; I didn't think there was anybody in the house right now, but the longer I remained, the greater the chance they would arrive home, perhaps pulling into their front drive even as I stepped out of their front door. Maybe in this reality they had the right to bear arms. Even if they weren't armed, I would have a lot of explaining to do

I hadn't taken on the enormity of my situation. I was about to emerge into a parallel world, with no way back except the way I had come - and that way meant getting past my would-be killer.

I turned the Yale latch and pulled the door towards me. It moved a short distance before jerking out of my grasp, and I realised it was on a safety chain. I fumbled with the chain, got it free, but by then my eyes had adapted to the dimness and I saw the crudely chalked sketch on the panelling of the door. It was a face, or more likely a skull, framed on either side by diagonal lengths of thorny vegetation or barbed wire.

I was outside. I had wits enough to leave the door on the latch before closing it quietly behind me. Doubling back might yet be my only option.

No, I wasn't outside. I was in some kind of corridor, maybe four metres wide and a similar height. The floors were flagstones, and the "walls" were stained glass windows, regularly interspersed with massive, fluted stone columns, and lit from behind by, presumably, more streetlamps. The windows displayed religious and Arthurian subjects, with human figures reaching almost to the ceiling twenty feet above.

I followed this corridor for some considerable distance. I looked back once and saw the front of the house I had come out of; it was as if a Photoshop artist had copied and pasted chunks of a cathedral onto the house's front drive. I found myself remembering the day I had gone with Dawn to Ebony the jewellers in Chichester to buy wedding rings, although I had no idea why this memory should choose to unbury itself at this moment. I quickened my pace. I expected the images in the stained glass to repeat, like backgrounds in a low-budget cartoon, but they did not.

The corridor turned right, then a short distance later turned right again. I supposed I was heading back towards the houses. I slowed to a walk, listening carefully; if the man without the birthmark was following, I should be able to hear his footfalls through the stained glass on my right. I heard nothing. No, that wasn't true. I could hear distant sounds, like snatches of whispers, and notes played on a shardy harp, if such a thing existed. It occurred to me that I was experiencing some form of synaesthesia, or else I was imagining the sounds I would associate with the pictures in the stained glass.

Further on I found my way blocked by a complex mesh of what appeared to be steel cables, each the thickness of a man's thigh. There were at least two dozen of them, stretched taut at every angle, mostly from the floor to the ceiling, but some passed through the stained glass window-walls. Closer up, I thought of it as more of a forest of cables rather than a single layer, although I could see far enough through the gaps to tell that the corridor continued, clear again, after maybe two or three metres.

These gaps were clearly not wide enough for me to squeeze through, at least not the ones close to the floor. I glanced over my shoulder; still no sign of my pursuer. What if I smashed my way through one of the stained glass window-walls on either side of me? I considered using my fists or my shoes, but quickly dismissed the idea; even if I managed it without lacerating my arms or being seriously injured by a falling shard, I doubted it would provide an escape route. I would find myself in another corridor running parallel with the present one, probably blocked by the same forest of cables, and it would be obvious to my pursuer which way I had gone.

Yet for all these practical, life-preserving reasons, the thing that really held me back was the thought of smashing the lifelike (though larger than life) figures in the glass; the thought of Lancelot, Elaine, Guinevere, Galahad and other readily identifiable characters lying broken on the corridor floor.

I turned my attention back to the cables. Some of the higher up gaps looked wider. Perhaps I could climb up and squeeze through.

I took hold of a cable with my gloved right hand. It was much softer than steel; it gave a little in my grip. And then I felt the cold of it. Even through the fabric of my glove it was like touching dry ice.

My fingertips stuck; I jerked my hand free, and saw that the cable had taken my glove, and a layer of skin. The glove slid slowly upwards as the cable absorbed it. I stepped back, shaken, sore and scared, and at a loss for what to do next. Blood was weeping from my fingertips, and I was aware of a figure standing beside me.

It was not the gunman. It was not exactly a man at all. It had the outer form and features of a corpulent, bald man with corpse-grey mottled skin. I immediately had the impression that this was just an outer skin, worn as a disguise (or perhaps for some other reason) by a grotesque creature. It wore torn rags, as corpse-grey as its skin, and which appeared to stick to the flesh – in places it was hard to say what was cloth and what was skin. It stared at me vacantly and unselfconsciously. It did not blink – or rather the outer eyes did not. I saw a twitch beneath the skin of each cheek, as if that was where the inner creature's eyes were located. It raised its left arm, which bent in two places, both the wrong places, and in the wrong direction. A band of skin on the wrist appeared to have grown over a wristwatch. It was reaching for my right arm, as if concerned about the skin I had lost when I touched the cable. I pushed the hand aside, but the creature persisted. I was reminded of a gypsy in London trying to plant "lucky heather" on me even after I'd said no. This time the creature put its hand on my sleeve. I felt the chill of its touch, exactly like the dry ice sensation of touching the cable. I knocked the hand aside again, seeing that burnt scraps of my coat sleeve were now stuck to its palm. I backed away – into another travesty of humanity. This one had a smooth face with prominent eyelashes but no eyes, not even sockets, and no ears or nose; it had a clean vertical wound for a mouth which extended from its forehead and passed between the eyelashes down to its chin. Its stomach was a parody of that of a heavily pregnant woman; it put me in mind of a bloated spider's abdomen. Two more abominations stood close by, and two more were climbing and slithering down the cables.

They moved like spiders. They stank of sweat and stale tobacco smoke and urine and excrement and drunkard's vomit. And something else I couldn't put a name to.

I was surrounded. Six of them stared at me in silence, an oppressive, all-pervading silence that muffled out the sounds from the stained glass and which seemed to last for several minutes. I thought of gangs surrounding their lone victim and engaging them in mock-friendly banter before getting down to business - an impression that persisted even though they did not speak. Then the one with the eyebrows opened its slit mouth; most of its head seemed to open and I got a glimpse of vertical lips that did not quite meet, and foul yellow sideways teeth and a tongue like a fat earthworm. The creature reached out a hand and gripped my left arm. Its cold touch burnt through my coat, my jumper, my shirt and finally the skin of my arm before I managed to shake it off. Another inhuman face pressed close to my own, and a hand pressed against my chest. Frantic, I kicked and punched at those nearest me, desperate to get them away and at the same time terrified of the sticky cold sensation from even that brief contact. They fell back as if afraid, but their apparent fear was clearly mockery.

I turned to retreat, back the way I had come. And that was when I saw him, the man without the birthmark. He had followed me into this disgusting, insane place. He was about ten metres away, and he was pointing his gun at me. He shouted; his words were muffled, but I thought he was telling me to get down. I dropped to a crouch and he fired.

The shot was deafening; I thought the stained glass windows would shatter from sound alone. The bullet hit the eyebrows creature in the face. There was no blood; the face just collapsed. It reminded me of some of my pupils kicking a burst football around the school playground. The creature did not fall, although the bullet left a wide, jagged hole. The man without the birthmark was still shouting at me as he ran towards me. I hesitated, still not entirely convinced his shot had not been meant for me. Then he fired again, and again. Not at me, not at the creatures even, but at the cables. He was aiming for the places where they criss-crossed. I thought of them now as something like veins, or nerves, or intestines, or even piano strings, and they had the sheen of silverfish. They twanged when the bullets struck. Each impact caused the creatures to spasm, as if a puppeteer were yanking their invisible strings. The eyebrows one now bled prolifically, and fell; two others also collapsed, convulsing, and two slithered their way back up the cable-things. The man fired once more and a cable-thing snapped; it whipped past me and decapitated the remaining creature.

The gunman was suddenly up close. "You owe me," he said.

I shouldn't be here, my mind screamed. *If you hadn't been chasing me, I* wouldn't *be here*. But he had the gun. I wasn't going to argue with the man with the gun.

I was in this way over my head. The fact that he was not my would-be killer gave me scant cause for relief.

He was regarding the monstrosities he had killed. "They've changed again," he said. "Why would they change again?"

"Are you asking me?" These were the first words I had spoken in this otherplace. My voice felt unfamiliar, both in my throat and in my ears.

"Did you bring somebody in with you?"

"You *saw* me." It felt as if I were thinking aloud; once started, my words were hard to stop. "You chased me in!"

He shook his head once, impatiently. "No. Not your first time. They wouldn't have changed if it was your first time."

I clamped my mouth shut, afraid of what thoughts I might let out. He grabbed me roughly by my injured right arm and directed me back the way we had come. I gasped in pain and shook his hand loose. He did not attempt to grab me again once it was obvious I was prepared to follow him.

We were silent while we made our way back past the stained glass giant figures, and in the silence I became aware once more of the sounds I imagined they were making. The whispers now sounded more like critical mutterings, and there was an aggressive vibe to the harp notes. Figures I had earlier noticed before took on a new aspect. A naked woman standing up in a steaming cauldron, her long golden hair preserving her modesty, looked at me as if concerned for me, and at the same time disappointed in me for a decision I was not aware I had made. A genuflecting armoured knight leaning on his sword in a green field with white tombs and a chapel in the background; before I had seen him as praying, but now it was a frozen image of him shaking his head in dismay.

There were others. I directed my gaze forwards and quickened my pace, making the man beside me (whose name I at some point learned was Tobias Quinn) hurry to keep up. We came to the house front, and once again I thought of the day Dawn and I had bought wedding rings. I remembered how I had thought my ring was a permanent part of me, not because of any lingering sentiment, but because I had been unable to get it off. Even with soap it would not pass over the knuckle of my ring finger. But one evening Montse had shown me a trick with cotton thread, and I was free of it at last.

Back in the hall Quinn appeared to remember something. He reached into the pocket of his yellow pac-a-pac, took out my mobile phone and handed it to me. "Yours. Showed initiative." Maybe I discerned reserved admiration in his tone. I briefly examined the phone. It came on but there was still no signal. There was a crack in the glass over the LCD display.

"I thought you were trying to kill me." I managed to force the words out; speaking was only slightly easier inside the house. He said nothing to this. "Did Dawn's brothers send you?" I persisted. He shook his head once, the way some people dismiss a stupid question. But it wasn't a stupid question, and I needed to know. "Tell me! Did William and Benjamin Price hire you to kill me?"

"I have *no idea* what you are talking about," he said at last, and it occurred to me then that maybe it was a stupid question after all. If the Price brothers had hired him to kill me, we would hardly be having this conversation.

I had supposed we were on our way back to the corridor of garages, and from there, back to normality. Instead, to my utter horror, he directed me to go upstairs.

The near-debilitating sense of apprehension I recall now may be something I actually felt at the time, or it might be something I have since added.

What did I expect to find at the top of the stairs? A crazed woman with an axe? A silent butcher with a cleaver and human body parts hanging from hooks? Another nest of slithermen? None of these were at all likely, least of all the last one, given that my companion had put himself at some risk to rescue me from the nest in the stained-glass corridor.

Perhaps as a result of my fear, I zoned out at some point, and my memory of the climb is confused and contradictory. I have a vague recollection of unending flights of stairs, and glimpses of landings with nondescript closed doors, and Quinn urging me on up when one of the doors began to open. I even recall the cold touch of a creaking aluminium loft ladder, although that is entirely absent from later memories of that place.

Eventually we reached the top flight of stairs. I was aware of breathing, slow and distant and far from effortless. I held onto the bannister, as if that could give me even the illusion of protection. This final landing had a burgundy carpet, old but still thick, and was lit by three or four dim bare bulbs hanging from the ceiling. There were doors on either side along its length. My initial impression was that this corridor was much longer than the hall on the ground floor - something I could well believe at this stage - but I was mistaken. The reason for my mistake was because the corridor narrowed.

The walls on either side ran straight, but not parallel. They converged at the far end at a sharp angle. The effect reminded me of the fun houses in American fairgrounds, built to give a false perspective. The similarity was not complete, however; there was no end wall, and the floor and ceiling remained level.

Directed by Quinn, I walked towards the angle. Two of the doors I passed were ajar; these ones, I noticed, opened outwards. Somebody had built this. Somebody had fitted these outward-opening doors, papered the walls, and, most disturbing of all, somebody had cut the carpet into a wedge shape with a Stanley knife and fitted it exactly into the tapering space between skirting boards all the way to the vanishing point.

Quinn motioned me to open the last door on the left. I did so; it did not open far before the handle was halted by the opposite wall. "Go on," he commanded. I removed my coat. I moved sideways, my back to the door frame. The inner handle of the door pushed deep into my stomach as I squeezed my way in.

I was inside a bedroom. Quinn followed me in with less difficulty and switched on the light. There was no furniture apart from a double bed and a bedside cabinet with a reading lamp on top, and a metal toilet bowl which lacked a seat and had a basin next to it. There was a man in the bed, old and bald and very fat. He lay on his back, in a heavy sleep, his breathing laboured. There was a jug of water and a glass on the bedside cabinet.

On the walls, red and white striped wallpaper, long overdue for redecorating. A window, the curtains open. A view of a garden, a garage at the end and houses across the street in night time Southsea. Street lamps.

I indicated the man in the bed. "Is he dreaming?" I asked, each word an effort.

"We all dream," Quinn said. Then he added, "He's dreaming this."

A sense of vicarious claustrophobia began to build in me. I was slim enough to squeeze into and out of the room with only a little effort. There was no other exit. For the fat man on the bed, it would be necessary to remove the inner and outer door handles. Even then it would be tight. It might be necessary to remove the door altogether, but even if someone were to fetch him a screwdriver I didn't think the door would open wide enough to access the screw heads for the hinges.

They must have been accessible at one time, though. Did that mean the walls moved? What if the door had been fitted when this end of the corridor was wider? The idea wasn't any more insane than anything I had seen so far. What if it moved while we were in here and the angle became even more acute and I could not squeeze out? I glanced back at the window. It was a sheer drop to the pavement below - not as far as my endless climb should have indicated, but far enough.

"Can we get out?" I asked.

Quinn stared at me but said nothing. I thought I saw an upward movement outside, a distant street lamp with its horizontal bar hinged like an old-fashioned railway signal. Quinn's stare moved from me to the man in the bed, then back to me again.

"Can we please get out of here?"

He gave a nod as if satisfied that I had got the message, even though I had not. I glanced out of the window again - the street lamp was back in its normal position - and followed Quinn out of the room. I retrieved my coat.

*

I remember a time in my teens when it suddenly became commonplace to see foxes in towns, car parks and residential areas. One time we saw a pair of them mating in the back garden of our house outside Guildford. They were oblivious to everything except each other; my mother told of how she had to step over them when she was putting washing out, and joked about pouring a bucket of water over them.

Sometimes when it was warm at night and I was sleeping with the bedroom window open I would be awakened by the cry of a lone fox. While in the hazy state of half-sleep, it sounded uncannily like the cry of an abandoned baby. The similarity was not complete; once I had roused myself to full wakefulness there was no question in my mind: it was just a fox.

But as I drifted back into sleep the irrational part of my mind became dominant again. What if it *was* an abandoned baby after all, desperately vulnerable? And nobody was doing anything to help it because they were all telling themselves it was just a fox.

One of the other rooms on a wider part of the top floor was a bathroom. Quinn opened the door to the cupboard under the wash hand basin. There was nothing inside the cupboard, no shelves or plumbing or even a back wall. At his behest I crawled into it, unsurprised that it led through a connecting wall and another empty cupboard into a mirror image of the first bathroom.

I soon discovered that the house next door also had a wedge-shaped landing, but this was not quite a mirror image of the one in the first house. This was more of a truncated wedge, with about a foot of the far wall remaining. I shuddered; this reinforced my impression that the wall moved.

We went down the stairs - only three flights, and no ladders - and into the dining room. There were parts of an engine on a cloth on the big table. Continuing the mirror image theme, there was a door in the wall that gave access to the garage.

This garage had an up-and-over door which was closed, and a back wall. It had never occurred to me that I would ever be so reassured by the sight of something as mundane as a back wall to a garage.

But we weren't out of the labyrinth yet. Before the proximity-operated fluorescent light had flickered on fully, we had crossed to a door in the opposite side wall, another access door that opened into a second garage. There was no light in this one, but I was aware of piles of boxes and assorted clutter which we had to work our way around. Somewhere in the darkness I heard the unmistakable sound of a slack chain being pulled taut, and a sound like the whimpering of a dog. It was intermittent whimpering, as if the dog knew it was supposed to stay in its place and keep silent but was unable to obey completely. I imagined Quinn firing his gun, and seeing the place momentarily illuminated by the flashes, the whimpering thing briefly revealed: not a dog at all.

It didn't happen, but I was as sure the creature was no dog as I was sure that the cry of the fox in the night time was not an abandoned baby.

I hurried after Quinn. We passed through the next connecting door.

Not unexpectedly, we were in another garage. I'd already seen a lengthwise series of garages so why not a sideways one too? However, this one did not have a back wall. Or, to be more precise, it did not have a *complete* back wall. This was not another infinite corridor of garages; rather, the back wall along with about a third of the roof had been partially demolished and was open to the air and the night sky. The moon, a few days past full, shone through occasional breaks in the moving cloud bank. We clambered over the rubble of broken bricks, and outside. Finally, I was *outside*. But where?

Could I walk home from here?

A path through a neglected garden led to a back gate in a wall. Looking back, there was no sign of the other two garages that we had just passed through. Frankly I would have been surprised if there had been. Nearby there was a house with a third storey window with the curtains open and the light on. I was fairly sure this was the room with the fat prisoner.

"I only meant the room," I said. It was easier to talk outside. Quinn did not respond; I continued anyway. "When I asked if we could leave. I just meant the room. Not the house." Still not speaking, Quinn led the way through the gate and onto a quiet street lined with parked cars. "Where are we?"

"Clarendon Road."

"Yes, I can see that." The street sign was just across from us. "I meant, is it *my* Clarendon Road?"

"I don't know what analogy you're working to."

"Can I walk home from here? Or am I in some parallel world?"

He shrugged. "That would serve as a working approximation this far out in the Common Land."

I had no idea what he was talking about, but our spoken exchange was at least resembling a conversation now, albeit a somewhat surreal one.

"Why here?" I asked. Quinn didn't respond. So much for the beginnings of conversation; I was really starting to hate him for his habit of ignoring my questions. But then I saw that he had raised a hand, both acknowledging me and asking me to pause. He was staring into the distance, in the direction I had been looking from the window when I thought I saw movement. A pair of streetlamps with the characteristic yellow glow of sodium towered over the intervening houses and shops. They were quite definitely moving up and down.

"It's the same that way," he said, stepping off the pavement and suddenly turning and pointing along the length of Clarendon Road.

I followed him. More moving lights, but much closer than the others. Quinn led the way along Clarendon Road, which was lined with "normal" street lamps. We passed parked cars, but I saw no moving traffic except for a single white van. We arrived at the object itself. A pylon. At the top of the pylon, a box with street lamps sticking out like a pair of arms. They continued to move up and down as we watched. A ladder led up to the box, but a locked barrier some ten feet up prevented unauthorised access.

It reminded me of the Martian war machine in Woking. Then realisation struck. "Semaphore towers," I said. This one was copying the moves being made by the first one we'd seen; somewhere further inland, a third was no doubt copying the moves of this one, and so it went on across the country, each tower presumably controlled by a vigilant operator.

Why would a society with cars and electric street lighting *need* a semaphore-based telegraph system? Surely they had telephones? On impulse I checked my mobile. The bars next to the aerial symbol were at nearly full strength. I wondered if the telegraph system and the mobile provider did not merely coexist, they were in some sense one and the same thing - or else the former was the personification of the latter, for want of a better word.

"Confused seas, secular skies," Quinn said.

"Pardon?"

"Escape or something more sinister."

"What are you..." Then it struck me. He was reading the semaphore.

"What does *that* mean?" He didn't answer. I repeated the question, letting an edge of impatience creep into my voice.

"I haven't the faintest idea." He smiled in the way some people do when they think they've scored a point. But then his eyes widened. "Recall," he read, almost spelling out the word. "Accelerated recall. Zero interval, accelerated imminent."

Then the semaphore arms froze in place and the sodium lights faded out. All the streetlamps along Clarendon Road faded out. There was no light in any of the nearby windows except for reflections of the moon. I looked at my phone again. No signal.

Quinn was pointing, not at the tower, but at the cable stretching from the end of one of the semaphore arms to the roof of a newsagent on the other side of the road. It had the sheen of a silverfish.

"We have to leave. Now." Quinn grabbed me by my injured arm once again and marched me back the way we had come. Shrugging him off but still following him I said, "Did the slithermen follow us out?"

"No. They found another route."

Unsure if his tone was sarcastic, I said, "*Can* they pass through the doorways?"

"Yes. It happens. Happens but it's rare, like people finding a way in. I told you, they've changed again. Now come on!"

"People like me?"

"*Not* people like you. People who find their way in by accident. The homeless, the desperate, the insatiably curious and the natural born intruders."

"Do they find their way out again?"

He said nothing.

I exhaled heavily. "I'm dreaming," I said. "I know it's a dream, but that doesn't help because I'm physically here too, aren't I?" We had arrived back at the garden with the partially ruined garage. "So what *is* this place?"

"Not safe."

Quinn began to clamber back over the pile of bricks, but I stood my ground. I didn't doubt that it was dangerous to remain in this world of confused seas and secular skies, but I wasn't convinced that the alternative - following an armed stranger into an insane, impossible maze - was the wiser course. Besides, I wanted to see if he'd go on without me.

He was in the garage when he saw I was not following. He looked back at me, anxious. "Come on!" he called.

"I want to know what this is. What's going on."

But once again he failed to acknowledge that I had even asked him a question. Whatever the reason for his waiting for me to follow, it was clear that his patience or indulgence was in short supply. And then I thought of the train journey on Kirsty's eighth birthday, and the beer mats on the table in my parents' kitchen. How much had I guessed already? How much had I got right - and how much had I got wrong? "Just tell me. Does it extend across the whole of Britain?"

"*Britain*?" He sputtered a laugh and shook his head. "Britain!"

I clambered over the bricks, back into the broken garage. I glanced back once. Alone of all the windows visible from this garden, the light in the room of the fat prisoner still shone.

Once through the door into the dark garage with the dog that wasn't a dog, Quinn seemed to relax, although he had gone back into his taciturn state. We retraced our steps, into the house through the dining room, up to the top floor, through the communicating cupboard doors between the bathrooms, and down through the dirty dining room into the corridor of garages. I thought he would leave with me through the up-and-over door of the first garage. Instead he stopped in the second garage and took out a key. He unlocked the side door. "When you are ready," he said, "take this doorway." He gave me an address on Highland Road, and the name Dan Spencer. He repeated these, and added, "He'll give you what you need, for a reasonable price. Tell him Tobias Quinn sent you. Don't mention the Common Land, he's not one of us." He handed me a key like his own, evidently a skeleton key. "You owe me. Don't you forget that: you *owe* me." Then he went through the door and shut it behind him.

Alone, I weighed the skeleton key in my hand. I didn't want to have it on me when I returned to the real world. I rested it on one of the rungs of the aluminium ladder in the first garage. I contemplated the garage's missing back wall and wondered if it would be restored when I came back here, *if* I ever came back. And I remembered the corridor in the Indian restaurant. That had still been there when I'd gone back.

I lay down on the dirty concrete floor and squeezed back under the up-and-over door, back into my own Southsea, my own world. The sky was clear and lit by the approaching dawn. Several hours had passed. The air and the ground were intensely cold.

Chapter 14. Dead Girl

I was barely out of Stanley Lane when the police picked me up. Two male officers, not ones I knew from the investigation into Kirsty's disappearance, although I explained to them who I was. They wanted to know why I had been wasting their time reporting an attempt on my life. I explained that I had been aware of someone following me for the past few nights (the Websters would confirm this) and that, due to my sleep-deprived state, I must have misread the situation. I told them that I had seen the man in *The Marmion Tavern*, seen the gun in his holster, but now that I thought about it, it probably was just a mobile phone. But my fear had been real enough at the time and I'd made the call while running away. Some revellers had snatched my mobile while I was making the call but I found it again much later – I showed them the cracked display to support my story. Between losing the phone and finding it again, I had hidden in a garage that hadn't been locked properly, and there I had fallen asleep.

I kept as close to the truth as I could. But the police were not stupid, and I wasn't a convincing liar. Mentioning garages was a huge mistake. They drove me back down Stanley Lane and asked me which garage it was. They clearly expected to find Kirsty inside it, imprisoned or dead. I told them it had been dark, and I'd been in a confused, panic-stricken state. "About halfway along," I said vaguely. We got out and an officer tried a garage door. It was securely locked. He tried the next one, and the next. And then a peculiar thing happened. He came to the garage door with the bollard in front, and he walked right past it. Plainly he could see it; they could *both* see it, but his partner did not comment on his failure to check it. It reminded me of a time when the mayor had come to my school to hand out awards to a group of children lined up in the playground, and he had walked past the boy in the wheelchair. The police officer went on to check the garage door after it, and the one after that – and as luck would have it, that one had indeed been left unlocked. It opened easily.

It was too early to feel relief. What if fate was playing a perverse game with me, and the garage contained the thing I most dreaded finding?

But they found nothing. Just a workbench with assorted motorbike parts scattered across it - I was reminded of the second dining room table - and the gutted remains of the motorbike itself. There was oil on the floor which matched the oil on my coat from when I'd squeezed under the door to the Common Land. I could almost believe my own cover story: I really had just slept on this floor and dreamt the whole thing.

They let me go. I had a feeling I was under suspicion, still; worse, my mental state might be taken into account when Kirsty finally did turn up. But there was a glimmer of hope. At last, I was starting to piece together what was really going on.

*

There were seven messages on my answerphone. I played the most recent first. It was from Miss Havers: "Ring me." I did.

"Where the hell did you go?" she demanded in lieu of a greeting. I was briefly startled; I wasn't yet used to caller numbers appearing on displays. It also occurred to me that I was interrupting her lesson. "I tried your mobile twenty times!" Without waiting for an answer, she went on to say, "I feel so *terrible* for you, you must be feeling *dreadful*. Let me know if you need company. I'll be round right after school."

So this was it. All over, finished. My throat felt paralysed; it was all I could do to croak out the words, "She's dead?"

"Oh God," said Miss Havers. "Oh God, they didn't tell you? Oh God, Philip, I'm so so sorry, I'm so sorry you had to hear it from me, like this. I didn't realise, I thought they'd have let you know, I..."

"Where?"

"St Richard's Hospital. Where she was taken after you found her. They say it was anaphylactic shock, poor little soul. She passed away in the early hours this morning."

For a long time I couldn't speak, couldn't think. Eventually I said, "Are you talking about Chloe Faulkner?"

"Yes of course, I... Oh my God, did you think I meant Kirsty?"

"Yes. Yes, I did."

*

I needed to get on with the mundane things – washing my clothes, cleaning my house, dealing with the rest of the messages on the answerphone – but instead I remained sitting, huddled into myself in my dirty damaged coat.

Kirsty was the one who got away after all. Poor Chloe was not going to grow up to be a beautiful woman.

I'd resented her for being more popular than my daughter.

Miss Havers let herself in. "You look absolutely terrible," she said.

"I don't doubt it. I don't know if I'm *ever* going to sleep again."

"You need a bath," she told me. She disappeared upstairs to start it running. She came back down, took my hands and drew me out of my chair. I responded docilely. She led me upstairs into the bathroom where the bath was slowly filling. She removed my dirty coat, pulled my jumper over my head, and began unbuttoning my shirt. She said, "Don't be getting ideas, Mr Hamilton. If any man is going to turn me straight, it's not going to be you." Despite everything, I laughed. She laughed too but stopped abruptly when she saw the burn mark on my arm. "Can you shed any light on this?" she asked. I shook my head. "Not now. Later, maybe, but not now."

She took away my dirty clothes. Shortly after I was soaking in the bath. It felt good and for a very long time I thought of nothing, except when I found myself wondering aloud, "How can you lose a room? How can you lose a whole building? How can you gain a doorway without knowing it?" I could hear Miss Havers moving around downstairs, putting the washing machine on, washing the dishes I had left stacked and dirty, hoovering the rooms. It was pleasant to have her around, and it gave me a twinge of conscience to think that I would never be able to tell her everything.

Two Christmases ago she had given me a Sudoku book, saying, "You're the mathematician, this should be right up your street." I couldn't make head nor tail of it. "What am I supposed to do with it - find the hidden formulae, or what?" She gave me her furrowed-eyebrows look and said, "Are you actually *from* this century, or did Leonardo lend you his time machine? Look, you can find these numbers by eliminating the rows and columns from the other blocks of nine, and that gives you more numbers to eliminate from the other blocks." It took me a minute or two to understand her explanation, but once I'd got it... "Ah, I see! But this one could be a five or an eight. There's simply no way of knowing." To which she replied, "The whole point is to work out the rules for yourself. If I told you the rules, it wouldn't be fun."

I wondered if the Common Land worked like this, although I doubted fun was going to be involved. I had found my way in by accident once, I had sought it and found it again eight years later, and then I had stumbled upon a different entrance last night. But how did it really work? Tobias Quinn had not been forthcoming; if I had learnt anything from him, it was from what he hadn't said. Was it a requirement that I work out its rules for myself? Would understanding come as easily as it had with Sudoku?

How was it that I found the "special" garage whereas the police officers - trained observers - had walked right past it? What were the slithermen, and what had they done to that "other" Southsea? Was that other Southsea even real? Were the other worlds as real as my own?

I held my breath, pinched my nose, submerged my head and shook it left and right to get the clean water into my hair. I stayed underwater as long as I could.

I thought again of the doors I had seen without noticing, all hidden in plain sight.

There was that elusive one that I still couldn't quite bring to mind. I recalled the image of the red pull cord in the toilets in the Chichester McDonald's, but no, that wasn't it; there had definitely been no doorway in that cubicle.

I exhaled in an explosion of bubbles, then surfaced and shifted my position in the bath. If sleep caught up with me unexpectedly, I didn't want it to happen when I was underwater.

So why didn't other people see the doors?

Wrong question. Of course they *saw* them, they weren't invisible. But what was different about me, and Tobias Quinn? What made us *notice* them? Was it insomnia? Quinn had hinted as much, but surely there had to be more to it than that. Most people experience insomnia once in a while. Quinn had followed me across Southsea Common in the dead of night, perhaps thinking my sleeplessness made me a contender. Before that he had stalked Tony and Mildred Webster, but presumably he had subsequently ruled them out.

If they only knew. They would have taken to the Common Land like ducks to water. They would have dealt with it far better than I had. Then again, I might have coped better if I hadn't been frantic with worry about my daughter.

Being a contender didn't mean I *had* to go back in. I could pretend it had never happened. But was it as simple as that? Was I even *safe*? I had lost skin and blood to the sticky cable. Did the slithermen have my DNA now? What if there was a hidden door in *my* house? I was aware of some of the doors, but was I seeing them all?

The knock on the bathroom door made me jump. "Mr Hamilton? Are you going to be all right?"

It was clear from her tone that she was wanting to get home.

"Give me a couple of minutes, I'll see you off properly."

"That *won't* be necessary."

"What's *that* supposed to mean? Look, I wasn't being suggestive – I meant I'd throw some clothes on."

She giggled. "I knew what you meant. Look, I've really got to rush. I've made you some sandwiches."

"You've been fantastic, Miss Havers. Thanks for everything."

Moments later I heard the front door slam and the sound of her car driving off. She must have stayed for more than three hours. The bath water had gone cold while I'd lain in it.

*

Dressed in a bathrobe I went downstairs. The kitchen was almost unrecognisable. There were work surfaces I hadn't seen since I'd moved in, and the Pyrex dish that had once had baked-on black bits now looked as good as new. My clothes were either in the tumble drier or on the wooden horse – what Kirsty called the clip-clop – and I could walk on the lounge carpet without anything crunching under my bare feet. Miss Havers had done more than clean up after me, her humour had brought me out of myself. If only Kirsty could turn up while the house and I were both in this state...

But I knew now that was not how it would work. I had to go out and find her.

I sat in my armchair with a cup-a-soup and the plate of sandwiches, the TV on quietly in the background. I wasn't going to strike out aimlessly, as I had been doing up till now. When something is missing in the house, you can ransack every drawer, every cupboard, every box and every shelf and still not find it; or you can relax and search your mind for the place where you last saw it or put it, and, having located it, make straight for that place in reality and find it there.

The insomnia dream that visited me after I finished my sandwiches was little more than a variation of one that had been recurring for the last few days. I was following the schoolgirl along the path. Again we stopped at the whalebone arch, and again the tips of the two whalebones drooped. I hadn't noticed it before, or the dream had always ended too early, but this time they formed a curved M, reminiscent of the McDonald's logo. I shook my head.

"It's not the restaurant, I ruled that out."

Without any sense of transition I emerged from the dream. On the TV a local reporter was standing outside a nightclub. Earlier tonight, he informed us, a fight had broken out, and escalated; there had been several arrests. It was typical local news, insignificant, hardly worthy of live coverage, and certainly not worth my attention. But then the camera angle changed, and I recognised the two bouncers who were arguing with a police officer. They were William and Benjamin Price.

I grabbed the phone and dialled Dawn's number. I got the "unavailable" tone - evidently they had blocked my number - so I rang it again from my mobile. Despite its ballistic flight through three garages, it worked fine, and soon Dawn's phone was ringing.

Had the footage of the nightclub been live? I wasn't sure. If William answered, I could hang up; he didn't know my mobile number.

The phone rang and rang. Eventually it was picked up and I heard Dawn's tired and irritated voice. "Who is this?"

"Dawn, *don't* hang up. This is important."

"Phil! Thank God! We need to talk, and we don't have much time."

Surprised by her tone, I said, "What do you mean?"

"Bill and Ben are out but Bill won't be late. They told me not to speak to you. I tried phoning you at night when they're out working or asleep but you never answer."

"You never thought to leave a message?"

"I needed to *talk* to you! I can't talk to those things, you know I can't. Anyway. What Bill said to you, it's not what you think. What he said about Kirsty not being your daughter... he should never have said that to you."

"Dawn, do you think I haven't worked it out?" I hadn't phoned for a confrontation, there was too much at stake, but I couldn't keep my feelings bottled up forever. Very calmly, then, I said, "Listen to me, Dawn. I resent the deceit. I resent the fact that ten years ago I lost forever the chance of a much better life because of that deceit. I resent the maintenance I could ill afford to pay over the last two years and which you *didn't even need.* But whatever deceit was involved in Kirsty's making – and I really, *really* don't want the details – she is not a part of that deceit. Do you understand me? Only Kirsty matters." Suddenly I was crying tears of rage and frustration. "Is that why they won't let me talk to you? In case you let slip what's already obvious? You've got to keep it in the family because you *kept* it in the family? Is that it?"

Dawn was sobbing uncontrollably at the other end. I was afraid her distress might trigger another epileptic fit. But at last she managed to talk between sobs. "If you already knew all this, why did you call?"

"I need to ask you something. Something important. Before Kirsty went missing, was she having trouble sleeping?"

"Yes, yes she was." Dawn was obviously surprised by the question. "I wondered if she was having problems at school. What made you ask?"

I would have told her there and then, but the words snagged in my throat. That which had been little more than far-fetched speculation was now all but confirmed. I had known for some time what was really going on, but I hadn't wanted to believe it. I hadn't been *able* to believe it.

"Philip? Philip, are you still there? I think I can hear Bill's car. Tell me Philip, quickly. Do you know where Kirsty is?"

"No," I said. "I honestly don't know where she is. But I do believe I know where to start looking."

*

In my bedroom I shrugged off my bathrobe. In the full-length mirror I regarded the burn mark on my left arm. I thought of Chloe's injuries. And I thought of the man who wasn't a man who had chased Kirsty in Whitby.

I asked my reflection, "What the hell have we got ourselves into?"

Chapter 15. The Wrong Labyrinth

I had to stay awake. I drank a strong black coffee as I dressed. It was gone ten o'clock at night when I got into my car. I had to get to Chichester, to McDonald's before it closed.

Sleep was behaving like a certain kind of lover. She had abandoned me when I needed her most. Now that I needed her to stay away from me, she was attempting to seduce me, promising me pleasures that no other lover could give. She was almost a physical presence in my car, a figure on my back seat that I might glimpse in the rear view mirror.

I wound down the windows, letting in cold blasts of air. I gritted my teeth, forced my attention onto the road ahead. I put the radio on and turned up the volume.

I came off Portsea Island and followed the M27 as it changed into the A27. At the beginning of the journey I drove through built-up places, but between Portsmouth and Chichester there were large areas of fields and marshes. Was the Common Land a single entity? Even allowing for multiple parallel worlds, it was hard to imagine how the Common Land could possibly connect the cities, towns, villages and petrol stations where I had already seen its entrances. Were there sprawling urban developments in worlds next door to my own? Or was there a simpler solution, just as I had found simple algorithms to complete the more difficult Sudoku puzzles?

McDonald's was still open. I ordered another black coffee from the youth who had served me on the evening when Kirsty went missing. He did not recognise me. I found a table.

The solution to the mystery of the red pull cord had come to me while I was on the phone to my ex-wife. It was so straightforward I could not believe I had taken so long.

What was the purpose of a red pull cord in a toilet cubicle? It was to provide disabled users with a means of calling for help in an emergency.

The last time I had sat in the eating area, I had looked at four doors marked Ladies, Gents, Disabled and Staff Only. At least I'd thought that was what they said. In this place, there really was a door marked Staff Only, and there was a Ladies and a Gents. But why would there be a door marked Disabled when they had already provided disabled facilities alongside the other cubicles.

I sipped my coffee - it was too hot to down it as I had wanted to - then got up and walked over to the door that was not, and never had been, marked Disabled. I pushed it open and strode through.

*

I was in a long, white tiled corridor, only a little wider than the door itself, and illuminated by white, chest-high lights in the walls. These protruded from the walls, and were covered in frosted glass. The place put me in mind of a temporarily vacated hospital wing; the staff, patients and visitors would be back, but not until the necessary maintenance work had been completed.

There was no maintenance crew to be seen. Nor, indeed, the constructor spiders that had so unnerved me in Guildford.

The corridor was, as I mentioned, long. Much too long to fit in the restaurant itself, but by now this sort of thing had lost most of its capacity to surprise me. Some of it, anyway. As I continued walking it occurred to me that by rights I should be crossing the access road and approaching the cinema complex. What if the corridor was not really located in a parallel world? What if I was only imagining the walls, and I was crossing the access road in the real world? I pictured people giving me strange looks, drivers slamming on their brakes to avoid hitting the sleepwalking idiot. But I was certain that this was not happening. I reached out and slapped my palms against the walls on both sides. The tiles were as solid and mundane as the ones in the bathroom at my grandparents' house when I was a child.

I was aware of distant sounds echoing through the walls. Repeated, not quite regular sounds, reminiscent at first of maybe a hundred people eating in a canteen or refectory: a place of metal cutlery and ceramic plates, not at all like the McDonald's that was a dozen paces and a world behind me.

The corridor ended at a blank wall, with swing doors in the walls on either side. I took the one on the right. Another corridor, similar to the first but with a hint of beige in the white tiles. The sounds were slightly louder. Distant sounds, mostly: now a grandfather clock ticking a little too slowly, a motor like that of a lift or an escalator, the rattlings of central heating or plumbing or floorboards responding to changes in temperature or humidity, a sound like the wind in the trees and a metal gate creaking and banging at irregular intervals against a gatepost. The acoustics made it impossible to locate or properly identify most of them.

There were more swing doors in the walls on either side of this corridor, each with its own circle of frosted glass in the middle. I pushed them open and glanced in, then let them swing back. So far every door had opened onto more corridors, some of which had more doors, and some of which had differently coloured tiles.

The sense of being in an impossibly strange environment overrode any feeling of monotony. At the same time, I was keeping my fear of getting lost in check. I had kept to the most straightforward route, and I had no doubt that I could find my way back. I could even picture my route as a map: all straight lines, some very short and some very long, but all parallel or perpendicular to each other, some crossing, some ending at t-junctions, some dead ends. It formed a ragged rectangle with a space in the middle.

So where was Kirsty? Had she found an exit to another Chichester? Or had she found a room in the space in the centre? Maybe I would find the room, and it would have a bed in it where Kirsty lay safe and sound and sleeping like a princess.

But I opened door after door and saw neither exit nor room.

Had anyone in the restaurant noticed my disappearance?

What if they closed and locked up while I was still in here?

Worried by the thought, I entered a charcoal grey corridor that I realised I'd been in already - I recognised a crack in the wall light opposite the door. The map in my head was not as reliable as I'd supposed. A lot of doors led off this one. I swung each open in turn and called out Kirsty's name each time.

Or rather I tried to. My words caught in my throat. I tried again, hyping myself up as much as I could.

"Kirsty!"

My voice was nowhere near as loud as I intended it to be. Nevertheless it echoed and re-echoed as I remained standing in the charcoal corridor. I tried with the next door, and the one after that. The echo died away each time as the door swung shut behind me.

But then everything changed. There was a subtle alteration to the background noises. I imagined I could hear slow, heavy footsteps, as if I had awoken something.

It was hesitant at first. Maybe my hearing was more acute than usual, but somehow I knew it was barefoot. Suddenly it was running. Crucially, it was *not running away.*

I'd already seen enough of the Common Land to know how dangerous a place it was. I understood why Tobias Quinn carried a gun. I had no gun. I didn't even have the Stanley knife I'd used to cut through the flock wallpaper in the Indian restaurant in Guildford. I didn't have a torch either. My map was about as reliable as my memory.

And something was coming for me.

Narrow corridors, nowhere to hide.

I backtracked, out of the charcoal-coloured corridor. Somehow the one I found myself in seemed different to before, as if the walls were shifting around me, though it is more likely that in my panic I was simply confused. I tried to get my bearings: if I had walked this way in the real world, I would have crossed the car park, and would now be close to the road where I had rescued Chloe from the speeding lorry.

I called Kirsty's name again, aware that I was giving the running thing a clue to my position. Once again, I had to overcome the constriction in my throat, and try as I might I could not raise my voice above conversation level.

The heavy footsteps were approaching. I pushed a swing door open and ran down the corridor on the other side. If my bearings were correct I was close to the space in the middle of the rectangle. Still the footsteps seemed to follow, and to draw nearer, but when I risked looking back there was nothing to see. I realised then that the footsteps were passing overhead. That was interesting; it meant this maze of corridors was on at least two levels, which suggested stairs, or maybe the lift I thought I'd heard.

Were the footsteps Kirsty's own? I remembered an occasion when she was changing into her pyjamas in her bedroom in my house in Southsea while I was sitting in the lounge below. She had a CD playing and she was singing something about living under water in the year 3000. As she sang, she danced, and the noise she made was entirely out of proportion to her size; it was a wonder there was no plaster falling from the ceiling. Nevertheless, the character of these footsteps were entirely different. I could practically read body language in them; I certainly didn't read a scared child running to be with her daddy.

There was a dark wood door at the end of this corridor, and another to the right. Unlike the swing doors, these had rectangular windows at eye-level, translucent glass with wire mesh inside. The door at the end was locked. The door to the right had the familiar chalked skull and barbed wire sketched on the wood.

Silence fell. Straining, I could make out sounds at the very limit of hearing: again, the distant whir of a lift motor, and the equally distant chiming of a grandfather clock. After that, nothing.

I thought of the coincidental silences that sometimes occur when pupils are gathered in the sports hall or canteen, short silences that invariably give way to laughter. This silence didn't. Instead, the sound of bare running feet returned, heading towards me from the other side of the end door. The sound grew louder, and faster. There was nothing between me and the running thing except for the door; if it didn't hold...

The running thing smacked into the other side of the door as if it hadn't expected it to be there, with a force that nearly broke it off its hinges. The frosted glass cracked, and blood appeared on the other side. The creature withdrew. I heard it panting - and, for want of a better word, lowing, which put me in mind of a cow. A running cow, in a corridor barely wider than itself.

The door held.

After some moments it retreated, running more slowly than before. I wondered what would happen if it got to the door that led back into the fast food restaurant before me. The image didn't strike me as funny until much later.

I turned to the door on the right, the one with the chalked skull and barbed wire. To my surprise it was not locked. It opened onto yet another corridor, the longest I had seen so far. Some of the lights in the walls were smashed, and others flickered on and off. I could just about discern a door at the far end, but there were none in the side walls. There was, however, a low archway in the right hand wall about halfway along, about waist height, and corresponding (as far as I could tell) to the edge of the space in my map. The running thing would be unable to pass under it without crawling; it was quite possible that it didn't even know the archway was there.

The ticking sound of the grandfather clock was back. I considered my options: Retrace my steps back to the real world, find a weapon of some kind and come back in a state of readiness. Or make for that archway, and hope it wasn't a dead end, and hope the running thing wouldn't be able to follow me.

I hesitated. There were so many swing doors between here and the McDonald's; the running thing could appear out of any of them. And even if I did evade it, I might not find the archway again. At the same time, the ticking clock sounded like a hint to hurry up.

So I strode forward, making for the archway. Above me, around me, possibly even below me, another swing door crashed open, and then another. I was convinced now that the running thing was blind. It wasn't stopping for doors. I wondered how much blood it was losing with each collision, and how much it could afford to lose.

Almost at the archway, the nearest lights flickered out.I halted. When they came on again, I saw that I was less than a metre away from the thick cable that ran from the middle of the ceiling to the middle of the floor.

Somebody had been this way before me. Somebody who had chalked the skull and barbed wire on the door to this corridor to warn of danger. I was not looking at an electrical cable, I was looking at a slitherman cable.

Indecision gripped me. Distant swing doors continued to smash open. For a moment I was sure it was above me, then behind me. A moment later it was somewhere to my left.

If I could squeeze past the slitherman cable, and crawl under that arch... Had Kirsty and Chloe done the same thing? Had their instincts alerted them to the danger of the cable?

I could see under the archway. The floor beyond it was carpeted, and wider than any of the corridors I had seen here. It was definitely a room. But had Kirsty and Chloe come this way? There was enough space between the cable and the walls for them to squeeze past without touching it. Enough space for me, though? Yes, I could do it, but I already had the impression that the cable was quivering in response to my presence; I didn't think it was necessary to actually touch it in order to trigger it. Maybe if I could slip by it quickly - and if I heard the door crash open behind me, I would definitely do it. I would roll under the archway, into the room, before the creature got close.

I pictured the two girls in their Halloween makeup, Chloe daring Kirsty to walk past the cable to the archway. I could almost hear their conversation. Then Kirsty, afraid of being a chicken in the eyes of her popular, temporary friend, squeezing her eyes shut, pressing herself against the corridor wall and sliding past, not daring to open them again until she was well clear. Chloe, realising Kirsty outclassed her in the bravery stakes, realising she was going to be left behind, running, misjudging the distance...

If a schoolgirl couldn't give it a wide enough berth, I wasn't sure I fancied my own chances. Maybe there was another way. There was a door at the far end of this corridor; I could come back and map the maze properly, and find my way to the archway the long way round.

As I was considering this, I saw something I had failed to notice before. There were markings on the tiled floor of the corridor: "C + K" in large green letters, and a green arrow pointing to the archway.

Green lipstick.

I would have risked squeezing past the cable there and then, but at that moment the door at the far end of the corridor crashed open. The running thing had found me.

It was female. It had very long matted hair. I had an impression of horns, like those of a cow. Eyes the colour of milk mixed with blood, clearly blind. Barely acknowledging the door it had smashed open, it ran towards me.

I turned to flee, aware that it would overtake me before I reached the door through which I had entered. But I was in no real danger; I looked back and saw it was keeping to the middle of the corridor. It would collide with the slitherman cable.

I got a closer view of it before that happened. It had women's breasts, four of them, in the place where a cow would have had udders – if a cow walked upright on its hind legs. In places its skin was the black and white of a Friesian, in others it was the white of a human albino. A woman's arms that ended in hooves, a cow's legs that ended in human feet. It was a cruel joke, a parody of a female minotaur in the wrong labyrinth.

When it collided with the cable it stuck. The slitherman dropped down through an unseen hole in the ceiling, clinging to the cable at first because the impact had set it vibrating. Then it leapt onto the back of the she-minotaur. This time I really fled, glancing back once to see the creature reduced to an unrecognisable mass of bloody wounds. The bovine screams and a smell like roast beef stayed with me for a long time afterwards, and I prayed I would never see or hear or smell its like again.

*

Sleep had become a subtly different kind of lover on the journey back to Portsmouth – a lover who had rejected me, and was now having second thoughts. But I had moved on. I hadn't found anyone else but I was content to be on my own for a while.

I needed a gun. I wasn't happy with the idea. I might get caught with it. Kirsty might find it and think it was a toy. Mistakes and accidents involving guns are irreversible. But if I was going to map that labyrinth, I had to be able to defend myself from the monsters of nightmare and mythology.

I arrived at Stanley Lane. My skeleton key was where I had left it on a rung of the aluminium step ladder in the first garage. For several heartbeats I was sure I was seeing a wall at the back of the first garage, but that was just an effect of the light. The fluorescent tube came on in the second garage, and Tobias Quinn stepped through the place where the wall should have been. It was for all the world as if we'd arranged to meet.

He gave me a long look, and said, "So what have you decided?"

"I'm going after her. I'm going to find my daughter."

He raised an eyebrow. "You think you know what you're up against?"

I said nothing. He looked me in the eye and said it again.

"Of *course* I have no idea."

"You really do have no idea what you're up against," he continued. "You think you've seen its dangers? You think there's nothing in the Common Land more dangerous than slithermen? You think you've scratched the surface? You've seen nothing!"

I exhaled slowly through my teeth. "All the more reason to find her then, isn't it?" I held his gaze. "All my life I've been doing the right thing. At least that's what I told myself I was doing. But all I was really doing was choosing the path of least resistance. I didn't want to offend anybody, and I wanted to avoid the really tough decisions."

I waited for him to respond. He did not. I continued. "But this time is different. I may not be her real father, but I love her *so much*! I love her as much as any father has ever loved his daughter. I don't care about the... circumstances of her birth. She means *everything* to me, and I am going to find her, even if I have to go to London Prime to get her back."

Despite himself, Quinn blinked in surprise at my last words. Maybe I'd picked up more than he realised.

"She sounds like a wonderful girl, your Kirsty," he said at length. "How old is she?"

"She's ten." Unsure if he was being ironic, I added, "And yes she is. Wonderful, I mean."

"Ah."

"What's that supposed to mean?"

His smile was surprisingly sympathetic. "Like you, she has a long journey ahead of her." But it wasn't helpful sympathy. It was all I could do not to grab him by the throat.

But I already knew better than to underestimate him. "What do you know? What can you tell me?"

"Learn to navigate. Learn to pick locks. Learn to shoot. But above all, use your instincts. Sometimes they'll be all you have. And one other thing. Never forget..." He trailed off, and looked away, as if he was embarrassed.

"Never forget *what*?" For one absurd moment I thought he was going to say something sentimental. He was going to tell me that whatever happened, he would be there for me. At the very least, he wasn't going to repeat what he'd said last time we spoke.

But he did repeat it. He said, "Don't forget you owe me."

Part 2. The Mirror Place

"We live, as we dream, alone."

Joseph Conrad, *Heart of Darkness*

Chapter 16. Outside

In a phone box outside the train station I dialled my home phone number. In the brief pause that followed I braced myself for the continuous whine that indicated "number unobtainable", but no, this time it was actually ringing.

I clutched the handset with a mixture of anticipation and dread. What if someone answered it this time? What if *I* answered it?

On the fourth ring someone picked up. "Hello."

My heart rate briefly accelerated. It was a man's voice, but the man was not me. He didn't sound like me - and I had heard enough recordings of my own voice to know how I sounded. With a mixture of relief and disappointment I pushed a coin into the slot.

"Good afternoon," I said. "This is David Grant from British Telecom Customers Satisfaction Survey. I understand there have been a number of nuisance calls made to this number. Can you confirm if that is correct, please?"

"Not that I'm aware of," the man said. "You'd be better off speaking to my... Wait a minute, that's her now, I'll just get her."

He put the handset down and called to the woman I assumed was his wife. I could hear him explaining what the call was about, and I heard her voice as she approached the phone. I wondered what their house was like. They had the same phone number as me but did that mean they have the same address? Did they have a daughter they both loved and cherished, and who lived in the room that was Kirsty's room in my world?

The wife came on and I repeated most of what I'd said to the husband. I added, "I believe it was somebody pretending to be a lost boy looking for his parents. Does that ring any bells?"

I'd changed the gender to make the call harder to trace back to me if things went wrong. I was also working on the assumption that people might be more forthcoming if they had a chance to correct me, a chance to say, "Actually there *was* somebody asking for their daddy - but it was a girl, not a boy."

But it didn't happen. The woman at the other end just said, "No, not that I can remember..."

"In the last couple of weeks," I added, as if she'd asked when. "Maybe a message on your answer phone?"

"We don't have one. Sorry."

I prompted her a little longer, hoping she'd suddenly remember. But she didn't, and eventually I closed the call after saying, "It must have been a false report. Sorry to have disturbed you, enjoy the rest of your day."

Kirsty wasn't in this world. Or if she was, she hadn't called home.

Chapter 17. Another Room 28

Standing at the window of my hotel room in the early hours of the morning, I watched the snow falling on the A27. Traffic was sparse and slow-moving. I pressed my hands on the window pane, feeling the cold through the double glazing. I prayed that Kirsty was indoors, or in a warmer world, and I wondered if she still needed to sleep.

I was learning about night. For the past few nights I had discovered new ways of using the extra time. Aimless nocturnal wandering was one of the things I did, sometimes outdoors, more often in the rooms and corridors of the Common Land, hoping I would simply chance upon Kirsty.

It hadn't happened yet.

I needed to understand how it all worked.

I was in Room 28 of the Premier Inn in Chichester again, but this was another Chichester, another Premier Inn, another Room 28. I was impossibly far from home. No, "far" wasn't the right word. I was impossibly *removed* from home.

When I let myself believe it, I experienced a mixture of thrill and fear.

As a history teacher, I was well aware of the idea of alternative histories, or counterfactuals as they were called in highbrow circles - "what if?" situations where the Axis forces had won the Second World War, or Queen Elizabeth I had been assassinated, or Harold had defeated William the Conqueror. That wasn't the vibe I was getting, though. Sure, there were noticeable differences between worlds, but they were mostly of a mundane kind. Sometimes the central part of Chichester was pedestrianised, for instance; other times there was busy traffic around the market cross roundabout where North, East, South and West Street meet. It wasn't always easy to find the library, which I needed to do in order to check the two most recent editions of *The Chichester Observer*. Usually the 1960s polygonal building could be found in the northwest quarter of the city, but sometimes it shared a site with the Festival Theatre, and sometimes it was a different building altogether.

Once - just once - there was no train station, no railway at all. In two others they still had steam trains.

How many versions of Chichester were there? Was it an infinite number? I had to assume it was not, because if it was my task was hopeless. So far I hadn't met myself, or spoken to myself on the phone. I hadn't bumped into any members of Dawn's family, or anybody else I knew in these other Chichesters, but presumably it was a statistical inevitability - in an infinite universe we are all mass-produced.

What if I found a duplicate Kirsty, and didn't realise? Given that I wasn't her biological father, she would have no reason to know me, and she would scream blue murder if I tried to drag her back to my world.

I forcibly stopped this line of thought. I was multiplying assumptions, and it really wasn't helping.

I stepped back from the window. My hand prints remained on the glass. I watched the long delays between cars in the wee small hours and listened to the sounds of the hotel breathing and shifting and creaking around me.

Most people don't really know the night. Sure, there are shift-workers and party-goers and ageing Goths like Mildred and Tony Webster, but their perspective is affected by the fact that they have to sleep some time. I no longer could. I still needed to rest, to physically relax my body, for an hour or two each day. From force of habit, and in order to make the best use of daylight hours, I took my rest at night. The hotel bed was warm and comfortable, and I was paying for the room as if the expense was no big deal.

Sometimes I watched TV while I rested. I remembered having trouble with the remote at first, and initially assumed it was because they worked differently in other worlds. But then I remembered having similar problems in the Room 28 of my own world, and concluded that TV remotes in hotels were weird by nature.

While channel-hopping I had caught a number of late shows over the last few nights. There was an incomprehensible comedy called *The Cousin Stretchers* which was set in and around a rundown farmhouse on a bleak hillside. A ginger-haired and ginger-bearded man dressed as a woman greeted passers-by with the repeated phrase, "You're not from around these parts, are you?" - to the apparent hilarity of the studio audience. I watched a news roundup, followed by an arts programme, all the time looking for the familiar in the unfamiliar, and for the most part not finding it. The Prime Minister was a woman called Sheila Braithwaite. A Tony Blair was mentioned, but he bore no resemblance to the man who was Prime Minister in my world: he was a black film-maker whose latest low-budget romantic comedy had grossed twenty-nine million in its opening week. A seventies rock group called Atreides-7 had reformed and released its first record in nearly three decades; they were unknown to me, but I got the impression that here they were as famous as Pink Floyd.

But not everything was unfamiliar. The global situation - as far as I could tell - was much the same as back home. Frank Pearson, the leader of the opposition, took Sheila Braithwaite to task for comparing herself to Winston Churchill. A production of Shakespeare's *Henry V* was mentioned, as was the Turner Prize. There was an advert for something called Entasis - I wasn't sure if it was a car or a perfume - which featured Bruegel's painting *Hunters In The Snow*, with the hunters and their dogs animated. It was as if the real history makers were somehow destined to be born into different versions of England, or at least in the ones I had visited so far. The English language tended to be the same everywhere, too, although I had noticed the occasional peculiarity in the alphabet.

Was this information really useful? Undoubtedly, but I had misgivings. Even if the Common Land wasn't infinite, it was still vast. Understanding how it worked would help me navigate, but some finite numbers are more overwhelming than infinity itself.

Where was Kirsty? Was she endlessly wandering? Was she outside in the dark? Had someone taken her in? Was she safe with them? Did she have any idea of what she had got herself into?

While I took my rest I tried to imagine what she was doing, what she was thinking. I hoped this would take me into an insomnia dream. They hadn't gone away, and I was learning to gain insight from them. But I was also learning that they did not usually come when you went looking for them. I remembered an astronomer friend showing me the trick of using peripheral vision to see faint stars that cannot be viewed directly. Could I apply an equivalent of this?

So I lay fully clothed on the hotel bed, listening to my surroundings and focusing on the events of the past few days.

*

In that final exchange with Tobias Quinn, he had given me directions, and a contact. We had then parted on terms that were polite, if not exactly friendly.

I used the skeleton key for the first time, on the side door in that second garage. Later I would come to appreciate the difference between through doors and access doors. Through doors were from one part of the Common Land to another; access doors led into or out of the Common Land.

That side door in the second garage was an access door. Going through it meant stepping into a world not my own on my own.

There were dangerous assumptions I had to question. Would they speak English here? Was my money valid? Did they have arbitrary and nonsensical rules that Quinn had not seen fit to mention - the death penalty for walking on the cracks in the pavement, perhaps? Did they dress up as Beefeaters, like those commuters on the Earls Court tube station? Was I expected to carry an identity card?

I stepped out into a narrow alleyway between garages. I was Neil Armstrong, I was Christopher Columbus. The alleyway opened onto a somewhat different Stanley Lane. This Stanley Lane had its own long row of garage fronts, but this row was interrupted by the aforementioned alleyway. There was no Waitrose on the other side, just a boarded-up plot of land and a sign with the name of a developer. There was a phone box nearby, the old-fashioned red type with the horizontal windows.

I rang Dan Spencer. He was in, and the phone accepted my twenty pence piece. He told me he was available for a one-to-one the following morning. I may have gasped out loud when he told me what his fees were; he then added that they were to be paid upfront, explaining, "I've had one or two clients who managed to disappear into thin air before they had a chance to pay me. It's not that I mistrust you, but I don't want to risk that happening again."

I agreed to his terms. He was going to have a good Christmas.

There was nothing I could usefully do until the next morning, at least nothing I could do safely. I got home without incident, set my alarm clock and lay on my bed, expecting to fall into a deep sleep.

I remained awake all night, of course, worrying that I would drift off in the early hours and sleep through the alarm. But when morning came there was no doubting that I really had broken through the barrier of sleep, and total insomnia was my normal state now.

It would have cost Tobias Quinn nothing to have warned me this would happen.

*

Dan Spencer met me off the bus when I arrived at the airport service road in the other Portsmouth. He turned out to be a capable and quite affable teacher. I spent the morning and half the afternoon learning how to pick locks and to handle a gun on a shooting range near the disused land that had once been Portsmouth's airport. In my world it had been developed some years ago - there was a PC World, a huge Toys R Us, and various others - but here the only structures were a derelict hangar and some outbuildings.

I got back to Chichester Gate in my own world a little after sunset. The access door in the McDonald's was still there, and so was the labyrinth beyond it.

My original plan was to systematically map the labyrinth, but that had been when I was defenceless. Carrying a gun made me feel confident, and I was impatient to find out what was on the other side of that archway.

I walked through the access door into the tiled corridor. Among the strange yet familiar distant noises, there was no sound of running feet heralding a second iteration of a minotaur. My confidence quickly diminished, however, as I realised I hadn't memorised the route as well as I thought, so I ended up having to retrace my steps two or three times. I eventually arrived at the corridor with the flickering lights and the low archway. I was still on the wrong side of the slitherman cable.

I kept my distance from the cable. In the steady light from my torch I could see fragments of skin and hair stuck to it. I also noticed a yellowish tooth. It was a molar, and from where I stood it appeared human. Some form of morbid curiosity compelled me to lean a little closer. As I did so, the cable began to quiver, as if aware of my presence. A large globule of a mercury-like liquid slid down the cable like drool down a glutton's chin, and some of the fragments of burnt skin were absorbed into the cable as it passed. I stepped back hurriedly, reaching for the Glock in my shoulder holster.

If I shot the cable from close up, it would snap and flail, and possibly do me a serious injury. If I shot at it from a distance, I could miss it, or merely graze it, and that might bring down the slitherman. With no other prey to distract it, it might come after me. If the sound of the shot carried into the real world, someone in the restaurant might call the police. If they searched me and found the gun...

I considered the Glock. In one day, Dan Spencer had taught me to draw it without accidentally discharging a bullet into my foot, and he had taught me to shoot tin cans and bottles on a low wall near the back of the hangar. He had not taught me to be a quick-draw marksman.

I looked at the message in green lipstick, and revised my earlier interpretation. Kirsty had slipped past the cable, and I was now fairly sure Chloe had too. If she hadn't, the message would surely not have read "C + K". Maybe they had both explored the space beyond the arch, and at some point Chloe had forgotten to be careful. Or maybe she had injured herself on another slitherman cable.

Without realising I was doing it, I found I was approaching the cable more closely than was safe, as if I fancied my own chances of slipping past, even though it was now beyond obvious that I was too big. It quivered again, more vigorously than before; another large globule of mercury-drool slipped down it, and suddenly the yellow molar was absorbed.

I backed away. Maybe I should bring sulphuric acid next time. Or holy water.

*

I needed to find another way. Either go with the original plan of mapping the entire labyrinth until I found a route to the door at the far end of the corridor, or else find another entrance to the Common Land.

At some point Chloe had separated from Kirsty and found herself back in the real world. She hadn't come back through the McDonald's, so she must have re-emerged some distance away.

The obvious course of action was to find the place where she had emerged. I had misgivings about that, however. For one thing, I did not know how long she had been wandering before I found her on Stockbridge Road. For another, I was now inclined to think she had sustained her injuries close to the exit. Otherwise, why wouldn't Kirsty have followed her out?

Unsure what to do next, I went back to my car. I must admit I was relieved to find the blue Fiesta parked where I had left it; it meant I hadn't taken a wrong turning in the labyrinth and come out through a different version of the McDonald's. I rummaged around in the glove compartment for an A5 notebook that I kept there. I found it under a pile of cassette tapes, including the stretched Blondie one that I'd not thrown away for some reason. I needed to start making notes and drawing maps. But I would need a backpack to carry everything as I needed to keep my hands free. I made some notes and sketches based on what I could remember - it felt like writing up dreams before they faded from memory - then put the notebook back where I'd found it.

On impulse I decided to try the cinema. As I entered the multiplex foyer I told myself I was following my instincts; they had served me well in the past, even if they didn't take me directly to where I wanted to be.

I found a new access doorway with surprising ease. There were some video game machines in a room off the main foyer. In the wall behind one of the machines, out of sight of the security camera, was a door which might have been a service door. Half a dozen people – not all young – were shooting aliens or racing virtual cars across deserts. I hesitated, wondering if I should be wearing overalls and carrying a tool kit, but decided the people around me were too absorbed in their own worlds to notice me. There was a lock in the door which presented no real challenge to my skeleton key, despite my minimal training in its use. I slipped through and locked the door behind me.

I was in the Common Land once again.

The place was in darkness. My torch picked out a flight of wooden stairs leading up. Their treads were sticky underfoot. At the top of the stairs, a door opened onto a long, unlit corridor that extended to my left and right. Instinctively I turned to the right, because that corresponded to the upper stories of the restaurants, bowling alley, pub and gym that formed the north end of Chichester Gate; I imagined the corridor in the other direction extending unsupported over the access road and the River Lavant.

There were doorways, similar to the one I had just come through, on either side of the corridor. Three or four were empty frames, with stairs leading down into darkness. Most had plain wooden doors in them, and some had symbols on them done in chalk or marker pen: the familiar skull-and-barbed-wire for danger, or converging lines leading to a rising sun to indicate a safe path. Another door had a square with a 45 degree line radiating from each corner which I would later learn meant a dead end. Two others had a circle with eight legs, four on either side, that I initially supposed indicated slithermen, but later decided meant there were constructors at work.

One of the doorways was boarded up; the safe path symbol was not quite hidden under the boards, and someone had drawn a very elaborate skull and a particularly vicious length of barbed wire. Evidently the corridors and doorways of the Common Land were subject to change.

In addition to the numerous wooden doors there was the occasional steel door, all located in the left-hand wall, all locked, and all far beyond my novice lock-picking skills. The symbols on these were painted on, and consisted mostly of arrows, zigzags and cross-hatching, all incomprehensible to me.

I chose the nearest door with a safe path symbol. Another flight of stairs with sticky treads led me down to a black-painted door which I thought at first was locked but just needed a push in the right place. It opened between two large bins behind a restaurant's kitchen. A surly-looking man in white overalls glanced at me through the kitchen window, then returned to his task of chopping meat.

*

So I had found ready access to a multitude of worlds. I'd already made plans for a systematic search of each world I entered; I could probably get through quite a few each day if I put my mind to it. There was a Premier Inn in this version of Chichester; I would make it my base of operations, assuming they used the same currency. If something went badly wrong - if, for example, I was caught carrying the gun - I could probably make a getaway.

The trail was cold but at least I was in a position to follow it now, although the sheer number of doorways made the task seem daunting. Nevertheless, I was optimistic as I strode to the far end of the car park and into the hotel. I asked for a room. They gave me Room 28. I decided not to read too much into the coincidence.

*

Now, lying on the bed in this other Room 28, I had to admit that my optimism was in short supply. I had been to a multitude of Chichesters, and didn't feel I was any closer to finding Kirsty.

But lack of optimism is not the same as giving up.

My hearing had become preternatural. The sound of cars on the A27 grew more frequent as dawn approached, but I filtered them out. I could be selective with what I was hearing. A woman three rooms away was tearfully murmuring in her sleep. Somewhere a baby cried, somewhere a toilet flushed. Somebody was using the lift; I could hear the whir of its motors and the metal slide of its doors when it stopped.

I frowned, aware that something didn't quite fit. I was pushing my senses to their limits, but I was sure the data was real, not just artefacts of imagination and wishful thinking. Nevertheless I was missing something crucial.

I tried to immerse myself into the insomnia dreamstate in the hope of finding answers. It was like clutching a soap bubble. My heightened senses returned to normal and I was like any other hotel guest who had been unable to get a good night's sleep.

Chapter 18. Stations

The railway guard was an overweight fifty-something who liked to do everything in his own good time. His scrutiny of Kirsty's picture was so prolonged that I began to resent the time he was taking up. He shook his head, said "No" quite decisively, then shook his head again and continued to stare at the picture.

After a further unnecessary long silence he said, "You say this is your daughter?"

"Yes."

"And *how* old did you say she was?"

"Thirteen." I was not a good liar. He moved his stare from the picture to me.

"Thirteen? That girl's never thirteen."

"I told you. It's not a recent photo. Besides, she looks young for her age."

"I'll say she does," he said, ignoring my first point and moving his stare back to the picture. "*Thirteen*?" He shook his head again. "She's not thirteen. Have you reported her missing?"

"Of course I reported her missing. Do you think anyone gives a damn about one more teenager on the run?" I put some aggression into my voice to compensate for my lack of credibility. "Now if you're *quite* sure you haven't seen her, I won't take up any *more* of your time."

*

Kirsty had been missing for two weeks now. I continued to phone my own number and check the *Chichester Observer* for a "Do you know this girl?" article and search the Common Land at random, but I had to find a way to search more effectively.

I'd been to numerous versions of McDonalds now, thinking Kirsty would have made her way back to the restaurant to rejoin the party, not realising she was in a different world. "My daughter's on a strictly controlled diet," I'd explain, "but unfortunately she loves burgers. I need to check she hasn't eaten in here until we've ruled out coeliac." I'd show her picture, then add that she might have come in wearing green make-up.

People were not going to remember one specific child for much longer. Not even if she was wearing green make-up.

Asking about a missing child was problematic. If I told the truth and said she was ten, they would wonder why her disappearance wasn't on national news. Raising her age to thirteen solved that, but it didn't get around the problem that she didn't look thirteen in her photo.

*

The railway guard was a plain-but-cheerful woman in her mid thirties. She looked at me sympathetically when I told her I was trying to track down my thirteen-year-old daughter. She took in my appearance at a glance, and quickly judged me by it. She judged me favourably: I was smartly dressed, clean-shaven, and my breath didn't smell of alcohol. I was presentable.

"How long ago did you say?" she asked.

"Over a week," I said vaguely. "The domestic situation has been a bit... complicated." I cast my eyes down and added, "My fault entirely. I could have handled things better."

She nodded sympathetically, clearly not believing the situation, whatever it was, was entirely my fault. "Do you have a photograph?"

"Nothing recent." I paused. "This is rather old, but it might help." I took Kirsty's picture from my coat pocket.

The guard studied the picture and shook her head, her lips fixed to indicate regret that she couldn't be more helpful.

Despite my earlier decision not to mention it, I added, "She might have been wearing make-up."

"Make-up?"

"She'd been to a party. Goth, or Emo, or whatever they call it these days. Green lipstick, that sort of thing."

The guard shook her head again. "No, I'm really sorry."

"Okay. Thank you for your time."

*

The railway guard was a short, overweight black woman with an infectious laugh which she suppressed when I told her my daughter was missing. She shook her head when I showed her Kirsty's picture.

"I must admit, I've got a bad memory for faces," she said. "Unlike Derek. He's got an eidetic memory. He'll know." She turned to the open doorway to the office. "Derek!"

If my heart lifted in response to her certainty, it quickly fell again. I recognised Derek - and evidently his colleague wasn't exaggerating about his eidetic memory. He was the suspicious fifty-something who had belaboured the fact that Kirsty didn't look thirteen. He stared at me for some moments, then went back into the office and picked up the phone.

*

The exit from that world was the back door of the bowling alley. A short distance away there was a doorway behind the Wetherspoons pub that I had used before. I'd made the mistake of assuming that each of the doors in the upstairs corridor led to different versions of Chichester.

As it turned out, two of the doorways led to the same world.

Back in the dark corridor, I resolved to be more observant, keep my wits about me, and not to make assumptions. Derek was obviously calling the police; if they had arrived before I'd regained the Common Land, things could have proven inconvenient.

It was a possibility I had considered long ago, when I had modelled the Common Land with my father's beer mats: two red houses in the same road. Which made the mistake all the more unforgivable.

It would have been worse if it had snowed. It was hard to see how anyone could fail to follow my footprints to the access door.

*

There was something different about the upstairs corridor. It had been in total darkness before; now, there was a square flicker of light from halfway up the north wall, and the muffled sound of voices. I went to investigate.

The light was coming from a ventilation grating. I looked through it into a partly filled cinema. They were showing an old black and white film, and after a minute or two I recognised it as *Brief Encounter*, with lead actors who did not resemble Trevor Howard or Celia Johnson.

Chapter 19. Coincidence

Being reasonably fit and energetic and having a room on the first floor, I had no occasion to use the hotel lift, and so the Out Of Order sign had not impinged on my consciousness. I had no reason to give it any consideration until I found my way blocked on the stairs by a very elderly and very slow lady.

"I'm sorry," she said, trying to make space to let me pass.

"It's okay, I'm not in a hurry," I replied. I was trying to be pleasant but my voice was tinged by the frustrations of the day. Among other things I was soaked from a rain storm in the last world.

"It's been three days," she said. "I'm not good with stairs, not at my age. Three days!"

*

The significance of the old lady's words didn't strike me until later, by which time I'd changed into dry clothes, locked my Glock in the Room 28 safe, and gone down for lunch. If the hotel lift hadn't been working for the past three days, what had I been listening to in the early hours?

Following my instincts, I finished my meal in the hotel restaurant and went to the McDonald's. It was busy, mostly with children on school holiday. I bought a diet coke and managed to squeeze in on the end of my accustomed table. The place was just like the one back home, with various minor differences, and one especially significant difference: there was a Ladies, a Gents and a Staff Only, but no fourth door, no entrance to the Common Land in this building.

But the sound of a lift had carried throughout the labyrinth. Was Room 28 somehow connected to it?

I considered going back to my room and checking for hidden doors. Again it occurred to me that there were some I wasn't seeing yet. But I dismissed the thought.

At times, during the insomnia dreams when my senses were heightened, I almost had a 3D map of the hidden places. Black and white and grainy, but accurate, I was sure. The sound of trapped air in the pipes triggered a visual image; I followed the pipes, through the gaps in the walls and the floor, and into the basement. They ran horizontally along a wall on the south side, a brick wall, blank and slightly damp, featureless except for the brackets which secured the pipes, and an air brick that led... where?

In my memory of the insomnia dream I could smell the crumbled dampness of the air brick. Its position was inconsistent with the structure of the hotel – this was not an outer wall!

Water was dripping on the other side of the wall. I focused on the sound, and I was through the wall. I was in a corridor. It was square in cross-section, barely three feet across, with crumbling plaster on the walls and short intrusions of piping (one of which was the source of the dripping sound) and unpowered electrical cable. The floor was submerged under two inches of dirty water. I was in complete darkness; I was "seeing" it the way I saw the traffic earlier. Where the corridor dog-legged a naked figure with frog-like skin crouched, breathing heavily. I followed the route in the other direction for a long time. It was straight for a while, then there was a sharp turn to the right. Eventually I came to a flight of stairs. The environment at the top of the stairs was less unpleasant; for one thing, I was clear of the dirty water, and for another, I had emerged from the darkness. The floors, walls and ceiling were covered in large, white tiles, and there were square light fittings in the walls. I came to a white swing door with a circular frosted window in it, and beyond it, a room with a low archway in one wall, and I knew at once that Kirsty had come this way.

"Are you going to be much longer?" The voice behind me made me jump. The fast food restaurant was heaving, and I had been sitting in a trancelike state, occupying a seat for no good reason.

I needed to get back in the labyrinth.

Snow was falling heavily again. I was covered in it in the short run around the cinema block and the unpaved ground to the door behind the Chinese restaurant. It hadn't fully melted by the time I emerged from the service door in the video game room off the cinema foyer. Maybe people noticed, because no snow had fallen in my own Chichester. More importantly, I was running low on dry clothes.

I'd decided not to get my Glock from the Room 28 safe for this trip. So far I hadn't encountered anything or anyone in the upstairs corridor, threatening or otherwise, and I didn't want the gun with me as I was heading back to my own world. Nevertheless, I had misgivings about entering the labyrinth unarmed.

It had only been a few days but it seemed weird to be back in my own version of Chichester. It reminded me of my first school trip to France, and returning to discover that my home town continued to go about its business, unaffected by my absence. I was a little concerned that I had made myself unreachable to the Family Liaison Officer, and worried that the police might draw the wrong inference from my prolonged absence, and might want to question me about my whereabouts. I hadn't allowed for that; I had been too confident of finding Kirsty within a day or two.

My mobile phone had a signal again. I rang home; I'm not sure why, maybe I just wanted to check I was in the right world. It rang; nobody answered. There was a way of accessing my answerphone messages, but I didn't know how; it hadn't occurred to me to find out.

First things first, though. Back into the labyrinth. One way or another I was going to enter that archway. I would map the corridors exhaustively and find a route to that door at the far end of the archway corridor. Failing that...

Failing that I was going to have to get past that slitherman cable one way or another.

The McDonald's in my world was as heaving as the one in the place I now thought of as Hotel World. No need to waste time queuing for food or drink, I made straight for the fourth door, opened it and strode in.

I stopped abruptly, shocked.

The door that wasn't marked Disabled opened onto the labyrinth as before, but this time there was something new and unwelcome.

There were two slitherman cables in the first corridor.

The first one extended from the upper part of the left wall to the lower part of the right wall. The second, a little further in, stretched at an oblique angle from ceiling to floor. In short, there was no way of getting past them without touching one or the other.

I stood staring for maybe half a minute. How had I allowed this to happen? I wondered irrationally. What if the slithermen found the access door? Was I supposed to warn the authorities? It was my understanding that the denizens of the Common Land were as blind to the exits as ordinary people were blind to the entrances, but it was hard to imagine they could miss it when they were this close.

There was nothing I could do. I left the corridor, but not before I'd heard the distinct sound of the lift in the distance. I closed the door, and in full view of the patrons I took out a black marker pen and drew the skull and barbed wire symbol on the door.

I left the restaurant.

*

My car was where I had left it. I thought about driving home and playing the answerphone messages - assuming I had any. I wasn't sure I wanted to do that, though. I'd been away for much longer than intended, and I didn't want to face the questions of the Family Liaison Officer, my next door neighbours or even Miss Havers.

I did want to move the car, though. I had left it in the car park close to a hotel I wasn't staying in - at least not in this world. Abandoned cars draw attention to their owners.

I drove it to the Avenue de Chartres multistory car park, which was less than five minutes' walk away on the other side of the railway. It was a pay and display car park. I bought a ticket that was valid until the following morning, that being Saturday. If necessary I would come back then and buy another ticket for the whole day. They didn't charge for Sunday parking.

From the car park I walked into the town. I found myself wondering what life would be like once I'd found Kirsty and things had truly returned to normal. With no reason to walk in the Common Land any longer, would my need for sleep return? Or would occasional visits meet the need? The extra hours available for marking and lesson preparation and paperwork would be an absolute godsend. But what if there were long-term consequences of sleeplessness? For that matter, what were the short-term effects? Was I experiencing them already?

There was undoubtedly a relationship between dreaming and seeing the entrances to the Common Land, but I didn't think it was a straightforward one.

In W.H. Smith I searched through a selection of newspapers. No headlines read, "Missing Girl Found." One paper featured a photograph of Dawn's family and some of her neighbours, and a caption declaring, "We will not give up hope."

I had to get on with the search. I hurried back to Chichester Gate, wondering if I could find some way of leaving a message for Kirsty or for anybody who had seen her. But that was another aspect of the Common Land that Tobias Quinn had chosen to let me learn for myself.

When you think you're dreaming, but you're not sure, one way of checking is to read something, look away, then attempt to read it again. If it still says the same thing, you know you are awake.

In dreams, it's generally impossible to read or write more than three or four words before the letters become jumbled. And so it was, I found, in the Common Land. I'd attempted to write a Missing poster whilst in the upstairs corridor but was unable to concentrate on the task. I'd wondered if the difficulty was akin to dyslexia.

Mapping my route was less of an issue, as long as I kept to simple rectangles and very short descriptions.

Brief Encounter was showing again when I arrived in the upstairs corridor. I watched it through the grating; a train was thundering past a station, and a miscast woman on the platform hesitated at the moment of suicide.

I turned away and paced along the corridor, shining my torch on the doors as I passed them. I wasn't intending to return to Hotel World yet, but as the beam from my torch fell upon the door to that place, I saw that someone had left a message.

The message was a single word written in large letters with white chalk. The word was, "Coincidence."

I frowned at it for several seconds. I shone my torch beam over the rest of the door. Nothing else had been written there. I checked the other doors. They were unchanged.

"Coincidence," I said aloud, then, "Hello? Is anybody there?" As before my throat constricted when I tried to raise my voice in the Common Land.

I went through the door. A vague, meaningless lead is better than no lead at all, I told myself, not sure I really believed it. I went down the stairs, out through the door behind the Chinese restaurant and into Hotel World, where it was snowing heavily.

What to do next? I'd already done my usual search here. There was the coincidence of being in the same hotel room as before; maybe I would find something there. It was too much to hope that Kirsty had been searching for me, and she'd guessed I would probably be staying in a hotel close to where she'd gone missing. But what if she was waiting there, and my search was finally over?

I hurried across the car park towards the hotel, but before I was quite halfway, I was brought up short by an unexpected sight.

Many of the cars were covered in snow, but a few were not. One of the cars clear of snow was a familiar blue Fiesta. I looked at the number plate in disbelief, and there was no doubting it: It was my car! Some prankster must have seen me drive it away; he had then followed me to the Avenue de Chartres car park where he proceeded to steal the car and return it to the Chichester Gate car park, to the very parking space it had occupied before.

But that didn't make sense. I'd moved my car in Home World. This was Hotel World. The doorways into the Common Land weren't wide enough to accommodate a car.

Could it have followed me through somehow? Or had it left a shadow of itself in this world because I had left it standing for so long?

No, the real explanation was clearly much more mundane. I was simply looking at this world's version of my car. Ordinary people were generally not duplicated in the different worlds, but Henry Ford hadn't been ordinary. The format of registration numbers was the same in most of the worlds I had visited, so there had to be a car somewhere with the same registration number as my own. The fact that it too was a blue Fiesta was nothing more than a coincidence.

With dread curiosity I tried my car key in the driver's door. It unlocked. I opened it, climbed in, and slammed it shut behind me.

There was the stink of stale tobacco smoke. I almost laughed with relief; I was not a smoker. I opened the glove compartment. There was no collection of cassette tapes, no stretched Blondie cassette. Underneath a small pile of cigarette packets were the owner's documents. I found a name. Not my name, not Philip Andrew Hamilton as I had feared; this car belonged to a Victor Simon Wright.

I was startled by a hard rapping on the windscreen. I shoved the documents back and closed the compartment as a man in his late forties yanked open the driver's door. "What the *fuck* are you doing in my car?" he demanded.

"I'm... I'm sorry," I said. "My car looks the same and... and the key fitted the lock. I'm sorry, I didn't mean any harm."

I showed him my key. I tried to get out but he just stood there, staring at me and blocking my exit. I thought he intended to beat me up, or at least intimidate me. Then his demeanour suddenly changed. Maybe it occurred to him that it was an easy mistake to make when most of the cars were covered in snow. Whatever the reason, he shook his head vigorously as if to clear it, mumbled a gruff apology and moved out of my way. Once I was out of his car he got in and drove away at an inappropriate speed.

Somewhat shaken by the encounter, I went back to the hotel and headed straight for my room. I didn't even register disappointment that Kirsty was not waiting there for me. I lay on my bed and switched on the TV and got the news.

A nine year old Chichester girl had gone missing during a shopping trip with her older sister. The girl's name was Eloise Wright.

Chapter 20. Eloise

Among other things, I was excited. This vague, meaningless lead had just become a little less meaningless, and a little more solid. It was the first real lead since I'd found the message in green lipstick on the labyrinth floor.

I was, of course, all too aware that the girl's disappearance was a potential tragedy; at the very least it was the cause for anxiety for her family. I knew well enough what they were going through. But I must confess that is not what was uppermost in my mind.

I showered, shaved, put on a fresh set of clothes and went to the library. They had computers with internet connection; I paid a pound and was given an hour's access.

The default search engine was Bloodhound, which I didn't think existed in my world. I typed in Eloise Wright's name and clicked the News button. With churning slowness, a picture appeared on the CRT monitor. It was a scanned page from yesterday's paper, indicating she had been missing for more than twenty four hours already. There was a colour picture of her smiling at the camera. She was a very pretty child with cascading blonde hair and brown eyes. She was the younger daughter of Victor and Samantha Wright, now separated. She had been shopping with her older sister Betany when she went missing.

The older sister's name made me pause briefly; I had never seen it spelled with only one T before. Strange, the things that stand out.

I found an address in the phonebook. There were a lot of Wrights, but only one with the initials V.S. The father lived on Caernarvon Road. I made a note of his phone number, although I didn't intend that to be the first means of making contact. I checked a street map; it was on the outskirts, roughly two miles away.

Two miles is quite a walk in the snow. More importantly, it's quite a long walk back if things go badly wrong. I didn't want to dwell on how likely that was.

On impulse I went for a haircut, and from the hairdresser's I phoned for a taxi.

The taxi driver was surly, bordering on obnoxious. There was a No Smoking plaque on his dashboard, but that didn't stop him. I considered getting out before he'd even pulled away, but I didn't want to delay this encounter any more than I had already. The afternoon was advancing and it would be getting dark in an hour or so.

It was not a long journey by car, but there was time enough to think. What if Eloise wasn't in the Common Land at all? Children went missing for mundane reasons too. What if Wright thought I was involved somehow? Even if we didn't get off on the wrong foot, how was he going to react when I brought up hidden doorways to parallel worlds? Was there any way I could avoid doing this?

The snow had stopped falling when we arrived at Chatsworth Road, round the corner from Caernarvon Road. I asked the driver if he would wait. "No more than an hour, tops," I said. He agreed, but insisted on being paid for his services so far. Then he switched his radio on and tilted his seat back, which I found reassuring.

Given that Wright and his wife were now separated, it seemed a safe assumption that Eloise had been living with her mother, making her the main focus for the police and the media. On the other hand, Wright would be an obvious suspect, so there was a possibility that I was walking into an awkward situation.

I paused by a hedge from where I could view Wright's house unseen. I took my phone out and pretended to text. There were no police cars parked outside; there was only the blue Fiesta with the same registration number as my own car.

That still felt weird.

I glanced back at the taxi. It was still there. If the driver reneged on his promise, I reflected, and Wright turned violent, it would be the easiest thing in the world to twoc his car. Unconsciously I felt the keys in my pocket.

As I was steeling myself for the coming encounter, a red Mini passed me. It pulled up outside Wright's house, and a slim blonde woman in her mid-twenties and wearing a yellow raincoat got out. The front door opened and Wright himself appeared. They embraced.

I watched the embrace, curious about the relationship. She was too young to be Wright's estranged wife unless she'd had Eloise when she was really young, and probably too old to be Betany unless there had been a huge gap between the two sisters. More likely she was the reason why Wright and his wife were separated.

The embrace was one of shared distress, prolonged and very awkward. I felt uncomfortable watching. Then they both went inside.

I gave it a couple of minutes, then strode up to the front door and rang the bell. Some seconds passed. Wright opened the door. He smelled of stale tobacco. "Yes?" he said.

He hadn't recognised me. That was probably for the best.

"Victor Wright?" I asked.

"Yes?" He looked bemused rather than suspicious. I wasn't a plain-clothes detective, or I would have shown my badge, and I wasn't a reporter, or I would have a camera or notebook or something.

"My name is Philip Hamilton. I wanted to talk to you. I know what you're going through. I know it because it happened to me too."

"What are you talking about?"

"I mean, my daughter went missing two weeks ago, not far from where Eloise was last seen."

There was a short silence. We were approaching the point, I thought, where he would either slam the door in my face or invite me in.

The silence was simultaneously broken by me starting to say, "I think we should talk," and by Wright starting to say, "I never heard anything about any..." and by a mobile phone going off in the house.

I got a glimpse of the young woman as she crossed the hall from the lounge to the kitchen to get it. Closer up, I could see the family resemblance, although Wright's hair was not blond. Most likely she was indeed Betany; Eloise had probably been an accident.

"Do you know something about my daughter?" he asked. There was aggression in his eyes, which abruptly changed to a look of vulnerability, which made me feel oddly guilty. "Anything at all? Do you have any idea where she is?"

"No, I'm afraid I don't. But I think she's... What I mean is, I don't think anything terrible has happened to her. Nobody took Kirsty, she just got herself lost, and I think that's what happened to Eloise."

"Lost? In Chichester?" The bewilderment in his voice was distressing.

"It's a deceptively big city."

He frowned, as if suspecting I was trying to be funny. "You mean she could have found somewhere safe?"

"It's possible."

He said nothing for some moments. In the pause I could hear the woman who was probably Betany in the kitchen saying, "He's talking to someone. No, at the door." Wright appeared to be considering my words, accepting for now the hope they promised. I wondered, how would I have reacted two weeks ago if a stranger had come to my door claiming to have information about Kirsty? Surely I would at least have invited him in.

Wright rubbed one eye with the heel of his hand. "Your daughter..."

"Kirsty."

"Kirsty. Where was she?"

I misunderstood the question. "She was last seen in the McDonald's restaurant. At Chichester Gate."

He frowned. "Last seen? What do you mean, last seen?"

"That's where she went missing," I said.

He pressed the palm of his hand against his forehead this time. Another silence; I was aware that Betany was also no longer speaking.

Eventually Wright said, "Do you mean she's *still missing*?"

I nodded.

"She's been missing for *two weeks*?"

I showed him Kirsty's photograph. "This is her. Kirsty. My daughter."

He looked at it but did not take it. "This... doesn't add up." Snow began to fall again. Still it did not occur to him to let me in. "A girl younger than Eloise goes missing near where Eloise goes missing and nobody even thinks to *mention* it? Did you even report it to the police?"

It was the problem I'd had with the railway guard all over again. "Of course I did. But this wasn't taken recently, Kirsty's older now. Look, she was having trouble sleeping before she disappeared. I think she found..."

"Found *what*?"

"An open doorway or something. She'd been sleepwalking." I was not a good liar at the best of times. I changed tactics, asked a question instead. "Did Eloise have trouble sleeping before she disappeared? It might be a clue."

He did not seem to hear the question. "How come the police never mentioned Kirsty? It was never on the news or anything. It just doesn't add up."

"Kirsty is thirteen. As far as they are concerned she's just another runaway teenager."

"Thirteen?" He grabbed my wrist to look at the photograph again. "*Thirteen*? That doesn't..." Realisation dawned, and he was angry. "I know who you are. You're the one who broke into my car! Now you come here with this... this *bullshit.* Do you really think I *need* it right now? Have you any *idea* what I am going through?"

"I assure you I know *exactly* what you're..."

"Listen to me, *Mister* Hamilton or whatever your real name is, I don't know what the *fuck* your game is, but you stay away from me and my family. You hear me?"

"Look, I swear it's true. Okay, I lied about Kirsty's age because the truth is too strange. She really is missing, I'm trying desperately to find her, but she's..."

He hit me in the face. Not hard, but hard enough. I staggered back, dropping the photograph. He raised his fist again, then restrained himself. We stared at each other for a second or two. Then I turned and ran.

I cried as I ran. I cried tears of rage and frustration. How could I be so *ineffectual*? This was the great father Kirsty was depending on, an ineffectual, useless *coward.*

I rounded the corner into Chatsworth Road. The taxi was gone. I'd been nowhere near an hour.

This was the lowest moment, the worst since Kirsty had gone missing. Darkness was falling prematurely with the increasingly heavy snow, and I was back to square one.

What the hell was I going to do now? The thought of going back to random versions of Chichester was soul destroying, and increasingly unlikely to prove fruitful as time went on. I couldn't give up, though. I'd told Tobias Quinn I would go all the way to London Prime (wherever that was) to find my daughter if that was what it took.

I needed to get back to the hotel and work out what to do next. The hotel bill was cutting into my savings; I couldn't keep it up for much longer. If I didn't find Kirsty soon I'd have to... what? Walk the streets, and take my short rests on a park bench? It would have been an option in summer, but not right now, and certainly not in this world. Besides the freezing cold, the wind and the snow, there was the certainty that Wright would have called the police by now.

I was going to have to get my gun, return to my own world and shoot my way past the slitherman cables. I'd finally reached that level of desperation. My courage had failed with Wright, but I hadn't been desperate then.

Of course, this assumed I ever made it back to the hotel. These were severe weather conditions, and it occurred to me that the taxi driver might yet prove responsible for my death. I checked my phone, with a view to calling another taxi, but it was still unable to get a signal. Visibility was poor. A sign told me I had reached the junction where Windsor Road met Florence Road, and in a very brief lull in the snowfall I saw that there was a recreation ground on the other side. If I could make for that, the police would be unlikely to follow me; my footprints would not last long enough to give me away.

As I was crossing Florence Road I was caught in the beam of the headlights of a slowing car. They had found me already. I made no attempt at evasion; the thought of a warm cell was beginning to seem quite inviting.

"Get in!" The voice was female, and familiar. She was calling me through the wound-down window on the passenger side of a mini.

With nothing to lose, I complied. As soon as I was in, she pulled away. I fumbled with the seat belt and the window winding mechanism. The warmth from the heater came as a welcome blast.

"Did Garcia Hollis send you?" the driver asked.

"Who?"

"Don't waste my time! I know you know about the Mirror Place. That's why I convinced Dad not to call the police, but if you hold out on me, I swear I'll..."

"I take it you're Betany," I interrupted.

Maybe I detected mild embarrassment in her tone. "Yes, yes I am," she said. "What you told Dad - was that true?" She reached behind her, took something from the back seat and handed it to me. Kirsty's picture; I was grateful to have it back. "She's your daughter?"

"Yes."

"And she went missing?"

"Yes."

"And she's not thirteen?"

"No. No, she's not."

"What is she, nine?"

"Ten."

"Ten, then. A sleepwalking girl of ten finds an open doorway somewhere in Chichester, and that's the last anyone sees of her. Is that what you were telling Dad?"

"Something along those lines," I said. "Look, it's complicated, and frankly it's hard to..."

"Complicated?" she echoed. "How could a child go missing for two weeks and nobody know about it? What did Garcia Hollis tell you? Did he tell you Dad had her?"

"Betany, I've never heard of Garcia Hollis. Honestly. I've never heard of the Mirror Place either. But I think I know what you mean."

"Maybe you don't call it that," she conceded. "But it's real, I know it is, I'm *sure* it is."

"What do you think is real?"

She checked her rear view mirror, then pulled over, but left the engine running. "Nobody *here* knows about your missing child because she's not *from* here. *You're* not from here. Am I right? There will be search parties for Kirsty in the Mirror Place, but they're not going to find her because she crossed over into this world, just as Eloise crossed over into the Mirror Place. Am I right?"

"You are partly right." There was another brief respite in the snowfall. I could see we had stopped outside a church. "It's a little more involved than that, but yes, you're on the right lines."

"I knew it," she said. "I *knew* it." She hit the steering wheel twice with the palms of both hands, and broke down in tears.

I sat there, unsure what to do. My instincts were to comfort her somehow, but I certainly wasn't going to risk touching her. Eventually I said, "I'd offer you a handkerchief but..." I gestured at myself, my clothes. I was soaked.

She forced a smile and leaned forward to turn up the heating. "I'm sorry," she said. "It's just... It's been so long. All this time I've been telling myself it was all a dream even though it obviously wasn't. Dreams don't make you..." She broke off abruptly.

Gently I suggested, "Why don't you tell me what happened? Then, if you drive me back to Chichester Gate, I can *show* you what I know."

She reached behind her again, found her handbag, and took a tissue from it. She nodded vigorously as she sorted herself out. "That would be perfect," she said. "After all, that's where it started. For me."

*

She drove as she talked. The windscreen wipers squeaked. "It says in the papers that Eloise is my sister," she began. "Well, it's not as simple as that. She's actually my daughter."

"I see." I thought of the clumsy embrace when Wright had met her earlier. "Eloise's father... was he your father too?"

It took her a moment to work out what I meant – or, more likely, to decide she had understood correctly. "That's horrible!" she said. "Of course he's not!"

"I'm sorry, I just..."

"Why would you say that? Why would you even *think* it?"

I apologised again.

"I was thirteen," she continued firmly. "I went to St Agnes Secondary School. Back then it had a playground and everything. Now its grounds and some of its outer buildings have been demolished, or become part of the Chichester Gate complex. But the school itself is still there.

"It was towards the end of the Christmas term. I was supposed to be handing in a project about a historical character who inspired me. Somebody I thought was a major figure in the making of our nation, that sort of thing. I'd had the whole term to do it in, but I'd done nothing. Nothing at all. I hated history, found it really boring. But Mr Crowthorn the history teacher was also my form teacher and he was really strict and I was in trouble for other things. If I didn't hand anything in it would be the last straw.

"I had two days left. I managed to borrow a book from my granddad which was really old and which none of the teachers would have seen. There was some stuff on Henry VIII. I copied most of it, changing a few words around, and I traced some of the pictures.

"I was up all night doing it. Literally all night. I even had a torch on under the bed. The next day I pretended to be sick so I could buy some time. By the evening I'd got something I could hand in the next day. It wasn't great, but it would do. So it was all over, I was safe, I'd made it in time.

"But I couldn't sleep. At all. Even though I'd gone one night without sleep. Every time I shut my eyes I had this image of Henry VIII in my head, or one of his wives, or one of the many 'interesting' facts about him – like, he threw chicken bones at people. It was driving me mad.

"I had to go in the next day, even though I was shattered. But when I got to school my body was tingling, like I had an electric current running through me, and the world seemed to take on a glow. It was snowing heavily, just like now, and I remember thinking that of all the billions and billions of snowflakes that ever fall, no two are ever alike.

"But that's not really relevant.

"I handed the project in. I think Mr Crowthorn was surprised, and maybe disappointed, because he wasn't going to get to expel me, but he didn't show it. At breaktime I told him I was still ill, and asked if I could go home, but he looked me in the eye and told me not to dilute water. I understand the expression now, but at the time I didn't have a clue what he meant. He told me to go outside and get some fresh air.

"I remember thinking I was sleepwalking. I was on my own because my friends had to go to the head teacher's office because they'd been caught smoking behind the bike sheds. I went into the girls' toilet and splashed cold water on my face but it didn't help me wake up. I stared at myself in the mirror for ages, and I seem to recall thinking the reflection behind me was wrong, but I may have added that later. Then I was outside. Snow was falling still, and I imagined I was walking in deep space and the snow was stars. There was a door that I had never noticed before. I was curious, so I pushed it and it opened. I found myself walking along a long corridor that seemed to go on forever, and then there was an endless series of stairs. Eventually I came out in the Mirror Place.

"I was sure I was dreaming by then. I had fallen asleep at my desk, and all this was happening in my head. So I was safe. I was in some sort of town, where some of the buildings were twenty stories high or more, like the Zurich building in Portsmouth, and fronted with dark reflective glass. There was no snow on the ground and the sun was shining, and people were saying things like, it's a nice day for the time of year. It wasn't warm, it was still winter, but it wasn't such a cold winter.

"There's not much I can remember about the Mirror Place. I remember asking some people where I was and they told me I was in Chichester, like I was really thick. There was a boy, about my age. He told me there was a place we could go. He led me down some alleyways, to a secluded place behind some shops. He started kissing me. He was a bit clumsy, and it wasn't exactly the most romantic location, but I didn't mind, because it felt nice, and I still thought it was a dream. Two years before, our head teacher had warned us all about the dangers of underage sex. We'd signed a pledge, some of us, promising we'd save ourselves until we were emotionally mature enough. Some of my friends signed it to appease the teachers, or their parents, but I signed it because I really meant it – I didn't want cervical cancer, or an unwanted pregnancy, or anything like that. If I'd known I wasn't dreaming, I'd have stopped it there, with the kissing. But he wanted to go further and I said, okay."

"Was the boy Garcia Hollis?" I asked.

Betany nodded. "He was my first." She paused, as if waiting for me to comment. I did not. She continued. "It was nighttime when I got back from the Mirror Place. There had been a panic at the school, and Mum and Dad – they were still together at the time – had gone to the school. Then I just turned up. I was lying there on the steps outside the gym, in the snow. Dad was demanding to know why Mr Crowthorn hadn't sent me home when it was obvious I was genuinely ill. To be fair, I'd thrown so many sickies that I was like the girl who cried wolf. The nurse wanted to examine me but I said no.

"I never told my parents about the Mirror Place. I told my friends, and some of them tried to help me find the place again, but we never did. Three weeks after it happened I had sex with a boy after a back-to-school disco. I told myself I'd do it once, just to see if it was the same as the time with Garcia.

"My period should have started a day or two after that. Well... you can guess the rest."

We came to some traffic lights. We sat in silence as we waited for them to go green. Betany turned into Terminus Road. A left turn at the next set of lights led to Chichester Gate.

"Was the baby Eloise?" I asked.

She nodded.

"She was Garcia's?"

"I had Eloise eight months after the disco, during the summer holiday. My parents adopted her, and moved me to another school. Everyone thinks she's my kid sister."

"What about the boy at the disco?"

Betany sighed. "I told my parents he was the father. I am not proud of that, but they would not have believed the truth - you of all people must understand that. They thought Eloise was three weeks premature, even though she weighed nine pounds and six ounces."

"Did you ever tell Eloise about the Mirror Place?"

She nodded. "Yes, I did." She drove into the car park and stopped close to where her father had parked earlier. I was right back where I had started. I looked over my shoulder at the school. I'd worked there, in another version of Chichester, and Kirsty would be going there next summer.

All being well.

We got out of the car. The snow had stopped. I led the way to the main school building.

"It feels strange coming back," Betany said. "All these years."

We turned a corner, to a part not visible from the car park. There was the doorway, in plain sight.

"What do you see?" I asked Betany.

She looked puzzled. "Nothing."

"This building isn't new, is it? It was here when you were a pupil?"

"Yes."

"You really don't see the doorway?"

She squinted, as if that would help. "No. Just a blank wall, the old fire exit, a drainpipe. That's it."

"So you do actually *see* the fire exit."

"Well of course I do. But it's hardly..."

"Tell me, have you *ever* seen anyone *use* the fire exit?"

“Not this one. Not that I can remember, no. We didn’t have that many fire drills.”

It was a blank door with blue paint flaking off in places. I put a hand on it and pressed. It felt locked. There was no handle, and no keyhole for my skeleton keys. I pressed other parts, feeling for and quickly locating the latch balance. I pushed up and a little to the right. The door swung open.

I felt like a magician, with Betany my awestruck audience.

“As easy as that?” she asked, incredulous.

“As you saw.”

We stepped through the door into a very long corridor, somewhat wider that the corridors in the part I had called the labyrinth; we could walk side by side with space to spare. Dozens of pipes ran alongside the walls and the ceiling. Our footsteps echoed. The background sounds that I’d heard in the labyrinth could be heard here too, but they sounded distinctly muffled. Every ten paces we passed under a gantry on which was mounted a yellow light. In the distance they cast a pale gloom. It could have been an ordinary service tunnel if it hadn’t been for the length.

“But... but it’s been there *years*,” Betany was saying. “In all that time, surely *some*one would have...”

“Someone did. *You* did.”

“You know what I mean.” She sounded irritated, unsatisfied by my glib answer. “And how come I didn’t remember it was there?”

I wasn’t sure about that one. My own experience was quite different; I’d managed to find the Guildford doorway a second time after a gap of eight years. “When Eloise disappeared,” I asked musingly, “did you get insomnia?”

She didn’t answer straight away, and I took it she wasn’t ready to talk about her daughter’s disappearance just yet. There was no need to force matters; it was quite obvious that we were both working under the same assumption: Eloise’s disappearance was somehow involved with the Common Land. "I slept really badly, but I did sleep."

"You hate history. I don't. That might be another factor."

"This is kind of how I remember it," Betany said, thinking aloud rather than talking to me. "Still dreamlike but this time I know it's not a dream."

"It's not," I confirmed.

"How can the corridor go on for so long? The building's only a few metres!"

"We're not in the same world any more," I explained.

Betany gave a staccato laugh. "Really? Mr Crowthorn was very strict about people going out of bounds. If only he'd known!"

We walked on, and the corridor began to take on a new character. The pipes, and some of the lights, were at first veiled, and then completely covered, with a familiar dirty white stuff. Like cobwebs, but so thick they had formed a crust.

"We may be too late," I said. "The constructors are here."

"What does *that* mean?"

I pointed at an almost-covered light. "They're closing off the corridor. It takes years, but they've *had* years."

The coating grew thicker, but we still had space enough to walk side by side, and just enough light to see by. By my reckoning we were close to where the corridor joined the one under the hotel – assuming I was right about them both being part of a continuous structure.

The corridor came to an abrupt end. Bemused, I felt the walls for a door, or at least a weakness. Finding none, I said, "Betany, you mentioned stairs."

She looked, and quickly found, a rectangle in the floor. A trapdoor. There was a ring sunk in it. Using a penknife I got it loose, and together we used it to lift the trapdoor open. It was hinged. We let it crash down on the floor. The opening gave access to stairs leading down, or at least it had done at one time. The room or corridor below had been filled almost to the ceiling with the constructors' stuff; they'd left a gap of about seven or eight inches, leaving the top step visible.

I knelt, and pressed down on the stuff; it was hard, and barely gave at all. If it had been soft or springy, like a pillow or a mattress, I might have imagined Eloise squeezing into the gap.

I considered the possibility anyway. Maybe the size of the gap or the softness of the material wasn't uniform. Still kneeling, I got my torch out and shone it between the constructor stuff and the ceiling. Betany crouched down behind me, resting a hand on my shoulder as she leaned forward.

There was movement. My heart skipped a beat. Something was scrabbling its way through the gap, attracted by the light. Maybe Eloise, maybe even Kirsty...

It registered with Betany first. "What is that stink?" she asked in disgust. Then it registered with me. "Get back!" I yelled, forcing her away from the rectangular aperture just as an arm thrust its way into the space, its hand reaching for us. A left arm; as I had seen once before, skin had grown over its wrist watch.

I ran around the trapdoor, again commanded Betany to get back, and with all my strength lifted it to its upright position and let it crash down on the arm. I stood on the trapdoor, looking for something, anything, to help weigh it down. There was nothing. "Come over here!" I barked at Betany. Somewhat reluctantly she joined me.

We stood together for some minutes. What if our combined weight was not enough? But I did not feel the trapdoor rise. Nor did I feel a freezing-burning sensation through the soles of my feet - something I had not considered beforehand.

"I don't think it can get past the frame," Betany said. "What the hell is it, anyway?"

"Slitherman," I said. "I should never have brought you here unarmed. I'm sorry."

*

As we hurried back to the entrance I looked for doors we might have missed, including trapdoors in the floor and even the ceiling. There was nothing.

Outside, the clouds had cleared and night had well and truly fallen. I hadn't thought it could get any colder than it already was, but it had.

"Can that thing get out?" Betany asked.

"No," I said. I got chalk out of my pocket and started drawing the skull and barbed wire on the fire door. "We've learnt two useful things this evening. One, the slithermen cannot pass through solid matter. Two, the Common Land sheds parts of itself like a lizard shedding its tail. That's a long corridor, given that it leads to nowhere now." I finished the drawing. I made no explanation to Betany, and she did not ask. Truth to tell, I should have drawn one on the trapdoor, but I was afraid the slitherman might force it open while I was doing it.

"So where could she have gone?" Betany asked.

"Not this way, obviously."

"You mean there's *another* route?"

I nearly laughed at the naivety of her tone, then reminded myself that we all have to start somewhere, and I was still a long way from knowing it all myself. At the very least I could give her a better introduction than Tobias Quinn had given me.

"Betany," I said gently, "where were you when she went missing?"

We were walking through the snow back to Betany's mini as we talked. We got in, not with any specific plans in mind beyond getting out of the cold. She turned the engine on. The heating came on.

I thought she would answer me then. She didn't. Still using my gentle voice, I said, "Betany?"

"If you must know she was being an insufferable little bitch!" she spat. "She'd come to stay with me for the rest of the Christmas holidays. I thought we'd go out shopping in Chichester. I don't know about your world, but here the January sales start in December. I thought we could get some nice clothes and things, go out as if we were really sisters."

"Does she know she's your daughter?"

"No. For a time I thought she did, but no, she doesn't. Didn't." She paused again, and this time she sobbed. She controlled herself. "She'd seen a bracelet in an accessory shop. It was horrible, and horribly overpriced, but she wanted it because someone on TV had one, and her friends all have them. I told her she shouldn't be dictated to by the media and by peer pressure. I thought she'd drop the subject and we could carry on with our shopping trip. But she went on and on and I... I wish I'd just bought her the fucking thing!"

She was in tears again. I sat there, once again unsure what to do. We were strangers; attempting to hug her was unlikely to be well received. Besides, I always felt awkward hugging someone in a car. When the sobbing subsided I said, "What happened?"

"She told me she hated me and she never wanted to see me again. I told her that was fine because the feeling was mutual. She started shouting and screaming, and I told her she was far too old to be having a tantrum, especially over a silly little piece of cheap and nasty jewellery. I told her I had had enough of her, I was going home, and she wasn't to follow me until she had learned to act her age."

"You left her in town?" I asked.

"It's not as bad as it sounds. I *live* in town – in a flat above a shop, on South Street. She has her own key and mobile phone and everything. It can't have been more than ten metres I walked. Just before the turning into the side entrance to my flat, I pretended something in a shop window had caught my attention. I was looking at the reflection, of course, so I could watch her without her knowing it. She was wearing a red coat with a hood and she had her back to me. She was just standing there. I thought, any moment she'll turn around. She'll be in tears, she'll be angry, but she'll know she has to apologise. That's what I thought."

Betany was silent for a long time, unable to continue. I was thinking, *red coat? Another coincidence?*

She continued. "It can't have been that long before she turned around. But when she did, when she turned I saw... I saw that it wasn't Eloise." She swallowed. "It was another girl, similar build, similar coat, out with her parents. I'd actually seen her earlier, I even remembered thinking she'd had the same coat for Christmas as Eloise. But right then I just wanted to know where the hell my daughter was.

"Then I saw her in the distance. She'd been walking away all this time. She was nearly at the market cross when I saw her. I couldn't run, not in those shoes, and not in the snow, but I moved pretty quickly, I can tell you. She turned right into East Street. I was absolutely livid then because I knew she was heading back to that stupid accessory shop.

"That's the last I saw of her. By the time I rounded the corner into East Street, she was nowhere to be seen. I wasn't worried at that point because I thought I knew where I'd find her. I thought she'd be cowering when I went in the shop. But she wasn't there at all. I asked the assistants if they'd seen her, but they just said there were young girls in and out the shop all the time. I described her, described the red coat she was wearing, but they just said the same thing, the exact same words. I thought she might have decided to walk to Dad's house. She lives with Mum normally but that's not walking distance. I was worried she'd lose her way, or get picked up or something, so I tried to phone her but her phone wasn't on. I even thought she'd doubled back to the flat, but... Well, obviously she hadn't." She hesitated, then added, "You think it's my *fault*, don't you?"

"That's not what I was thinking at all," I said. She seemed to accept that.

"There was something else," she started to say, "something I never mentioned to anybody because... because it didn't sound relevant, but now..."

She seemed reluctant to continue, as if she were slightly embarrassed. I nodded encouragingly.

"When she was walking away, I was sure it really was her this time, even though I could only see the back of her. But the way she walked, it was like..."

She broke off. Her mobile was ringing.

It was her mother. She wanted to know where Betany had been for the past few hours, and why she had had her phone switched off all this time. I could only hear Betany's side of the conversation but it was easy enough to infer what was being said. Betany explained that she had been looking into places where Eloise might have gone, and she'd only been about an hour at most. Her mother pointed out that that sort of thing was better left to the police, who knew what they were doing, whereas she, Betany, should have more sense than to be out on the streets late at night when there was a child abductor at large. To which Betany retorted that she was twenty four for God's sake and knew how to look after herself. And so on, and so on.

The conversation eventually ended. "She still treats me like a child," she complained. "I'm a mother myself." She glanced at her watch. "And it wasn't 'hours and hours', it's not even half past five."

"Actually..." I said.

"What?"

I glanced at the car clock. She followed my look. "It's nearly ten o'clock! How is that possible?"

"I'm not sure how it works exactly," I said, "but there seems to be a time differential between inside and outside."

"A time differential? What sort of explanation is that?"

"As I said, I don't know how it works. All I know is, it varies in different parts. What were you going to say, before your mother rang?"

"About what?"

"About the way Eloise was walking."

"Oh yes. She seemed to be sleepwalking."

*

Having digested the information that there could be more than one doorway into the Common Land, Betany was anxious to go into town. She didn't want to drive any more than she had to in the dark and in the deep snow, and it wasn't all that far to walk. Reluctantly I got out of the warmth of the car.

We exited Chichester Gate through the gap between the school and the fitness centre, onto Stockbridge Road where in another world I had found Chloe Faulkner. At some point Betany took my arm, obviously for balance rather than a desire for closeness as the snow made walking much more difficult than she'd anticipated. We crossed the railway close to Chichester Station, and proceeded on to South Street. We passed her flat - she pointed it out to me - and went on to the market cross, retracing Eloise's route now, and turned right into East Street.

"I wish I'd followed her footprints," Betany said. "I probably could have done if I'd had my wits about me."

The accessory shop on the other side of East Street was locked. Not just locked, it had steel shutters, as if the owners were afraid that ram raiders were going to target a beads and handbags shop. Betany explained that it used to be a jewellers. I reckoned I could have picked the locks, I was eager to try even, but the shop was probably alarmed; in any case there was no guarantee that I would find a doorway inside. Maybe in other circumstances I could have sensed the route of the Common Land, but not then. I was damp, and hungry, and so cold.

"Perhaps the shop will open tomorrow," I suggested.

"It's New Year's Eve tomorrow," Betany said.

"Shops open all the time these days. And young people will need their accessories for the New Year parties."

Betany nodded. "Let's go back to my flat. I'll make us some supper."

In her flat Betany directed me to hang my wet clothes over a radiator and to take a shower. I steamed up the mirror and the window but still felt the cold creep in. She told me to use the dressing gown that hung on a hook on the bathroom door. It was a man's dressing gown, a little big for me. I didn't ask whose it was. When I came out, I could hear the humming of a microwave in the little kitchen. Betany was in the smaller of the two bedrooms, which contained a small bed – the one belonging to Eloise when she was staying with her "sister". There was a desk with a computer, scanner and printer. I was quite taken aback when I realised what Betany was doing.

An image of Kirsty filled the monitor screen. It took maybe a second to realise Betany must have scanned the photo. But she'd made... changes.

"You've done so much for me," Betany explained. "All these years of wondering if I was mad. You put an end to that. I thought I should do something for you in return."

"You've *aged* her," I said.

She nodded. "It's a public domain program. I got it for Eloise last time she came to stay. We spent an afternoon making her older and me younger, so that we could be twins. The quality's not great but Kirsty makes a convincing thirteen year old, don't you think?"

She clicked on the Print button and a glossy photo of my daughter, three years older, came out of the printer. "You're not happy with what I've done?"

"It's not that, I... I'm just not comfortable with the idea of Kirsty being..."

"Pubescent?"

"No. I mean yes. I mean... She's a child! She's *my* child! I understand why you've done this, but... But surely you can understand it's not something I want to think about. Thirteen! Some girls are sexually active at thirteen."

"Girls like me, you mean?"

"Oh for God's sake! I'm not judging you. But she's my daughter!"

"Seriously, Phil. How much longer can you show people a picture of a nine year old girl and tell them she's thirteen?"

"She's ten. Nearly eleven."

"Whatever. The point is, I've changed her as little as possible. You show this to people and say she's thirteen, they'll believe you. At the same time, if they *have* seen her, they'll probably recognise her from this."

"Yes, I said I understood. But... Look, I do appreciate it. Really, I'm grateful, but surely you can see it from my point of view?"

The microwave oven pinged. "I hope you like curry," she said, and went out.

I lingered in the room for a minute or two, reminding myself that Betany was going through the same as me. Her manner was almost carefree compared with how it had been, doubtlessly because I'd given her hope. This hope would of course die for her as it had died for me when I learned just how vast the Common Land was. But for now, let her keep her hope. After all, she might get lucky. I looked again at the picture of teenage Kirsty and nodded acceptance. I looked around the room, at the shelf above Eloise's bed. Evidently the *Horrible History* books were popular over here too; she had the whole set, and a book called *A Treasury of Celtic Legends* on her bedside table.

I joined Betany in the kitchen. We ate without speaking, but I sensed that the silence was on Betany's side, as if she were building up to something. When we were finished she said, "Phil. I don't want to be alone tonight. Not after... everything."

I was not aware that my expression had changed in any way, but Betany lowered her eyes as if ashamed, and disappointed in me. "*Please* don't misconstrue my request. I need you to be there for me. After what we've seen. I need to be with someone who understands. You know what it's like to lose your daughter. And you know about the Common Land. I don't pretend to understand it, but I get that it's real, and it's a hell of a lot to take in."

"It's still pretty new to me too."

"Okay. One other thing. I used to have a reputation for being an easy lay. I can't say it wasn't justified. But I *have* grown out of it now. So... So please don't judge me by what's gone before."

"I told you, I'm not judging you."

She nodded. "That's okay then."

*

Nights without sleeping pass with glacial slowness. This night was glacially cold, too. I could feel it, even in the double bed, even with the windows closed and the radiator on. Betany lay close to me, so close I could have touched her without seeming to reach out.

I was naked save for a dressing gown in bed with a woman I had met mere hours ago. This sort of thing was a normal weekend situation for some of my acquaintances, including the Religious Studies teacher, if their boasts were to be believed, but for me it was unprecedented. She had told me not to misconstrue her request, but seriously, it was difficult to imagine she wanted me to lie there inert all night. For all that she had undressed in the bathroom and come back in a nightie that looked like something out of a docudrama about Irish convents of the 1920s.

I had an almost painfully hard erection. That couldn't be helped; I couldn't control that, but I could control what I thought and what I did. In other circumstances, it would have been okay. We were adults, and this was not a situation that wasn't what it looked like.

But Kirsty was still missing. *Eloise* was still missing for that matter. It wouldn't be right.

I thought of Dawn. She was prematurely middle-aged, trapped in an unequal and illegal relationship, and no doubt feeling the loss of Kirsty every bit as keenly as I was.

Betany's sleep was fitful. I could almost imagine I knew what she was dreaming. Then the breathing took on a more peaceful rhythm. I fancied I could hear her heartbeat. Whenever she turned in her sleep I hoped she would move closer to me, cuddle up to me. But the distance remained.

God, I wanted some *joy* in my life.

To take my mind off this, I made myself think about how time worked in the Common Land. I was getting used to the differentials between time spent in it and the time that passed outside, but for Betany it had come as something of a shock, and my explanation had been inadequate. I needed to get it clearer in my mind.

Much as I loved music, my understanding of music theory was poor. Until a friend at university had actually let me play one, I thought guitars had five strings because there were five lines in a stave. I'd sort of got the idea that you could tell which note to play by the position of an oval on a stave, but I could not get my head around the concept of rests, and I assumed the speed at which you played was determined by how closely the notes were grouped together - after all, that's what frequency was.

There were bells in the Common Land. I never saw any of them, I only heard them through the walls, often muffled, sometimes echoing along corridors, and once I was sure the bell was on the other side of a locked door.

Although I didn't see the bells themselves, I saw the sound they made. It was a kind of synaesthesia. Somewhere, behind a locked door, there was a long room with a long stave suspended in midair, five long taut wires with a note resembling an egg on the middle wire like a bead on an abacus - the B, I supposed, remembering the "every good boy deserves fruit" mnemonic, although I had no idea if that was the actual sound of the bell. When I first entered the labyrinth, I approached the stave from an oblique angle, and it tolled out the time at a rate that seemed natural to me. When my movements took me into a more broadside position, the intervals between chimes became longer, corresponding to a slower rate of time. Conversely, when I moved towards the ends of the metaphorical stave, I was seeing it edge on. The effect was a foreshortening; the interval between chimes approached zero, and the speed of time was theoretically infinite.

Theoretically. In practice, it was fast, but nowhere near that fast. Small mercies...

My movements were of course constrained by the corridors, and the losses and gains in time more or less averaged themselves out, although the losses generally won.

More to the point, depending on the corridors, it was sometimes possible to go round the end to the other side of the stave. There, the tolling rate began to slow down again, sounding more or less the same as it had on the side I had first approached.

More or less the same, but not exactly the same. The interval between chimes was similar for similar positions, but on the far side, it was like listening to a recording of a bell played backwards. The decay came before the attack.

Like most analogies, this one was not perfect, but it was workable.

That was just relative speed, though. That was not the whole story. The Common Land tended to link to abandoned rooms and buildings, and that sometimes meant crossing into the past, or the future. Quinn had actually told me this; it was one of the few occasions he'd been forthcoming. I had no working model to explain this, no analogy, I simply had to take it on trust.

"Are you awake?" Betany asked suddenly.

"I am always awake," I replied.

"Oh yes. You told me about the not-sleeping thing."

"What about you?"

In the dark, it seemed that she shrugged. "I haven't acquired your superpower," she said. "At least not yet. My circadian rhythm's a bit mixed up, though. My body thinks it's four hours earlier than it is."

We lay quiet for a time. This was not the time to talk about musical staves and synaesthesia.

"It's so cold," she said. "How can it *be* so cold? It's like the cold is alive. If that makes any sense."

"It's not the same in every world," I said. "You saw that for yourself."

"Do you think Eloise and Kirsty are indoors?"

"I hope so. That's one thing the Common Land has going for it."

"Do you think they're alive?"

"I know she's alive," I replied. It did not occur to me that I was answering only half of her question, or that there was no evidence to support my assertion. "She's out there, and she's all right. I can feel it. Can't you?"

"Yes. Yes I can." But I could hear the doubt in her voice.

"She's in another world, but remember, *we can get there too.*"

"Okay."

We lay quietly for a little longer.

"What did you tell your father?" I asked. "To stop him calling the police."

"I told him I knew you. I told him someone close to you had died three years ago, and you had issues about it."

"How did you say you knew me?"

"From the hospital."

"Are you a nurse?"

"No. Receptionist. When you were talking to Dad I heard you say Kirsty was thirteen. So I said three years to make it fit."

"He believed you?"

"He *always* believes me."

"A receptionist, eh? We know so little about each other."

"That is true. But I think I trust you."

We moved together at the same time then. I was kissing her, on the mouth, on the neck. She was wriggling, then she was pulling away, pushing me away. I thought she'd changed her mind, or she'd been deliberately leading me on, or I actually had misconstrued the situation. Seemingly reading my mind she said, "No, wait!" She was reaching into the drawer of her bedside cabinet. For condoms.

Soon she was on top of me, opening my borrowed dressing gown and guiding my erection into her. She screamed in ecstasy as we came together.

Afterwards we lay naked and entwined, still aware of the creeping cold but now proof against it in our mutual warmth. We were strangers, with nothing in common, nothing to bring us together except for a shared ordeal – and it was wrong that an ordeal should be bringing us together in *this* particular way. But it was happening, and it happened three more times during the early hours of the morning.

Chapter 21. Something Wrong

The next day, the unthinkable happened. I overslept.

It wasn't possible. Sleep was something I didn't do any more. But there was no denying it; I had just woken up and was looking at a red LED bedside clock that told me it was 10.53.

I shot out of bed. I roused Betany, who was equally taken aback by how late it was. It was still cold in the bedroom. I hurriedly washed and began putting on my yesterday's clothes. They still did not feel completely dry. Betany put on dungarees, a faded red jumper and a jacket.

"I had the alarm set," she was saying. "I can't believe we slept through it. And there are messages on the answerphone, and on my voicemail. Mostly from Mum. Not the police, thank God."

"None of that is going to matter if we get a result today," I pointed out as I pulled my trousers on.

We descended in the lift that the flat shared with the shop and out into the side street where it was as cold as expected. We made our way to the accessory shop on East Street, discussing our plans as we walked. First, find the doorway, then do a brief check of the corridor beyond. If there were chalked warnings or any other hint of danger I would go back to the hotel and get my gun from the safe.

Just before we arrived at the shop, Betany said, "What happened last night... I wasn't planning it, or hinting it, at least not consciously. But I don't regret it. We were good, don't you think? I mean, *really* good."

Unsure what to say, I eventually came out with, "I think we needed each other. In a good way. And it *was* good. Very good."

"We didn't do anything wrong, did we?"

"We did nothing wrong."

The accessory shop was open. We went in. An assistant asked if she could help us. We told her we were just looking.

And I kept on looking. Fruitlessly. In frustration and near panic I hissed at Betany, "I can't find it!"

"So where *could* she have gone?"

"No, I don't mean there's no door here. I mean, even if the door *is* here, I can't see it!"

"That makes no sense. How would you know?"

"I don't know *how* I know. I just know that I know! It's like... it's like you not being able to see the door at the school yesterday."

Betany giggled. I glared at her. She restrained herself, then giggled again. I grabbed her by the arm and would have dragged her out of the shop if she hadn't followed willingly. She was laughing hysterically by the time we got outside. "My daughter's in another *universe* and we can't get there because you can't find the door! It's like... it's like that song about parties that go on till four."

"It's not funny!"

"I *know* it's not funny! God knows, I'm not thinking it's funny!"

I felt a rage building up inside me. But it wasn't her fault. Instead of shouting at her I hugged her. For a moment I thought she was offended by the gesture, but then she pressed herself into me, her face against my shoulder, and she sobbed. We stood like that for a while.

"I'm all right now," she said, and gently ended the embrace. "But what are we going to do?"

"I'm thinking."

"Can't we just go back in and try everything that *looks* like a door?"

"I don't think it works like that. If it did... well, other people would have found their way in at your school. *You* would have found it again."

"So what do you suggest?"

"We go to my world." We walked as I talked. "If I can find the way, that is. I *should* be able to, it's a route I know well. If I can make it there, it might jog my memory, or reestablish my relationship with the Common Land."

"What if you can't find the door?" She giggled once more. She tried to control herself but it got worse. I ignored it.

"I don't know."

"You could be stuck here. This isn't your world. You'd have no job, no money, no identity, *nothing*."

"Thank you for pointing that out, Betany."

"I'm sorry. I'm just... worried for you."

Her concern was genuine. If I *was* trapped in this world, her concern might be all I had. "I know," I said gently. "And I do appreciate it. Really I do. But let's just wait till we get there."

"Phil, if you can't find it, I might be able to find the door in the school again. That might help."

"It might," I said doubtfully. "We'll keep it in mind."

Outside, a crowd had gathered for no apparent reason, making progress difficult. On South Street, a man carrying a microwave oven in a box approached us at speed on the narrow pavement; we barely had time to get out of his way. When we got to the level crossing the gates were down and the footbridge was closed for maintenance. We waited, and waited. Eventually a goods train thundered through. The gates remained down after it was gone. We were soon surrounded by irate pedestrians, and there were very long queues of traffic on either side of the crossing.

"Why's this happening?" I said aloud. "Why now?"

Betany squeezed my hand. "It gets like this sometimes. Since the incident with the footbridge last month. It seems much worse when you're in a hurry."

"Yes, I know." I pressed my eyes with thumb and forefinger. I didn't know what she meant by the incident but didn't think it was relevant. "Yesterday, in the Common Land, you said you knew you weren't dreaming. But... I know it sounds silly, but I'm not sure *I'm* not now."

"You're not, believe me, Philip. *I'm* real!"

I laughed mirthlessly. "You would say that either way. But it's not what I mean."

"Then what *do* you mean?"

"I know I'm here, really here. But what if I'm making this happen myself? I read somewhere that in dreams, everyone is an aspect of you. The things that happen happen because you *make* them happen. Now normally that only happens when you're asleep, but you have to have a special relationship with dreams to get into the Common Land in the first place. I had that special relationship. But this morning I slept properly for the first time in weeks. Does that mean the relationship is changing?" I forced a smile. "I'm probably not making any sense. Put it down to lack of regular sleep."

"But if you're making things happen, why are you putting difficulties in your way?"

"Perhaps I'm punishing myself." I frowned. "We did something wrong."

A passenger train thundered through in the opposite direction to the goods train. Several pregnant seconds passed, and then the gates finally lifted.

I walked so quickly that Betany had trouble keeping up. We arrived at the Chichester Gate complex. I was feeling confused, for all the world as if I was sleep-deprived - as if the real sleep I had experienced served only to remind my body how much more I needed.

Betany headed at first for the school building before realising I wasn't going that way. I headed for the cinema. There was a delay on the automatic doors, so I had to break my stride before going in. I was almost at the video games room when I remembered: this was the Home World entrance to the corridor, not the Hotel World entrance.

I abruptly turned, nearly colliding with Betany. "We need to go round the cinema block, get to the back of the Chinese restaurant." She followed without speaking.

I found the door. My heart pounding loudly, I reached for it. It stuck. I pushed harder. It opened.

"Inside!" I shouted.

We piled in. Up the wooden stairs to the door at the top, and into the long corridor. I was back in the Common Land! I was almost overcome with relief.

"It's okay," I said. "It's going to be okay."

"This is... different," Betany said.

I hadn't got my torch out yet, and she'd noticed the flickering of light from the grill that overlooked the cinema. It suddenly occurred to me that I really shouldn't be moving in the dark like this. Slitherman cables appeared in unexpected places, and there was no reason to assume this corridor was sacrosanct.

I switched my torch on. Betany was standing at the grill. "It's *Brief Encounter*!" she said brightly.

I grinned at her in the torchlight. "It's always *Brief Encounter*."

"It's my favourite film. Mum and I used to watch it on Sunday afternoons, whenever it came on, and later we got it on video. I didn't know it had been remade."

"It's not a remake," I explained. "It's a different version, made in a different world, with different actors."

"Oh."

"I thought you'd have guessed that. After all, why would they remake it in black and white?"

"Are you being funny?"

"What do you mean?"

"I mean, how would you *know* it was black and white?"

"Well you can see it is!" I joined her at the grill. It was the cafe scene. One of the men sitting at a table looked oddly reminiscent of the younger brother from the sitcom *Only Fools and Horses.*

"Yeah, but *everything's* in black and white. Here in the Common Land. Even you."

"Colours don't really show up well in torchlight," I pointed out.

"What was the colour of the lights in that corridor yesterday?"

"Yellow."

She shrugged. "To you, maybe."

I was intrigued by this curious fact, this basic difference in perception. But it was important we didn't become distracted. I needed to know that I could get home, and move in and out of the Common Land with the same freedom as before. Instinct told me all was well, but I needed to be sure.

Turning, my torch beam fell upon the door to what I had designated Hotel World but was now thinking of as Betany's world. The chalked word "Coincidence" was gone, no trace of it left. In its place was the word "Hope".

"Hope," I read aloud.

Betany was looking at the chalked word. "Is that your writing?" she said.

I turned to look at her, dazzling her with the torchlight. Her eyes were blue, I noticed for the first time. Like my own. "How can you *know* that?"

"I didn't. I said *is it* your writing. It was a question, not a statement."

A memory flashed into my mind. I was telling my class about the Flying Dutchman, and how his home was the Cape of Good Hope. I wrote the words on the blackboard; the letters in that final word, then and now, were joined up, the O not quite closed at the top, a distinct loop in the tail of the P. But did that *really* mean anything? "I *can't* have written it here. I didn't have the opportunity."

But hope. It had said coincidence, and there had *been* a coincidence. A massive one. Now it said hope.

I needed to hope. I needed to stop preparing myself for the worst, to stop trying to insulate myself against disappointment, because that was why I was having no success in my search. Impulsively I took out the picture of Kirsty - the one Betany had doctored - and shone my torch on it. "It ends this year," I said decisively. "For *both* of us. We're going to find our daughters."

"It's New Year's Eve today," Betany said, a slight tremor in her voice.

"I know."

*

It was noticeably warmer in my own world when we came out of the cinema. There was no snow, and the sky was a deep blue.

"I probably ought to go home and check my answerphone for messages," I told Betany, "I should be able to do it remotely, but I can't remember how."

"What about the voicemail on your mobile?"

I hadn't thought of that. I got my mobile out and she tsked in disapproval; it wasn't exactly top of the range and the display was cracked. "Look," she said. "That symbol means you've got a message."

It was from Dawn. Evidently she'd phoned just a few minutes after my previous visit to my home world. I played it.

"If you are there, Philip, pick up. Pick up the phone, Philip. Please, Philip, pick up the damned phone!"

My heart raced. Why would she be phoning me? Why the urgency? Unless...

The message continued. "Philip, it's me. Dawn. I've seen Kirsty, I've *spoken* to her. She's alive! But Phil, she's *changed.* She's..." Her voice suddenly seemed distant, most of her words rendered incomprehensible by sobbing. "...Said she couldn't stay, she's looking for answers... meet her at London Prime... didn't even know what she was talking about..." Then there was the unmistakable clatter of the phone being dropped. I could hear a male voice in the background - William or Benjamin - and Dawn saying, "No! *Please*!"

Then silence.

I played it again. And again. I turned to Betany. "She's been here!" I headed rapidly in the direction of the Avenue de Chartres car park.

Hurrying after me, Betany said, "Yours or mine?"

"Mine!"

It was staggeringly, heartbreakingly unfair. The nightmare was supposed to *end* with the safe reappearance of Kirsty. It should have been relief, reunion, and gratitude to a God I would be prepared to believe in. I should be thanking God; instead I was berating Him. *How much more of this do you think I can take?*

But Kirsty was alive. How she'd changed, and where and why she'd gone, I didn't know, but these things could wait. She was alive. No matter how many times I'd told myself she *was* alive, it was nothing like having confirmation.

"I need to get over to the Price Estate," I told Betany. "Find out what's going on." I didn't know what sort of reception I'd get from Dawn's brothers. Probably not a good one, given how they - or William, anyway - seemed to be treating Dawn. Then, almost as an afterthought, I added, "After that we'll resume the search for Eloise."

We continued on in silence. I felt I was on the brink of something, a crisis point where I might make the worst decision with the best of intentions, or else through cowardice. Maybe there was no point in going to the Price Estate - why get beaten up again when Kirsty had already left?

That she had returned to the Common Land was pretty much a given. Dawn hadn't said where she'd seen her, but my guess was probably Chichester. For all I knew Kirsty had been in the corridor shortly before or shortly after I had; maybe she was the one who had written the cryptic messages. Or perhaps she had slipped past the slitherman cables in the labyrinth. Had she been injured, the way Chloe had? Is that what Dawn had meant by "changed"? I didn't think so; I was sure she would have said "hurt" or "injured" if it had been the case. So what did she mean? Was it possible it hadn't been Kirsty at all?

We were entering the multistory car park when I remembered my ticket was only for the one day. I had intended to move it today – but I had not allowed for oversleeping. What if it had been clamped, or towed away?

"What the hell is *Dad* doing here?" Betany said, startling me.

"What?" I had no idea what she was talking about.

"That's his car," she said, pointing. "How the hell could he have driven here?"

Realisation dawned. I gave a short laugh. "It's not your dad's car, it's mine."

"Huh?" It was her turn to be bewildered.

"Same model, same registration, different universe. I don't know if it's fate or the biggest coincidence of all time, but for some reason my car is identical to your dad's."

"Okay, so just one more thing to take on board, right?" She frowned, her eyes narrowed. "There's something wrong with your car."

I'd got the keys out when the sight through the windows registered. The car had been filled with fresh cobwebs, so tightly woven they looked like hundreds of very thin dirty white sheets. Between the seats, from the seat fronts to the steering wheel, from the seat backs to the ceiling, across the footwells, from the rear view mirror to the windscreen, even from the slot in the cassette player. I hesitated, afraid to touch the vehicle.

"Constructors?" Betany asked.

"Maybe. I'm not sure." It looked like an act of vandalism – if vandals went around pouring spiders into people's cars.

"Maybe it was bananas."

"Bananas? What are you talking about?"

"Sometimes when they're shipped over here there are spiders in the packing. Maybe someone parked a van with them in."

I checked the surrounding cars to see if any of them had been affected. None had. Perhaps it had happened overnight

"We *did* do something wrong," Betany said, as if thinking aloud. "I don't think it was the lovemaking." Her use of the quaint expression struck me as quite endearing.

"What if we're imagining them?" I said.

"We can both see them, Phil."

"No, I need a witness, someone who hasn't been in the Common Land." There was a couple nearby, a bearded man of about my age and a much younger woman. They were both tanned, which suggested they'd spent Christmas in sunnier climes. They were carrying Waitrose carrier bags. I called to them. "Excuse me, can you help us? We've got a problem with our car."

"Gonna have to be quick," the man said. "Couldn't get a space in the Waitrose car park, and these aren't going to stay frozen long." He raised the bags to indicate what he meant.

"Are you needing a push?" the young woman asked.

I said, "Have you ever seen anything like that?"

The man looked in through the windscreen. "Good grief!" he said. "That's just... too weird."

The woman asked, "Did you leave bananas in the boot or something?"

The man said, "I don't think the AA covers this sort of thing. I hope you're not an arachnophobe." A moment later he winced as if embarrassed and nodded. "You are, aren't you." Seeing my blank look, he said, "You don't remember me, do you Philip?"

Then it clicked. "Howard?" I said in surprise. "Sorry, I didn't recognise you."

He grinned. "I think I've changed more than you have. Anyway, good to see you, but we really have to dash."

They hurried off.

Evidently Howard had been out of the country when Kirsty disappeared. I shrugged; he had long since ceased being relevant. I turned back to my car, unsure what to do. I had no wish to get into a car filled with spiders (although I could not see any actual creatures in among the webs) and I had no desire to visit the Price Estate. If Dawn had told me our daughter was still with her, then nothing would have stopped me, but the truth was, she probably knew less than I did.

"They're warning me not to continue in this direction," I said, decisive at last. "It makes sense. Kirsty's okay but she's not in this world. Dawn's message was more than a day old, and she was talking in the past tense."

"Maybe Kirsty found Eloise."

"It is possible." I gave my car one last look, then shook my head. "Let's go back. I think I can navigate again."

But before we arrived back at the cinema complex I phoned the police, and asked to be put through to the FLO. I had to field a number of questions, including basics such as my name, address and relationship to the missing person, for all the world as if they'd all had amnesia and lost all the files. I briefly wondered if this was in fact my own world after all. But eventually I got put through to one of the FLOs I had dealt with before, and I told her all about the voicemail message I had received from Dawn. She was surprised and interested; evidently the Price family had not informed them of Kirsty's brief reappearance.

I embellished nothing; if anything I played down the fact that Dawn was practically a prisoner in her own home. But I was pretty sure they got the message.

Maybe I'd improved matters, maybe I'd made things worse. Maybe I was only delaying the real showdown with Dawn's brothers, but for now, there were other, more pressing matters.

Chapter 22. The Novikov Model of Time Travel

We returned to Betany's World. I retrieved my gun from my hotel room. I'd left a few items of clothing in the wardrobe, toothbrush and deodorant in the en suite, but I didn't think I'd be coming back for them. One way or another, this ended tonight.

On our way back into town the railway gates opened at our approach; the crowds had dispersed, as if by magic. In the accessory shop itself, I headed straight for a display of overpriced tacky bracelets – it seemed so *obvious* now! The display was screwed in to some wood panelling. I pulled at it and the panelling swung open, hinged on the left edge. I ushered Betany in through the opening, followed her, and closed the panelling behind me. I chalked our initials on the wood in case we had difficulty finding our way back.

The corridor we found ourselves in had bare floorboards and dusty shelves along one wall, and sixty watt lightbulbs hanging from the ceiling. I suddenly felt uneasy, and Betany picked up on the fact.

"What's the matter, Phil?"

"This is too easy. I'm not sure this is actually the Common Land. My instincts are all over the place. I don't want to get caught trespassing in a store room!"

"One way to find out." She took her mobile phone from her pocket. I thought she was going to check for a signal, but no; she was looking at the back of it, at the case.

"Does this look pink to you?" she asked.

"Yes."

"Well it looks grey to me. So we're in."

At the end of the corridor was a plain metal door. By my reckoning it was positioned in line with the shop fronts that included the accessories shop itself, so I wondered if it would open back onto East Street, or into another room or corridor. I wasn't sure how the latter could work here. In every version of Chichester I had visited so far, East Street had been broad and clear, and usually pedestrianised. In no version had I seen a building jutting out of the shop fronts;

then again, I only had the sketchiest idea of how the Common Land related to the exterior buildings that contained it.

I pulled the door open, only to reveal another door sharing the frame in a sort of airlock arrangement, but without space for anyone to fit between the two doors. I reached to push the second door open, but hesitated. At some gut level I could see the logic of such an arrangement, but it contradicted everything I had seen before.

Betany noticed my hesitation, so I decisively opened the door and stepped through. I was neither in the street nor in an awkwardly-placed building.

I was in a portacabin.

Betany's slightly amused look of surprise reflected my own as she followed me in. Both doors swung closed behind us.

The place had a recently-vacated feel about it, as if the manager of a construction team had gone out for an early lunch and wasn't coming back any time soon. There was paperwork on a desk, which I tried to read but could not, a couple of hard hats and high visibility jackets, and some dirty coffee cups on a filing cabinet. A venetian blind covered a small window behind the desk. Betany parted two slats and looked out. I joined her, and saw a different version of East Street. A jewellers occupied the space that had been the accessories shop, and the snow was, if anything, even deeper than in Betany's world.

Opposite the window, halfway along the long wall, was a door, locked from the outside. I could probably have picked it but saw no reason to do so. At the end of the portacabin was another metal door. Again, it proved to be the first of two doors sharing one frame. We went through this doorway into a second portacabin, similar to the first. I looked through the blind in this one too, mainly to reassure myself that it was in a different world to the first portacabin. There was no snow on the ground. In fact it had rained quite heavily, leaving puddles almost deep enough to count as flooding. That confirmed what I suspected; the two portacabins connected end to end, but each one was located in its own version of East Street.

The side door to this one was locked as well. Nevertheless I was getting a sense of how things fitted together. Unlike the fire door in Betany's old school and the garage door in Stanley Lane, passersby in this partially flooded Chichester would notice the portacabin extending halfway across East Street, much as they would have seen the red houses I had once represented with my father's beermats. If they noticed that no work was going on inside the portacabin or nearby, they would no doubt shake their heads and make some disparaging comments about workmen or councils, then move on. I did wonder what they'd see at the portacabin's end. A blank wall, I supposed, or else a door that would not open. The side door was another matter; a traveller like myself would recognise it as a means of access into or out of the Common Land.

Maybe I would pick the side door's lock later, to confirm my surmises. But that could wait.

There were no more of the double doors once we had entered the buildings in the south side of East Street. We followed stretches of wood-panelled corridors, similar to the one behind the accessories shop. They had sloping ceilings for the most part, giving the impression we were walking along the eaves of a very long bungalow. These alternated with stone corridors with cobbled floors and vaulted ceilings, and occasional flights of stone steps leading down into underground tunnels, and back up to the surface again. By my reckoning we had passed Betany's flat, gone under South Street, and were heading more or less in the direction of her old school in Chichester Gate. That was her reckoning too, and I was impressed by her sense of direction, given how new to this she was. Sometimes I needed to use my torch to find our way, other times there were skylights, or electric lights in the walls or ceiling. From time to time we passed doors. I tried a few. Most were locked but three or four opened onto darkness. I marked them off in my pad for future investigation, should that prove necessary.

We eventually came to a narrow passageway ending at an arched gateway with vertical bars. It swung open onto a square courtyard with very high walls, overlooked by barred windows in the second or third story. Wall-mounted plant pots displayed dead vegetation.

Directly overhead was late afternoon sky. In the middle of the square was a sundial that never saw direct sunlight.

There were similar gates in the left and right walls, but it was the heavy oak door in the wall opposite our entrance that caught Betany's attention. It had been painted blue a long time ago but the paint had largely faded or peeled. A child had drawn on it in chalk: a house with a fenced garden, a path from the front door to the gate, flowers, smoke spiralling out of the chimney. As we crossed the square of the courtyard and saw the drawing close up, Betany gasped out, "Eloise has been this way!"

"How do you know?"

"I just know. It's her style."

I tried the handle. The door was locked. "Lots of children do drawings like this," I said.

"There's no people in it. She never draws people." She pointed at the almost set sun, and the crescent moon hanging over the roof, its illuminated edge towards the sun. "It's astronomically accurate too."

"I take it we're working on the basis that Eloise can't pick locks?"

"Of course she can't, she's nine years old. But somebody might have locked the door *after* she went through."

"It's possible," I conceded doubtfully. "But it would be time consuming to unlock every door we come across." I thought about the unlocked side doors we had already passed. For all we knew Eloise could have gone through any one of them.

"It's definitely her drawing. Any other child would have included their family in the front garden."

I sucked in air. It seemed too tenuous; I might even have said that aloud. I thought of how Kirsty and Chloe had left their initials, and an unambiguous arrow, in the labyrinth. "She might have passed through this courtyard, but that doesn't mean she went through this door."

Betany nodded without meeting my eyes. "Whatever."

“Betany, I’m talking about priorities here. It would make more sense to try the straightforward routes first. We can always investigate the side routes later.”

“All *right*! I *get* it!”

But I tried it anyway. I pushed at the door in several places. It did not give in the slightest; it might have been fixed to a wall. I knelt, and looked at the keyhole. It was quickly obvious that even the proper key would not have got this door open.

I stood up and mimed drawing the picture to try and get a sense of Eloise’s thinking, and an idea as to which way she would have walked upon completing it. Nonsensical thinking, of course, but instinct told me it was to the right, and a wrong decision was better than no decision. It occurred to me that the picture was at chest height for me, and I wondered if she had stood on a chair or something to draw it.

We took the right hand gateway out of the courtyard.

There followed another long series of wood-panelled corridors and stone passageways. By the reckoning of both of us, we crossed the railway at some point; I half expected to see tracks in the cobbled floor, or spaces in the floor where they had been. I recalled visiting a Chichester where there had been no railway, and wondered what kind of Dr Beeching that world had produced.

For an indoor journey we had walked some considerable distance. It occurred to me, not for the first time, that it must have been a long walk for a little girl; indeed, the thought had crossed my mind even before we’d seen the flimsy evidence of the chalk drawing. Betany must have thought it too, but had made no mention of it. Finding a secret passageway in the accessory shop was one thing; following it from the city’s centre to its outskirts was quite another. So what was it that motivated the child? Sheer curiosity? Fear of the wrath of her older sister? Had someone followed her in, and she had fled from him? Unlikely, if she had stopped to draw a picture. Had something called to her? Not impossible. I had already encountered a minotaur in the Common Land, so some form of siren didn’t seem especially unlikely.

The corridors were quiet for the most part, the only sound being the echoes of our footsteps. At length we came to a corridor that ended at a blank wall, with two doors on either side. The door on the right was unlocked, but it did not open far; there was some sort of obstacle on the other side, and barely enough of a gap between the door edge and the frame to fit my arm through to find out what it was. Not that I had any desire to do something as risky as that.

"Could Eloise have squeezed through that?" I asked.

Betany shook her head and tried the other door. This one opened easily, and towards us. On the other side it was the ubiquitous wood panelling. It had hooks in it from which hung kitchen utensils - a fish slice, serving spoons, two slightly rusty frying pans and so on. We walked into the back of a walk-in pantry. I swept my torch over the shelves. They were empty except for a few abandoned items: a torn sieve, a tin of past-their-sell-by-date prunes, a burst bag of pasta shells and parts of a dismantled food mixer.

Emerging from the pantry, we found ourselves in the kitchen of an empty house. There was no furniture, and the windows and back door were boarded up. The hall was uncarpeted, as were the rooms leading off. Our footsteps on the creaking floorboards echoed in the empty space. The front door was also boarded up.

There was a staircase in the hall, and a cupboard under the stairs. The back of the cupboard should have been the wall the house shared with the adjoining house next door; instead, an opening gave us access to a similar understairs cupboard in the next house. This next house was more or less a mirror image of the first, also unfurnished and uncarpeted, and boarded up – and it too had a walk-in pantry with a hidden door at the back.

The character and layout of the third house was different. The hidden door took us through a broom cupboard into a utility room; we had to step over bottles of cleaning fluid. Darkness was falling; the low crescent moon and a streetlamp shone through an unboarded window. Across the road we could see a row of bungalows with neat front lawns and lamplight at some of the windows. A man in a fur coat and hat was walking his dog. He glanced over at us. Maybe he saw us; maybe he registered surprise seeing that the house was occupied. Or maybe I was reading too much into his expression.

There were carpets in the other rooms, and furniture. The central heating had been switched off, but I reckoned this had been recent.

"Let's hope the owners don't get back from holiday while we're here," Betany said.

"They won't," I assured her.

"Why not?"

"It doesn't happen. It's something to do with the way time works in here. It's as if it's in suspension."

"Suspension?" Betany laughed. "It's going like the clappers!" She gestured at the window. "Look at that! It must be that differential you told me about. It should be early afternoon but the day's nearly over already."

"The *year* is nearly over."

"That's weird. I can see that the streetlights are yellow. Everything outside is in colour. Everything indoors is in black and white."

She indicated a picture on the wall. It was a lonely train station by a railway whose vanishing point was the setting sun, with orange clouds above the horizon. I confirmed that it was not a black and white print.

There was no hall in this house; the stairs were in the lounge, which was separated from the kitchen by the dining room. The cupboard under the stairs here had a partition wall, but a vertical line of dim light indicated a narrow gap in the panelling. I pressed one eye to it. I was looking through the back of the understairs cupboard of the adjoining house, through the partly open cupboard door into a lounge. I could see a fireplace with Christmas cards and tinsel on the mantelpiece, and an old television. An old man carrying a tray crossed my field of view, then continued out of sight. I could hear a brief, muted conversation between him and (presumably) his wife. There was a short silence. Suddenly the cupboard door opened wider and the man thrust his face at mine. I jerked back; I almost cried out. But he was not aware that I was inches away from him; he was merely getting a vacuum cleaner from out of the cupboard. Moments later he was gone.

I told Betany what I had seen.

"It's a voyeur's paradise, isn't it?" she observed. "It makes you wonder who's been watching *us*."

She pressed her eye to the gap but there was nothing to be seen now; the old man had closed the cupboard door. We could hear the sound of the vacuum cleaner.

I checked the floorboards of the cupboard. As I expected, they formed a trapdoor. Most of the items in the cupboard had been put to one side, leaving the trapdoor clear, which made me wonder if it had been used recently. Remembering my last experience with a trapdoor, I got my gun out before lifting it open. A flight of stone steps descended into darkness. I shone my torch, wiggling the beam around. Nothing stirred, nothing responded to the light. Even so, I felt uneasy. I closed the trapdoor, regretting the fact that there was no way of fastening it shut, and led the way out of the cupboard and back into the house.

By some unspoken agreement we decided to stop in the house for a while. We had not eaten since the previous evening, so we returned to the kitchen. I shut the door so that cooking smells would not spread throughout the house, and Betany filled the electric kettle from the tap. While the water boiled we rummaged through the cupboards and the freezer. We found a tin of beans, a tin of pilchards, some packet soups, tea that smelled like Earl Grey, some biscuits, a frozen loaf of sliced bread, and several frozen containers of food with labels we could not read.

Betany fished in a kitchen drawer, then brandished a menu from a local Indian restaurant. "Let's just phone for a takeaway," she said. We laughed heartily at this, then proceeded to make the most of what we had.

We had supper at the kitchen table. I boiled the kettle again for washing-up water. I was concerned about the rubbish, particularly the pilchard tin, which would get smelly quite quickly, and I was tempted to take it out. There was a key to the locked back door hanging on a hook beside the door to the broom cupboard, but I was uneasy about leaving the Common Land without a good reason. We'd already been seen by a dog walker; there was no sense risking an encounter with a neighbour. And the fact that the key was still hanging on the hook suggested Kirsty and Eloise had not gone out this way.

Betany, meanwhile, was clearly excited by what we were doing. Intruding in someone's house was one thing; to do something as *mundane* as make a meal was paradoxically thrilling.

She swallowed her last forkful of pilchard on toast and said,

"When all this is over, let's come here again."

"I'd like that."

"We can make a weekend of it. Dad can look after Eloise and Kirsty."

"I don't know about that. I don't think I made a very good first impression. Or second impression."

"Oh, he'll take to you all right. It's the ones he *doesn't* punch in the face who have to worry!"

We both laughed again. I took her plate to wash it. Somewhere in the distance, a church bell began to ring out the hour.

"There's a whole world out there," Betany said in a low voice, almost an awed whisper. "It might be yours, or mine, or the Mirror Place, or another world entirely. We'll never know."

"It's best we keep to the through doors for now," I said. "I'd rather play it safe until I've got a better understanding of how it all works. I'm still very new to it myself."

"So you keep saying." The church bell pealed a ninth time and then stopped. "How confident are you?"

"What do you mean?"

"It's just it's... so *big*. Like playing hide-and-seek on different planets. Speaking of which..." She indicated the moon, in crescent phase. "I don't think this is my world. That shouldn't be there. It's wrong by about four days."

"What do you mean?" I said again.

"It should be new."

"It *is* new."

"No, I mean only the far side should be illuminated right now."

"You're into astronomy, are you?"

She shook her head. "Not me. Eloise. Having the moon in the wrong phase is just so... I mean, it would hardly seem more strange if there was a miniature Saturn up there."

"I know Kirsty is alive. I believed it before but now I know for sure."

"Do you trust your wife?"

"Ex-wife. Yes, I do, I really do. She can be evasive, downright dishonest even, but she was never one for direct falsehoods."

"What about my girl? What about Eloise?"

"We saw her drawing, remember."

"I didn't think you..."

"My instinct is to trust your instinct, Betany."

"Even assuming it was hers, it only tells us she *was* there. We don't even know she came this way. She might have been heading in the other direction."

"One way or another we'll see an end to this tonight," I promised. "Before the new year. Even if it means doubling back and taking the left gate from the courtyard."

"I wish I could share your op–" She broke off. We were both startled by a noise from upstairs, the sudden sound of metal sliding on metal.

In a whisper Betany said, "Something's in the house! Something's on the... I think the owners really have come back!"

"Did you check the bedrooms?" I whispered in turn. Betany shook her head. "Neither did I. They could have been fast asleep all this time."

"You said..."

"I know - I also said I was new to this."

At that moment I recognised what the metal-on-metal sound was. "It's a loft ladder!" It rattled and creaked under the weight of whoever was climbing it. I whispered, "We should get away while they're up there." But Betany was listening keenly, frowning in puzzlement. Then she said, "That's not someone going up – they're coming down! They're coming into the house through the loft itself!"

Something knew we were here. Stupidly I had put my gun down on a working top. I gestured Betany to move away from the kitchen door as I went to retrieve it. There were rapid footsteps on the stairs, across the lounge and dining room. And then the kitchen door flew open.

For once, time in the Common Land really did seem suspended. A woman of about sixty was standing in the doorway. She was small and grey-haired, but looked remarkably fit. She held a walking stick which she almost certainly did not need; I wondered if it was a sword-stick. She wore what appeared to be mountaineering clothes, keeping her warm without encumbering her movement.

"What the *hell* d'you think you're doing?" she demanded.

Her dialect was broad but unrecognisable. She glared at Betany, then turned the glare back on me.

"A follower. Of all the idiotic... Do you have the slightest *idea* of the kind of danger you've put us all in?"

Without thinking, I said, "I wasn't exactly briefed." Whatever I had expected, whatever I had feared, it was not to be admonished the way I admonished my more commonsense-challenged pupils.

I thought I saw a flicker of sympathy in her eyes. "Mentored by Tobias Quinn, huh?" she asked. I nodded. The sympathy lingered for a long moment, then evaporated. She called over her shoulder, "Gareth, man's got a follower."

A slightly older man appeared in the doorway behind her. In looks and dress he resembled the woman – he was probably her brother or cousin. He too carried a stick. "You okay Hannah?"

"Well that depends how long he's been here, doesn't it?"

"Excuse me," I cut in, not a little annoyed at the way they talked of Betany as if she wasn't there, "Do you think you could tell me what we're supposed to have done wrong?"

"You brought a follower in here," Gareth told me angrily.

"A follower?"

"One of Quinn's," Hannah explained over her shoulder to her companion. He acknowledged this with a nod. "One who sleep-dreams," she told me. When I continued to look blank, she added, with heavy patience, "No special relationship with the Common Land. You think there aren't serious repercussions if you bring someone in who can't find their own way in? You learn the rules here or you stay out!"

Gareth had gone into the utility room. He opened the broom cupboard, took one look, and slammed it shut. His anger tinged with panic, he told Hannah, "We need to get out of here. Now!" To me he barked, "Find an exit. Not this one, obviously. Don't follow us, and don't waste time!"

They fled from the kitchen, back upstairs and into the loft again. They did not pause to pull the ladder up after them.

It was clear from the pair's behaviour that we were in serious danger, but without any idea of what the danger was, it was hard to know how to react. I recalled a fire drill at Guildford Borough Council, how colleagues packed their bags, finished their coffee and so on while the alarm wailed. I'd retrieved my gun; I grabbed my coat and backpack while Betany grabbed her things, then I wasted precious seconds just wondering what the hell I was supposed to do next. Gareth had told me to find an exit. A way out of the Common Land.

The back door was an access door, but it was locked. The key was still in the place I had first seen it, on a hook next to the broom cupboard. I made to grab it, then saw that the wall was *wrong*. It had changed; now it was sweating, and it was flat. Not flat the way a wall should be, but flat like a photograph. The cupboard door, the frame, even the hook with the key on it, had been rendered 2D. The back door itself now looked painted on, and beyond the window was only darkness.

"Front door!" I yelled. Betany was ahead of me. But when we got to it it was locked in the conventional sense. It was not one of the old Yale locks you can open from inside, and there was no key to be found. There was nothing else for it: We were going to have to use the trapdoor in the cupboard under the stairs.

I took the lead, running down the steps into darkness, fumbling for my torch. Even if there weren't unspeakable horrors down here, there was the danger of running into mundane obstacles. But I'd heard strange, unpleasant sounds from the utility room, and had no intention of waiting around to discover what was causing the sounds.

I managed to get the torch on. We were in a cellar filled with junk, including an old workbench and a stack of shelves filled with tins of paint. There were archways in two facing walls. We took the archway in the east wall, the one that led in the general direction away from the broom cupboard.

Through the archway was another cellar, this one fitted with a dim bulb that came on in response to our presence. An archway in the far wall suggested we were in a corridor of cellars.

Through the next archway we found ourselves in an actual wine cellar, with dust-covered bottles stacked on shelves from floor to ceiling. I risked running up the steps to the trapdoor in the ceiling, but either it was locked or there was a heavy weight on top of it. Betany had stopped to look back through the archway we had just come through. Horror suffused her voice when she said, "Get down here, Philip! We need to get out!"

I complied, aware that she had now seen one feature of the Common Land that I had not. We ran without stopping through five or six more archways, into a succession of similar cellars.

The corridor of cellars ended in a room that was as wide as the previous cellars and about three times as long, and illuminated by yellow overhead lights. Immediately to our right, in the south wall, was a pair of lift doors. Betany's face lit up at the sight of them. "I'd forgotten all about the lift!" she said. She pressed the call button, but nothing appeared to happen. In the opposite wall at about chest height was an inspection hatch, roughly a metre square.

While we waited for the lift to arrive we observed the rest of the room. This was a dead end: walls without windows or any other features, except for two steps near the far end of the left hand wall.

"Those are the steps I came down all those years ago," Betany said. "It's been blocked."

There was a hint of panic in her voice. I saw now that apart from the bottom two steps the stairway had been filled with constructor material that was flush with the wall, with a gap of a few inches near the ceiling. The trapped slitherman we had seen earlier was in the gap; we caught its stench as it thrust one arm and its hideous head out, thrashing painfully in its eagerness to get at us but it could not get free.

I jabbed at the lift button again. Still nothing happened. Commanding Betany to follow, I ran back into the cellars we had just come out of. I directed her to run up the stairs to see if she could get the trapdoor open while I tried the one in the next cellar. I fumbled for a lock, pushed up with all my strength, but there was no movement at all. At the same time I heard Betany calling, "No luck!" I ran down the steps into the next cellar, and was just about to mount the steps there when I sensed a change in the background noise that I had not registered before. It was a low sound like an organ note, an oddly mournful tone. And that's when the walls here began to sweat. The steps were a ramp, the treads and risers a mere trompe l'oeil. I backed out the way I had come, unable to pull my eyes away from the sight. The walls were curving, the way the insides of your mouth would curve when blowing up a balloon. Bumps appeared on the walls' surfaces, reminiscent of the nipples on a dog.

There was a time when Miss Havers had insisted she was going to take me to a nightclub, and I had eventually given in. While waiting to be served at the bar, two young mothers got into a lactation fight, much to the amusement of most of the nearby lads, but it was one of the few occasions I had seen Miss Havers embarrassed by other people's behaviour. I recalled this now as a milk-like substance squirted out of all the wall-nipples simultaneously, luckily not in the direction of the archway. The milk, I realised, was not liquid, but some form of crystal thread. I hit one strand with my torch. It shattered like a glass rod. If I had remained in the room I would have been impaled.

"Use the inspection hatch!" I called.

I was fairly certain it connected with the labyrinth somewhere. If we could reach that, we could probably outrun the crystal threads - I knew the way, and this time I had no qualms about shooting any slitherman cables we might encounter. We would come out into the McDonalds in my world.

The wall in this cellar was beginning to go sweaty. I ran until I reached the long room. When I arrived, Betany had just managed to get the inspection hatch open - it had a hinge at the top - and was climbing into the passageway beyond. There was barely space to crawl, let alone run. There was no possibility of outracing the glass threads.

I glanced back at the cellars, and then at Betany's disappearing legs. It suddenly occurred to me that I didn't have to outrun the glass threads.

*

One time I showed my class a slideshow of the Bayeux Tapestry. I told them this was the closest we could get to using a time machine to go back and watch the Battle of Hastings.

A pupil called Mitchell said, "If I was there I'd nudge the archer who shot Harold in the eye."

There was a ripple of laughter from the class. I smiled. When the laughter died down I said, "It wouldn't help. Either you'd nudge the wrong archer. Or - and think about this - your nudge would correct his aim."

A short silence followed. Most of them were familiar enough with time travel paradoxes from the likes of *Star Trek*, but it was a novelty to have it applied in an actual history class.

Another pupil said, "But surely if you can go back once, you can keep going back, and keep trying."

This was a class I also took for maths, and I had recently delivered a lesson on vectors. I drew a slanting line on the board and added an arrowhead.

"History," I said, "is like a vector." There was a collective groan, but I persevered. "The history we get in history books is the final, resultant vector, but that's made up of a sum of smaller vectors - wind speed, the archer's aim, what he had for breakfast that day, and so on." I drew a series of nine or ten smaller vectors, attached head to tail, going off in random directions but beginning at the tail of the big vector and ending at its head. "The more we look into history, the more we learn about these contributing vectors, but we can never know them in enough detail to change history, not even if we had a time machine." I pointed at one of the smaller vectors. "Say this vector is the archer shooting Harold. You nudging him is a smaller contributing vector coming off here -" I drew a line from the tail of this vector "- but his own aiming is *this* vector -" I joined the new vector to the head of the archer's vector.

I explained that this was Novikov's model of time travel, hoping my interpretation of it was correct. Later, I thought about the things that can never be undone, even the things without consequence, such as praying for Kirsty's death when she was a baby. Even if Novikov was wrong and I could have gone back to stop myself, there was still the fact that I had done it to serve as the motive for me needing to stop myself in the first place.

Whatever good I might do in the future, nothing was going to undo what I had planned for Betany.

Gareth had told the two of us not to follow them. But it didn't matter what I did. I wasn't the intruder, Betany was.

The glass threads were filling each cellar, but I didn't think they would reach the far end of this room. I had merely to stand there while they overtook Betany as she crawled along the passageway.

The beauty of it was, I wouldn't even be sacrificing her for my own sake. There was no way we could outcrawl the threads in that passageway, whatever we did. It would be a simple case of one person dying instead of two.

And that is how I would have left matters were it not for the fact that an incongruous *ding* sound announced the arrival of the lift.

I pulled open the inspection hatch, yelled at Betany to back up, then let it fall back as I ran to the lift. In that short time its doors had opened, paused, and begun to close again. I dived forward, and at the last possible moment thrust my left hand between the doors. Unlike the doors of a normal lift, there seemed to be no safety feature; I screamed in pain as they crushed my hand. Then they relented and opened again.

Betany had managed to reverse out of the passage. I urged her to run. She turned and ran. The last of the cellars was filling up with glass threads. I caught Betany before she hit the back wall of the lift, and slammed my injured hand against the button for the ground floor. There was a long pause before the doors began to close again, as slowly as they had been rapid when I needed time. The interval was long enough for me to see a sheen of sweat appear on the part of the wall occupied by the inspection hatch; I wondered if it had failed to catch up with the fact that Betany had doubled back. Maybe her climbing into the passage had bought us precious seconds.

Betany recovered her breath. "Are you okay?" she asked, concerned.

I checked my fingers. "No bones broken. Actually... well I don't think they are. What about you?"

She nodded. “I’m fine.”

The lift doors were finally closed and the cage began its upward journey. It moved with glacial slowness.

“Does this take us straight out into the real world?” My voice was harsh from the pain in my hand.

“I think so. I don’t remember a lobby or anything.”

Eventually the lift *dinged* again. The doors opened with painful slowness, and then seized up. The walls of the lift went sweaty - but by that time we had squeezed out through the gap. There was the sound of stressed metal as the walls warped inside the lift shaft, but neither of us looked back.

We were outside. We had escaped. We were safe.

Chapter 23. In A Cold Place

We were in an alleyway in the Mirror Place. The air was bitingly cold and a thin, patchy layer of snow lay on the ground. Betany was almost deliriously happy. Any concerns she might have about getting home were temporarily on hold. For now, it was enough that we were alive.

She slipped her arm through mine. "This way," she said, leading me to the end of the alleyway. "We should find a large square with a fountain in the middle."

We did. The square was surrounded on all four sides by buildings with reflective glass fronts, with a tower block at each corner. Some of the buildings were shops, and some of them were still open, despite the fact that it was after ten o'clock on New Year's Eve. The fountain in the centre of the square was frozen. The place was unlike any Chichester I had known.

I nodded vaguely at the reflective glass of a nearby building. "Is that why you gave it the name?"

She nodded. "The Mirror Place." She was silent for a long time, and I saw there were tears in her eyes. "I'm really, really here!" She hugged me tight, kissed me with uninhibited affection. "Thank you for everything, Philip. It was *never* just a dream, I know that now. Ten years of wondering and now I *know*!" She kissed me again and again. "It really happened. Garcia Hollis really exists - what's he going to say when he hears he has a daughter?"

I confess to feeling a pang of jealousy at the mention of her former lover.

Eager to show me around her secret world, she led me across the square. It was pedestrianised, except for a tram line which passed close by the fountain. The tram itself shortly appeared, stopping nearby and disgorging people in apparently real fur coats and hats.

"The trams looked futuristic when I was here before," she said casually. "Now they've gone for a retro look." We stopped at the fountain, a huge stone bowl with silver coins visible under the ice. "It's beautiful, isn't it!"

She took my arm again and we headed towards a pub called *The Hat Maker*. Live music drifted from its doorway whenever someone opened it to go in or come out.

"That's where I met Garcia," she told me.

"What, in the pub?"

She giggled. "No, of course not. I was only thirteen. He was just coming out."

"Wait a minute – how old was *he*?"

"In his twenties, I think. Thirty tops."

"I thought you said he was about your age."

Betany reddened. "I told you, I thought I was dreaming at the time. You said you weren't judging me, remember."

"It's not *you* I'm judging!" But she had let go of my arm.

We went down a side street near the pub. After checking that nobody was watching, she turned left into an alleyway. I followed her in silence. We were behind the shops, between a high blank wall and a chainlink fence. A little further on we came to a secluded spot behind some tall bins. It was an unprepossessing location; even in the freezing cold air, the smell of rubbish was strong, and there was a pile of dirty white rags on the ground.

"This is where it happened," Betany told me. "This is where Eloise was conceived."

It didn't seem to cross her mind that I didn't want to hear about it, how a man had taken advantage of a confused, sleep-deprived child. But it occurred to me that she needed to tell me. She was a victim of abuse, unable to tell anybody because she was not in a position to identify her abuser. So she was confiding in me, less than an hour after I had considered abandoning her to her fate in the Common Land.

So she told me the details. How he had initially seemed concerned for her, asking where her parents were and which school she went to. She hadn't invited him to kiss her, but she'd liked it, and because of that she later thought she had been to blame, even after learning she hadn't been dreaming.

I let her get it all out. By the end she was in tears, and we were hugging again. I was in tears too; this was no play-acting. The immediate question was, where do we go from here? I *liked* her, could imagine being in a relationship with her. For now she was restricted to the Mirror Place, but we could sort something out, and, assuming the Common Land would settle down now that she was out of it, I would be able to move freely between home, her home and here.

It could work. If it was what she wanted.

But something I had seen and pretended not to *really* notice was fighting its way into my awareness. Here in this place where Betany had lost her virginity to a pervert behind some bins, I had seen a pile of off-white rags. I remembered Kirsty in Whitby in her red jacket, and how it had been drained of its red colour.

"She's changed!" Dawn had told me on my voicemail.

Even as I hugged Betany, I could see how the pile of off-white rags might be covering a sleeping child. Suspicion turned to near certainty. Gently I ended the embrace. Betany watched, curiosity turning into horrified realisation as I crouched down and touched the material. I hadn't told Betany about Kirsty's jacket, but somehow she knew.

Eloise had also worn a red jacket when she first went missing.

The rigid body lay face down. As I made to turn it over, the sleeve shifted to reveal a frozen hand and a stolen bracelet on the wrist. Eloise's brown eyes were open. Her skin was solid to the touch.

"She's been dead for some hours," I said. "Maybe since..." I thought of the moment when Betany and I, in her bed, had touched, had begun to make love. "No, none of this makes sense. Children are more resilient than that, they don't *suddenly* die of cold."

I realised I was sounding like someone pointing out mistakes in a film. This was Betany's daughter I was talking about. I stopped, and turned around to meet her eyes.

That's when I finally lost it.

*

Frantic, I ran through the streets and alleys of the Mirror Place, calling out Kirsty's name. Outside the Common Land, my throat did not contract; I was *loud.* I ran into pubs, including *The Hat Maker*, interrupting New Year's Eve parties and demanding to know if anybody had seen my missing daughter. I thrust the doctored picture in people's faces, telling them she was ten but she'd been made up to look thirteen in the picture. At first the patrons and staff were sympathetic, but I ranted, sprayed spittle, and even mentioned the Common Land, and soon lost their good will. I was forcibly ejected from one pub, and politely asked to leave two others.

Back in the main square, I had calmed down through sheer exhaustion. I found myself outside a supermarket with an ungrammatical sign in the window that read, "Were open till midnight." The automatic door slid open as I approached it, and I stepped inside.

There were four very long aisles, three staff on duty, and no other customers at all. I approached a woman who had the bearing of a manager.

"Have you seen this girl?" I asked, showing her the photograph. "She's my daughter. She went missing two weeks ago."

The woman took a close look. "No," she said apologetically. "I... No, wait a minute, she does look familiar." She spoke into a device like a mobile phone which was clipped to her lapel. "Nigel, are you busy?"

Nigel proved to be in charge of security for the supermarket and half a dozen other shops. He was an affable forty-something with a thick beard and large belly. The manager showed me into his domain. He seemed perfectly content to spend his New Year's Eve in a windowless room filled with monitors and consoles.

After a short search he found what he was looking for. Security footage of a girl coming into the store. She was wearing a baseball cap the right way round, a dark jacket and jeans. She looked around, then began taking things off the shelf and putting them into her bag. The girl could have been Kirsty, but the resolution was blocky and she was too far away to be sure.

"When was this taken?" I asked.

"Last night. Just before we closed."

"The camera's following her. Is someone operating it?"

"Ah, that's the latest technology, you see!" Nigel beamed. "The camera is fitted with neural networks which recognise the body language of a would-be shoplifter."

"She's stealing *food*. Do they cut people's hands off for that?"

Nigel chuckled, oblivious to the venom in my voice. "The nets have made their diagnosis, so now they're dedicating bandwidth to the best-placed cameras. You see?"

The view changed. Apparently they had placed a camera somewhere below eye-level precisely because shoplifters tended to wear baseball caps. In place of the blur was a crystal-clear close-up of the visible part of Kirsty's face. My heart hammered in my chest.

"We can extrapolate the rest of the face," Nigel said, clicking on an icon. He looked at my reaction and said, "I think we can safely declare positive identification."

"It can't be her," I said. I was losing it again. "It's just not possible."

"She looks just like the girl in your photo."

"I know that! She looks *exactly* the same. But she can't *be* the same. Kirsty is only ten years old!"

She's changed.

There was no doubt about it. I was looking at a thirteen year old girl who happened to be my daughter Kirsty. As I watched, she became aware of the camera. She looked straight at me. There was no mistaking those fiercely intelligent eyes. She turned to run, then stopped and looked back at the camera a final time. Silently mouthing words, she pointed to her eyes with the index and second fingers of her right hand, then pointed them at her chest. She rotated her right index finger once around her right ear, and held up the finger as if to indicate the number one. Finally she touched her chest with both hands, followed by a gesture that was an unmistakable offering of her heart. After that she fled, a pair of security guards in pursuit.

"Did they catch her?" I asked. "Is she here?"

Nigel shook his head. "No, they couldn't find her. Seemed to think she disappeared into thin air."

*

The lift doors were wide open when I found the alley again. Inside, the walls of the cage had been restored. I considered going in search of Betany - maybe if we retraced our steps as fast as we could, stopping for nothing, I could get her back to her home world before the Common Land started reacting to her again. But even as I considered this the lift doors began to slide closed; as there was no call button in the alleyway, and there was no way of knowing when they might open again, I slipped in.

The lift went down, stopped, and the doors slid open. I strode out. The long room had been restored, but the slitherman had got free somehow. Without breaking stride I shot it in the chest, the throat and the face. I heard it crumple behind me as I entered the corridor of cellars.

I couldn't remember which steps led up to the house where Betany and I had shared a meal, but I found a door in the north wall of a cellar that I did not think had been there before. A series of corridors led me to a heavy wooden door that took some considerable pushing to get it moving. Once it was open I stepped through into the courtyard with the sunless sundial, letting it swing shut behind me. The door I had just come through was the old blue one with the chalked picture, the last picture Eloise ever drew.

*

I couldn't blame Quinn for my mistakes. The thing about unwritten and unspoken rules is that they are obvious; they don't *need* to be written or spoken. If I had listened to my instincts I would have known not to take Betany into the Common Land. I needn't have met her in the first place; I'd known Eloise had gone missing during a shopping trip, so all I needed to do was search the shops a nine year old girl is likely to want to go round. That way I might have found her a day earlier, and got her home alive. She might even have been able to tell me where Kirsty was.

Instead I had allowed myself to be distracted by a replica of my car, and all that had followed. Even though the chalked message had warned me it was all just coincidence.

I thought of my last view of the Mirror Place as the lift doors closed on the sound of church bells ringing in the new year, and the wail of an ambulance on its way to pick up a grieving mother and her dead child. I told myself I really had to raise my game; I had to do better next time, because Kirsty was depending on me.

Part 3. All Roads

"You don't just stumble upon London Prime."

Chapter 24. Domestics

Two weeks after my return from the Mirror Place, I invited Dawn Price to my home. I met her at the Portsmouth and Southsea train station after school on the Friday. She was carrying an overnight bag and wearing a headscarf. We hugged each other tightly but did not kiss. I put her bag in the boot of the Fiesta, and drove us the short distance back to my house in St Peters Court.

"How have you been?" she asked.

"I'm back at work," I told her. "It's not been easy but... well, everyone's been really supportive. Nearly everyone."

"That's good."

"What about you?"

"I'm okay," she said, a little too quickly to be convincing. She followed that with a long pause which I did not interrupt. Eventually she said, "That phone message. It was a mistake. I shouldn't have made it. And *you* shouldn't have gone to the police with it."

"I needed to know. What else was I supposed to do?"

"The police don't like getting involved in domestics. You know that."

"Oh come on! It's not like the police weren't *already* involved. Besides, it worked out for the best, didn't it?"

"That was more luck than judgement and you know it. If Bill hadn't got himself into trouble like that, things could have turned out unpleasant. They still might!"

"Then let's hope they don't."

"Please don't do anything like that again."

At the house I made us a pot of Earl Grey tea. While it was brewing I put Dawn's suitcase in the guest room, the room where Kirsty used to sleep when she came to stay. I poured the tea and carried it into the lounge on a tray.

Dawn wasn't ready to tell her story just yet. Not beyond the summary she'd given me in the car of what I already knew: "What's to tell? Kirsty turned up out of nowhere, three years older than she should be. She stayed a while and then she left. As I say, what's to tell?" I wanted to squeeze every last drop of meaning out of her encounter, but I had to be patient, and I had to accept the likelihood that there really wasn't much more to it.

So once we were settled I began my story. Over the course of the evening I told Dawn everything. When I got to the end I took out my copy of the security footage of teenage Kirsty stealing from the supermarket in the Mirror Place and put it in the DVD player.

I was moved, almost to tears, by Dawn's stoic acceptance of it all. Her nearest concession to scepticism was her statement, "It's almost too much to take in," which she repeated two or three times. When the camera zoomed in on Kirsty, Dawn asked, "What's she saying?"

"She's saying, 'Look for me in London Prime. I love you Daddy.'"

"You can read sign language?"

I shook my head. "Not me, Yasmin. My next door neighbour's daughter is deaf. She interpreted it for me."

"You *showed* her this?"

"No, of course not. I copied Kirsty's signing as best I could. Anyway, Yasmin's interpretation ties in with Kirsty's mouth movements."

Dawn watched the security footage over and over again, until I gently took the remote from her hands and suggested she go to bed. She obeyed, and I cleared away the barely-touched remains of her meal.

When she had gone up I did the things that needed to be done. I did housework. I marked homework. I prepared lesson plans and completed reams of admin - there was an upcoming Ofsted inspection. I updated my assessments of various pupils' progress.

Teachers who sleep have to do this also.

Afterwards I lay in my own bed, listening to the sound of Dawn breathing in the next room. She fidgeted throughout the night, asleep but unable to find a restful state. Occasionally she whimpered, reminding me of a dog dreaming. It seemed strange, having her under the same roof as me again after all that had happened. She was not my wife any more. Kirsty was not my daughter any more. Kirsty was not a *child* any more. And aside from that one occasion in Betany's flat, I did not sleep any more.

Dawn and I were in a temporary state of equilibrium. It felt oddly pleasant. Her brother William was out of the picture for the foreseeable future, serving time in Winchester Prison. William's sideline as a bouncer at a Bognor Regis nightclub had come to an abrupt end when he ejected a black youth with more force than was strictly necessary, breaking two of his ribs in the process. The incident had been caught on camera, and the language William used left no doubt that it was racially aggravated.

The police were keen to know why the Price family had failed to report the reappearance of Kirsty. They had, after all, expended considerable resources into finding her. The police might not like getting involved with domestics, but they had liaised with social services who had looked deeper into the family situation. Things did not look good for William. If Kirsty did turn up again on a permanent basis... but there were too many unknowns to follow this train of thought. Everything was in a state of flux now, including Kirsty's status. *Especially* Kirsty's status. Kirsty was ten. Kirsty was a teenager. Kirsty was missing. Kirsty was found, and gone again. Who do you believe? *What* do you believe? Most rational people reject contradictions, but what do you do when the facts *are* contradictory?

Matters would resolve themselves into a new normal. This much I was sure of, although it hadn't happened yet, and I didn't know when it would happen. In the meantime, I had no choice but to accept everything without question. Or, to put it more accurately, accept things without expecting an immediate answer to my questions.

As these thoughts played out in my mind I heard Dawn get up in the night. Unfamiliar with the layout of the house, she stumbled against a bookcase as she tiptoed across the landing to the bathroom. She swore in a whisper, and closed the bathroom door carefully so that the latch would not click. I was amused at the thought that she was trying not to awaken me. Evidently she had forgotten, or did not quite believe me, when I told her I did not sleep.

But I still dreamed. I still dreamed the insomnia dreams.

*

I am lying on my side on a park bench with my eyes closed. It is a cold day, but the sun is shining and I am wrapped up in warm clothes. There is the tinkling sound of a fountain nearby. I am not sure if I am awakening from some kind of sleep, or experiencing an insomnia dream within an insomnia dream. Behind me an elderly American female voice is saying, "They never did find the body."

I am suddenly wide awake within the dream. *What body?* I open my eyes but I can see nothing in the glare of the sun. *Whose body?* Who is she talking about? Eloise? Surely not. They found *her* body within a day of her death.

The elderly American woman's husband is evidently hard of hearing because she is repeating herself for his benefit. "I said, they never found his body."

His body. Definitely not Eloise, then. And not Kirsty either, although I had not thought of Kirsty. So who *is* she talking about?

Sunlight is reflecting off a white building in a white glare. My eyes are very gradually adapting to the light. The building has tall arched windows, six in all. There is a tower. It must be a church, then.

The husband has spoken but his words are hard to make out. Meanwhile, the wife's voice continues to dominate. She seems to be paraphrasing from a guide book. "They carbon dated the cat. They say it's too recent to be the one in the story. Don't you think that's a shame?"

I am being incredibly obtuse. What the *hell* are they talking about?

Church bells are ringing. There is a distinctive rhythm to the peal, a double sequence: *Ding-dang-dong ding-ding-dang-dong* repeated over and over. They sound like syllables; I try to find the words that fit them before I emerge into a state of true wakefulness, but they elude me.

*

In the morning, our last vestiges of hostility were forgotten. Dawn and I sat at the breakfast table in our dressing gowns. I toasted crumpets for us and poured us hot cups of Earl Grey tea from a pot. Dawn devoured the crumpets faster than I could deliver them, and I remembered how little she had eaten last night.

"I don't pretend to understand everything that's going on," she said. "But as long as we're working on this together..."

I assured her we were. I reminded her that she had seen our daughter in the flesh at the end of last year, whereas I had merely seen her on some security footage from a parallel world.

Dawn looked uncomfortable. "She turned up as if she'd never been away," she told me. "She was at least three years older than she should have been. Three years! She stayed a short time, then she said she had to leave. She said she had to find London Prime."

"Whereabouts did she actually appear? Was it in Chichester?"

She shook her head. "At home. She knocked at the door. Of the main house. I didn't hear her straight away, I was on the phone. When I answered... I didn't know who she was. I did, but I didn't, if you know what I mean."

"I know what you mean. Did she say *why* she has to find London Prime?"

"She just said she needed to find answers. I asked her what answers. She told me I wouldn't understand. Just like a teenager, Phil. *Just like a teenager.*"

"Did she say how she would get to London Prime? How long she would stay? Anything at all?"

Dawn just shook her head.

"What about when she left? Where did she go?"

"She said she needed to go outside, get some fresh air, some time to think. I let her go, thinking she'd calm down."

"You had words?"

She nodded. "I couldn't help it, Phil. I'd been worried sick for all that time, then she just turned up as if nothing had happened. She may be a teenager now, but she's still got the emotional maturity of a child. I didn't think she'd just leave, though." She frowned, and as if the thought had just occurred to her, added, "I don't know *how* she left. It's not like there was a car waiting for her or anything."

"There used to be a train station in Singleton, when there was a direct line to Chichester," I mused. "I wonder..."

"I gave it five minutes, then went out to look for her. There was no sign of her, but the security light was on. I went to check the barn conversion, even though she wouldn't have had a key. I changed the lock back when... you know."

I nodded once.

"There were wet footprints on the carpet in the guest room. Leading out."

"The new lock," I said. "Can you open it from the inside and leave it on the latch?"

"Yes."

I thought of the darkness I had sensed, or imagined I had sensed, on the evening when Kirsty disappeared. Had she come from out of that darkness?

Another batch of crumpets popped out of the toaster. I passed two to Dawn, and the butter. We talked some more, but it quickly became obvious that she had little in the way of substantial information. I wondered if Kirsty had hoped to find me at the Price Estate, although this had more to do with wishful thinking than likelihood.

Two things I did glean from Dawn's account, although I wasn't certain about either. One was that Kirsty had been in a hurry, whether to get somewhere or whether to get away from something I couldn't say. The other was that she hadn't simply been aged; from her point of view, she'd lived those three years. This, despite Dawn's assertion that she hadn't developed emotionally. Surviving three years in the Common Land tended to dictate one's priorities.

"Will you go after her?" Dawn asked me.

"I don't have a lot to go on. I don't know where London Prime is – I don't even know *what* it is."

"But will you try?"

"Of course I'll try."

Suddenly she was begging. "Bring my daughter back," she pleaded. "Whatever it takes. Bring her back."

I flinched. If only she'd said *our* daughter. Our eyes met and I could see that she knew what I was thinking. She could have corrected herself there and then, and everything would have been all right. But she did not.

After breakfast I drove her back to the station. When the train arrived we hugged each other tightly again. When we ended the hug she took both my hands, and I noticed for the first time that she was still wearing her wedding ring. For a reason I am unable to explain I kissed her on both her eyes.

"Promise me you'll call as soon as you hear anything," she said.

"I promise," I said, and I meant it. I resolved not to let her earlier slip of the tongue drive a wedge between us. It had taken us a long time to join forces, but now that it had happened I was determined to keep it that way. We were in this together at last.

But three months passed before we spoke again.

*

A week before the end of the Spring term, Dawn came to stay with me a second time. It was a Friday. I picked her up at Portsmouth and Southsea as before. She wore the headscarf she had worn on her previous visit, and a pair of dark glasses, although it was a fairly dull day in April. She looked like an ageing film star, I thought, or a victim of domestic violence. When we hugged it occurred to me that she was wearing them so that I would not kiss her on the eyes again.

"How's work?" she asked me in the car.

I shrugged. "Not good at all. They've been carrying me all term. Everyone has been really understanding, but... It only stretches so far."

"You've not been easy to get hold of."

"I know."

"You never answer your phone. I even tried to phone you at the school. Just in case you were... *delayed* in the Common Land. I spoke to the secretary, Ms Marshall. She said you were teaching, but she told me she'd get you to ring me back. You *did* say you'd let me know if anything happened."

"I know," I repeated. "I'm really sorry about that. I was going to call you, but..."

"But what? It was never the right time?"

"No, Dawn, it never was the right time."

"All right," she said coldly. After a short silence she said, "Did you know Bill's out of prison?"

I was taken aback by this news. "What? Already? It's only been..."

"Three months. It's been three months, Phil."

"When was he released?"

"Two days ago. I *did* try to call you to let you know. But as I say, you never answer your phone."

"You could have left a message on my answerphone."

"I don't like talking to those things. You know that. Besides..." She let the line trail off, knowing I'd fill in the rest myself. *Besides, remember what happened last time I left you a voicemail message?*

"Does he know you're here with me?"

"He's on parole, Phil. He's not going to do anything stupid."

I was liking the situation less and less. I seriously considered telling her this wasn't working out and turning the car around. But I had promised, and I had let her down. If she was going to begin all of our meetings with bitter reproaches, I could hardly blame her.

When I stopped the car outside my house I turned off the engine and released my seat belt but remained seated. "Let me explain it to you," I said.

"For the first two weeks after we last spoke, I had nothing to tell you. Then things got hectic. Teaching during the week, an Ofsted inspection, and searching the Common Land at weekends... It got out of hand. On occasion I *did* get delayed. I was nearly killed. And even then I came back with nothing to report. When at last I *did* have something to tell you, I didn't know *how* to tell you."

In a voice barely above a whisper, Dawn asked, "Did you get to London Prime? Did you *see* her? Did you *speak* to her?"

"I found London Prime. Kirsty was there, waiting for me." I swallowed and looked away. "She won't be coming home."

Dawn's eyes widened. "Why..."

"It's a graveyard."

I got out of the car and went into the house. Dawn followed me in.

Chapter 25. Laura Theresa

That first time, after I'd dropped Dawn off at the station, I drove back home then went out for a walk wearing my backpack.

On Castle Street there is a half-timbered shop with a magnificent clock tower. Across from it is - or rather was - a second hand bookshop. Inside the shop a doorway may be found between the philosophy and spirituality bookcase and the one for poetry and plays. The door looks like it opens onto a cupboard. Nobody notices it, not even the proprietor.

By now I was quite familiar with the challenges of doorways located in enclosed public places such as shops and restaurants. The biggest challenge by far was closing times. Entering the Common Land, and emerging from it unseen, was actually not that difficult; the same tendency of people to overlook the doorways also applied here too. Bumping into someone you hadn't noticed is commonplace enough even in the mundane world. Nevertheless, I would not be tempted into complacency.

The proprietor of this shop was inclined to sit behind a desk in a corner out of view of the philosophy and poetry section, or else he would be out the back sorting stock. But he was alert and observant, and worst of all, the door to the shop had an old fashioned bell which rang whenever someone came in or went out. If I was the only customer in the shop (as was sometimes the case) and he noticed me gone without the bell having rung, he was likely to be curious, if not outright suspicious.

Nevertheless I still preferred the bookshop entrance to the garage in Stanley Lane.

There were several other customers that Saturday. I didn't think any of them were looking in my direction, but just for my own peace of mind I adopted my practised body language of "meant to be doing this" as I opened the door between the bookcases.

This took me to a long corridor with half a dozen doors on one side, including the one I came in, and lockers on the other. There were locked double doors at either end of the corridor. I wondered if this place had once been connected to a gym or a swimming pool. Some of the lockers were open and empty and had a numbered key in the lock. Most were locked.

I retrieved my gun with its shoulder holster from locker number 7. I put it in my backpack and went out through another of the doors. I strode through a Betamax video rental store and out onto Castle Street. The shop opposite had no clock tower; it had been destroyed during the war. For this or other reasons, my world was the only world accessible from the locker corridor that had a clock tower. It made it a useful landmark when I wanted to be sure I was home.

In this world I walked to Portsmouth and Southsea Station, taking a somewhat different route to the one I had taken in my car in my own world. I noted differences both small and significant along the way. I passed this world's version of my house, and wondered if I'd ever phoned its occupants from the call box in Chichester.

I bought a return ticket to Waterloo and boarded a train.

*

Look for me in London Prime. Kirsty was being chased by security guards when she'd mouthed and signed this message. Maybe if she'd had time she would have given me some indication of how I was supposed to do this.

I didn't have a lot to go on. Just a working assumption that it was a version of London - presumably *the* version, if that meant anything at all. I had a decade-old memory of Earls Court appearing on a TV set, and I had an instinct brought on by a recent insomnia dream.

Realistically, the best I could hope for was to stumble upon an actual clue whilst following a false trail. After all, this was what had happened last time.

*

From Waterloo I travelled by tube to Cannon Street. I emerged blinking into daylight, not far from the north bank of the Thames, and found my way to St Michael Paternoster Royal. This was the church in the insomnia dream.

Distant bells were tolling, the way they had tolled in the dream. *Ding-dang-dong ding-ding-dang-dong. Ding-dang-dong ding-ding-dang-dong.* This time I could make out the syllables without difficulty: *Turn-a-gain Dick Whit-ting-ton.* There were no American tourists present, but I knew I had come to the right place.

Richard Whittington, when he was Lord Mayor of London, had rebuilt the church in 1409. It had subsequently been destroyed in the Great Fire of London, but the present church had been built on the same site.

I had expected a graveyard outside the church. There was not. Instead, there was the Whittington Garden, a paved area enclosed by hedges and a low wall and consisting of several park benches, a fountain, and a rather odd pair of black sculptures. The mayor himself had been buried inside the church, in 1423. His body had been moved several times since then; eventually it had disappeared altogether. In 1949 researchers discovered a mummified cat in his grave. But if the historical Whittington had ever owned a cat, there was no evidence to suggest that this was it, and plenty to suggest it was not.

If Kirsty wanted me to find her, she would have made for a location like this. Whittington was of course a significant figure both in terms of history and mythology, and therefore bound to appear across worlds. Kirsty might even be here right now, on the very bench where I was sitting, in another London. Maybe London Prime itself.

Quinn had told me I hadn't scratched the surface of the Common Land, but that was before my time in Chichester. I didn't doubt I had more to learn, but neither was I going to dismiss my experiences. Betany and I had seen the moon in its wrong phase, which reinforced the idea that time in the Common Land did not run in the conventional sense. This in turn suggested that a rendezvous could be a simple matter of turning up at an agreed location, with no regard to when or in which world.

But Kirsty was not here. So it really wasn't that straightforward.

I turned my attention to the door to the church. It was locked. Nothing about it suggested it was anything more than a mundane door to a mundane church, but I didn't want to give up on it yet as I was sure it was significant. I applied pressure to different positions on the panels, but the lock did not snap open, and the doors remained closed.

I headed off, overground, in the general direction of Waterloo station. If I could find a way into the Common Land, I could make my way back here. I was working on the assumption than the church was a nexus point, a means of access to London Prime. Perhaps I would emerge into the one true version of Whittington Garden, where I would find Kirsty waiting for me.

In the event, I walked for hours in a haphazard spiral, unable to find a doorway.

*

I persisted with the idea the next day, and the following weekend, when I passed through a different doorway behind the bookshop, and caught a train to another London.

In the capital, doorways were scarce, though there was no doubting the presence of the Common Land. At Cheapside and Gresham Street I could almost sense it directly. At the National Theatre it was closer still, and outside the Imax Cinema I could swear I heard a through-door slam.

After a lunch at Nandos I followed the distant echoes through shops, museums and art galleries, but still the doors eluded me. It felt deliberate, as if the Common Land was setting out to tease me in new and innovative ways.

A wide alleyway off Blackfriars Road formed a gap between a sandwich shop and a bicycle shop. I stepped into it. I was so close. One world away, the space I was standing in was occupied by a boarded-up hairdressing saloon - I could swear I could smell the chemicals. There was a through-door on either side of the saloon, leading to a place occupied in this world by the adjacent shops. But the through-doors could not be seen in this world; there was no point in trying to get in through the sandwich shop or the bicycle shop.

I lingered for some minutes, picturing the inside of the saloon. Linoleum on the floor, still, the long mirror still fitted to the wall and covered in dust or cobwebs. But however vividly I imagined it, I could not will myself into it.

In Southwick I found a doorway in the outside wall of a closed-down restaurant. Unfortunately someone had parked an old delivery van right in front of it. The door opened outwards; I could not open it wide enough to squeeze through.

I tried the tube station at Earls Court, as I had done the previous weekend. Nothing, again nothing.

It sometimes happens that the very act of giving up marks a change of fortune. And so it turned out. After another hour of aimless searching I'd decided to call it a day and was heading back to Waterloo when I got lucky. In the Underground, at St Paul's Station I found a door with a circular frosted window to one side of the automatic ticket machines. Nobody paid me any attention as I pushed it open and stepped into a fluorescent-lit white corridor. I was back in the Common Land at last!

But this time it was different. This corridor was no more than a few metres long. There were no turns, and no doors in the side walls; just a single door at the far end, a twin of the one I had entered, which led out into another version of St Paul's Station, where long lines of people were queuing for tickets. I had to ask someone to move out of my way.

Up till now I had assumed that the corridors of the Common Land were all interconnected, apart from the ones which had been taken "out of service" and partly or wholly filled by the constructors. But this one appeared to be operational – an isolated link between two Londons, the Common Land equivalent of a stray thought.

The map of the Underground resembled the one in my own world at first glance, with its symbolic representations of railway lines, stations, and an unnaturally geometric River Thames. But there were differences too. There was no Jubilee line, but there was a Disraeli line, which linked strange and familiar stations alike: it went through London Bridge, then Shakespeare's Globe, before it passed obliquely (or so it seemed) under the Thames, then on through Embankment, Lincoln's Hart, Sufferance Row and Mornington Crescent.

In my sketch pad I named this place Disraeli London, and the previous place Doorless London. I bought a ticket from a machine - to my relief, my money was good here - and caught a tube train to Shakespeare's Globe. As I sat on the train I was aware of the furtive glance of the elderly lady beside me as I flicked through the sketch pad, and wondered what she made of the disordered array of maps, corridor plans, arrows, question marks, skull-and-barbed-wire symbols, names such as Mirror Place, Cinema Nexus and so on.

At Shakespeare's Globe Station there was a mosaic on the platform wall showing the Bard leaning over parchment with a quill in his hand. Otherwise the place was unremarkable. I went up the escalator to street level, and headed for this world's Cannon Street, crossing the Thames via Southwark Bridge as the Millennium Bridge did not exist here. A light drizzle was falling by the time I got to St Michael Paternoster Royal. The church looked much the same as the one in Doorless London. There was no sign that Kirsty had ever been there, and by the time I'd spent ten minutes or so looking around for doorways (there were none), the rain was falling heavily.

Clearly there was little to be gained in travelling from one world to another checking out different versions of St Michael Paternoster Royal. I needed a new strategy.

There was a doorway on the other platform at Shakespeare's Globe. I nearly missed it because of the noisy milling crowd waiting to catch the train. It was late afternoon and I was tired from walking all day, but I wanted to know if this was a route worth exploring. I pushed the door open and walked through.

The door swung closed behind me, mostly shutting out the noise of the crowd. The passageway on the other side was arched, in the manner of the passageways in most Underground stations. There were white tiles on the walls, and faded posters advertising generic action films and comedies starring actors I'd never heard of. About forty feet away, a flight of steps with a central handrail led up. There were doors set in smaller archways on either side of the passage. Some had chalk markings on them, including the skull-and-barbed-wire sign on two. With considerable difficulty I read the strange words and names that were written on others, ranging from the relatively familiar such as "Gogmagog" to the obscure and meaningless such as "Ghe attash". But one particular door caught my attention because the writing on it formed coherent sentences.

It was a message, perhaps, or an attempt at what Miss Havers would have called a prose poem. It read, "We keep the outside outside. How beautiful to watch the rain on the window and the birds settling on the blasted oak from the comfort of the fireside, consciously oblivious to the forces that beset us from either side."

The writing was distinctly feminine and very neat. Underneath it was signed, "Laura Theresa." I read it through once, then again. I considered the repetition of "outside" in the first sentence, and the "consciously oblivious" oxymoron in the second. I read it through a third time, silently mouthing the words that did not scramble. So thrilled was I by this discovery, this exception to the rule of not being able to read inside the Common Land, that I did not immediately react to the sound of one of the doors opening behind me. By the time I turned, a figure had crossed the main corridor and was disappearing through another doorway. The door swung shut, and I saw it was one of the two doors with the skull and barbed wire symbol.

I took my gun from out of the backpack and pushed the door open.

Even without the warning sign on the door, it would have been obvious that this was not a good place. Like the main passageway, this was tiled and arched, but there was a darkness about it that went beyond the poor lighting and the dirt on the tiles. A telephone hood in the left wall appeared partly melted; the receiver, also deformed, hung from its cable, swinging gently. A glass-fronted vending machine looked as if it had not been refilled in years. Packets of crisps and bars of chocolate in faded wrappers rested in their coils. There was movement in one of the crisp packets, as if it contained a wriggling tarantula. I hurried past.

I caught up with the figure. She was a middle-aged woman in a grey raincoat. She had the appearance of a sleepwalker who had just woken up in a strange place.

"Not safe," I told her. "You leave here. I'll help." My throat was constricted and my eyes were still adjusting to the dim light. Further along the blackened remains of a busker sat leaning against a wall, an undamaged guitar resting on his lap and a hat with some coins in front of him. I wanted the woman to get away before she caught sight of the corpse, but she had already seen it.

"These aren't my dreams," she said crossly, as if I were somehow responsible. "I don't dream filth like that!"

"Laura Theresa?"

"My name is Mrs Bowden. Mrs *Mavis* Bowden," she added, as if that would clear up an ambiguity.

"Not a Common Land traveller."

She gave me a blank look, then continued, "I've lived here for more than forty years and I've never seen anything like it. Or *that*!" She indicated the gun in my hand. Under her breath she added, "There's nothing common about me!"

"Follow!" I barked, leading the way back to safety.

I did not point the gun at her, but she obeyed as if I had. I repeated the word as we drew close to the vending machine as I did not want her to look closely at it and see what I had seen. She did not slow down.

When we emerged back into the main passageway I sensed that someone was watching us. I looked across at one of the doors - not the other one marked with skull and barbed wire - just in time to see it close. Whoever it was, they were not the only ones who had been this way. At the far end of the passageway, two people were walking away from us. They were climbing the steps, one on either side of the central railing, so I only saw their lower halves. They were wearing trousers but it was clear from their walk that they were both women.

In other circumstances I might have gone after the watcher, or the two women, but first things first. I had to get Mrs Bowden to safety. Since leaving the side passage I found I could speak in proper sentences again.

"Mrs Bowden, my name is Philip, and I'm going to get you out of here. Were you waiting for a train?"

She nodded.

"At Shakespeare's Globe?"

Again she nodded, adding, "I'm going to be terribly late. And my daughter has always been one for worrying."

I guided her back out onto the station platform. There were no other passengers, just two railway staff having a conversation at the other end of the platform. One saw us, shouted, "Where did you spring from?" adding, "We're closing up."

"This lady got lost," I explained vaguely as they led us to an escalator. Mrs Bowden explained, "I couldn't get a signal." She took a large mobile phone out of her large handbag.

The escalator had been turned off for the night. It always feels strange walking up an escalator when it is stationary, similar neither to stairs nor moving escalator. Eventually we reached the exit, which was closed; the guard unlocked a latchgate to let us out.

Time had passed at the wrong rate again; it was getting on for midnight. Mrs Bowden got a signal, and I stayed with her until her daughter arrived by taxi over an hour later. I explained to the anxious daughter that her mother had wandered into a disused part of the station and had got lost.

*

As the year progressed I would once again consider saving money by not staying in a hotel. To begin with, though, it was simply too cold to get my hour or two of rest on a park bench, and I hadn't developed an instinct for which places were safe in the mundane sense. It was warm in the Common Land, or at least sheltered, but it carried its own dangers which I didn't understand well enough yet. If I took my rest inside the Common Land itself, I might fall asleep, like the obese man trapped in the room in the house in Southsea, the house I now thought of as the House of Shards.

There were other considerations that made staying in a hotel appealing. A shower, a shave, brushed teeth and a clean change of clothes, not to mention a clean toilet and a cooked breakfast.

I lay on the hotel bed thinking about the events of the day.

I'd been able to read the prose-poem of Laura Theresa, and I was intrigued. Even her name was fascinating. In my time as a teacher I had had female pupils with double first names, not always hyphenated: Sally Anne, Sarah Jane, Ann Marie, Kelly Jay. But never a Laura Theresa. Could Theresa be her surname?

My ability to read while inside the Common Land did not extend to anything beyond Laura Theresa's message. As a rule, anything longer than two words was virtually impossible, and I struggled to read even my own notes in my sketchpad. The names of manufacturers on the chocolate bars and crisp packets in the vending machines were beyond me. Walkers? Golden Wonder? Cadbury? Galaxy? If I could read the words "coincidence" or "ghe attash" why could I not read these?

While waiting for Alice Bowden, Mavis's daughter, to arrive, I had taken the mother to an all-night cafe. Little details: when I tried to pay for the coffee with coins, they had rejected them as foreign, but had accepted a ten pound note. Mrs Bowden wasn't a follower; she had simply stumbled upon an entrance, and had subsequently failed to stumble upon an exit. Her eyesight was poor, and she had lost her glasses, otherwise she might have asked me for help. Our conversation in the cafe had been stilted, at first, with lengthy pauses. It was similar to, but not the same as, the experience of being in one of the dangerous corridors where my throat constricted and I could only blurt. I wanted to tell her not to call the police; if she did, she was not to tell them about the dead busker, or the fact that I was carrying a gun, but I could not do so without reinforcing the reality of what she had seen. So I mostly talked about mundane things, asked her about her family and so on, in the hope that her memory of the Common Land would recede, be remembered, if at all, as an unpleasant but nonsensical and harmless dream.

Just before the taxi arrived she said, "There is something important missing from your life."

"Yes, I know. My daughter."

She smiled. "They mean so much to us, don't they?"

"They do."

*

So, I'd rescued someone from the Common Land. Someone I had not put in danger in the first place.

I thought of Betany, stranded in the Mirror Place. I could tell myself that that had not been my fault, and I could tell myself that I had got her to safety, and that any attempt to rescue her would simply put her back in danger.

None of that helped.

Sometimes I considered planning a route for her that would get her home, an optimal route that would mean she spent as little time as possible in the Common Land. But I had no idea how long it would take to react to her presence.

Without such a plan, visiting her was out of the question, at least until after I was reunited with Kirsty. For all that it had ended in tragedy, Betany's story was over, at least. Mine was not.

*

The next day I returned to the Shakespeare's Globe Station. Laura Theresa's message was still there, unchanged and unchanging. I tried the door on which it was written. It creaked open and I shone my torch into darkness. It was not a corridor, as I had expected, but a room filled with tables and upturned chairs stacked on the tables.

There was a door in the far wall, but there was no way to get to it without shifting the tables a little at a time, and there was no urgency to do this. Evidently nobody had been this way recently. So I made for the steps at the end of the passageway, the ones where I had seen the two women ascending yesterday. Part of the ceiling had collapsed, and there was a thick layer of plaster dust and broken pieces of tile on the ground. There were footprints in the dust, presumably those of the two women, but the dust on the central handrail remained undisturbed. There followed a long empty corridor with alcoves, the occasional doorway, and a mostly intact ceiling. In places the fluorescent lighting flickered in an irritatingly repetitive manner, and sometimes I imagined I could see movement out of the corner of my eye. Once a swing door creaked open and a large white dog with pink eyes, an albino Alsation, loped out. Unnerved, I took the safety off my gun. But the dog was well fed and paid little attention to me.

At length I found myself inside a disused power station. If my instinct was correct, it was the building that corresponded to the Tate Modern gallery in my own world. Most of the turbines and other equipment had been removed, and the huge vertical windows were boarded up, but I could see out through a gap, onto a square where commuters and shoppers were going about their business.

Galleries overlooked the place where the turbines had been. I went up the stairs to the top one, and I was surprised to see what appeared to be a loft hatch in the ceiling. A pole with a hook leaned against one of the boarded-up windows. I used it to pull the hatch open, and a wooden ladder unfolded. I went up it.

If I'd expected to find myself in a loft, I wasn't disappointed. It was a huge area with bare floorboards which had a fresh, pleasant smell to them, as if they had only been put down recently. There was a forest of steel pillars evenly spaced every three metres, their purpose presumably to suspend the floor rather than support the flat roof. It was a spacious loft in terms of height as well as area; I could walk without having to duck.

Parts of the loft were partitioned off, but my attention was drawn to the centre, which was lit by daylight shining through a large skylight. I guessed the glass was tinted, because there was a turquoise quality to the light, which fell upon a cluster of furniture.

As I got closer, I had the impression that this was the studio flat for a student with rich parents. There were fewer steel pillars here, which put me in mind of a clearing in the forest. There were two sofas and an armchair facing a bank of a dozen large plasma televisions, four across and three high. There were rugs on the floorboards, two standard lamps, several cupboards, an easel, and numerous paintings stacked leaning against most of the cupboards. Rifling through half a dozen portraits, I recognised one of the subjects. It was Tobias Quinn, the man without the birthmark, except he still had it in this picture: a port-wine stain that covered the lower part of his face.

Confirmation, then. He *was* the man the Websters had seen in Whitby. A significant piece of information? Maybe, maybe not, but it was satisfying nonetheless.

The turquoise light shimmered, reminding me of something. I looked up to see a glass dome, some ten metres across. That's what I was reminded of: the sea! The dome was completely submerged, the surface of the water at least a metre above its highest point. Mid-morning sunlight shone down through the water and the dome into the studio flat.

I was in a version of the world where London was under water.

Just how strong was that glass? I wondered. What if a ship's hull brushed against it? Were there even ships? Was the whole of England covered? I'd read somewhere that London was low-lying, but even so...

I might have fled back to the loft ladder, but curiosity competed with my fear, and eventually won. I strolled over to one of the sofas, stood on a rug, and stared up at the glass dome. Feeling suddenly blase, I decided that it would hurt my neck less if I lay on my back on the sofa. So I did.

Clearly the glass *was* strong enough to hold back that pressure of water – and presumably the situation had not come about recently. On the other hand, if the glass *did* crack, the consequences would be catastrophic. The loft hatch was a through-door - I was certain of that because I'd seen an unflooded London through the gaps in the boarding over the windows downstairs.

The loft hatch was clearly not waterproof. I imagined water pouring through it, rapidly filling up the power station, bursting out of the downstairs windows in an explosion of glass and boarding, and flooding the inhabited streets outside, eventually drowning the whole of this particular London. Perhaps the force of the water would cause the walls of the power station to collapse, and that would sever the link between worlds, in which case the cataclysm would be localised. Or perhaps it would continue to pour through the tunnel to Shakespeare's Globe Station, its unlimited supply inundating that version of England; in turn it would flow through all the other doorways into the Common Land, eventually reaching my own world.

And so on, and so on. But surely, if something like that *could* happen, it would have done so by now?

Even if there was a mechanism that prevented the water from spreading any further than the power station, I was in terrible danger so long as I remained here. Yet still I remained. Why was I doing this? Was it in any way helping me in my search for London Prime, for Kirsty?

No. I was here for another reason. I had been lured here, drawn off course by something akin to the Siren song. Were there Sirens in the Common Land? Did they sing? I listened intently, but there was no sound at all in that studio flat. Not even the sound of water, or the strange background noises I had heard in other parts of the Common Land.

There was a safe next to the easel, the sort with both combination lock and keyhole. I wondered if my lock-picking skills were developed enough to get it open, but decided not to try. There was nothing on the easel itself, but the artist's work was everywhere. I had noticed framed paintings, both landscape and portrait, on the partition walls. Other, unframed works hung from some of the steel pillars. The landscapes were mostly of forests, office blocks and desolate beaches. The portraits were of men and women, young and old, and also slithermen, and three other kinds of creature I had not yet encountered - and hoped and prayed I never would. I knew little of art, and did not have the vocabulary of appreciation beyond the trite phrase, "The artist has captured life." But he had. Even in his hurried and unfinished sketches, many of which were stacked on a coffee table or leaning against the side of a sofa. I remember thinking, *How can anybody so talented be so prolific?*

Kirsty did not feature in any of the portraits that I saw. I was as much relieved as disappointed by this. One subject appeared more than any other - possibly more than all the rest put together. It was a woman. Most of the portraits of her were close-ups of her face, although there were a few in profile, and one showed her neck and part of her shoulders. She had a round face, and long, straight hair, probably longer than shoulder length. It was brown, but such a light brown it appeared almost blonde. She never smiled. She had brown eyes, the saddest eyes I had ever seen, perhaps because I was reminded of dead Eloise. She was quite, quite beautiful. And she was everywhere.

This artist is a man in love, I thought. Or a man obsessed. She could have been his wife, but I doubted it. He was trying to consummate in art what he could not consummate in life.

She was Laura Theresa.

I found a sketchpad devoted to her. She appeared on every single page; sometimes he managed to fit her twice on a page. Between two pages I found a slip of paper. It was in her handwriting. It said, "When your sleepless rest is disturbed I will kiss your eyes. In the early hours the chimes of the clock say Gone. Fear Gone. All Fear Gone. Laura Theresa."

The words in the first sentence startled me. Was eye kissing a practice among Common Land travellers? Was that the reason I had kissed Dawn on the eyes - to tell her not to be afraid? If so, how had I picked up on it?

I understood the rest of the message well enough. Clearly they were addressed to an insomniac who hears words in the chimes of a clock as the hours of the night wear on and still sleep eludes them. Laura Theresa was reassuring someone who had lost the ability to sleep but had not yet acquired the special relationship with the Common Land that meant sleep was no longer necessary. One o'clock: Gone. Two o'clock: Fear Gone. Three o'clock: All Fear Gone.

If only I'd had someone like Laura Theresa when I was going through the change.

On impulse I took my own sketchpad out of my backpack and started copying Laura Theresa's message. This didn't quite go to plan; evidently the rules of the Common Land still applied when I tried to write her words, even if they didn't apply when I read them. I flicked through the artist's sketchpad to see if there was anything else she had written. There was. It began, "We dream the architecture. We dream the architecture. We lose ourselves in the killing distance." It occurred to me then that I could photograph text with the camera in my mobile phone, so I began to fumble for it as I read. Then the single most frightening thing imaginable happened.

A trickle of water ran down my neck.

I fled. Without pausing even to pick up my sketchpad I ran back to the loft hatch, banging my left elbow on one of the pillars; down the ladder to the gallery, down the stairs to the ground floor of the abandoned power station, along the long corridor (and startling the large white dog), not stopping until I reached Shakespeare's Globe Station. Once I was back in Doorless London I caught the first train back to Portsmouth, and regained my own world through the doorway behind the secondhand bookshop. I breathed a sigh of relief at the sight of the clock tower, and walked home. I went straight to bed and shut my eyes. I pretended to sleep; I pretended I was not listening out for the roar of an alien sea rushing to join the one near my home.

My elbow hurt like hell.

Chapter 26. Living Without Dreams

On Monday morning as I was delivering a lesson about the Somme to an unruly Year 10, Geoff Sandhurst, a long-haired and particularly obnoxious pupil, interrupted to say he had mislaid his homework.

"It's up to you to keep track of your work," I told him.

"What, like it's up to you to keep track of your daughter?" he retorted, adding, "Sir."

An uneasy laughter rippled through the class. Even Sandhurst realised he had overstepped the mark.

I gave him a long, thoughtful look, which I think discomfited him more than shouting would have done, or sending him to the head teacher's office.

The world at large had moved on, it seemed. As far as the media was concerned, Kirsty had been found, safe and well, and she had returned home. *The Daily Mail* had published an article about the effects of fast food on prepubescent girls, citing Kirsty as an example of a victim of early onset puberty. It had angered me when I first saw it, but then I dismissed it as a typical example of their ill-informed agenda-led shameful excuse for journalism.

Where my friends, acquaintances, colleagues and pupils were concerned, the world had not quite moved on. It would in time but it hadn't happened yet. In the meantime I had to focus on my job whilst my mind was preoccupied with wondering what the hell had happened to Kirsty, where she was now, and would she ever return home for good.

But for the first time in months she wasn't foremost in my mind. She was *in* my mind, to be sure, but the thing I could not stop thinking about was the *crack!* noise that the glass dome must have made. Granted, I had not heard it, but it was a matter of my mind filling in the gaps.

My sketchpad was lost. Not that it really mattered; I had used the school photocopier to copy the earlier pages, and I could remember most of what I had added on my last expedition. Luckily I had not lost the gun.

Nobody would ever know what was in the artist's safe. Unless a diver in the flooded world found their way down and somehow got it open.

Had Laura Theresa drowned? Or just her pictures? Had the sea spent itself by flowing in through a succession of doors into the Common Land and out into a hundred other worlds? What if it reached London Prime?

"Three million men fought in the Battle of the Somme," I resumed. "A million were killed, or wounded, or maimed."

*

On Tuesday there was flooding in London. My heart skipped a beat when I heard this news, but it turned out to have an entirely natural explanation - torrential rain.

I coasted for the rest of the week. In Maths I talked about the three kinds of average, happy and sad quadratic curves, and prime numbers. In History I talked about the Industrial Revolution, Anne Boleyn's extra finger, and the evidence for the existence of King Arthur.

At the weekend I cautiously entered the Common Land at the bookshop and visited another St Michael Paternoster Royal. This particular London showed no signs of flooding, and it had doors everywhere, so many it was hard to understand how anybody could miss them. I got complacent here, and nearly got myself killed. A doorway that was at ground level on one side proved to be nearly three metres above the floor on the other. I fell through, landed on a soft pile of rubbish, but still managed to injure one ankle. The door by which I had entered was too high to reach, and the passageway leading off was blocked with slitherman cables.

I was trapped for a long time. Eventually I escaped, of course, but not until early on Monday morning. I bought pies and sandwiches at Waterloo and caught the first train to Portsmouth. Throughout the journey my mind was occupied with images of slithermen faces (for want of a better word) getting up close, and the memory of nearly getting cut in half by a snapping cable.

My supply of ammunition was going to need restocking.

The bookshop didn't open until 10am on a Monday. Fortunately I was able to do a reverse break-in. Even so, it was after 9am that I was finally able to phone the school. I had a difficult class first thing on Mondays; on this particular Monday the admin staff would be rushing around trying to organise cover.

"Where the hell are you?" demanded Kerry Marshall.

I told her I had gone to London for the weekend, and had fallen ill; I'd forgotten to charge my mobile so I wasn't able to phone from the train on my way home.

There was suspicion in the secretary's tone, and I didn't know why. I later discovered there hadn't been any trains running on the Waterloo line since Saturday. When I limped in at lunchtime, however, there was no doubting that I was really ill. As they had already paid for a supply teacher, they sent me home.

That evening I received some distressing news. My cousin Martin had died of a heart attack that lunchtime in the kitchen of his restaurant in Edinburgh.

I made it in to work the next day, despite everything, to the surprise and relief of Kerry Marshall. She'd already phoned the agency, asking for the supply teacher who had come in yesterday, only to be told he'd reportedly said he would rather remove one of his own kidneys with a rusty steak knife than do another day at Southsea Grammar, adding that he wasn't too keen on the kids either.

"She's not pleased you're taking Friday off," Miss Havers told me as we sat in the cafe after work.

"She does get that it's a funeral I'm going to, right?"

"You know Kerry Marshall. She might have been a little more understanding if it was your own."

*

On Thursday evening I was on a plane to Edinburgh. It seemed strange to think I wouldn't be spending the weekend searching the Common Land for Kirsty. I wasn't forgetting about her the way the world had, far from it, and I certainly didn't feel less worried about her than before. She was still my baby, my princess. But she had lived for three years without me, without her mother, without the dubious support of the extended family. She had survived the horrors and the insanity of the Common Land, she had been able to look after herself and, I supposed, Eloise, until the latter's inexplicably sudden death.

Kirsty and I had holidayed in Edinburgh soon after my divorce. We'd stayed for a week at Martin and Phoebe's place in what proved to be a near-perfect holiday. Perversely, the thing that stood out in my memory was the one thing that made it not quite perfect. One evening after Kirsty had gone to bed and after I'd had one glass of wine more than I'd really needed, I happened to make a derogatory comment about Dawn. For this I received the gentlest of reprimands from Martin which, because of its very gentleness, I found quite mortifying. He really had liked her, and was saddened that things hadn't worked out for us.

I wondered if Dawn had been invited to the funeral. I doubted it. Even if she had been, I doubted William would have allowed her to go.

I read for a while but I wasn't in the mood for the book. I put it down, reclined my seat a little, and shut my eyes, willing myself into the reverie state that I still thought of as insomnia dreaming. I was walking in the Common Land, but in the ancient past - a version of Roman Britain that probably had more to do with Hollywood than actual history, as I hadn't studied it in any depth. I was in a long, seemingly unending corridor with columns on either side. The corridor was illuminated but there was darkness beyond the corridors. Someone was stalking me, a figure in a white toga, almost certainly female; she hid behind columns, running across the gaps between when she thought I wasn't looking.

Abruptly I came out of the reverie, as suddenly as if someone had woken me from sleep with a bucket of water. I looked around, but nothing on the plane had changed. A father and his son across the aisle from me were talking. The son, who I reckoned was about fourteen, said, "Can we see Hadrian's Wall from up here, then?" The father replied, "We passed that a while back."

I was unable to get back into my reverie.

Phoebe met me at the airport. She thanked me for coming while we shared a prolonged hug, then drove me to her house. I had offered to stay at a hotel, as most of the other mourners were doing, but she would not hear of it.

The house was almost immaculate. Almost. If she had gone to pieces the way I had gone to pieces when Kirsty disappeared, it would have made sense. It was the little things: dust on the mantelpiece, a dirty coffee mug on a windowsill, shoes under the dining room table - things that would have gone unnoticed in my house but which were out of character with Phoebe.

There were recent photographs of Cousin Martin. He had put on so much weight since I had last seen him that if he hadn't already died I would have feared for his health.

Phoebe showed me to the guest room, where I had stayed last time. I put my overnight bag on the bed and freshened up while Phoebe made a light supper. We sat together on the sofa after and talked about Martin, and we talked about Kirsty. "It's a shame it wasn't your weekend with her," she said at one point, making me wonder what she thought was going on.

It reminded me of the time in Whitby when she and I had thought Kirsty was with Dawn and Martin, and they had thought she was with us. That seemed to be the way the Common Land handled everything - hidden doors, disappearances, contradictions. While Sinead O'Connor's "Nothing Compares 2 U" played in the background we kissed five or six times, and somehow it didn't feel as if my cousin's widow was coming onto me on the night before his funeral, and neither was I trying to take advantage of her while she was at her most vulnerable. She thanked me. I asked her what for.

She said just being there for her. We kissed once more, intimate and prolonged, once we'd decided to turn in.

At two in the morning Phoebe tapped on my door and asked if I was asleep. I told her I did not sleep. She told me she had forgotten to get an extra blanket from the cupboard in the spare room, and hoped she was not disturbing me. I repeated that I did not sleep. She said it was cold for the time of year, which struck me as amusing, given that she was wearing a nightie but no dressing gown, and asked me if I needed anything. It reminded me of the time Dawn had thought Phoebe had put a spider in Kirsty's room just so she had an excuse to parade in her nightie. I told Phoebe I was fine. She said, "Okay, but let me know if you need anything," and she went back to her room.

I was not fine. I desperately needed to sleep but I had lost the skill. I did not know what was going on, but I had some idea.

It's a common misconception that Hadrian's Wall marks the border between England and Scotland. The first thing I had heard when I was yanked out of my reverie on the plane was a boy asking his father if we could see Hadrian's Wall, and his father replied that we'd flown over it some time before.

We must have crossed the border at that point. In leaving England I'd lost the link with the Common Land. Sleep was a means to an end; as long as I had the link with the Common Land, I didn't need to sleep to dream.

Now, I couldn't sleep, and I couldn't dream.

Everything that had happened since I'd crossed into Scotland was subject to my uncertain interpretation. Miss Havers had told me about novels with unreliable narrators, and I wondered if I had become an unreliable narrator in my own story.

Hours passed. I had duties tomorrow. I had promised Phoebe I would read my own eulogy of Martin at the service. I had written a draft that I was reasonably happy with, but it had been my plan to polish it during the night. Instead I lay on my back staring up into darkness. I hadn't realised before how much the insomnia dreams relieved the monotony of night, even those nights I spent reading, watching films or getting up to speed on marking and lesson preparation. This was a stark reminder of the early days.

When day came I walked like one of the living dead. In the chapel, where Cousin Martin's coffin lay on the conveyor belt, I was sure I could smell flames; I wondered if the furnace had got out of control. During the church service, when the time came for me to deliver the eulogy, the words on the page broke apart the way they did when I tried to read in the Common Land.

A lot could be excused on the grounds of grief, but that only went so far, and things got worse. I drank heavily at the reception, perhaps hoping to find oblivion. My last memory of Phoebe sees her at the front door of her house late at night, tears running down her face, saying, "Just go."

*

On my return flight, I was more myself again when the plane crossed the border back into England.

Once home, I emailed Phoebe a short but sincere apology. I read over it two or three times before clicking Send. I waited by the computer, hoping she'd get back straight away. I was still there an hour later.

I checked the next day, and the day after that, then every few days, then weekly. From time to time I still skim my inbox looking for an email from her, wishing I could turn back time.

Chapter 27. The Sea in London

Watching a documentary late one night about music halls, I was surprised to learn that there had once been a popular song called "Why Can't We have the Sea in London?" They played a recording of the song performed by Billy Williams. The quality was poor, and it was hard to make out the words, but the gist was clear.

A number of weeks had passed since the cracking of that skylight glass, assuming time in that version of England was in synch with my own. If something catastrophic had happened, it had had time to settle down.

I needed to find out what was going on there. My searches up till now - mostly centred around different versions of St Michael Paternoster, for all that I had dismissed this as a strategy - had continued to prove entirely fruitless. Whereas the portrait of Tobias Quinn in the attic of the power station was some sort of connection at least.

Somewhat diffidently, I travelled to the London of the Shakespeare Globe the next weekend, taking a different route that was mainly above ground. I stopped off at the coffee shop, not the one where I had taken Mavis Bowden, but close by. I drank black coffee while waiting for the rush hour to end. It could be argued I was procrastinating. Evenings were staying lighter longer now, and from my window seat I had a good view of two bridges - Millennium and Southwark - stretching across the Thames.

I became aware of someone watching me from another table. A tall woman of mixed race, not young but very attractive, and oddly familiar. She was wearing a maroon hat that looked like something out of the 1920s. I gave her a shy smile, and to my surprise she got up and came over.

"It's you, isn't it?" she said, striding over while carrying her coffee. She had a very cultured London accent. "You did a very brave thing."

This was entirely unexpected. Had she mistaken me for someone else? Had I done *anything* recently that could be considered brave or in any way admirable?

"I'm sorry, I can't quite place you," I said.

She smiled apologetically. "Forgive me, I have you at a disadvantage." She put her coffee down on my table, then leaned over, took my face in both hands and kissed me on my eyes. "My name is Miah Proctor." She released me and sat across from me.

"Philip Hamilton," I said, somewhat bemused by the greeting. "Where are you from?"

Her smile faded at that. "I was born right here in London. My father was English, my mother is from Kenya." It sounded like a recitation.

"No, I didn't mean... I meant, are you from this version of England?"

"Oh, I see. Yes I am." She gave me a stare. "You look surprised. Why?"

"Because I think I know you. From long ago. Long before I even knew about... you know."

"Where do you think you know me from?"

"I don't know. You look familiar, but as I say, I can't place you. From my own world, obviously."

"Obviously," she echoed. There followed an awkward pause, which I was actually quite glad about because it put us on more or less equal footing. At length she explained, "You followed a bystander through a door marked for peril and brought her out to safety. That was a very brave thing to do."

"You were watching me from the opposite doorway?"

She nodded.

"If you saw me, why didn't you make yourself known to me?"

"I thought it best that Mrs Bowden didn't see me. She'd got it into her head that I was the danger she was fleeing from." She hesitated, then added, "It was a misunderstanding."

"It's kind of you to say I was brave."

"Maybe. To be honest I wondered if you even knew what you were doing. You looked... new to it. Was it your first time or did you have a mentor of some sort?"

"Tobias Quinn was the closest I got to a mentor."

She gave a look of distaste. "Okay, well that explains a lot!"

"Everyone seems to know him. Is he famous or something?"

"That's not the word I would use. What's your job, Philip?"

"I teach. Mathematics and History."

She nodded, seemingly interested. "You'll know, then, there are many different styles of teaching. If Quinn were a teacher... Well, let's just say his approach is hands off. He'd argue you can't teach someone about the Common Land, they have to find out for themselves, and to an extent he's right. But that's no excuse for being a jerk."

"Maybe he has another excuse," I ventured.

Miah gave me a look as if she had never considered that before. "Maybe so. Be careful who you get indebted to, Philip. That's free advice."

"So what do you do?" I asked.

"I'm a private detective."

I raised an eyebrow. "Are you on a case right now?"

"Several, but one in particular." She showed me a photograph of a young man with an irrepressible smile and short blond hair, hugging his equally happy-looking young son and daughter to him. "I don't suppose you've seen this man on your travels?"

"I'm afraid not," I said after scrutinising the picture. "You think he's in the Common Land?"

She shrugged. "Going by his wife's account, he shows some of the signs. But in the vast majority of cases it's something sordid and boring."

I showed her my picture of Kirsty, the one in which she had been aged. Miah looked long and hard, but eventually she shook her head. "Sorry, no. Is she your daughter?"

"Yes."

"You think she went missing in the Common Land?"

"I *know* she did. She told me to look for her in London Prime." I briefly explained what had happened.

"And that's what you're doing now? Looking for London Prime?"

"Yes."

"Okay. Listen, Philip. You don't just stumble upon London Prime. If you could find it by chance, I would have done so a long time ago."

"So how *do* you get there?"

"You talk to people. People in the know. Have you met Douglas Lamb?"

"I don't know the name."

"He's an artist."

"Ah."

"He gets things done. He grants wishes."

"Wishes?"

"Wishes. Literally. People wish for things, he grants them."

"Do you mean like in *The Godfather*?"

"I don't know what that is."

"I mean, someone who knows powerful people and who can call in favours. Or do you mean he's like an actual wizard?"

"You sound sceptical."

"I'm not sceptical exactly. I've just had a lot to get my head round lately. It occurs to me that believing all of it is as dangerous as believing none of it."

"Be very careful of Douglas Lamb," she admonished.

"Why?"

"Because everything comes with a price. He'll get you what you wish for, and the price won't be very high at all. Not the first time. Like a drug dealer outside the school gates. The first one's free. But you'd be surprised how addictive wishes can get when you know they can be granted, Philip, and you'd be shocked how steeply the price goes up."

With that she finished her coffee and got up to go. She had an appointment, she told me. I remembered seeing her face among the portraits in what I supposed was Douglas Lamb's attic. But I knew her from earlier than that, I was sure of it.

Before she left I told her briefly about the blackened corpse of a busker in the perilous corridor. She now had the unenviable task of finding out if her client's missing husband played guitar.

*

Three or four years ago, Kirsty, Dawn and I spent a Saturday afternoon watching a VHS tape of short Laurel and Hardy films. One sticks out in my memory, mainly because it made Kirsty laugh so hard she was nearly sick. It was an episode called "Brats", and it featured the duo both in their regular roles and also as child versions of themselves. At one point the child duo left the shower running before going to bed; with comically unrealistic rapidity, the water overflowed the bath and filled the bathroom. Inevitably the episode ended with Hardy opening the bathroom door.

Every door was like that bathroom door as I attempted to retrace my steps to that attic. But I reached the power station without drama, seeing no indication of recent flooding. When I finally arrived at the loft hatch, it was clear that my fears were entirely irrational. A loft hatch was not going to hold back an ocean.

I opened it with the pole I had used on the last visit. The vast attic-cum-steel forest-cum-studio flat was the same as I had left it. But this time it was occupied.

My first impression was that he was young, not long out of school, but that impression would change. He was heavily built, but not exactly fat. His hair was black and floppy. He wore white trousers, a black shirt and a white tie, giving his clothes the appearance of a photographic negative. He lay back on one of the sofas, underneath the dome, bathed in the light that filtered through the unchanged sea above. Eleven of the twelve televisions were on, but they were all muted. He was listening to music from a personal stereo through a pair of ear pieces. The music was loud; I could hear its tinny sound even from the loft hatch.

I walked slowly through the forest of steel pillars. He acknowledged me as I approached him; he raised an eyebrow and gave a casual wave. I sensed that he considered himself some kind of king of the Common Land, or at least this part of it. There was a metal object lying on the sofa beside him which made me think of a sceptre, or possibly a mace, though it was not the right shape for either. A moment later I realised it was four or five TV remotes welded together. Each one was made of steel, and gave the impression it was a military prototype. Not that I believed there *was* such a thing as an army-grade TV remote.

"Can we talk?" I asked. He looked at me blankly. I mimed taking the earpieces out. He took one out.

"Yes?"

As a teacher I had experienced behaviour like this. But here I had no authority. I was playing by his rules.

"You are Douglas Lamb?" I asked.

He grinned. "That I am!" he said, as if I had passed a test. "What can I do for you?"

"My name is Philip Hamilton. I was told that you..." I hesitated.

"You were told I what? Grant wishes?"

"Yes. Yes, that was it."

He grinned again, then nodded. "So what is it you wish for?"

Suddenly the sheer unreality of the situation hit me. "Look, I can't deal with this. I thought I'd be able to, but it turns out I just can't. I'm sorry to waste your time, but..." I turned to go but his words held me.

"You cannot deal with *what*?"

"All this. Everything. Your manner. This conversation. There's a billion tons of water above our heads and we're talking about things from a *fairy* tale!"

Lamb narrowed his eyes for a moment. "I'm sorry about my manner but it's the only one I have. However, I had no intention of deceiving you, let alone intimidating you. At least, not at this stage."

He switched off his personal stereo, took the other earpiece out, then picked up the TV remote control mace. He pointed it up at the glass dome, pressed a button, and all the water vanished. The dome was gone; in its place was a huge circular monitor screen, switched off. On impulse Lamb removed something from a slot between two of the banked TV sets - a thing I recognised as a USB memory stick - and replaced it with another one that he took from an inside pocket. The dome was back, but the water was not. Overhead was a blue sky with white clouds drifting in the breeze.

"But... the water!" I said stupidly. "When I was here before, it got in!"

"Rainwater gathers on the roof. There was a leak. I've had it fixed. Though not before it did some damage." He indicated a mark on one of the sofa cushions. "By the way, is this your sketchpad?"

Wordlessly I accepted the sketchpad. My mind was reeling. All these weeks, worrying about *nothing*. Despite what I'd said to Miah Proctor, I had believed too much. I'd known enough physics to realise a glass dome wasn't going to hold back that much water, but I'd believed it anyway. And the worst of it was, Douglas Lamb wasn't even trying to deceive me.

At least that's what he'd told me.

He was businesslike all of a sudden. "We're going to talk terms now. You tell me what you want, I tell you the price."

So this was it, the final surrender to irrationality. I said, "Kirsty, my daughter, went missing in the Common Land. Later she sent me a message. She told me to look for her in London Prime. She also told me that she loved me."

Douglas Lamb nodded. "So that's what you want. The means of reaching London Prime."

"Yes," I said. "Is that something you can...?"

"Yes."

"Let me get this straight. When I get there, will I find her there?"

"If she keeps her side of the bargain, then yes."

I hadn't considered the possibility that she might not. I dismissed it at once.

"How do I pay you?" I asked.

"You pose for me while I paint your portrait."

That didn't seem too onerous. "Now?"

"Now."

*

He was fast, but not supernaturally fast. I sat for over three hours.

While I sat I was able to watch the eleven television sets out of the corner of my eye. What they showed was random, and largely unremarkable: a time-lapse sequence of a flower growing, a nature programme that focused mainly on colourful birds, a hospital drama, another nature programme that appeared to be filmed from the viewpoint of a wasp entering its nest, a science fiction show about a man and a woman climbing a rope ladder between planets, CCTV footage of the streets outside a pub in the late evening, *Brief Encounter*, a first-person viewpoint of a tour of the Common Land, and various others. Occasionally Lamb would put down his brush, pick up the mace and change one of the channels, then resume his work.

I was committed, but doubts passed through my mind. I was well versed in myths, legends and folklore. I knew about wishes that were granted to the letter but not to the spirit. I knew about the Monkey's Paw and the Sausage Nose, and many, many others, but from what I understood, Lamb wasn't about pedantry or unprovoked spite. However he granted wishes (and so far I had it only on trust that he did) he was getting something for them in return. It was in his interest to ensure customer satisfaction.

At length he was done. He invited me to look at the finished portrait.

At first I was struck by the photographic realism, and by the intensity of my blue eyes looking out from the canvas. But there was more to it than mere realism, though I could not at that stage have said what it was. Some aspect of my personality that I could not have identified in myself, and which would not have been manifest in a mere photograph.

"Are you free next weekend?" Lamb asked.

"Yes. Yes I am."

"In that case, do exactly what I say, and you'll visit Kirsty on Saturday."

Chapter 28. Connecting Trains

They still had trains with slam-door carriages in this world, something that had been phased out a few months earlier in my own world. There was a corridor along the left side of each carriage and compartments on the right. Each compartment was accessed through a sliding door, except for the one at the front of the third carriage. This one was locked, and a sign in the window said, "Out of service."

It wasn't seven o'clock yet and the sun had not long been up, and the train was not crowded. The compartment adjacent to the locked one was occupied by a middle-aged woman. She looked up as I entered, flashed me a pleasant smile, then returned her attention to her Ian Rankin hardback. Outside the carriage window a light rain was falling as the countryside rushed past.

I had made it through the week. I had been an emotional pendulum, one moment confident that I could take Douglas Lamb at his word, the next convinced it was a cruel trick, an overly literal interpretation of the way I had phrased my wish.

I was going to see my daughter.

Pupils and staff alike picked up on my state of mind. Miss Havers had come close to asking me outright if all was well. I could not tell her the truth, could not tell her that the miracle of Kirsty turning up safe and well had been immediately followed by her disappearance on a more permanent basis. We had skirted around the topic on occasion, as we had once skirted around the gender of her partner; evidently she supposed I was not getting custody of my daughter until matters had been settled, including Kirsty's reason for disappearing on the day she was meant to be coming to stay with me.

Miss Havers was patient and tactful, prepared to wait for me to open up to her on the subject. I might have done, might have breached protocol and told her about the Common Land, as I had told my ex-wife, but for one thing. I was afraid I might discover that Miss Havers "remembered" that Kirsty was now a teenager, despite the fact that she had known well enough that Kirsty had only recently reached double figures.

Just before the train stopped at Haslemere the woman put her Rebus book in her bag and left, so I had the compartment to myself. I untensed, not realising how tense I'd got myself. Two more stations till Guildford. Then I would carry out the first of Douglas Lamb's instructions.

If he was a man of his word, I would have no further need of wishes once I reached my destination. Silly thoughts had passed through my mind - "I wish for a million pounds", "I wish to live forever", "I wish for unlimited wishes" - but Miah Proctor had warned me how steeply the price rose.

In point of fact I had asked Lamb about a second wish. During a short pause while he was painting my portrait, I'd said, "Speaking purely hypothetically, as a matter of interest, what would I have to do to get a second wish?" A fleeting smile crossed his face. It was not a pleasant smile; I guessed my question was one that everybody asked, and he'd been waiting for it. For a long time I didn't think he was going to answer. For a long time I thought he wasn't going to resume painting my portrait, and the deal was off. But then he got back to work. "The price is pretty much the same as for the first wish," he said. "You sit for another portrait. The difference is, the first portrait is before you have killed. The second one: After."

After Guildford I unlocked the out-of-service compartment with a skeleton key. I went in and locked the door behind me. This compartment differed to the others in that it was visibly old, both in style and (for want of a better word) agedness. It wasn't just visible either; it *smelled* old, the way only trains and buses can.

There was nothing remarkable about the compartment otherwise, except for one thing that had become commonplace to me by now. There was a communicating door that appeared to provide access to the compartment I had just vacated, although there was of course no corresponding door to be found there. To make room for this door, the seat, along with the overhead luggage rack, had been shortened to accommodate two passengers rather than the usual three.

I sat down on the short seat, feeling self-conscious about occupying the out-of-service compartment. The partition that separated it from the corridor was partly glass, and although the "Out Of Service" notice covered most of it, it was possible for a passenger or even a guard to peer in. I sat still, reasonably confident that it wouldn't happen, that this was one of the things the Common Land dealt with in its own way.

The rain was falling heavily now, and the morning sky had darkened. I was restless and fidgety, aware that every second that passed took me closer to Kirsty. I'd picked up a copy of *The Metro* before boarding the train at Portsmouth and Southsea Station, but I'd been unable to read it since entering the out-of-service compartment. I should have anticipated this, but I had not, perhaps not quite believing Douglas Lamb's instructions.

More than anything else, I was nervous about what I was going to *say* to Kirsty. She hadn't simply been aged, she had, as best I understood it, *lived* three years in the less than four months since I had last seen her. I'd seen close friendships end as if they had never been after less than a year apart; what was three years going to do to a father-daughter bond?

I took out the artificially aged picture of her and stared at it, imagining her in school uniform. What had three years in the Common Land done to her education? How much had she learned about the Common Land itself? Would that be our main common interest now? Did she know it somehow worked on trains too?

I thought of Kirsty coming home from school, in the years before Dawn and I split up. She would go upstairs to change out of her school uniform. She had her own TV in her bedroom. She would start watching it while she changed, and sometimes she would be so engrossed in what she was watching we would have to call her down for her evening meal.

My mother, who was of course still alive at the time, reminded me that I did the same when I was Kirsty's age. I smiled at the memory, and I almost - *almost* - remembered where I knew Miah Proctor from.

The train was pulling in at Worplesdon Station. (The name of the station always made Kirsty laugh.) The next of Lamb's instructions was coming up. A lot of passengers boarded so the train would be quite crowded now, but nobody even tried the door of my compartment. There was a short delay, then the sound of metal on metal which I suspected couldn't be heard by passengers in the other compartments. This was my cue; I could open the connecting door now.

I pulled it towards me. It was a double door arrangement, similar to the one I had seen with the portacabins in Chichester. I pushed the other door open.

"There will be people on the other side," Lamb had told me, "but they won't pay you any attention." So Lamb had a sense of humour. I'd expected another compartment, occupying the same space as the one I had shared with the Ian Rankin reader, but instead found myself in an undivided carriage without windows. Dim fluorescent lights came on, triggered by motion sensors.

There were coffins stacked everywhere.

*

Perhaps time passed more slowly because I couldn't see out, but the final stage of the journey, from Worplesdon Station to Waterloo, seemed much longer than usual. I sat on a bench listening to the clacking sound of the wheels, waving my arms from time to time whenever the lights went off. After a while I stopped doing this, content to sit in the dark among the dead.

Douglas Lamb had been very precise about when to enter the out-of-service compartment, and when to come through the communicating door. I guessed it was a matter of trains in different worlds moving into synch; it possibly involved coupling and decoupling carriages too. I thought about the times I had sat on a train waiting for it to start moving, delayed for no apparent reason. Or trains that left before they were even due to arrive. Were these events all part of the synchronisation? The idea intrigued me, but I didn't really believe it. It didn't take Occam to realise the unremarkable explanation was almost always the correct one.

If the routes did diverge, then it was presumably no longer possible to get back into the compartment. I tried the door; it had opened without resistance before, but now it was firmly shut.

I was confined to this carriage until we reached London Prime.

Chapter 29. City Limits

We had arrived.

The large doors that I had thought of as the carriage's walls slid open noisily, and mid-morning sunshine shone in unexpectedly. I was aware of a work gang outside, maybe a dozen men in hi-viz jackets waiting to unload the coffins. I waved a blue card that Lamb had given me; it appeared to be a pass of some sort, because the men stood aside.

There was no station platform. I climbed down from the carriage, holding onto a brass railing for guidance. Gravel crunched underfoot. The other sound I recognised was the idling of a steam engine, the one that had brought me from Worplesdon Station.

My emotions were heightened, and my eyes were taking an inordinate amount of time to adjust to the sunlight. I was walking on an overgrown lawn now, the unmaintained outskirts of an immense graveyard that seemed to stretch to infinity when I shaded my eyes to see it as a shining silhouette. Most of these nearby graves were old and dilapidated. Looking back, still with my eyes shaded, I could see that the train from which I had disembarked had stopped short of a huge old building. The railway continued on into the building through a huge archway. Another train occupied the space inside; it was the reason my train had stopped short.

I turned away and walked determinedly through the long grass. Behind me there was the sound of men unloading coffins.

This was outside the main part of the graveyard, but I felt the occasional gravestone that I likened to trees outside a forest. At length I came to the end of the waist-high grass.

The area beyond it had been better maintained, though not all that recently. I had arrived at a place of children's graves, and my instinct was to skirt around them, but I quickly realised this was out of the question. There were just too many.

I did not at first understand the reason for my acute discomfort. Was it fear? I doubted it; I wasn't expecting vampires or zombies to dig their way out of their graves. If anything, I was afraid of what I might see. I was relying more on touch than on sight to find my way between the graves, shading my eyes with a hand only when it was absolutely necessary to do so.

Still my eyes had not adjusted, and still my emotions were heightened. I was in London Prime, or on the outskirts at least. I thought of what Miah Proctor had told me: "You don't just stumble upon London Prime." I thought of Douglas Lamb's insanely complicated instructions to get here, and this set me off laughing hysterically. Laughing in a graveyard, and still dazzled. I continued to laugh until I bashed my ankle on a low stone cross, to which I responded by shrugging and saying aloud, "You can't miss them all."

It was the cuddly toys I could not cope with. Teddy bears, penguins, puffalumps, their sole purpose to be loved. Unloved, they mark the absence of the child. I thought of Kirsty playing with a tea set with her teddies, then imagined the teddies without her. Is that why bereaved parents put them on their children's graves, to make others share their pain?

I walked on, following my instincts. I walked for what seemed like hours, and may well have been; one of Lamb's instructions was that I was not to wear a watch or have any other means of telling time. I was not to carry a camera either. Even now my eyes had not fully adjusted to daylight, for all the world as if I had been confined to the darkness of the coffin carriage for days on end, although that clearly was not the case.

Something Lamb had said struck me then. He had used the word "visit": *you'll visit Kirsty on Saturday.* Why had he not said "see" or "meet"? This, together with his joke about the occupants of the carriage not paying me any attention, alarmed me. Was I going to visit Kirsty's grave?

I thought of the last time I had visited a grave, other than during a funeral. A few years before, when my parents were still alive, I had attended a stag party in Lyndhurst. While wandering through the village I noticed that a lot of shop windows displayed figures from the Lewis Carroll books. When I asked Dave the groom about this, he explained that Alice Liddell, the real-life inspiration for the main character in *Alice In Wonderland,* had lived here, and in fact was buried nearby. It being early evening, Zac the best man took us on a detour to visit her grave. It wasn't much of a detour - it was practically en route to the first of the pubs - but it took us up a sloping path to the graveyard outside the church of St Michael and All Angels.

Alice's grave was a small rectangular plot. It wasn't the most impressive grave; it wasn't elaborate, even by the standard of the rest of the graveyard. It wasn't maintained, and you had to look close to find her name.

Alice was iconic, immortal. She wasn't supposed to grow up to be an old lady; she wasn't supposed to die, and be buried in an obscure and unkempt grave. But she had. Looking at her scruffy resting place, I got quite tearful, even though we were a long way from the maudlin phase of the evening.

It was irrelevant, I told myself. I wasn't going to find Kirsty's grave, I was going to find Kirsty. We had a bond; if she was dead, I would know about it.

There was a tomb, with a stone angel. A figure sitting on the tomb. There were dots in my vision, but I was beginning to see clearly. The figure was a girl, no, a woman. Maybe twenty. My heart leapt into my mouth as I recognised her. No, *thought* I'd recognised her. I thought she was Dawn, my ex-wife. *What the hell is Dawn doing here in London Prime?* But she was too young, too slim to be Dawn.

I knew who she was. Fate was playing a trick on me. I wasn't going to react, I wasn't even going to act surprised. I wasn't going to give Fate that satisfaction.

"Kirsty," I said, accepting without question that my daughter was now twenty years old. At least.

She jumped down. "You came!" She ran into my arms and I hugged her tight. She was too big to be my daughter. But she was my daughter. I crushed her to me, she crushed me to her. "Daddy, it's been so long." Maybe the thought *Whose fault is that?* crossed my mind. Maybe I said it aloud, maybe I did not. Nothing was going to take anything away from this longed-for reunion. It was happening, I wasn't dreaming it, and it mattered to her as much as it mattered to me.

Eventually we had to let each other go. I held her shoulders at arms length. Without piling on the irony too much I said, "You've grown."

She laughed, a tinkling laugh that was new to me. "It happens." She added, "I've been through a lot since we last spoke. I'm not even sure where to begin."

*

I had barely scratched the surface of the Common Land. Kirsty had gone deep. Kirsty had been in history, and she had been in myth. I asked her what she meant by this; did she mean she had travelled in time? She grimaced at that, then assured me my question was not stupid, merely difficult to answer, which indicated to me that she was still a kind-hearted soul. She then added that it would be like a ten year old asking if higher calculus was like having to learn the thirteen times table.

She told me many things. Some I could understand, many I could not. She used analogies to make it easier, but sometimes these relied on unfamiliar terms or references. She had earned citizenship in London Prime - that was easy enough to understand - but this had had something to do with crossing the North Wilderness Tower, which meant nothing to me. Three or four times she shook her head apologetically, as if to say it would take too long to explain.

I thought of how it must have been for Dawn when I told her about my own experiences in the Common Land. Dawn didn't even read science fiction, so talk of parallel worlds must have been a hell of a conceptual leap for her. Now, listening to Kirsty, I had some inkling of how far short I had fallen from real understanding, despite the fact that she was really trying to help. The idea that the Common Land gave access to parallel worlds was a fiction, but a workable one, like the idea that atoms are tiny solar systems - a useful model when studying Physics and Chemistry for GCSE, but dangerously misleading beyond A-Level. Or as Kirsty put it, "The idea of a flat

Earth is perfectly reasonable if you never travel any farther than your nearest town."

Kirsty had certainly travelled.

She had taken care of Eloise for a time. The younger girl's sudden death had badly shocked her, not least because she could not account for it. It was then that she had broken her resolve and paid a visit to her home world.

"What resolve?" I asked, upset by the implication that she could have come home, but had chosen not to.

"When you travel as much as I have, you make enemies as well as friends," she explained. "Not always people, not always *tangible* even. But some I believed were following me, and I did not want them to find the people I love."

She had expected to find me at the Price Estate. She had honestly believed Dawn, her family and I would have joined forces in the wake of her disappearance. It was the one and only time that she came across as the naive one.

"Yasmin," she said, referring to my next-door-neighbours' child. "I didn't want her to see me, a teenager while she was still a child. I don't think she would have taken that well." Her brow furrowed; she started to say, "Even though..." then broke off, shaking her head once. I waited for her to finish saying whatever it was she had started. There was a short, uncomfortable silence. "Even though I had news that would have interested her."

I gave her a saddened look. Kirsty shrank back, aware that I had caught her in a lie; it was obvious that that was not what she'd been about to say. "What news?" I asked gently.

"I met someone. Someone special. Our paths crossed many times, once before I was in my teens, and sometimes after intervals of many months. He saved my life three times and I saved his twice."

"He?"

"His name is Andrew. We are an item now."

The expression that normally made me wince actually made me smile. Kirsty continued, "I would very much like it if you gave us your blessing."

Just like that. I vaguely remembered a song from the 1970s about a man who had to cram his entire life - education, relationships, mourning even - into a single day. "Do I get to meet this Andrew?"

"He will be here shortly." Kirsty glanced at her wrist - only to remember she wasn't wearing a watch. I wondered if this was a general directive, one that Douglas Lamb had merely passed on rather than instigated. She smiled, embarrassed. "I'm actually a bit limited on time. Here he is now."

With that, Andrew stepped into view. He was slim, quite tall, slightly wayward brown hair, and he wore a shirt and tie. He was diffident, but successfully overcame that; his handshake was firm, and he addressed me as Sir. He was, quite probably, the daughter's boyfriend every father hopes for. Perfect but for one detail.

He was barely seven years younger than me.

In the past few months I had performed acts of physical courage, and I had done shameful things. But on the day I saw my daughter aged a decade, I found it in myself to talk to her fiance in a friendly, slightly paternal manner, as if that were perfectly normal.

It occurred to me, but not until later, that it might have been difficult for him, too. For the sake of the love of his life, he had to make an impression with her mysterious unageing father. Maybe "unageing" wasn't quite the right word; the events since Kirsty's initial disappearance had taken their toll on me.

Andrew's parents had been high-fliers in London - that is to say, his mundane London. His mother was from Eastern Europe. They had gone skiing when she was four months pregnant with him and his twin sister, who now had a job as a model. Andrew himself had qualified as an architect, and had crossed paths one final time with Kirsty at the university where she got her maths degree.

Kirsty watched us talk, seemingly torn between delight at seeing Andrew and her father getting along famously, and concern about the passing time. There was so much she didn't know, and if there was ever a right time to tell her, it wasn't now: her real parentage, the death of Chloe Faulkner, the death of Cousin Martin. Other things. Maybe Kirsty and Andrew would have the relationship that Sarah and I would have had if events hadn't happened, if Dawn and William hadn't needed me for a cover story.

But then I too became aware of the shortness of time. My dazzled vision cleared. A gentle mist rolled between the graves in the vast graveyard. Not the mist of horror films, but morning mist. The sun was low now, but this was not sunset, this was a sunrise in reverse.

I took in my surroundings. We were on a hillside, overlooking the city. It was recognisably London, but there was an indefinable simplicity to it, as if it were a little less sprawling, a little more geometric. In fact it put me in mind of a fractal simulation of a tree, a cloud or a coastline; recognisable for what it was meant to be, while at the same time unmistakably not that thing. I quickly located St Paul's Cathedral, but there was no Gherkin, no London Eye and no Telecom Tower.

By some unspoken agreement the three of us began walking down the hill, still conversing, but with a sense of an ending. I was waking up. I was physically here, on the outskirts of London Prime, but I was also dreaming, and I knew the dream would end soon. I was suddenly aware of railings, at least four metres high, that appeared to surround the entire city. There were gates in various parts of this perimeter fence, ranging from the person-sized one to which we were heading to a giant pair that controlled entrance and egress via the Thames itself, standing proud of the river surface and do doubt reaching down to the river bed. Other people, dressed in suits and elegant dresses, were making their way to the gate, maybe a dozen or two.

One I recognised.

*

Although I had not been asleep, I awoke on a train heading back to Portsmouth. I was alone in a compartment not unlike the one I had been in earlier (later?) that day. The aforementioned unmistakable smell of old railway carriage. I was coming out of a dream within a dream.

Nevertheless, that which had happened had happened.

I'd recognised an old school friend on his way to the gate. Chris Lawrence was his name. We'd been close in childhood, often staying at each other's homes. He outperformed me in every school subject I cared about. He literally left me behind in cross-country runs. He got himself a girlfriend when I was too shy to talk to girls. We lost touch when we left school but I did hear he'd got a first in a science subject at Oxford or Cambridge.

Later in life I reminded myself that he'd introduced me to some truly great authors, bands and video games, helped me with my physics homework, defended me against some bullies, had been sympathetic when my first girlfriend dumped me, and all the other things that mattered at the time. But the taint of envy remained. I recognised it was my own problem, one I should grow out of in time.

He recognised me. He looked somewhat younger than I would have expected, which may or may not have been because of the way time works in the Common Land. He made no attempt to conceal his surprise at seeing me there. He addressed me by name, and asked if I was going in too. I didn't know, and then I realised that not knowing meant no.

Andrew was shaking my hand, and then Kirsty was hugging me, crying without restraint and telling me she loved me. I thought again of the things she didn't know about, and I thought of the time I had prayed for her to die. And I wondered if that was the reason I would not be going through the gate.

Chris Lawrence was gone; he was briefly visible on the other side of the railings, then out of sight. Gently, Andrew touched Kirsty on her left shoulder, gesturing for her to let go of me and reminding her that time was very short now. Reluctantly she complied. The pair walked the remaining distance to the gate. Kirsty, still weeping, turned three or four times to wave another farewell. I could have run, I could have overtaken them, I could have forced my way in. But I made no attempt.

The thing that was killing me was what had not been said. There had been no exchange of phone numbers or email addresses or rendezvous points, no promises to keep in touch, not even the well-meant but ultimately empty parting words, "Don't be a stranger."

Douglas Lamb's instructions for getting home were as convoluted as those for getting to London Prime in the first place, so I needed to keep my wits about me. But for most of the return journey, the thing that occupied my mind was the sound and image of the gate slamming shut. And after that, the impression that might have been imagination but which I was sure was not: the impression that the streets of London Prime had been paved with gold.

But the closing of the gate had been just that: closure, symbolic and literal. My quest was over and it was time to move on.

Part 4. The Narrow Folk

"They can't cross silver when the moon is up."

Chapter 30. Even Though

Southsea, April 2006

People talk of different kinds of silence. Sometimes they are trying to be funny, sometimes they think they are being profound, but there is undoubtedly truth in the observation. There's the silence in the classroom when the pupils know the teacher means business, church silence, the comfortable silence between old friends on a journey, the embarrassing silence when a joke or anecdote fails, the "you're in trouble" silence, the silence of a walk in the country or praying at a funeral or inside an anechoic chamber or underwater or in space or in hiding.

I had never known a silence like the one I was experiencing now. Would it have been better if I'd lied to Dawn, told her I'd found Kirsty's grave? I honestly didn't know.

Dawn broke the silence with a word: "Why?"

I shook my head, not knowing how to answer, not knowing which of several *why* questions she was asking, although there was one I was sure she was not asking: "Why didn't you know how to tell me this?"

Perhaps, after last time, she was asking why I'd doctored a picture of Kirsty to look twenty. I hadn't. But this put me in mind of Douglas Lamb and his prolific artwork. Did the creation of images really cause events to come to pass? Maybe, but events come to pass anyway. People have heart attacks without voodoo priests thrusting needles into dolls' chests.

"Why what?" I asked at last.

She shook her head. "Nothing."

She went to bed. I remained downstairs, the TV on with the volume low, and got up to date on my schoolwork. It was marking, mostly, and mostly Maths, which was less time-consuming than History as answers were either right or wrong.

It occurred to me that Dawn had not asked about London Prime. Or perhaps her question was why I had said it was a graveyard. My description was more or less true, depending on whether you considered the outskirts to be part of the city, but I had to admit I had intentionally misled her.

If Dawn had asked me about London Prime I would have told her it was the true heart of England, and the graves had been for the many, many people who had fallen in its service. Kirsty, having lived more than half her life in the Common Land, had grown beyond being able to come home, although I did not understand why.

I could sense that Dawn was sleeping fitfully, if she slept at all. I left my bedroom door open when I went upstairs for my rest. I hadn't been in the bed for weeks, but I'd rested my head on the pillow; now, the pillowcase was overdue for a wash. I turned the pillow over.

Dawn wasn't snoring. That was another kind of silence. Outside, I was aware of a car driving past very slowly, which at three in the morning was sufficiently unusual to make me mildly curious. No doubt the teenage son of my neighbour three doors along on his way back from a party, although last I'd heard he was between cars. Looking out the front window, I saw a Hyundai, stopped but not yet parked, further away from my neighbour's house than it needed to be. Evidently the driver thought so too because the car suddenly reversed, and finally stopped, still not quite in the logical parking place. I had no doubt he was well over the limit. I watched for a few moments, but he did not get out. I wondered if he was delaying, preparing himself for an earblasting from his parents, or simply willing the contents of his stomach to stay down.

Dawn had come into the room behind me. I turned at her approach.

"I couldn't sleep," she said redundantly. "I get that you don't either. So."

"So," I echoed.

"What did Kirsty mean by 'even though'?"

I sat down on my bed. "I don't know, Dawn. I told you, she broke off and then evaded the question."

"Yes, I get that. But what do you *think* she meant?"

"Seriously? You want me to read meaning into two words? You do understand I may have been paraphrasing?"

"She must have meant something. Otherwise, why say it?" A beat. "You weren't paraphrasing."

I did not reply. She went over to the window, ostensibly to see what I'd been looking at, but I knew it was to hide her tears. After a time I got up and joined her at the window. The Hyundai was still there but as far as I could tell the driver had still not got out.

"Come on, Dawn," I said. She turned to let me see the silently-falling tears on her face. She submitted to a hug, but neither of us prolonged it. We moved away from the window and sat apart on the bed.

"The world will forget about her," she said between now-audible sobs.

I nodded agreement. "It won't be a complete forgetting. She'll come up in conversation from time to time. Now and then people will remember that you and I had a daughter, but they'll assume she's with the other one of us. There will be no mystery, no curiosity."

"In some ways that's worse."

"Yes, it is."

"I won't forget about her. I'm her mother."

"I won't forget about her either."

"I'm sorry, I wasn't implying... you know."

"I know. It's okay."

There was a long pause between us, a silence broken by the sound of smashing glass. I leapt up, realising at once that someone had just put a brick through my car window. I got to the window in time to see the driver door of the Hyundai closing. The car pulled away at speed and was quickly out of sight.

“What the hell?” A moment later I was downstairs and out the front door. My car windscreen was cobwebbed with a hole in the middle. There was a brick on the passenger’s seat. One of my neighbours - not the one with the teenage son - was having some building work done. Evidently that was where the brick had been taken from.

“Is there a message with the brick?” Dawn asked.

“Is there *what*?” I answered impatiently. “What do you think this is, Robin fucking Hood? Of course there isn’t a message with it. The brick *is* the message.”

“Who do you think it’s from?”

“Who do *you* think it’s from? It’s from your cretinous brother. Probably saw us at the window.”

“He drives a Mercedes, not a... whatever that car was.”

“Oh right. Because he couldn’t rent a Hyundai. Or more likely nick it, knowing him. He’s hardly going to risk his Mercedes being seen on CCTV, is he? Even William’s not that stupid!”

“Keep it down a bit, Phil. You don’t want to upset your neighbours.”

She had a point. It was gone three in the morning and lights were coming on in people’s windows. Angrily, I went back into my house. I’d failed to note the car’s registration, and the colour wasn’t distinguishable in street lighting.

Eventually I found a bin bag to cover the hole in the windscreen, and held it in place with duct tape. When the garage up the road opened I would see if they did replacement windscreens. Another needless expense. God, I hated Dawn’s family. I felt like sending Dawn home, but didn’t think there would be taxis running at this hour. I would have driven her home myself if the bin bag had been transparent.

My temper gradually settled. I suggested coffee. Dawn shrugged and said, “It’s not like it’s going to keep me awake, is it? Or you.”

I said, "What about your epilepsy? Aren't you supposed to get a certain number of hours sleep?"

Dawn shrugged again. "It's not like I turn down sleep when it comes looking."

So I made us coffee and we went into the lounge.

Dawn sipped her coffee. Her face contorted in what I was surprised to realise was pleasure. "You always made good coffee, Phil. Look, I've been thinking. You've told me time works differently in the Common Land. What if you could find Kirsty *before* she gets older? Bring her home while she's still ten?"

I shook my head vehemently. "What's happened has happened. She's not a little girl any more. I can't change that any more than... well, any more than anybody can. If I tried... well, at best I would simply fail. The worst doesn't bear thinking about."

"But it might not *be* changing! When I saw her at age thirteen, it was an older Kirsty who had somehow come back from three years in the future. When you saw her you were seeing a Kirsty from ten years in the future."

"Yeah, but that's just a way of looking at it. Marking points on a timeline. What difference does it make?"

"These things can still happen! Sure, she can be travelling in the Common Land when she's thirteen, but in the time before that, the ten year old version can come home. We will know some of her future, we'll know she'll disappear for a time when she's thirteen, and we'll know she'll always be safe at least until she's twenty."

"Why would you even think that's possible? Dawn, we're talking about *time travel* here."

"When Kirsty said 'even though' to you, I think she was going to tell you that she did come home. I think she was going to say she'd met up with Yasmin after her disappearance but while she was still ten. I think what I want to happen has already happened from Kirsty's point of view. So it's not changing anything."

"No, Dawn. Just... *no.*"

"Why not, Phil? Give me one good reason."

"Look, Dawn, I know the Common Land goes against everything we thought was true, but that doesn't mean everything is equally possible."

"Show me the flaw. You've always told me if it's not logical it's not true. So what's the flaw in my reasoning?"

And the truth is, I couldn't see one. Not immediately. But my gut told me, *No!* The Common Land couldn't be manipulated that way. Or if it could, it would require far more understanding of it than I currently had. Most of my search for Kirsty had been aimless and dangerous, and I had only succeeded - insofar as it could be called a success at all - as a result of luck and meeting the right people. To suddenly raise the game and find an earlier version of Kirsty - that was asking the impossible.

But Dawn *was* asking the impossible. "Find my daughter, Phil. Find her while she's still a child and bring her home."

*

As I dropped Dawn off at the train station in the middle of the afternoon, it occurred to me that she'd done it again. "Find my daughter, Phil." But the thing that most concerned me this time was not jealousy, or resentment at being reminded that Kirsty was not my biological daughter (although these things were all part of it too). It was the thought of my little girl living in a household with William. He'd got his own sister pregnant, he'd done time for racially motivated assault, he'd beaten me up and he'd vandalised my car. And those were just the things I knew about. Assuming I did manage to find ten-year-old Kirsty, how safe was she going to be from him? How safe had she *been*? Maybe taking her chances in the Common Land had been a more inviting prospect than living in the Price Estate.

I had to accept things the way they were. Kirsty was an adult now. She was happy, a decent man cared for her, and she had earned citizenship in London Prime. I missed her terribly but that was to be expected.

Meanwhile I would go about my mundane life. It was raining, but the windscreen wipers didn't leave a smear on the replacement windscreen the way they had with the old one. I just had one more week to get through until the Easter holiday. Then I might start looking for another job. I no longer had any reason to walk the Common Land, so in time I would need sleep again. Among other things I was sick of the workload that came with teaching, the quickness to blame and the slowness of praise, if it ever arrived at all, and the lack of support. I just wanted a job with a regular salary and a work-life balance. Size of salary wasn't so important, now that I wasn't paying maintenance for Kirsty. I had no reason to see Dawn again, so William would have no cause to "punish" me for having her at my house.

I'd been divorced for over two years, but only now did I finally feel free.

But God, I missed Kirsty.

*

I bought a new pillowcase and went to bed that Saturday night. I didn't sleep, I didn't even have insomnia dreams, but getting back into normal habits seemed the right thing to do. *Be patient,* I told myself.

The week went by smoothly. Nearly everybody, staff and pupil alike, was in good humour. I even got quality work out of some of the more difficult boys.

I still didn't sleep.

Friday was half day. There was lunch laid on for all staff members at a restaurant owned by the partner of one of the teachers. Much alcohol flowed, although I drank in moderation. After lunch, a space was cleared to be used as a dance area, and a hired DJ was set up in a corner where he played mostly 70s and 80s hits. People danced, and alcohol continued to flow. School secretary Kerry Marshall, who was straight and known to be somewhat homophobic, got very drunk by early afternoon; by four o'clock she was snogging Miss Havers.

Not counting Cousin Martin's funeral, it was the first social gathering of any kind that I had attended in months. I liked being at ease with people. This was normality, and it took a long absence from it to really appreciate it. Maybe the people around me weren't going to be my colleagues for much longer, and maybe I'd gradually lose touch with all of them, even Miss Havers, but all that was a matter for the future. For now, I would *enjoy* the now.

I felt a twinge - more than a twinge if the truth be told - in the heart at the thought that I would never hear from my not-so-little girl ever again. I sat down at an unoccupied table and checked the wine bottles to see if any of them had anything left in them. A minute or so later Miss Havers sat down beside me.

"I don't know which of us is going to be the more embarrassed next term," she said, indicating Kerry Marshall who was staggering off to find the toilets.

"That's assuming she even remembers," I said. "Everyone else will, though." I glanced behind Miss Havers towards the entrance of the restaurant, smiled, and in a tone of pleasant surprise said, "Why, Laura! I didn't know you were coming!"

With an expression of guilty shock, Miss Havers turned. Laura was not there, of course. Miss Havers punched me lightly in the chest and said, "I've never liked you, Mr Hamilton."

"Some days you're just too easy," I said. The banter hadn't been this relaxed since the day Kirsty vanished. (It kept coming back to Kirsty. It always came back to Kirsty.)

The DJ played *Sailing* by Rod Stewart. The restaurant owner had set up a karaoke system, so one of the teachers was singing along, doing a bad imitation of Stewart's gravelly voice. Miss Havers started telling me about a time her father had taken her sailing in Langstone Harbour when she was ten or eleven. She would have enjoyed it, she explained, except for having to keep dodging the pole thing that swept across the floor of the boat. That, and having to remember all the boaty names for everything.

I would never get to take Kirsty sailing. I wouldn't get to take her to archery club when she turned eleven, because her turning eleven was something that had happened a long time ago.

"Are you even listening to me?" Miss Havers asked.

"The boom."

"What?"

"It's the proper name for the so-called 'pole thing' that sweeps across the deck. Incidentally, nobody, but *nobody*, calls the deck the floor."

"Whatever." She resumed, and her story segued to a time she'd gone fishing with her school, how she'd been the first to bait a hook despite her reputed squeamishness, whereas Dominic, a boy who'd always given her a hard time, managed to catch his hook between the webbing of the thumb and index finger of his left hand. Miss Havers had then said, "What's the matter, Dominic? We all had you down as a *master* baiter!"

Then again, what if Dawn was right? Adult Kirsty was in the future. The child version still existed somewhere, somewhere accessible in the Common Land. Maybe I could still find her; maybe I was *meant* to find her. Perhaps my part in her later upbringing had helped her earn citizenship of London Prime. Maybe one day I might even earn it myself.

No, this was stupid. The Common Land was vast, and I'd nearly burnt myself out before in my fruitless random searches. Why would it be any different this time?

But it was different. I understood the Common Land much better than I had. Before, I'd merely had blind faith that Kirsty was alive; now, I knew it for a fact. Come what may, she would be hale and whole for at least the next ten years.

I also knew where to go if I wanted a second wish granted.

I hadn't been through a doorway in nearly two weeks, yet I still hadn't started sleeping again. Why would that be unless I was *meant* to return to the Common Land?

Kerry Marshall was back from the toilet. She sat at a vacant table looking the worse for wear, pretending not to see Miss Havers' friendly, flirty wave. Terry the Religious Studies teacher sat down beside her and handed her a mug of coffee.

"Mr Hamilton, you haven't listened to a word I just said!" Miss Havers barked.

"Yes I have," I insisted. "Hook had to go right through and out the other side because of the barb. Everybody laughed at your erudite pun."

She gave me *the look* over her glasses. "A lucky guess," she eventually said.

Kerry was nuzzling Terry's neck now. Terry was gently pushing her away. He kept metaphorical notches on his bedpost, but not when the woman was drunk, and definitely not the school secretary. At least not this one.

The afternoon was wearing on, and soon the restaurant would be opening for the evening shift, so we needed to clear out. Someone suggested a pub, another suggested their flat. Everyone headed out. I went with them.

Tomorrow I would update my CV and send it out to agencies. This evening I was planning on enjoying myself. This was the real world, the mundane world. This was where I lived. No matter how much I missed Kirsty, and no matter how great the temptation, I would not be going back into the Common Land. The bird had flown the nest and I needed to get on with my life.

Chapter 31. Just Theresa

Douglas Lamb was not at home. I'd announced my presence from the top of the loft ladder but there was no reply. It felt uncomfortable, walking in without invitation, but knocking on a loft hatch doesn't really work.

Seven of the televisions were on, showing the usual random selection of silent programmes. One showed heart surgery being performed on a conscious patient - I hoped it was just a horror film. Another showed a succession of views of roofs, mostly of terrace houses. In each shot, birds were crowded on a single roof, as if it was the only warm house in the street and all the others were abandoned.

Overhead, the skylight dome provided a view of bright nebulae in deep space. It was animated, giving the impression that I was inside a spaceship drifting slowly through the universe.

The mace, consisting of heavy-duty welded-together TV remotes, lay on the sofa. Curious, I picked it up, cutting a finger on one of the sharp edges. It was as heavy as I'd expected. I turned it over in my hands. I recalled a Swiss army knife I had once owned - actually an imitation one I had bought on holiday - which didn't close properly, and on several occasions I had cut myself when I'd thrust a hand into the pocket that held it. But there was a safe way of holding the mace. Several ways in fact. I'd seen Douglas Lamb throw it, spinning, into the air, and catch it as it fell.

"What do you want?" The voice startled me. It was not Lamb; it was not male at all, and it certainly wasn't friendly. I realised I had pressed one of the buttons on the mace and turned a television on. Sound too.

"I-" I began, then recognised the face that almost filled the TV screen; I'd seen it in Lamb's portraits. "Laura Theresa?" I said in surprise.

She grimaced. "Just Theresa. I asked you what you want."

"Nothing, I... I must have activated a connection or something." Evidently this was a two-way closed circuit arrangement; I noticed a tiny camera located above the active screen.

"You're at Lamb's place. What are you doing there?"

"I came to see him."

"He's not there, is he?" She sounded like a teacher dismissing an unconvincing explanation. I suddenly sensed that she had someone in the room with her. A child, mentally handicapped, making noises it could not control. Outside the field of view, but almost certainly a girl.

"I didn't know that," I said. "I came on the off-chance."

"Enough with the evasion." She jerked sideways, as if the unseen girl had tugged at her. She turned to her left, raised her right hand and said, "I'm warning you." To me she said, "What are you doing at Lamb's place?"

"I came to see him," I repeated.

"Enough with the fucking evasions!" The unseen child whimpered more loudly in response to Theresa's raised voice. "And you shut the fuck up too!"

I considered looking for an off switch on the mace, a red button that would shut off this unpleasant, abusive woman. There were in fact several red buttons, but it wasn't obvious which did what.

"Well?" she said.

"I wanted to thank him. He did me a favour."

"Nobody thanks Douglas Lamb."

I was getting fed up with this unprovoked confrontation. "Yeah, well maybe you don't."

Her eyes blazed at that. "Oh yes? And what the fuck would *you* know about it?" She jerked again, raised a hand again to slap the unseen child who had tugged at her again, then thought better of it, maybe because I was watching. "Nobody *just* thanks Douglas Lamb.

Nobody comes back and says, 'Thank you so much, Mr Lamb,' and then goes on their way. Nobody."

I said nothing.

"What's your name?" Theresa asked.

"Philip Hamilton."

"Philip Hamilton? You're the one whose girl went missing? Kirsty, wasn't it?"

"Yes."

"Okay." She nodded once, as if this fact somehow changed things. "Can you..." she broke off as the girl with her let out a howl. When this stopped Theresa held a printed sheet up so it filled the screen. "Can you read this?"

The words were large enough to read, but they formed and swam as I tried to concentrate on any one of them: Carpet, crave, instil, flier, negation. "No," I said. "No, I can't."

"What about this?" She held up a sheet of what I recognised as her handwriting. "Quaint coffee shop off Campbell Square. Take doorway beside kitchen. Follow corridor. Brown door after low ducting." There was also a simple sketch that gave some indication of which route to take from Lamb's residence to get to Campbell Square.

"Yes, I can read it when it's your handwriting."

"Good. You need to get over here. You need to see what I'm going to show you. I'm not showing you over a TV screen, it's got to be live. Don't commit yourself to *anything* until you've seen it."

She leaned forward and the TV went off.

*

Whatever impression I'd built up of Laura Theresa (as I had thought of her) in the last few months, the reality had proven altogether different. She was undoubtedly beautiful - or rather, to use an expression Miss Havers had taught me, she had a beautiful resting face. Her manner towards me and her readiness to slap a mentally handicapped child made her seem thoroughly unpleasant. I wondered if there was an equivalent of Social Services in the Common Land.

Of course, it was possible that she'd simply had a bad day and I was seeing her at her very worst. I had no idea how I would have coped with a handicapped child; I recalled the fear when Kirsty contracted meningitis.

I needed to see Theresa. I needed answers. Clearly, when she talked about committing myself, she meant in relation to Douglas Lamb. If Lamb could grant wishes (and he clearly could) then he was powerful. He appeared to be something like a cross between Don Corleone and the Wizard of Oz. So what was he doing living in a loft that was open house to any passing traveller? Was it more in the nature of a shop floor, or a reception area, rather than his residence? Could he monitor and somehow control his realm through his banks of televisions? Was he answerable to someone?

Was he answerable to Theresa herself?

The sensible thing was not to go and see her. The sensible thing was to go home, and stick with the resolution I had made at the end-of-term party. I'd gone to bed that night, and I could swear I'd felt sleep coming on. It hadn't arrived, but it had been a close thing. If I'd given it one more night...

Still undecided on my course of action, I made for the loft hatch exit. Before I reached it I heard footsteps on the ladder, and a few moments later Douglas Lamb himself appeared. I must have reeked of nonspecific guilt; I'd been using his equipment to talk to the woman I knew he was obsessed with. I thrust my right hand into my pocket, remembering I had wrapped a white handkerchief around the cut on my index finger. Had Lamb noticed? Probably, just as he was probably going to notice the traces of blood on the mace.

"Hamilton," he said. "I can't say I'm altogether surprised." He had reached the top of the ladder and was walking towards his sofa as he talked. "How did it go with your daughter? Did you see her?" His interest seemed genuine enough.

"I saw her, yes," I replied. "It didn't go quite as expected."

He raised a quizzical eyebrow. "No?"

"I got there a few years too late, you could say. She'd aged a decade since I last saw her."

"Ah, that is unfortunate. Very unfortunate indeed. A question of synchronisation, I would think." He seemed to be thinking aloud rather than explaining to me. "I kept my side of the bargain; nevertheless I prefer transactions to result in satisfaction on both sides."

"What do you mean by synchronisation?" I asked. I had a feeling I partially understood already.

"You don't suppose she was waiting for you all this time, do you? She will have gone to the meeting place maybe once a year, probably the same date each year from her point of view. Some years she might not have kept the appointment for one reason or another. From my side of things, it was a matter of arranging a route to London Prime; the lines converge when you get close to the city so timing isn't an altogether strict matter. Does that make sense?"

I nodded, more in recognition that another explanation from him wasn't going to make any more sense.

"It's akin to the coincidental meetings that happen in dreams," I suggested.

"Exactly right!" Lamb said.

"So where does that leave me?" I asked.

"In what sense?"

"I mean, can I meet my daughter while she is still a child? Or would that be some sort of," I waved my hands vaguely, "violation of causality?"

"You're asking for a second wish?"

I shook my head. "Not yet, no." Not without seeing what Theresa had to show me. "I'm just wanting to know what's possible at this stage."

"Do I need to remind you of the price?"

That brought me up short. "No, not at all, I'm speaking hypothetically."

"Hypotheticals also take up time, Mr Hamilton. My time is not free."

"Sorry, perhaps I could come back later."

Lamb waved a magnanimous hand. "It's an important decision. Take all the time you need."

I nodded my thanks and made to leave. Then I hesitated. I would waste weeks in indecision, knowing that as long as there remained a possibility I would be unable to let it go. Even if it meant killing.

I'll make no secret of the fact; I'd given it a lot of thought. The price of the second wish was that I kill. It had to be a deliberate act with immediate results. Lamb hadn't been specific, but he undoubtedly meant a human being; the slitherman I had gunned down did not count.

On the other hand there was no reason it couldn't be self-defence. Pre-emptive self-defence. I turned back to Lamb.

"How about we make it not hypothetical?"

"Do you have someone in mind?" Lamb asked.

I nodded. "Yes, I have someone in mind."

Chapter 32. What The Shower Scene Meant

There was no going back after that interview. I was committed.

We had talked for nearly two hours. Lamb wanted to know everything. I talked about my feelings towards William Price. Did I hate him? Yes, but more in principle than as an emotion. Was I scared of him? Definitely - smashing my car windscreen might have been a warning to stay away from Dawn, or it might have been a promise of more random violence to come, regardless of what I did. He had, after all, told me it wasn't over after he'd beaten me up. What effect had William Price's incestuous act and subsequent lies had on my life? I wasn't sure where to start with that one. I talked of an alternate timeline, what I thought of as the original one, in which I was now celebrating my tenth wedding anniversary with Sarah Compton, and Dawn was merely the last entry in a fairly short list of past girlfriends.

As for the real timeline, the fact that William Price had jerked the carpet out from under me by taking away my role of father on the very day that Kirsty disappeared... *That* was what I would focus my hatred on.

Lamb wanted to know everything about the incest, why Benjamin Price and their mother had not intervened, where it had taken place, had there been blood, and much else that I could only conjecture. It occurred to me partway through the questioning that there was no lurid curiosity involved, it was as if the information was somehow of practical use to Lamb. This made me uneasy. He went on to ask if I thought William's dislike of me from the beginning was a straightforward matter of jealousy, and whether I should have been more understanding towards him. This last point struck me as more of a provocation than a real question, so I made no attempt to answer.

Finally Lamb asked for a picture of William. I told him I had none to hand, but should be able to get hold of archive pictures from *The Chichester Observer*. This was not what he meant, however. He was wanting a picture based on my impressions. In other words, a photo-fit.

We worked together for maybe an hour on the photo-fit. Even from my vague descriptions he was able to capture the man's likeness.

He then asked me to frame my wish. I said, "I want to find my daughter while she is still a child." Remembering the words Dawn had used, and how they had stung me, I made a point of saying "my daughter". I was confident that Lamb would not quibble over the fact that Kirsty was not my biological daughter; he knew well enough what I meant.

I left Lamb's studio with two thoughts uppermost in my mind.

I was going to be reunited with Kirsty for real this time.

And before many days passed I was going to have blood on my hands.

*

I found the quaint coffee shop off Campbell Square. Miah Proctor was inside, settling her bill. She had her back to me; I recognised her partly because she was wearing another of her 1920s style hats - and I slipped past her unseen. If she had seen me she would probably have guessed I was on my way to see Theresa, and no doubt would have guessed why.

I found the brown door after the low ducting. I pushed it open and walked into a windowless bedsit. I announced my presence but there was no reply. A door by the bed was partway open and from beyond it came the sound of a shower.

I went into the kitchen part. On the wooden table was an old-fashioned portable TV that reminded me of the one I had seen in the room off the corridor in Guildford. It had a webcam on top but no keyboard; it was doubtless the means by which Theresa had contacted me. There were dirty coffee cups and plates on the table and in the sink, some chipped.

At the other end of the room was a double bed with an undersheet and pillows but no covers. Beds seemed incongruous in the Common Land; not for the first time I wondered what would happen if you tried to sleep on one, and again remembered the obese sleeping man trapped in the bedroom in the House of Shards. Did he dream within the dream? Was there some kind of underland, as real as the Common Land?

There was a pile of clothes on the bed, and another on the floor. Two identical sleeveless yellow dresses caught my eye. Picking one up, I noticed there was a clasp on one of the shoulder straps but not the other. There was a similar shoulder clasp arrangement with a brassiere.

I was uncomfortable. For all that I was here by invitation, I felt I was intruding on my hostess's privacy. Theresa would be coming out of the shower any minute now; what if she didn't realise I was there?

I called through the doorway, "It's Philip Hamilton here. I can call back later."

"Come on through," Theresa's voice replied. Her accent was slightly similar to Dawn's.

"Are you sure? As I say, I can..."

"I said come on through!"

It occurred to me that the pile of clothes didn't mean she was naked. Maybe she was cleaning the bath. Or perhaps she was washing the child.

I pulled the door open and went in. I stepped on tile; I was in a wetroom. Billowing steam reduced visibility, but did not conceal the fact that Theresa was indeed naked under one of several shower heads at the far end of the room.

Theresa was not at all embarrassed by my presence. She was not alone either. She was in a sideways embrace with another woman. She was running a soapy hand up the other woman's body, passing over her right breast.

I was speechless for several moments.

"Seriously?" I said when I got my voice back. "This is what you called me over to see?" I wondered what the hell was the point of this performance. Was it intended to shock or embarrass me? Or even arouse me?

"What do you think you *are* seeing?" Theresa demanded, and as I looked through the shifting gaps in the steam I realised there was a lot more going on than I'd supposed.

The other woman was *also* Theresa. Her expression had a vacant look, but it was the same face for all that. The original Theresa was not fondling her, she was *washing* her. And they weren't in a sideways embrace.

They were conjoined.

Theresa's left arm ended a little above the elbow. The other woman had a right arm that ended just below the elbow. As if each had undergone amputation, not quite symmetrically and not quite perpendicularly, and the raw stumps had been brought together. *Welded* together. I didn't need to be told they had not been born like this, and even before Theresa spoke again I knew who had done it.

"You think I should be *thanking* Lamb for *this*?" she demanded.

"Laura Theresa," I said, looking from one to the other. The Laura sister responded with an inarticulate series of noises, but I had already worked out that she was the one I had thought was a child. "You didn't keep your part of a bargain," I said. I didn't mean it to sound judgemental, I just wanted Theresa to know I understood.

Theresa abruptly shut off the water flow and marched over to a towel rail. Her motion caught Laura by surprise, causing her to stumble and whimper as she hurried after her twin. They left the wetroom.

I stayed behind for a few minutes to give them time to dry off and dress. This felt back to front, given that I had begun by seeing them naked, but I was in no hurry to follow them into the main part of the bedsit. I could hear them through the open doorway; Theresa telling Laura, "Put this on!" Laura responding with anguished noises. Theresa repeated, "Put this *on*!" and there followed the sound of a slap. Laura howled; I cringed. The purpose of this display was clearly to disturb me, to dispel any thoughts I might entertain of reneging on any deal with Lamb. To dispel any thoughts that I might not kill William Price.

So there it was, I was a murderer. Without having raised a hand in violence, without having planned the killing even, I was a murderer.

Perhaps if I had not delayed when Laura Theresa invited me over, and they'd played out the shower scene then, I might not have made the commitment.

Laura Theresa looked elegant in burgundy dresses, the red handprint on Laura's face notwithstanding. The dresses had sleeves; I guessed they used velcro on the shared arm. I wanted to leave but was at a loss as to what to say in parting. I think I mumbled something to the effect of, "I appreciate what you have done for me." Then for no reason I could think of, Laura stepped forward (this time taking Theresa by surprise) and took me in a one armed embrace, to which I submitted. Realising it was expected of me, I kissed her on both eyes. The embrace might have gone on longer but Theresa barked, "Alright, that's enough," and jerked her away from me.

*

Heading home on the late evening train I was alone in the carriage except for a middle-aged woman in a brown coat. After what I had seen that day, I could not shake off the impression that her reflection in the window was her twin. I thought about moving to a seat where I could not see her, but didn't in the end, partly because I was tired and partly because it seemed foolish.

I had a killing to plan.

I would of course be making use of the Common Land. I had no illusions about the difficulties of getting away with murder, and I would certainly be a suspect, but William had made other enemies, and if all went to plan there would be no corpse for the police to find.

I considered trapping William in a room with slithermen, but quickly ruled that out. I had to kill him directly, not merely cause his death, and I had to be sure he *was* dead afterwards. I had a sickening image of opening the door to the room after what seemed like a reasonable wait, and William, enraged and covered in cold burns, coming out at me and grabbing me by the throat.

The train stopped at a station. I looked out of the window and recognised it as Guildford. I looked back across the aisle and saw that the woman in the brown coat was gone, but her reflection in the window was still there. I almost cried out before I realised there was a simple explanation - we'd stopped alongside another train, and I was looking at a woman in a similar coat on the other train.

There would be no question of anybody dying besides William. I was not a psychopath or a callous pragmatist. If anybody else got in the line of fire, I would not pull the trigger. I would not kill witnesses to silence them, not even if that meant getting convicted in my own world, although I sincerely hoped it would not come to that.

If I were a psychopath, I told myself, I would not be considering these things. And, sophistry aside, it really was for the best. If Lamb kept his side of the deal, young Kirsty was coming home. She would want to see her mother, so she would be spending time at the Price Estate. In which case there was no question of allowing William to be around. A man who forces himself on his sister can never be trusted with children. Granted, Kirsty had never given any hint that her uncle was guilty of inappropriate behaviour, which suggested William wasn't a paedophile at least. But Kirsty was approaching puberty, and William might consider that the beginning of adulthood, the point at which she became fair game. It would be a crime to put her at risk.

Kirsty was approaching puberty... This was difficult to get my head around. In another location she was in her twenties and getting married. That wasn't going to change. I tried to think of the encounter outside London Prime as a scene from near the end of a film that I'd seen in a preview; I was still near the beginning of the film.

Once I had Kirsty back, there would be no more wishes, no more killing, no more Common Land, no more insomnia. I really meant it this time.

Eventually the train pulled in at Portsmouth and Southsea Station. I couldn't remember where I had put my ticket so I thrust both hands into my coat pockets, and was surprised to find a small book in the one on my right. I took it out. It was a leather-bound notebook, very old fashioned and, I would have guessed, decades old. I cracked it open; the pages were filled with tiny handwriting, done in fountain pen. There were numerous pencilled drawings. Douglas Lamb's name was on the front page.

Deeper down in my pocket was a yellow USB stick. I didn't find it until later as it was caught in a hole in the lining.

Chapter 33. Stolen Property

In Portsmouth I entered the corridor of lockers and stowed my gun in locker number 7, as usual. I considered stowing the notebook there too, but decided against it. In the light of the flickering striplight overhead, I leafed through the pages. The words blurred and danced and slid as they usually did when I attempted to read in the Common Land. Not all of the words, though. A single phrase, appearing on several pages, remained stable and clear: "The Narrow Folk."

I thrust it back into a coat pocket and went through the door into the secondhand bookshop in my own world. The shop was unoccupied at this time of night. The bell jangled as I went out the front door, and I headed home.

I was surprised and angry about the notebook, and not a little puzzled. That Laura had slipped it into my pocket I did not doubt, but how had she got hold of it in the first place? I thought of the safe in Douglas Lamb's studio flat. Was I to suppose Laura had cracked the safe without Theresa realising? Absurd, of course, but on the other hand I didn't think Theresa knew what her conjoined sister had been up to when she embraced me.

Perhaps it was Theresa who had stolen it, possibly before Lamb had inflicted his terrible punishment on the sisters.

Whatever the story behind it, the fact was, it was Lamb's property, and it was now in my possession. Up till now, he'd had no quarrel with me, and I'd intended it to stay that way. So what was I supposed to do with it? Give it back to Lamb and tell him I'd found it? I wasn't a good liar, and he'd soon get the truth out of me. Whatever I thought of Laura Theresa, I had no wish for them to be punished further. Should I hide it somewhere, or destroy it?

It occurred to me that I might find the answer in the notebook itself. When I got home I got comfortable in an armchair, opened the notebook and proceeded to read.

The opening lines read, "When I was eight I watched my family die in an air raid. They were not killed by German bombs, they were massacred by the Narrow Folk."

*

But if I was expecting a straightforward narrative, I was disappointed. Like many well-used notebooks, its content was very varied; it was a combination of diary, memoir, sketchpad, and even shopping list. Less typically, the narrative parts seemed to be addressed to someone, with phrases such as, “You’ll no doubt remember...” and “As you probably guessed...” Here and there Lamb referred to people using one or two initials. The letter J came up repeatedly, referring to at least two different men and one woman, depending on the context. I also found a single third-person reference to LT, which confirmed that Laura Theresa was not the intended recipient of the notebook. There was a reference to the North Wilderness Tower, which Kirsty had mentioned when I met her outside London Prime, but I was none the wiser about where or what it was.

The information about the Narrow Folk was in there, but it needed piecing together. At times it was unclear if Lamb was describing what he thought at the time or what he learned later, so my reconstruction required some guesswork. Nevertheless I was reasonably satisfied that I’d got the gist.

Lamb’s father had done a deal with the Narrow Folk. Lamb did not state what the deal involved, but it probably had something to do with the fact that his father won a silver medal for the sprint at the 1936 Olympics. That had been four years earlier, and now payment was due. Lamb’s father had clearly intended to settle his debt, but whatever it was he’d had in mind, the Second World War got in the way of his plans. Unfortunately he had offered himself and his family as collateral.

The Narrow Folk came to collect on the night of a full moon, while he was home on leave. There had been an air raid the previous night, and Lamb had been unable to sleep. The siren sounded again just after sunset. It was a long, darkening street in Surrey. This was the time of blackouts; no lights shone from behind curtains, and the streetlamps (gas lamps as far as I could tell from Lamb’s exquisitely detailed drawings) were unlit. Lamb, a boy of eight, stood at the open front door watching in bewilderment as his father ran. His father was the fastest runner in England - and I realised this was no childish hyperbole. Later, Lamb would think he had been running from the threat that had come for him; later still he would recognise that he had been trying to draw the threat away from his family, but he had misunderstood how the Narrow Folk operated, and he had not run fast enough.

Near the end of the road, past the post box, half moons appeared in either side of Lamb's father's body. Another half moon appeared in his upper left arm, so that the limb was hanging from a strip of flesh. Another appeared in his right leg - details, again, that Lamb painstakingly recorded in a series of overlapping frames. Then his mother drew him into the house and told him they must make for the Anderson shelter.

Lamb asked, "What about Daddy?"

His mother replied, "He can take care of himself, Douglas." Lamb understood, but not straight away, that she had not seen what he had seen. He was sleep-deprived and young; the irreversibility of it had not had time to sink in.

When Lamb and his mother reached the kitchen, his brother Jamie had already gone out the back door and was running along the garden path. He was six. He passed the shed where the garden was in shadow. Between the apple tree and the cabbage patch, still running, he stepped into moonlight, where he was cut into five clean vertical slices.

(Looking at the pictures, I was reminded of the egg slicer in my grandmother's kitchen. Cousin Martin used to pretend it was a tiny harp.)

Lamb's mother caught him in the doorway, drew him back into the kitchen and slammed the door shut. This time she *had* seen what he'd seen. Up to that point Lamb's fear was an abstract thing; the deaths of his father and brother had an almost cartoon-like quality. But when his mother spoke, the calmness of her voice filled him with terror. Not just because her voice was calm, but because he understood that she knew what was going on.

"He made a deal with the Narrow Folk," she said. "He didn't keep his word. He didn't keep his word!"

Without locking the back door she pulled out the cutlery drawer and scattered knives, forks and spoons on the doormat, and the windowsill. "They can't cross silver when the moon is up," she said.

Lamb didn't think their everyday cutlery contained silver. His mother must have belatedly come to the same conclusion, because she suddenly grabbed his hand and dragged him into the hall. If they could get into the dining room, there was the sideboard where they kept the best cutlery, and his father's trophy case...

But the curtains were open in the dining room and moonlight flooded in. Windows wouldn't stop the Narrow Folk when there were pools of light from the full moon.

There was a pool of moonlight on the stairs from an upstairs window. It was fading, as if a cloud was crossing the full moon. From the kitchen came the sound of cutlery being kicked aside across the tiled floor - clearly it didn't contain silver. Lamb's mother considered, made an immediate decision. She half carried, half threw her surviving son up the stairs, following on as fast as she could.

But the cloud had been small and fast-moving. When Lamb reached the top of the stairs he knew he was now an orphan. His mother's last words had been, "Don't present an easy target."

Lamb himself had not reached the landing entirely unscathed. He was wearing long trousers, but the Narrow Folk had sliced through his left calf, through the trouser material and his skin. Despite their proximity, he hesitated outside his bedroom door. His room was north facing, so moonlight would not shine through his window, but he made for his parents' bedroom instead. It was south facing, but the blackout curtains were closed. He ran in, seized the ceramic piggy bank from his mother's dressing table and smashed it against a wall. Silver half crowns spilled out. He spread them over the windowsill and on the threshold of the door. Working by touch he found rings and chains in his mother's jewellery box. Some were silver, and some were not. Either way, they were added to the barricade.

While he fumbled in the dark, Lamb knocked over a perfume bottle, which smashed on the floor. It was expensive perfume; it seemed strange to Lamb that he would not be punished for the damage he had done.

Once he was as secure as he could be, he sat shivering next to his parents' bed, his knees drawn up under his chin, the quilt from the bed wrapped around him, a pillowcase pressed against his calf to stop the bleeding. The Narrow Folk were outside, in the garden, but unable to get in. He heard them snuffling and whining like dogs deprived of their food. German bombs were falling, mostly in the distance, but now and then one got close. The night wore on.

If Lamb were to sleep, there would be a possibility of him waking up to find it was all a dream, that his parents and his brother Jamie were all alive and well. But he did not sleep.

The air raid ended in the early hours of the morning. The all-clear sounded, and neighbours emerged from their Anderson shelters. Still Lamb remained huddled in his parents' bedroom. He understood that when the moon was full it would set at around the time the sun rose. When the moon was up, the Narrow Folk could not cross silver, but how did it work when the moon was not up? His mother had not explained that, and he could not ask her now. The cut in his leg had healed, but the injury had given him an inkling of how it would feel when they killed him.

There came a point when he realised he had nothing to lose. He got up and went over to the window and drew back the curtains. Moonlight flooded the bedroom through the diagonally-taped glass, but the items of silver on the windowsill maintained the barrier. There were six of them in the garden. They were flat, like cardboard cutouts, approximately the size and shape of a man or a woman. Edge-on, they were infinitely thin; face-on, they put Lamb in mind of Pathe films of the targets used by soldiers during shooting practice. Unlike these targets the Narrow Folk had features projected onto them, faces with big eyes and far too many triangular teeth in grinning mouths too big for their faces. Sometimes the way their features moved was at odds with the way the bodies moved. They were aware of Lamb watching them.

The siren sounded again. Another air raid. The Narrow Folk, milling about the garden, paid it no attention. Lamb returned to his huddling place beside the bed. (It never occurred to him to get onto, let alone into, the bed itself.) But before he got there he saw - or perhaps a better word is *noticed* - the cupboard door above the headboard.

There was a built-in cupboard in his parents' room that he had never seen before.

A cloud bank covered the moon. An hour or so later the moon shone free again. It flooded the room through the open curtains, but as long as the silver remained in place it did not provide a bridge to the Narrow Folk.

In later memories he would recall a silent build-up to what happened next. Maybe it was something the Narrow Folk influenced, maybe it was sheer bad luck. The silence was broken by a bomb exploding very close to the house. The window shattered, and the half crowns and silver rings were scattered

Time hesitated. Lamb had nowhere to go. His only hope was to hide in the cupboard that, until that night, had not existed.

*

I shifted in my armchair and glanced at the clock. Nearly 4am. Probably 4am in the story too. It had been a long night for young Douglas Lamb. I had a feeling I knew what was coming next. Everybody wants to know if their first time is typical.

*

It was an L-shaped room. A door in each end, and a door in the wall opposite each end. Sometimes the doors were full-sized and panelled, sometimes they were cupboard doors like the one that had appeared in his parents' bedroom wall. The pattern (or a variation of it) was repeated in each succeeding room, regardless of which door he chose as he passed through each iteration.

Along one length, there was a single bed against one wall, and a curtained window in the other. The curtains were a lush velvet in each case, and the carpet was thick pile. In the other length was an armchair, a table, and a wireless on the table.

Each time he passed through a door he found himself in another L-shaped room. There were superficial differences - the carpet or the curtains were a different colour. Once he burst in on a couple making love on the single bed; he backed out quickly and chose another door.

He was uncomfortably aware that the L-shaped rooms might form a swastika as seen from above. At other times it struck him that he was moving like a knight in a chess game.

Music was playing from the wireless. Now that he thought about it, he was sure he had faintly heard it during his vigil in his parents' bedroom. The song was easily recognisable; Vera Lynn was singing "We'll Meet Again". The realisation came to him that he would not be meeting his parents or Jamie again. It made him weep.

Once he pulled the curtain aside. Logically he should have seen the outside of the L-shaped rooms. Instead, he saw a rectangular tower with row upon row of windows. There were lights on in many of the windows, and there was no ARP warden shouting at them to put them out.

Had the Narrow Folk found their way into this strange labyrinth of rooms? Maybe they had, but if he continued to choose doors randomly they would find it almost impossible to follow him.

Again he stopped to pull back the curtain. Moonlight shone in, which made his heart leap, but, inexplicably, it was a waning crescent, not a full moon.

The labyrinth of L-shaped rooms seemed to go on forever, and Lamb was concerned he might have doubled back. Each time he opened a door there was the chance that he would run into the pursuing Narrow Folk. Maybe they would be edge on, as they had been for Jamie, invisible and infinitely sharp.

The wireless became more modern with each room he entered. Judging by the drawings, the wooden valve set gave way to a transistor radio. The music gradually morphed, too; Lamb's notes described a song about a lonely man from the top estate leaving a note for a local girl.

Realising he might be doomed to run through L-shaped rooms forever, Lamb finally decided on another tactic. Stopping at the next window, he managed to slide it open, and climbed out onto a fire escape. This led down to a street behind a pub and an office block. The moon was midway between full and waning crescent. Lamb sensed he was a long way from home.

*

Here the narrative ended. There was no indication of where he had arrived, nor - apart from the description of the song on the radio - when. If he had travelled through time, it would explain how a man born in the early 1930s could still be a young man in 2006. That, however, could not explain how he was so prolific with his artwork. I had seen him work; he was fast, but not supernaturally so.

And what of the Narrow Folk? I recalled Tobias Quinn warning me that there were worse things than slithermen in the Common Land. Were they still after Lamb? I had no doubt that they were, or at the very least, Laura believed they were. Otherwise, why would she have given me the notebook?

Clearly she intended me to use this knowledge against Lamb.

Chapter 34. The Ghosts of Connecting Buildings

I bought a second hand bicycle in another Chichester. It was the folding type, ideal for carrying through doorways. I had some map-making to do.

I considered the key I had to the barn conversion on the Price Estate. It would have been so much easier if I could have gone directly to the destination and worked backwards. But that would have drawn far too much attention to myself. Besides, Dawn had told me they'd changed the lock, and I had no reason to think she was lying.

That didn't stop me driving past the place in the early hours of a Tuesday morning. My instinctive sense of the Common Land had developed considerably since the days of stumbling around in the McDonald's labyrinth. Mapping it was still like trying to assemble an immensely complicated jigsaw, but at least the pieces were picture side up now.

I was home for 8am, then showered, shaved and dressed for a job interview at a company in Fareham. I'd been using my considerable spare time to get qualified as a data analyst. I already had maths qualifications from the Open University from when I had become a teacher; since then I had learned Python, and a language named R. It was a promising interview; out of ten candidates, I was one of the three they wanted to see again. In the evening I drove back to Charlton and made the questionable decision to visit *The Fox.* None of the regulars that I'd known from a decade ago were there, and the bar staff had changed several times, so nobody knew me.

There was always the chance that one of the Price brothers would call in, so I sat by a window with my drink and kept a wary eye on the car park for a black Mercedes. Among other things, I was in no mood to have my windscreen smashed again.

Six years ago, *The Fox* had been featured in a fantasy miniseries called *The 10th Kingdom.* Back in the seventies it had appeared in a *Doctor Who* serial, the one in which aliens invaded Scotland, apparently. Given the pub's credentials, it struck me as ironic that there were no strange doorways to be found in it. This may have been for the best; had there been, I might have planned to shoot William Price in the pub itself, and make my escape into the Common Land. There were so many things that could go wrong with that scenario.

I finished my drink, drove to the Chichester Gate car park, and got my folding bike out of the boot. I used my regular doorway in the cinema complex and found a world where there was still a railway line between Chichester and Singleton. I bought a return ticket.

There was a real possibility that I was following in Kirsty's footsteps.

*

From Singleton Station I went for a leisurely ride around the countryside. I found no doorways, but I could sense the ghosts of connecting buildings. At one point I cycled for half a mile along a dirt track that I knew occupied the same space as a very long corridor in another version of England.

I found the Price Estate in this world. On impulse I pulled in on the front drive, which was paved rather than gravelled, and rang the doorbell of the main house. The owner proved to be an extremely pleasant fiftysomething widow by the name of Charlotte Bell. I explained that I had lived here when I was younger, and happened to be in the area. She gave me a guided tour of the property, treated me to tea and homemade fruitcake, and showed me her artwork - landscapes and seascapes, mostly, and nowhere near Douglas Lamb's level of accomplishment, but nevertheless very pleasing to the eye and to the imagination.

Before I left she made me promise to call in if I was in the area again.

I noticed with interest that the barn conversion was still a barn. I suggested she do something with it (given that it wasn't being used to accommodate animals) and she said she would consider it.

I cycled back to Singleton and caught the last train back to Chichester.

*

Thursday afternoon was third time lucky. There was a doorway in the waiting room at Singleton Station with a long, impossible corridor on the other side which was lit by moss-smeared skylights. Kirsty had been this way. She had written a K and an arrow on the wall with her green lipstick, which she must have been carrying for three years. This corridor eventually opened onto a high-walled square courtyard like the one in Chichester. There was a door in the middle of each of the four walls; Kirsty's green initial and arrow was on one.

From the point of view of the Kirsty I had met outside London Prime, she had been this way seven years ago. I tried not to dwell on the fact.

The corridor on the other side was being rapidly narrowed by constructors. I would have to move fast. It was actually very straight, but irregularities in the layers that the constructors applied gave the impression that it twisted and turned. I passed a half-open side door opening onto a room with boarded windows and no other exits, and a bed. I spared it no more than a glance. The corridor came to an abrupt end: a doorway that opened towards me.

On the other side of the door there was a bedroom which I knew well. It was the one in the barn conversion that I had slept in when my marriage to Dawn had come to an end.

*

In some sense I was home. It felt almost nostalgic.

Leaning the bike against a wall in the corridor, I emerged from the Common Land and entered the room. The strange doorway was hidden behind the mundane door. It wasn't hard to find, but I had slept here, night after night, completely unaware of its existence. I could have decorated the room and not noticed the doorway.

There was a single bed that could be made into a double bed if you slid the secondary bed out from under the main one and extended its legs. There was a bedside table with a lamp on it, and a copy of a Dan Brown novel. Coincidentally I had bought a ticket to see *The Da Vinci Code* in the cinema complex in case I needed an alibi today. The book was not one of mine; I guessed the room had been rented out to a lodger.

I looked in the wardrobe and in the chest of drawers. They were empty. There were no lodgers at the moment.

I listened at the mundane door. Silence. I reached for the door handle then remembered: fingerprints! I donned gloves; it was way too late in the day to be overlooking things like that. I opened the door and went out into the hall.

I heard the sound of car tyres on gravel. I got my gun out and made to open the front door, but the latch was unfamiliar. Opening the original lock from the inside was a straightforward matter, but with the new one, I needed the key. It was hanging from a hook, but by the time I'd fumbled with it and got it in the lock, the car had stopped and the driver had got out. He was scrunching across the gravel path towards the main house.

I got the door open. It was William Price; I recognised him from behind readily enough. I took aim at the back of his head, then hesitated. I hadn't reckoned on him being here, not this time of day, and I hadn't been planning on killing him. Not yet. This had been intended as a reconnaissance mission, not the actual execution.

While I dithered he continued to walk towards the house. If I shot now and missed, I would not get a second chance.

On impulse, I stooped to pick up a handful of gravel. I threw it forcefully at his car, recalling how he had thrown a brick through the windscreen of my car. I slammed the door shut just as he began to turn so that he would have seen it closing, and retreated to the spare room. I opened the window and left the door ajar so it would keep banging in the breeze. I kept the door to the Common land open; I stood in the frame and faced the window. My gun was in my hand in my coat pocket.

There was the sound of a key in the lock of the front door. It opened. I heard William's voice demanding, "Is that you, Russell?" I had no idea who Russell was, but it struck me as a godsend that I wasn't the first person he suspected.

William paced about in his heavy boots. He was calling out, "Russell! You know you can't hide in here forever!" He was moving slowly, kicking doors open. The room I was in was the obvious hiding place; he was leaving it till last deliberately.

"What are you going to do, Russell? Are you going to fight me? Man to man?" He gave a derisory laugh. "Sorry, I don't know the politically correct term for the likes of you." There was a pause. "Hang on, what's that?" He went silent, as if something had distracted him. He was moving as quietly as he could towards the room where I was waiting. He stepped on the floorboard that creaked; not loudly, but I heard it because I was listening for it.

Nothing happened for a very long time. I didn't know Russell, but I didn't doubt he would have considered looking round the door to see what was happening. I considered shooting William through the door. The thought that I was going to become a killer today, *right now*, made me feel utterly sick. The lesson of the shower scene was a nonsense; until this moment there had always been a chance that I could have got out of my commitment to Lamb.

My knees buckled and I felt as if I was about to vomit. That was the moment when William kicked the door open. It crashed against the frame of the doorway to the Common Land. I heard William grunt in surprise; if Russell had been hiding behind the door as he had supposed, he would have been crushed by the door, and the door would not have swung round so far.

Recovering slightly, I heard William walk across the room to the open window, clearly wondering if Russell had climbed out and made a run for it. I could step back, close the door to the Common Land and leave, maybe come back another day. But I might not get a chance like this again, and besides, the constructors were making the corridor narrower.

I pushed the mundane door closed. William heard it click shut. He spun, saw me, and his jaw dropped.

"You!" he said in astonishment.

"Yes," I said weakly. My hands were out of my pockets; if he rushed me I would have no time to use my gun.

He sat down on the bed. "Philip," he said. "Philip. I... I don't know what to say."

"This is the room where it happened," I said. "Before it even was a room. Isn't it?"

"Yes." He was holding his head in his hands.

"The darkness. The *incest.* Kirsty's conception happened in here, didn't it?"

William was nodding slowly. "We should never of... we should never of blamed you. That wasn't right. I'm... sorry."

This was real. This was *real.* Of all the scenarios I had run through my head, none of them had William Price *apologising* to me.

William was still talking. Despite the turmoil in my mind I heard snatches of what he was saying: "We were in so deep there was no turning back... had to cover it up... needed someone to..."

How could I kill him when he was apologising?I had to kill him. I was committed. Kirsty needed to be safe from him when she returned.

"So, where do we..." He frowned, squinted at the open door to the Common Land, seeing it for the first time. "What the hell is..." I pulled the door shut behind me. His glance darted around the room. He shook his head as if to clear it of something, or as if he'd forgotten something important. "Where do we go from here?" he eventually finished.

"What do you mean?"

He shrugged. "When she comes back for good. Can we... can we at least be civil?"

Comes back? Did he know something, or was he just holding onto hope?

"Besides," he said, going off at a tangent, "it was consensual."

"Consensual? What was consensual?"

His gesture indicated the room, the place where it had happened.

"You mean Dawn asked for it?" I said in disgust.

My tone surprised him. "Yes, of course she asked for it. Come on, Philip!"

Those were the last words William Price ever spoke. Almost the last. Before I could allow myself to process what he said next, my hand was back in the coat pocket and I shot him through the fabric. The noise was deafening. William was clutching at his bloody chest. I took the gun out of the pocket and shot him again, in the stomach. Although I was doing him terrible injuries, he was not dying. I wasn't enjoying this. His gasps were pitiful, and I would have given anything to reverse the events of the last few seconds, but my only option now was to end it quickly.

From point blank range I shot him in the brain. He slumped, finally dead.

I stood there panting, crying. Nothing I'd imagined prepared me for the reality. A man was dead because of me, because of my actions. Nothing he had done to me justified what I had done to him.

I didn't hear the sound of the wheelchair, and I didn't hear the bedroom door open. I turned around to see Mrs Price in the doorway.

She had time to say, "What..." before I shot her between the eyes.

Chapter 35. Delirium

In a dream I stormed into Laura Theresa's place, holding up Douglas Lamb's notebook and saying, "Either you return it to him or I will." As if I was in any position to take the moral high ground about anything, ever. "No punishment he metes out can compare with the way I feel right now."

Laura Theresa was no longer conjoined. Each woman's missing arm was restored, but there was something wrong with them. The skin was the wrong colour, and they were jointed in the wrong places. In unison the sisters said, "It's not about how you feel though, is it?"

In another dream I was in a park outside a familiar church with all three versions of Kirsty sitting together on a bench: the adult, the teenager and the child. All three were inconsolable when I told them their grandmother had died.

I was on a bed. No, *in* a bed. This was neither the familiar experience of insomnia dreaming, nor the mundane experience of sleep dreaming. I was delirious. I was ill. The room shifted around me, at one point seemingly my bedroom at home, another a very old bed in a bare room in the Common Land with boarded up windows. In another it was one of the L-shaped rooms from Douglas Lamb's account, and in another it was Room 28 of the Holiday Inn in Chichester.

Suddenly there was hope. If I was delirious, maybe the terrible events were part of the delirium. Maybe they never happened.

"They happened," said Sarah Compton.

"I never meant to kill Mrs Price. It was reflex, pure reflex. I wasn't going to kill *any* witnesses. Not even if... I never intended to pull the trigger."

"You pulled the trigger," said Sarah.

"How am I going to live with myself?"

"It's not about how you feel," said Sarah.

"She had terminal cancer. From smoking. She wouldn't have lived much longer. I might even have spared her suffering. At the end."

Sarah said nothing this time. She just gave me a look of disgust.

In a low voice, almost sympathetic, Miss Havers said, "She lived long enough to see her son dead."

"I am dreadfully sorry about that."

Miss Havers shook her head. "You screwed up badly, Mr Hamilton."

*

Time passed. I had no idea how much.

I was in my own bed. The room stank. There was a bowl of brown vomit beside the bed. It was so full it seemed that only surface tension was preventing it from spilling.

Someone was hammering on the front door.

The rest of the room was immaculate. Had Miss Havers' voice been real and not just my delirium? Had she cleaned the house again?

Still the hammering on the door. It had been going on for some time.

I was wearing a t-shirt and underpants. I had not shaved for days. I threw on a dressing gown and went downstairs. I opened the front door. Daylight flooded in. Not direct sunlight but bright enough.

A man in a suit came into focus. He was holding out an ID badge. "Levinson, CID," he announced. "Are you Philip Hamilton?"

"What? Yes, yes I am."

"Can I have a few words with you, please?"

"Sure, come on in."

He followed me in, passing the coat rack. My coat with the bullet hole in the pocket was hanging there - I might as well have handed him a laminated confession - but he didn't glance at it. As I led the way into the kitchen I wondered if I'd left my gun on the working top.

I hadn't.

"Coffee?" I asked.

He was about to say no when he saw that I'd got a coffee maker. "Don't mind if I do."

We sat on stools at the kitchen table while the coffee brewed. I had sat here with Mrs Price two years earlier on the occasion of Kirsty's first visit. He said, "I take it you know why I'm here?"

I nodded. "It was on the radio." I hadn't heard it, but it seemed like a safe guess.

"A nasty business," he said. "So where were you on the afternoon of 6 April?"

"You'll have to forgive me, I don't even know what day it is today." I'd seen myself in a mirror; I looked as ill as I felt.

"Last Thursday."

"Thursday, yes. I went to the cinema. In Chichester."

"What film?"

I honestly couldn't remember the title. "The one with Tom Hanks. Based on the Dan Brown novel."

"*The Da Vinci Code*?"

"That's the one."

"Did you go with anyone?"

"No, I went on my own." I found my wallet. The ticket stub was in it. I handed it to him. He gave it a long, hard look, then handed it back. "Does that put me in the clear?" I asked.

"For now. I understand there was bad blood between you and your brother in law?"

"William? Yes."

"And your mother in law?"

I tensed. "She didn't deserve to die."

"But William did?"

"Maybe not. Let's just say I won't be weeping at the graveside."

Levinson nodded. "What can you tell me of Michael Russell?"

"I know nobody of that name. There's a *Mark* Russell in my history class. I can't remember his father's..."

Suddenly the smell of the coffee caused me to retch. I got up and hurried over to the sink just in time. There were two plates and some cutlery in the sink; I vomited over them. I rinsed it all off, washed my face and continued, "I can't remember his father's name but I can find out for you."

"I don't think that will be necessary. Maybe forget about the coffee if you don't mind. What's the matter with you, anyway?"

"Man flu," I said with a weak smile. "It's been a stressful spring term."

*

I was back under the duvet. The bowl was still beside the bed but it had been emptied of vomit and rinsed out. I didn't remember doing this. In the absence of anyone else, I had to assume I had done it myself. I was living my life in fragments, in a house haunted by other fragments of me.

I hoped this would end soon.

Levinson apparently believed I was innocent. Had I suddenly got good at lying? No, it was obvious he had been convinced of my innocence before he even interviewed me; he was just going through the motions. Nevertheless I had done my homework; a CCTV camera would have recorded me entering the cinema complex. I wasn't seen leaving before the time of the killing, and the fire exits were alarmed. Levinson didn't ask me why I'd taken a folding bicycle to the cinema; either it wasn't clear what I was carrying in the CCTV footage or he simply didn't think it was relevant. Either way my alibi was watertight.

Where was the bicycle now? I couldn't remember.

After I'd killed Mrs Price, and before I escaped into the Common Land, I'd dabbed a tiny amount of William's blood on the window frame with my gloved left hand to make it look as if the killer had fled through the window. My main reason for doing this was to draw the police's attention away from the strange doorway; I still couldn't quite believe a team of detectives could overlook it.

Time passed. It occurred to me I had never reckoned on getting ill. It had not occurred to me that there might be a third dream state.

The bed was in a room with no wallpaper and no carpet. I was wearing the coat with the bulllethole, and one of the gloves I was wearing had William's blood on it. The folding bicycle was leaning against a wall.

I got up. The room seesawed, then settled. The bedroom door opened to my touch. Beyond it was a long corridor I recognised. To the right it led to the crime scene - I could see the door in the distance. If I listened at the door, would I hear the voices of a forensic team on the other side? I had no intention of risking it. To the left, in the direction of the courtyard, the corridor narrowed, and continued to narrow as the spiderlike constructors covered the wall in their webbing, layer by layer. I had never seen them work so fast.

How had I got here? Teleportation? I shrugged at the thought. I'd visited parallel worlds and I'd visited my daughter in the future. Why would I have a problem with teleportation? What was next, space aliens?

Carrying the bicycle, I squeezed my way between the narrowing walls. I had to keep the coat because I knew I would still have it when I came to be interviewed by Levinson in the near future. Novikov rules.

The walls were so narrow I had to walk sideways. Constructors crawled across my face and under my clothes. Did I mention I was arachnophobic? I had to move as quickly as I could in case someone stumbled upon the strange door and discovered this corridor.

Logic told me (and tells me now) I had not been teleporting, I was simply remembering things in the wrong order. Years after the event, I realise I am adding details to the memories that had simply not been present at the time.

But sometimes I wonder if this is all rationalisation.

*

It wasn't about how I felt, I got that, but the fact remained that I had to find a way of living with myself. Mrs Price had been part of the family conspiracy. If the intelligence level of William and Benjamin was anything to go by, it was probably all her idea in the first place, so ultimately she was responsible for me being torn away from the life I should have led.

But none of that justified that single impulsive act. I had to own responsibility for it. Chances were, I wouldn't be going to prison - unless Levinson was tricking me into thinking I wasn't under suspicion so that I would slip up - but I would be paying for it every day in my own way as long as I lived and memory endured.

*

I recovered from my illness in time to attend the second interview for the data analysis job. I listened to the news on the car radio on the way to Fareham. Michael Russell had been charged with three counts of murder.

Chapter 36. Lucid Dreaming

"I am here for my second portrait," I told Douglas Lamb.

"You killed Kirsty's real father?"

"I killed William *and* his mother," I replied. "The latter wasn't intended, and I'm not happy about it."

"Sit."

Something about his manner was off. He was nervous. I didn't expect that. He saw me seeing it in his eyes; he controlled himself so quickly I almost doubted what I'd seen.

He turned the sound on on one of the televisions and began to work on the portrait. The television was playing generic rock music, not anything I recognised but probably from the 1990s or later. Music he'd grown up with? Suggesting he'd fled across thirty or forty years to escape the Narrow Folk.

Overhead, on the circular screen that I still thought of as a glass dome, a silent thunderstorm was raging, presumably chosen to match the music on the television. The music was bland and irritating but after a while I was able to blank it out and think about other things. When I wasn't dwelling on the terrible acts I had committed, I found myself wondering why Lamb had wanted me to kill in the first place. He didn't know the Price family; how was he going to benefit from a random murder? I didn't think he was a psychopath, any more than I was, and I suspected he would have balked at the idea of pulling the trigger himself.

I was suddenly aware that he'd stopped working. Like a teacher stopping teaching to see how long a misbehaving pupil will take to realise - I had been that teacher, and that pupil.

"What?" I asked.

"You're hiding something."

My throat constricted. What did he know?

"You've been to see her, haven't you?"

"Who?" I asked, genuinely puzzled.

“Laura Theresa.”

“Oh. Oh yes.” I might have guessed who he meant if he’d said “them” rather than “her”. “I wasn’t exactly hiding the fact, I just wasn’t sure... I wasn’t sure I should mention it.” If I sounded defensive enough, if I sounded as if I was protesting too much, maybe he’d think that was all I was hiding. “And anyway, I’ve kept my side of the bargain.”

“You still want to see your daughter?”

“Of *course* I do.”

That sounded wrong in my throat, as if I was trying to convince myself. The last time Lamb painted me, seeing Kirsty again was the entire point of my existence. She was my little girl, my princess, my joy, my delight. And this time she was going to be my little girl again, unchanged by time.

But I was not.

Lamb showed me what he had done so far. He’d concentrated on my eyes. It struck me that nobody could possibly look at those eyes and not know what I had done. If Kirsty saw them she would know at once that I had murdered her Uncle Bill and her grandmother.

If it was that obvious from my portrait, how much would it show in my face?

But if child Kirsty were to see it when we were next reunited, then adult Kirsty would have known. Had she known and not revealed it? Because she understood that for me it had not happened yet? Was it the reason why the gates of London Prime were closed to me, for a crime I inevitably would commit?

Lamb was quiet as he worked. I sat uncomfortably; this was much more of an endurance exercise than last time. Last time he’d delivered what he’d promised but not what I’d asked for. Would he do the same thing again? Would he corner me into making another wish, with an even steeper price?

Still concentrating on his work, Lamb suddenly asked, "How did Laura Theresa reveal herself to you?" He was still using singular pronouns for the sisters.

"I was invited into the shower room..."

Lamb barked a laugh and put down his brush. His face was illuminated by a flash of lightning from the pretend glass dome overhead, giving him a crazed look. "Always the shower with her! Between you and me I think she gets off on it." He laughed some more; he stopped abruptly when he saw that I wasn't convinced by it.

"Anyway. You know what I had to do. A bargain is a bargain, and sometimes that has to be enforced, or penalties paid when it isn't. Besides, she hid things from me. You understand what I'm getting at? I don't begrudge anyone a private life, but... She hid things from me. I think you know what I'm talking about."

"I would have mentioned it if I'd realised," I insisted, keeping my eyes downcast. "When am I going to see my daughter?"

"Soon enough. I have some finishing touches to do." He picked up his brush again.

"Do I still need to be here for them? It is quite uncomfortable sitting still for so long."

"Just a little longer."

The "little longer" went on for forty minutes, long enough for the overhead video of the storm to repeat. I could tell from the position of the brush that he was working on background details; I really didn't need to be there for that. I thought I caught a smile, as if he knew I suspected what he was doing.

"Are you nearly done?" I asked at last.

"Just a tiny bit longer."

More time passed. Eventually I reached the limit of my endurance. "You know, I really need..."

"Finished!" he declared. "Come and have a look!"

He picked up the mace and pressed buttons on it. The generic rock music went silent and the storm froze. I gazed at Lamb's portrait of me.

I had built up in my mind the image of a caricature, the sort satirists use to demonise politicians. This was much more restrained. As before it was almost photographic realism, but the thing with my eyes was more unmissable than before, and a slight twist in my smile made me recoil. Would I trust this man to babysit for me? I wouldn't even trust him to wash my car!

"A portrait of a man who will not take a hint," said Lamb.

"I'm sorry?"

"Yes, I'm sure you will be. I told you before, my time is valuable. But I gave you all that extra time just now. I was *so sure* you would realise why, and come clean. I was *so sure* you had the common sense. You know, we could have concluded our business without any unpleasantness, and then we would have gone our separate ways."

"I honestly don't know what you're talking about."

"Really? I'm sure it will come to you in time." With that he swung the mace and it hit the side of my head with considerable force.

*

I was in a dark place. My head hurt as badly as expected. My exploring fingers touched still-sticky blood.

Knocking people out through blunt trauma is never a good idea. If you don't do it hard enough, you merely provoke your victim; too hard and you do them serious damage, possibly permanent, possibly fatal. Either Lamb was adept at this sort of thing, or he didn't care about the outcome.

There was a faint, familiar stench. Slithermen. I couldn't see and I didn't have my gun. I was lying on some sort of slab-like bed next to a stone wall that radiated cold.

From high overhead came the creaking sound of someone carefully stepping from rafter to rafter in an unboarded loft - an impression that was confirmed when a loft hatch was lifted, and light flowed out. A child's voice said, "Is that him, Mummy?"

The child was a girl, but it was not Kirsty's voice. The light in the loft lit one side of her face. Definitely not Kirsty, but familiar nonetheless. Where did I know her from? Maybe she was the little sister of one of my pupils, dragged along to Parents' Evening because they couldn't get a babysitter. No, that wasn't it. A part of my mind was screaming at me that I really should know her, but I couldn't place her at all. Was I suffering from concussion? Quite possibly; I didn't know how it worked.

There was a brief, muffled whisper from (I assumed) the girl's mother. In an alarmed tone the girl said, "He's coming back!" and the loft hatch was dropped shut.

Back in darkness, I risked sitting up. There was evidently a motion detector in the room, because my movement caused wall lights to come on. I was aware of footsteps on a ladder under the bare floorboards a short distance away; I had just enough time to take in my surroundings before a trapdoor opened up.

I was in a rectangular room about six or seven metres long. The walls were unplastered. The bed I sat on was hinged to a side wall, a chain at each end holding it in place. Bars divided the room into two, giving my not-quite-half the appearance of a prison cell. The appearance was not quite complete; the bars were sufficiently far apart that I could have easily squeezed between them, had they not been Slitherman cables.

The trapdoor was located in the floor on the other side of the cables. It rose. Tobias Quinn emerged and closed it behind him. He stared at me through the barrier of cables for several long seconds, then shook his head as if to say, "I'm disappointed but not surprised." Without a word he left the room through a door at the far end of the room.

There was a certain symmetry about the room. There was a door at the back of my cell. Keen to put as much distance as I could from the cables, I opened it, surprised to find it unlocked, and went through.

My world, I quickly discovered, was three rooms, or parts of rooms: the cell, a bathroom and a kitchen. I'd considered confessing to Mrs Price's murder to Levinson, but it looked like I was doing time already. The rooms were each in a different England. The bathroom had an exit door that was blocked by a single cable, perfectly vertical like the ones in the cell room. So far, no Slitherman had appeared.

There were dirty dishes in the kitchen sink. I washed them with lukewarm water and washing up liquid from a nearly empty bottle. There was a bit of dried-on food on a plate that I could not remove. A window over the sink gave me a view of a blank wall. I made a meal of tinned fish and tinned peas, heating the latter up in a saucepan on a gas stove. The bin under the sink was already overflowing with empty tins left by a previous inmate. I found a packet of tablets in a drawer crammed with useless items. I could read the word "Paracetamol" easily enough but the font was strange. I washed them down with a glass of rusty water and sat at a table to eat.

I felt woozy. Partway through my meal I felt quite sick. I rested my elbows on the table and my head in my hands. I was aware of movement behind me, and knew I was dreaming. Having a head injury in the Common Land evidently gave rise to a fourth dream state, this one closer in feel to the type I thought of as insomnia dreams. I was someone else, the previous inmate perhaps, throwing an empty tin into a not-quite-full bin.

He turned and looked at the table and chair, but he did not see me; I was in the future, I had not arrived yet. He was aware of an unseen something that definitely was present. Reaching out, he touched something so thin it cut his finger. It rotated like a lifesize cardboard man, a profile projected onto it. A Narrow Folk.

(I wondered if there was a singular form of "folk".)

He was not its quarry. With its mouth closed it looked bizarre but not threatening. With a liquid lurch it passed through the closed door into the bathroom. Opening the door, he followed it.

He caught his reflection in the bathroom mirror and I saw that he was Tobias Quinn, the man without the birthmark, only now he still had it. I thought of the look he had given me an hour or so earlier (in my timeline). Had he forgotten that he had done time here himself? I didn't like the thought that I was using a plate and cutlery that he had used.

The Narrow Folk continued its liquid lurch through the door into the cell. Quinn opened the door but held back.

Five slithermen slid down their cables. Douglas Lamb was standing on the far side of the room, watching the slithermen, Quinn and the Narrow Folk. The slithermen were in a frenzy. I was reminded of dogs on one side of some railings watching a cat walk past on the other side. They moved like dogs too. The Narrow Folk casually stepped through a slitherman, cutting it in half, and took an impossibly large bite out of another. Strangely, it made no attempt to harm the cables. A third slitherman pounced onto its back, and lost all four limbs in the process.

But the fight was not one-sided for long. A sixth slitherman dropped down behind the Narrow Folk (if "behind" can have any meaning in this context) and somehow managed to bite the flat side. The Narrow Folk shuddered, screamed in silent agony, and crumpled.

The slithermen disappeared back up their cables, except for the limbless one which bled out a black ichor. Douglas Lamb, who had stood his ground all this time, nodded in satisfaction. He beckoned Quinn towards him; another gesture and two of the cables slid aside like curtains to make a wider gap. Quinn walked out of the cell, and the dream ended.

Back in the kitchen and the present I forced the rest of my food down. Then I rose from the table, and looked for the bloodstains on the floorboard where Quinn had cut his finger. I quickly found them.

*

The bath took ages to fill. I would be naked and vulnerable in a room with a slitherman cable across the door. I would have to dry myself with an old towel that Quinn had used, and then dress in the clothes I'd been wearing before. But it was better than nothing.

As I lay in the lukewarm, rusty water it occurred to me that Quinn might not have been an inmate here. Maybe Lamb had shown him this set of rooms as a warning of where he'd end up if he didn't keep his end of the deal, much as Quinn had shown me the sleeping man in the House of Shards. I remembered Quinn remarking that the slithermen had changed again; they had moved like spiders when I first encountered them, but in the dream-memory they moved like dogs.

Lamb hadn't kept his side of the deal. I had not seen Kirsty.

I did not know how much time had passed. Two days? Three? Besides the injury to my head itself, the concussion dreams made it hard to keep track. In addition to how much time had passed here, how much time had passed in the mundane world? Had I lost the job in Fareham? Would I have to tell them I'd been assaulted and kidnapped and hope they'd just believe me?

I slipped into a reverie. Another concussion dream; I was somebody else, looking for a way out. I saw his reflection; it was not anyone I recognised. He reached for the handle of the door, his wrist too close to the cable...

I forced myself out of the dream.

I had explored the possibility of escape. The loft hatch in the cell room was much too high to reach, but what if I made a pile of items to climb onto? The cooker, the table, the cupboards if I could get them off the walls. The girl and her mother had not been back, so presumably the loft led somewhere.

Why was Douglas Lamb doing this? Why had he locked me up, why had he punished Laura Theresa so severely, and what was Tobias Quinn doing for him? There had to be a reason for it all. The reason was not in itself difficult to guess; the only trouble I had piecing it together was that it was based on premises that were themselves insane.

Lamb needed power. I didn't think he wanted to rule the world, or even the Common Land necessarily, but he did need the power to protect himself. As far as I could tell the Narrow Folk had been pursuing him relentlessly since World War II. He'd survived up till now first by fleeing, then by hiding, and finally by means of defence barriers. Presumably he'd strategically placed silver in various parts of his studio flat for whenever the moon was up. He had gained some kind of control over the slithermen, to the extent that they could be used as guard dogs. No doubt he had other forms of defence that I knew nothing of. He'd used magic, for want of a better word. Lucid dream magic, the act of influencing the "reality" around you when you know you're dreaming. When you know you are dreaming, anything is possible, but not everything is credible. If you try obviously impossible things like flying, you either forget you're dreaming or you wake yourself up.

Lamb had got it down to a fine art. His ability to grant wishes enabled him to recruit people, putting them in his debt and threatening them with sanctions if they tried to renege. Some ended up in here. Others... well, others ended up like Laura Theresa, but I was fairly sure she was a special case when it came to cruel and unusual punishments.

Why had he been so interested in William Price? Why had he wanted me to kill him?

Again, the answer was as obvious as it was insane. He was using the power of myth. The cuckolded husband killing the incestuous father of his beloved daughter... Actually that sounded more like a storyline from *Brookside* or *EastEnders*, but it was what Lamb believed that mattered. Now that I thought of it, he had seemed anxious, almost desperate when I had sat for that second portrait, as if a lot depended on the story playing out.

Well, it had played out. What came next?

I didn't know. But while I searched my mind for other things, I randomly remembered where I had seen Miah Proctor before.

In the late 1980s, when I got home from school, I would watch the portable TV in my bedroom while I changed out of my school uniform into my evening clothes. On Thursdays ITV had an American or Canadian sitcom called Amber which I enjoyed because the lead character was attractive. She had a brother, Reg, whose wife Mavis had an eating disorder. We only knew this from dialogue, because Mavis was one of those unseen characters that TV shows often employ as a gimmick. Sometimes you would hear her calling from another room, or she'd walk into shot carrying a huge cardboard box that concealed her face, or she'd arrive at an airport check-in walking alongside a giant basketball player who always got between her and the camera.

But then there was one episode in which Amber was a guest at a party. One woman appeared in shot several times, often with two or three others, each time loading up her plate from the buffet. It was nearly halfway into the episode that Amber casually said, "How's the diet going, Mavis?"

In the following episode, Mavis resumed her unseen status. But I remembered seeing her credited at the end as being played by Miah Proctor - as I lay in the tepid bathwater I could actually visualise it, and read the memory, even here in the Common Land.

It was somehow reassuring. History makers and mythical figures tend to be like hills and mountains, visible from every world, whereas the rest of us are as interchangeable as pebbles on a beach. But once in a while one of us pebbles succeeds in getting a second turn on the stage.

My reverie was suddenly interrupted by the abrupt appearance of a figure standing over me. My heart leapt into my mouth. A slitherman?

"How's the head?" It was Lamb's voice. He spoke as if genuinely concerned. I felt acutely uncomfortable having him stare at me. I had to consciously resist the urge to cover my privates.

"I'll live," I said, my voice weak. How long was it since I had last spoken?

He crouched the way an adult sometimes will to confide in a child.

"It has come to my attention that when you withheld information from me, you were motivated by a wish to protect."

His sentence seemed to trail off, so there was an awkward silence while I worked out whether I was meant to reply.

"Are you apologising for hitting me?" I eventually asked.

It was the wrong thing to say.

"No," said Lamb. "I was giving you an opportunity to come clean."

"About what?"

"We are so far past this!" he angrily said, and strode out.

I got out of the bath, grabbed a dirty towel and followed him through the door into the cell. By the time I'd wrapped the towel around my waist and fumbled with the door handle, he had passed between the bars. They had opened like a curtain, leaving me in no doubt that my dreams had been visions of the real. They were finished closing before I got near. He looked back at me through the bars, then gave me a dismissive shrug, stepped over the trapdoor and headed for the door at the far end of the room.

I called after him.

"Wait! What about your side of the bargain?"

Over his shoulder he said, "What about it?"

"You didn't keep it!"

"Didn't I? Are you so sure of that?" Then he went through the door and closed it behind him.

For several minutes I stood as close to the bars as I could without bringing down the slithermen. I seethed with unexpressed thoughts. Laura Theresa wanted him dead, that much was obvious. And he was the one who had pushed me into being a killer. Well guess what. That wasn't all he'd pushed me into. He'd just pushed me into Laura Theresa's camp.

When my rage passed I went back into the bathroom and dried myself off. I got dressed. I put my coat back on for the first time since my imprisonment. It was the coat I had worn when I first met Laura Theresa, not the one I had worn when I executed William Price and murdered his mother; I had since burned that one.

To my surprise, the USB memory stick was still in it. It had fallen through the hole in the pocket and into the lining. Lamb had missed it.

Chapter 37. Not the Expected Reunion

The USB memory stick had a single file on it which occupied almost the entire memory. When I first discovered I had it, I didn't want to risk infecting my own computer with a virus. So I tried running it at a library. It didn't run in my world. It required an app (whatever that was) that hadn't been developed in my version of England.

I tried it in libraries in other Englands. I got an error message each time, except for one occasion when I found a partly compatible video app, "partly" being the operative word. A very loud noise came out of the computer's speaker, causing everyone else in the library to look round at me. The noise sounded like that of a roaring motorcycle. The image on the screen was mostly black with a circular light in the centre, which I took to be the headlamp of the motorcycle. It appeared to be racing along a country road, possibly filmed by a camera on a stick in front of it. In among the glitchy horizontal lines of static and flickering double images I could make out what appeared to be wisps of fog, or possibly exhaust fumes.

I remembered hurriedly pulling the USB stick out of the computer but the noisy film kept on playing. I tried jabbing at buttons to get it to stop before a librarian came over to tell me off.

Douglas Lamb had picked up on the fact that I was still withholding information. Was it the USB stick, or was it that other thing, the thing I was withholding even from myself?

Fully dressed, I went back into the cell. Maybe I could make the bars slide apart at a gesture. Lamb could do it, and I understand how he operated.

I gestured. I affected impatience and said, "Come on! I don't have time for this!"

I stepped forward as if expecting them to respond like sliding doors in supermarkets. They did not. The nearest two began to quiver, and mercury drool ran down one. I stepped back quickly, but too late. A slitherman was sliding down the cable, and I had nothing with which to defend myself.

I didn't hear the loft hatch opening, nor was I aware of the unravelling rope ladder until it hit me on my left shoulder.

"This is more than you deserve, Philip Hamilton!" shouted Betany Wright from above. "Now move!"

*

I'd only once climbed a rope ladder before. It was at the house of a friend who owned a treehouse. I was twelve. It proved much more difficult than anticipated. The clue was in the name; it didn't stay rigid as I attempted to climb. Two decades on, having a slitherman at my heels didn't make it any easier. But somehow I managed.

Betany directed me to the rafters, which could take my weight, and drew in the rope ladder before the slitherman got any ideas. She closed the hatch behind me and I followed her to a boarded part of the loft. I was free.

I was also overcome with surprise.

"You escaped from the Mirror Place?"

"No thanks to you! You lied to me. You used me, abandoned me, and then ran off back to your adoring wife!"

"My *what*?"

We were hurrying along a seemingly infinite triangular corridor, boarded in places and not in others, and lit at intervals by a bare light bulb on a vertical beam. From time to time we had to pick our way across overflowing boxes of old clothes, teetering piles of books, a standard lamp, Christmas tree lights spilling out of boxes and so on but most of the time our path was clear. Betany switched off each light as we passed it. Despite concentrating on my footing, and wondering where we were headed, I took time to pause and process what Betany had just said, and what she was thinking. The very brief embrace between Dawn and me in view of the front window of my house. The driver of the Hyundai seeing us...

William hadn't been the one who'd put a brick through my windscreen, then. I'd killed him, and I'd misjudged him.

"Come on, Philip! We need to move quickly!" I was unnervingly reminded of the time when we had to make a fast exit into the Mirror Place. But Betany wasn't a follower now; evidently she had learned to walk the Common Land in her own right. I hurried after her. Eventually she stopped at an open loft hatch and lowered herself onto a stepladder on the landing below. I followed.

"You found your way back in," I said once I had stepped onto the landing carpet.

"That was nine years ago. Close the hatch after you! And be careful with the ladder, there's a rung missing."

I complied. Once I was on the landing floor she folded the step ladder and leaned it against a wall. This wasn't going to stop anyone who came after us, but it would make it difficult to enter the house quietly. For the first time I got a proper look at Betany. She was visibly older than when I'd last seen her, almost my own age now. "I didn't mean to abandon you in the Mirror Place," I said apologetically. "My options were... limited."

"Don't talk to me about limited options!" But the urgency had lessened now that we were out of the corridor of lofts. "Douglas Lamb is out of control, and we have to stop him."

"We? How?"

She didn't answer that, and I sensed that it was simply too big a question at this stage. As I followed her down the stairs I said, "Are we in the Common Land now?"

She stopped at the foot of the stairs. "Yes. This is rented accommodation. It's temporarily linked, with the front door as access. Lamb won't be able to find it for at least four hours."

"But why the urgency?"

As if hesitating over something she'd already decided, Betany said, "There's someone you need to meet."

We were in a hallway. The front door had frosted glass panes, and I was surprised to realise it was daytime. Betany turned to open an internal door, and again hesitated.

"What's going on, Betany?"

Betany opened the door to a lounge which was lit with evening sunlight. A blonde girl of about eight sat in an armchair. She was the girl I had seen looking down at me from the loft hatch a few days earlier.

"Hello!" she said, a friendly smile brightening her face.

"No!" I said, realisation dawning.

"Mummy warned me you might be shocked, but it's quite all right. I assure you, it will all make sense when she explains it to you. It seems quite evident that you recognise me."

I nodded. "Yes, I recognise you." And I did. Not just from a few days ago.

She was the dead girl Betany and I had found frozen in the Mirror Place among the bins behind a pub.

"You helped me find her after all," Betany told me. Then, turning to her daughter, she said, "Eloise, this is your father."

Chapter 38. The Long Way Round

I was showered, shaved, wearing a clean set of clothes and carrying a torch and a loaded gun. I was on my way to put a stop to Douglas Lamb. Evening was turning to night, and in a gap between houses I could see that the crescent Moon was nearly setting. It had to be below the horizon before I arrived.

Betany had drawn me a map to Lamb's place. It covered twelve A4 pages. Her route was very indirect, and it wove in and out of the Common Land at unlikely locations. She insisted I follow her route as it greatly reduced my chances of being caught early. There were other considerations too. Timing was critical.

I considered the gun. I had no liking for Douglas Lamb, I only had it on trust that he was dangerously out of control, and I really didn't like the thought of killing again. Furthermore, how likely was I to succeed? How many James Bond villains, or for that matter real life gangland bosses, get dispatched because they didn't take precautions against some barely-trained gunman's assassination attempt?

Lamb had kept his side of the deal after all. Thanks to him I had been reunited with my daughter while she was still a child. Even if it wasn't the daughter I had expected.

That preternaturally cold night, when Betany and I shared a bed, the original Eloise died. No, it wasn't as simple as that. She didn't just die, she was *reconceived.*

"But," I'd said, incredulous, we used protection!"

Her disbelief matched my own. "That's the part you're having trouble with? You didn't know condoms aren't a hundred percent reliable?"

"Oh I get it," I said. "Eloise's original father was Garcia Hollis. You got pregnant by a man from a different England. Then you got pregnant by me, a man from yet another different version of England. For some reason that's too confusing for the Common Land, so it resolves matters in its own special way."

If I still had my sanity at the end of all this, it would be a miracle.

The new Eloise had blue eyes, like Betany and myself, whereas the original had brown. Apparently the rules of genetic inheritance still applied.

"She remembers things," Betany told me. "New things, as she reaches the equivalent age."

"I remember Kirsty," Eloise piped in. Despite a warning glare from her mother she continued, "I suppose she's my half sister this time around."

"It's made her quite precocious," Betany said. "On top of being an insufferable little bitch." Eloise giggled at this. Betany went on, "But there aren't going to be any more new memories. By my reckoning, they end tonight."

"Why?" I asked.

"Why do you think?"

I thought.

"Oh."

"I estimate some time in the next four hours she'll be exactly the age the original Eloise was when she... you know."

"When I died?" Eloise asked cheerfully.

Betany winced. "I have no idea what effect it will have. But one thing you can be certain of, Lamb is going to use it to his advantage."

*

A light, continuous drizzle was falling. Betany's directions took me down an alleyway between the chain-link fence enclosing a skateboard park and the side wall of an office block. There was a door about halfway along. Someone had chalked the skull and barbed wire sign on it. It hadn't smeared in the drizzle so it was recent. What to do? Betany had included some alternative routes for just such an eventuality, but not for this particular door. There was nothing for it, I was going to have to take my chances. I pulled the door towards me. It moved, but was heavier than it looked.

The slitherman was clinging to the other side of the door. I'd half expected this; I leapt back against the chain-link fence and shot the slitherman twice. The gunshots echoed around the neighbourhood; nobody could mistake them for a car backfiring. I prayed that this was an area where shootings were commonplace, and unlikely to be reported back to Lamb. I pulled the trigger a third time while aiming at the top of the cable which was just inside the passageway on the other side of the door frame.

The dead slitherman lay on the ground in the alleyway, preventing the door from swinging closed. I couldn't leave it here, not in the real world. At the same time I didn't want to risk touching it, even when dead, and time was ticking.

In the end I found a very old vacuum cleaner in a cupboard in the passageway. I was able to get the cord wrapped around the slitherman's body and under its armpits. Dragging it into the passageway and out of sight was a difficult and unpleasant task, and black ichor stains remained behind.

I reloaded the gun.

*

There were other things Betany and I discussed before I set off. She took me into another room where Eloise would not hear.

"Did you ask Lamb for wishes?" I asked.

She nodded.

"He made you pay?"

"Of course," she said, her eyes lowered. And it suddenly occurred to me that I had not seen any portraits of Betany.

"Did he make you kill?" I asked.

She nodded, unable to speak for a while. When she finally did speak I recognised the name more from reading her lips than from hearing what she was saying: "Garcia."

My heart sank. Lamb had her kill Eloise's original father. Did he have any plans regarding Eloise's new father?

"I didn't care about him," Betany continued. "He took advantage of me when I was a child, barely a teen. I could justify my action readily enough. I was ridding the world of a menace to young girls." She paused for a long moment. "It wasn't just him, though. That's something they don't make clear in films. Bullets don't just stop when they hit their target. They keep going."

"There was a bystander?"

Betany nodded without speaking.

"Killed?"

She shook her head. "Not killed." What she said next she spoke so quietly that I had to ask her to repeat it. Again, I lipread better than I heard.

"Life-changing injury."

*

I crossed the Thames via an unfamiliar bridge, and crossed back through a tunnel designed for trains and pedestrians, passing under a sign that said "Tubeway Access". Sometimes the time of day would change; I called in at newsagents to check the dates on newspapers, and saw that the day itself varied too, sometimes by as much as a month. One time I couldn't read the newspapers at all, and I wondered if the shop had become part of the Common Land.

I came to an office block which was twenty stories high. Although it was late evening there were still lights on in some of the windows on every floor, except the fourteenth. That entire floor was currently a part of the Common Land. I had to get to it. My only issue was getting past reception. There was a slightly overweight man in a security uniform behind the desk, and magnetic badge-operated turnstiles. When she was mapping my route, Betany had probably sweet-talked the guard, maybe claimed to have forgotten her badge. I knew only too well how poor I was at lying, so I ended up simply vaulting over one of the turnstiles while the guard was preoccupied with the late delivery of a parcel.

He called after me, but I kept running. As long as I could find the stairs and climb fourteen flights without being caught, I could move on; it wasn't as if I'd be coming back this way. For good measure I shouted, "First aid emergency, can't wait!" before disappearing around the corner.

It was when I reached the sixth floor that I remembered how out of condition I was. Unfortunately the lift wasn't an option; on the first floor I'd seen a tape across the doors and a sign saying "Do Not Use". I wasn't sure what I would have done if the guard had come after me, or phoned someone upstairs to intercept me. It occurred to me then that I wasn't entirely clear what was at stake. Was my life in danger? Possibly. Was Eloise going to die a second and final time? Again, possibly, and I didn't know how I felt about that. Unlike Kirsty, she was my biological daughter, but I simply hadn't had time to develop an emotional connection beyond the basic wish to protect a child. What about Betany? Would Lamb know or guess that she had freed me from his little prison? There were a lot of unknowns, none of which promised a happy ending.

Having caught my breath, I resumed my climb. The door with a big 7 on it suddenly opened, and my heart skipped a beat, but it was just two men and a woman, all in suits, finishing for the day. One stepped aside for me. I said, "When are they going to fix that lift?" The woman said, "Tell me about it!" And we continued on our separate ways.

Another six flights of stairs, another six doors with a big number on indicating the floor. There was no number on the door to floor 14; indeed, the door looked as if it had been sealed up years ago. A few flights below, somebody puffing and panting even more than me was following. If it was the guard, he was probably having to stop off on each floor.

No matter. I pushed the door open and strode into the dark floor 14, taking out my torch with one hand and my borrowed gun in another. This floor had its own reception lobby, unoccupied of course, and double doors to the out-of-order lift. According to my map, a door to one side of the reception desk gave access to a central corridor which in turn gave access to all the offices.

With a certain feeling of weariness I saw that the skull and barbed wire sign had been drawn on the door in marker pen. The pen itself lay on the reception desk, the lid lying nearby. With an absurd feeling of irritation I put the lid back on; there was no sense in letting it dry out for no reason.

I faced the door and wondered for a moment if Betany was sending me to my death. She'd been nearly killed, she'd found her daughter dead, and she'd been abandoned, pregnant, in a parallel world with nothing but the clothes she was wearing. It wasn't all my fault, and she knew it - if I'd tried to rescue her we would both have died - but I wasn't exactly blameless either. Maybe, when all this was over, if we both survived, we would talk this over, along with our daughter if she survived too. Eloise had a pair of murderers for parents. We weren't bad people, we had only done bad things because circumstances had forced us to... And I couldn't help thinking that half the prison population could say the same.

I kicked the door open, torch and gun at the ready. The corridor was long and dark, office doors (some open) on either side, and three slitherman cables at evenly spaced intervals.The slithermen themselves lay sliced on the carpet tiles.

Treading warily, I looked in each office. They had a recently-abandoned look - mostly cleared desks, but an old CRT monitor with a yellow sticky on the screen and the word "BROKE!" written in red. There was movement in the third office. A pair of Narrow Folk; they looked exactly like the ones in Lamb's notebook, and the one I had seen in the memory dream. I stood absolutely still. They either wanted me dead or they didn't; if they did, I prayed they wouldn't toy with me.

A third one rotated into existence. The projected figure was in profile. It turned to face me, as did the first two. I put my gun away, held up Betany's map (I was now on page 11), shone the torch on it and said, "Follow me." Or rather I mouthed the words; in this part of the Common Land, I was unable to speak aloud.

Three mouths like those of cartoon sharks smiled. Three heads nodded their thanks. And I remembered that Lamb had never done these Folk any harm, he was paying for the sins of his father. He had been driven by circumstances to do bad things.

Unsure if they were following me or not, I took my leave and crossed the corridor into a fourth office. A spiral staircase led down into the thirteenth floor of an identical office block in another London.

This thirteenth floor was very similar to the fourteenth. Two doors led to other parts of the Common Land but my route didn't take me that way. Before leaving I looked out of an office window and saw that from this location the moon was a thicker crescent and had not yet set.

The lift was working in this version of the office block. There was a call button in the reception lobby, but no button for floor 13 inside the lift.

Leaving the office block was much easier than entering the previous one. A button released the turnstile, and there was no security guard. Outside the sky was clear, and there was no moon in the location where I had last looked.

Page 12, the final page of Betany's map. A private house. I used a credit card to get the front door open and went upstairs to a bedroom that had been vacated very recently. A couple had made love rather messily on the bed, and I wondered when Betany had added this location to her map. I supposed it was one of those parts where time only passes when it's occupied.

There was no door here other than the conventional one, and a wardrobe that proved to be just a wardrobe. Was I in the wrong house? The curtains were half open, and I could see the lighted houses across the street. I could also see yet another moon in the wrong phase and wrong part of the sky. Should I be in the next street? And yet I could just about sense the route that passed this way.

After wasting more time looking for a door, realisation struck. I opened the right hand curtain fully to reveal an open casement. The view through this one was different to the view through the rest of the window: I could see another casement a very short distance away. It reminded me of the medieval houses we'd looked at in History class. I climbed out the window and in through the one opposite. The kitchen in this house had a walk-in pantry with a door in the back.

I followed a long corridor, knowing I was now back in synch with Betany's location. The moon was below the horizon again here, and the Narrow Folk, should they have chosen to follow me, would be able to enter Lamb's studio flat even he'd put silver under every floorboard in the place.

But in the end, it proved to be all for nothing. Betany's carefully drawn plans and my attempts to follow them added up to abject failure. I was overpowered by Lamb's henchmen long before I had a chance of putting a stop to him.

We had badly underestimated him.

Chapter 39. The Power of Image

Lamb's two henchmen led me, blindfolded and handcuffed, along the corridor, through doors, up flights of stairs, and so on. At one point they stopped and one of them made a phone call. "We've got Hamilton," he said, and strain as I might I could not hear what Lamb was saying in reply. As they spoke I checked how constrained my arms were behind my back. With a bit of surreptitious wriggling I could reach my coat pockets without them stopping me. There was no real doubt that they'd taken my gun, but I had to check.

They had. They'd taken my torch, too.

We were moving again. At length we were walking up a loft ladder, one man in front and one behind me. I wondered if I was being brought to Lamb's studio flat, my intended destination, albeit in unintended circumstances. But then I caught the faint stench of slitherman cables, and supposed I was simply being returned to my prison via the trapdoor that Quinn had used. I doubted the cables would move aside at a gesture from Lamb's underlings, so I guessed Lamb himself was close by.

But then they walked me a much greater distance than would have been possible in the prison.

"Philip Hamilton." The unmistakable tones of Douglas Lamb. "I didn't expect to see you back here quite so soon."

"I get around," I said.

"So it would appear. So what brings you here this time?"

"Your henchmen."

"Very amusing."

"Actually I'm not trying to be funny. I genuinely don't know where I am, although I have a pretty good idea." As best I could I indicated my blindfold.

I guessed Lamb had gestured to one of his henchmen. A moment later my blindfold was removed. The handcuffs were not. Lamb was sitting back on one of his sofas, lit by the light of the overhead circular screen. I looked up and saw it was the Underwater London scene. I winced.

"Could you please change the screensaver?" I asked. "It makes me uncomfortable."

Lamb remained where he was, and did not reach for the mace. "Right now, your comfort is... fairly low on my list of priorities."

"I'm not your enemy," I said.

Lamb raised an eyebrow.

"You took a labyrinthine route to get here. That's unusual for you." I started to speak and he raised a hand. "Very unusual for you, in fact. One might even call it suspicious, given that you know at least two much more direct routes. You were also carrying a gun."

"I always carry a gun in the Common Land. It's a dangerous place!"

"Have you any idea how many people have tried to usurp my position here?"

"I have no wish to kill you."

Lamb smiled. "You really aren't a very good liar, are you Philip?" He laughed, genuinely amused. "What were you expecting? Did you think you'd catch me napping? Have you any idea how long it is since I last slept?"

"I was hoping to reason with you."

"With the gun as insurance?"

"With the gun as protection. Look, can you please change the video?" I gestured with my head up at the dome under uncountable tons of water.

"I had you down as a rational man, Philip. You know it's a video. You're not a savage tribesman who believes the camera can steal your soul."

"Images carry power," I said.

Lamb gestured with one hand, gracefully conceding a point. But still he did not change the video.

"You gave me a chance to come clean," I said. "I haven't betrayed you, but I have withheld crucial facts. You know this, and I am prepared to disclose them to you."

This time Lamb's gesture was dismissive. "All in good time. I understand you encountered some old foes of mine."

I said nothing, but I wasn't even good at lying through silence.

"I can see it in your eyes," he said. "Almost literally! I know you read my notebook. You know all about the Narrow Folk, don't you? You could probably list their abilities and limitations, almost as well as I can. They can teleport short distances into moonlit patches, but they can't cross silver when the moon is up. Which is a pretty major limitation when you think about it. They can be invisible, but only from one direction. They are as narrow-minded as they are physically narrow, and relentless. So, you came here when the moon was down. Did you think my defences would be down too? But you forgot something. Silver isn't the only thing that stops them."

He pressed a button on the mace and a light came on in the ceiling above the loft hatch. From where I was standing I could just see that a ring of eight or nine cables had appeared around it since my last visit.

"You control the slithermen now?"

"I control a lot of things."

He pressed more buttons on the mace and lights came on to illuminate a second and third ring of cables surrounding the first. "So you underestimated me. I think we've established that. But you're in good company." He pressed another button on the mace, and one of the screens on the bank of televisions came on. It was a view of the lounge where Betany had introduced me to Eloise. I had not noticed a camera in the room; my daughter and her mother became aware of it as we watched. They'd been playing chess on a glass table; in unison, they turned in shock to look in our direction. There was a heavy click, the unmistakable sound of a lock, and they hurried over to the position below the camera where the door would have been.

Lamb pressed the button again and the screen blinked off.

"What are you going to do to them?" I asked, unable to hide the anxiety in my voice.

"Betany's got a few good years of child bearing yet. And Eloise has got..." He glanced at his watch. "A little over an hour. Maybe I'll pay her a visit when we're done here - if I time it carefully I could be Eloise's next father. I understand Betany doesn't take a lot of persuading as a rule." He grinned. "Can you imagine what a precocious, insufferable bitch Eloise will be with *three* sets of memories? Then again, maybe I'll release them unharmed. Yes, that's probably what I'll do." He paused for a long time before adding, "It depends."

I nodded once. Nothing I said or did was going to change the outcome, at least not in a predictable way. Not at this point. I had no idea where this was leading, and I could only hope for the best while preparing for the worst. What did he have in mind for me? An overly elaborate punishment? An attempt at recruiting me? If the latter, would I have to prove my loyalty through some unspeakable act?

"Have I underestimated you in return?" he asked, suddenly staring into my eyes from very close up. If he was a James Bond villain, I was not James Bond; my one advantage was that I didn't feel obliged to hide my fear. On the other hand, I could *divert* my fear. I pictured the dome cracking, the first stream of the water that drowned London trickling in, then the inward burst of glass as the flow increased catastrophically. My terror was genuine; here in the Common Land the image could become real.

But the imaginary dome continued to hold back the imaginary water.

Lamb was shaking his head. "No, I haven't underestimated you. That's not to say I dismiss you. I think I have you weighed up. Are you a danger to me? Possibly. Can you be useful to me? Undoubtedly. In fact, you already have been. The balance of power is with me, and you played no small part. Soon, I'll no longer need to run or hide. It's the Narrow Folk who will be running and hiding, and they won't be doing that for long."

I found my voice. "What power are you talking about?"

"The power of myth." He pressed another button on the mace and all twelve televisions came on. On every screen, a crucifixion. Men, women, some children. Most dying, some dead. Some nailed to crosses like Jesus, some tied to trees like Odin. There were more crucifixions than there were televisions; the picture on each one changed every half minute or so.

"This..." I began, initially at a loss for words. "This isn't myth, this is just murder." The two henchmen to either side of me became more alert in response to my tone, but I was also aware that the tone was wrong. I wasn't outraged! I was criticising Lamb, not for being evil, but for being *unimaginative.*

"No matter. It works." Did I detect a defensiveness in Lamb's tone?

"That's like dismissing criticism of a book or record because it sells," I countered. "Yes, there's mythical symbolism in what you've done, obviously, but there's so much more to myth. People needn't have died, at least not in such numbers."

"They're nonentities," Lamb said with a dismissive sweep of an arm.

"Not to themselves. Not to those who care about them. Not even to you. You're no psychopath."

"So what do *you* think myth is? Passing fair knights killing dragons with swords taken from lakes? Arms clothed in white samite?" Lamb's sneer was unconvincing.

I had looked away from the television screens. I was concentrating once again on the image of the glass dome cracking.

"It's the interface of history and dream. Stories told and told again, each time losing another part that doesn't resonate, sometimes at the expense of accuracy and logic, but that doesn't actually matter. It's why the phrase 'dream logic' is not an oxymoron."

"So what do you dream about?"

"I dream of lifts."

It struck me that the question didn't seem strange, nor indeed that I was answering at all. Nor did the fact that I was using the present simple for something I hadn't done for months. "Glass lifts. Lifts that move along rails both vertically and horizontally. Absurdly large lifts, with furniture in them. And stair cases the wrong way round so the top meets a blank wall instead of the landing floor."

He smiled. "Go on."

"I dream of my parents, still alive but knowing about the traffic accident that killed them. I dream that my dog is still alive, even though I never owned a dog. I dream of being unable to start a new relationship because I am still with my ex. I try to phone the police or the fire brigade but the phone comes apart in my hand."

"Does any of that sound like myth to you?"

I ignored the question. "When I'm watching a film, I become a character in the film. Sometimes it's the other way round."

On one of the twelve televisions there was a large tree in a misty and otherwise empty landscape.

"Yggdrasil?" I asked.

The picture expanded to fill the twelve televisions. At a gesture from the henchmen I stepped forward. Gravel crunched under our feet. I was grateful for my coat as the air was chilly. The tree was not occupied, but as we drew closer I could see that there were straps in place for the next victim.

"No," I said, and the scene changed.

Another tree, this one occupied. There was thick snow on the ground in this scenario, and the crucified man wore a crown of thorns that was obviously plastic - it made me think of military uniforms done as children's playsets. He wore bright colours, except they were monochrome - I only *knew* they were bright. It made me think of Betany's perception of the Common Land.

The scene changed once more, this time to a land of drizzle, and a tall wooden crucifix. The woman nailed to it was Miss Havers. She was naked except for her glasses. I didn't doubt for a moment that this was real, as real as anything I had experienced in the Common Land. I reached up to her (despite knowing my arms were still handcuffed behind my back - I could feel the steel on my wrists) and touched her leg. It was cold. She had died up here.

There was no taunting commentary from Lamb. He didn't know of our friendship. His selection of this particular victim was the kind of coincidence that happens in dreams.

My rage was building up inside me like a scream, but I had to keep it in check, because only that way would I be able to use it against him. Douglas Lamb had just signed his own death warrant, and I was going to be his executioner. I had the means, and now I had the motive. Very soon I would have the opportunity.

"Thank you," I said quietly, as if in prayer.

"For what?" asked Lamb from his sofa.

"For making it easier."

"Is that some kind of threat?"

"Yes."

I was back in his attic. Over by the hatch, through the forest of steel pillars, I could see that two slithermen had climbed down their cables in the inner ring. They moved jerkily and I could hear them hissing.

Lamb stared at me for some moments, perhaps unsure whether to acknowledge the threat. "I think you've seen enough," he eventually said. "So what was it you were going to tell me?"

I glanced up at the circular ceiling monitor. Still it showed the dome and the water above it. I shuddered, a genuine reaction. "I wish you'd... Never mind. Before I begin, if you would be so good as to indulge me, I need to explain something I learned when I was observing another teacher's science class."

"Go on."

"When we're listening to somebody talk, there's a delay while the brain processes what it hears. It's only a fraction of a second, but it's real enough. Whereas sounds that don't need processing - a door slamming, for instance - these arrive straight away. If, for example, you spoke a sentence, then slammed a desk shut as soon as you finished speaking, your listeners would miss the last part of the sentence, even though the sudden noise occurred afterwards."

"I didn't know that. You live and learn."

"Before I killed William, I confronted him about the incest. He didn't deny it. Why would he? We were in the room where Kirsty was conceived. William told me it was consensual."

Lamb raised an eyebrow but said nothing.

"This took me by surprise. He's a great hulking brute. I mean, he was. I'd always imagined he'd forced himself on Dawn. But it was clear that he thought it was consensual - it never occurred to him I would have thought otherwise. So I asked him, 'You mean Dawn asked for it?' I was being sarcastic, of course. I thought I would get a rise out of him. But what did he say in reply? 'Yes, of course she asked for it. Come on, Philip!' And that's when I shot him.

"But the thing is, that wasn't the last thing he said. Even though I shot him after he said it, the gunshot drowned out the sound of his final words before I could process them. However, I've got quite good at reading lips."

Lamb sounded genuinely interested. "What were his final words?"

"He said..." I glanced up at the dome again. "Look, will you please just switch that off!"

Lamb did not move. I said, "Well if you won't, I will!"

I turned abruptly. I'd visually located the position of the USB memory stick in the bank of televisions; I had only to grab it with a handcuffed hand. I got my fingers around it and pulled. The dome became a flat circular monitor, emitting a dull grey glow.

"Put that back!" Lamb shouted, leaping up off his sofa. His henchmen grabbed my arms. The hissing of the slithermen - now three of them at the hatch - grew more intense. I quailed before his anger.

"Okay, but I'm not going to be able to locate the slot with these on."

"Hand it over right now."

One of the henchmen checked my hands. As he took the memory stick I had been holding and handed it to Lamb, I said, "William's final words were, 'Of course she asked for it. Come on, Philip! You didn't think he raped her, did you?'"

The shock on Lamb's face appeared almost instantly. The man I had killed was not the biological father of my beloved Kirsty. Yes, her conception had been the result of incest, and yes, it had been consensual. But it had been Benjamin, not William. Lamb had painted my second portrait after I had killed the wrong brother.

How much had he invested in this mistaken assumption? Would it prove to be the chink in his armour that would bring him down? I doubted it, but it had shaken him. Perhaps it had shaken him enough that he would fail to realise that the memory stick he was about to put in the slot was not the one I had just taken out.

"You killed Miss Havers," I said.

"What?"

"You crucified my friend."

"Really? Which one was she?" Without waiting for an answer he went on, "Well that was genuinely unfortunate."

Having replaced, as he supposed, the memory stick, he moved away from the bank of televisions and returned to the couch. I glanced up at the ceiling monitor nervously, a nervousness I happily didn't have to conceal. It occurred to me, then, that I could lie after all; I simply had to bury the lie in a similar truth. But what if Laura

Theresa had got it wrong? What if the video file was incompatible with the app, or only partly compatible as the app in that library had been?

Lamb continued, "But that's no excuse for rude..."

The video file *was* fully compatible. Overhead, it was not the headlamp of a motorbike in fog. It was a full moon casting its pale light through a glass dome and into the space below. For a moment Lamb stood, bathed in the recorded glow of moonlight.

Then the Narrow Folk came to finish the job they had begun more than six decades ago.

Epilogue

Chichester, July 2007

In the passenger seat of my Audi, Eloise sang along to her Pussycat Dolls CD until I parked in the Avenue de Chartres car park. She took my hand as we walked towards South Street. She was ten now; I cherished that she still did this, while wondering how long it would last. I said, "I was thinking we could take your mother to the Chinese restaurant, and over lunch you can tell her how well you did at archery club."

"Okay."

We were silent for a while. Then Eloise said, "You miss her, don't you?"

"Of course I do. Incidentally, how did you know I was thinking about her?"

"You held my hand tighter when you said about archery club." After a pause she added, "I sometimes dream of her when I'm sleeping."

Eloise sleeping... Betany and I had agreed that our daughter should have as normal a childhood as possible now that Douglas Lamb was no longer a threat. Even so, it had been a difficult decision. One night we had kept vigil over her, not sure she wasn't faking it, until the early hours of the morning. Then, as the sun was beginning to rise, Betany put on her coat and said, "You take it from here." She kissed me on the eyes, left the house and drove away in her Hyundai. Eloise slept on until eight o'clock; when she awoke she described the experience as "strange but nice".

"Do you know which dreams are memory and which are only dreams?" I asked Eloise.

She just shrugged.

*

We looked in the window of Ebony, the jewellers. A member of staff who was putting a bracelet back on display saw us, recognised us and beckoned us to come in. "Betany is just finishing with a customer, then she's done for the day," she said.

Betany's customer squeezed past us on his way out as we went in. Betany herself was in the back part of the shop. Behind the counter was a facsimile of the shop front, but from an earlier era. This had fascinated me when I had bought Dawn's ring all those years ago; I could imagine vaulting over the counter, going through the door of the facsimile, and entering a version of the shop from maybe forty years ago. This in turn would have a facsimile of a still earlier shop front at the back, and so it would go on.

Small potatoes compared with what I had experienced in the last year and a half.

On seeing us, Betany leaned across the counter, and I kissed her on the cheek. She was putting away a selection of wedding rings. Pointing at one, I said, "I reckon that would look good on you."

"Philip," she said, a gentle warning tone in her voice. With less of an edge she added, "Let's just keep things the way they are, okay?"

"Okay," I agreed. "We were thinking of Confucius for lunch. Are you up for that?"

At the restaurant Eloise told her mother all about her archery skills. After lunch the three of us went to see *Stardust* at the cinema, and afterwards Betany invited me back to her flat for the first time in over a month. "Don't be getting ideas, though," she said to me.

As it turned out, Betany invited me to her bed as soon as Eloise was asleep. She insisted I wear protection, despite the fact that I had had a vasectomy several months before.

"It won't be for long," she said apologetically. "I've got an appointment to get my tubes tied."

"You're certainly not taking any chances, are you?" My tone came out more flippant than intended.

"You wouldn't take chances if you knew what it was like to give birth to the same child twice. I'm never going through that again."

After we'd made love I lay on my back while she lay on her side against me and I stroked her back. We could get drowsy but there was no danger of either of us falling asleep.

I liked being in her flat. Unlike the one in her own world, this one was on the outskirts of Chichester, conveniently placed for a doorway in the side of the public toilets across the market car park. That one had appeared quite recently. The one in the cinema where we'd been that afternoon was still there - it still led to the long corridor - but the one in the McDonalds was gone. Betany had started to fill the walls of her flat with artwork, mostly her own, and mostly portraits. She wasn't in Douglas Lamb's league, but she definitely had talent, and her ability to work with images might prove useful in the future. So far as I knew at that point, nobody had taken over after Lamb's death, but a power vacuum like that wasn't going to remain unfilled for ever.

"I got invited to the end of year party," I said suddenly.

"That's a bit early," said Betany, puzzled. "It's only just July."

"No, at the school where I used to work. Kerry Marshall, of all people, got in touch."

"But you're not going, are you?"

"No."

"You should. You liked the staff. Especially..."

"No," I said again, more vehemently. "I can't face meeting Miss Havers. Not after seeing her... you know."

Betany sucked air through her teeth. "You know she wasn't the same one. Duplicates are rare, but they happen. You're always telling me I should be more rational, that we can't afford not to be in our situation."

"I *know* the crucified one wasn't her. But that's kind of the point. She was just as real as my one. She would have been as funny and as loveable, and as huge a loss to her friends. If I see my one alive again after being so sure she was dead, it's as if the other one didn't count. I'm not making myself clear, am I?"

Betany kissed me, and said, "No, not at all."

We made love twice more, but then Eloise cried out from her room across the landing. I threw on a dressing gown and went to check on her. It was nothing, just a bad dream, but when I returned Betany was already applying spermicidal cream. "You'd better go," she said gently. "This is my weekend with Eloise, after all."

I knew better than to protest, or to point out that Eloise preferred it when her parents were together. I quickly showered and dressed. Before leaving the flat I looked in at my daughter one final time. She was sleeping peacefully once again, and my heart clenched just a little bit.

Weekends were still a novelty to me, after more than a year. No marking to do, no preparation, no writing reports about difficult pupils, no defending myself against malicious allegations, no reams of paperwork for its own sake. Sometimes I took work home out of habit but mostly I enjoyed my leisure hours. I had so many of them.

At 3am I drove over to Singleton and went to visit the graveyard. By the light of the nearly full moon I found the Price family plot. David Price, Dawn's father, who had died before I met her. David's wife Vanessa and their two sons William and Benjamin. Three victims of murder. Michael Russell was doing time for all three although he had only killed Benjamin.

Why had he killed Benjamin? I didn't know for sure. I had tried to avoid following the case too closely, but a picture had emerged nonetheless. Russell had worked with the Price brothers on a job involving drugs or a robbery or possibly both. At some point, Russell had made a pass at Benjamin, and Benjamin had outed him. This would not in itself have given Russell a motive for murder; if my suspicions were correct, the clincher was that Benjamin *hadn't turned him down.* But Benjamin had denied it afterwards, and William had believed him. He hadn't had a problem with Benjamin having sex with their sister, but doing it with a man was beyond the pale.

From my own point of view it was a blessing that Russell had used a Glock. I spared a thought for Dawn. Her daughter was gone for good, and she had lost her mother and both brothers on the same day. I spared a thought for Vanessa, too. Maybe I could have spared a thought for Benjamin while I was at it. But frankly I didn't give a shit.

Last I'd heard, Dawn was still living at the Price Estate, but she'd moved back into the barn conversion. Maybe she'd find the secret door while cleaning the guest room, if it hadn't already gone; maybe she'd piece together the crimes I had committed, or maybe she'd succeed where I had failed and find Kirsty at some earlier point on her timeline. I didn't think it was likely, though.

"Philip Hamilton. I thought I'd find you here." The female voice behind me made me jump out of my skin. I braced myself and turned.

I'd half expected Dawn. The voice had been like hers, and her home was a short walk from the graveyard. Or it might have been a police officer, hoping to hear me beg forgiveness of my victims - which would have made her a pretty incompetent officer, given that she'd announced her presence before I'd had a chance to incriminate myself.

The woman was neither Dawn nor a police officer. In fact it took me a moment to recognise her, given that there was only one of her. She wore jeans and a t-shirt, the early morning air being just about warm enough to allow that. She had a round face and long hair, brown but light enough to be nearly blonde in the moonlight. Her right arm was prosthetic from below the elbow - I could see through the rods and cables - but her hand looked real. Real enough that, had she been wearing long sleeves, I would not have known it was prosthetic at all.

"Laura Theresa," I said.

"Just Laura," she replied.

"So what happened to..."

"It wasn't what you think. I was never a twin. What Lamb did was much weirder than conjoining two people. Perhaps I'll tell you about it some day, but not tonight."

"What about your arm?"

"It's good, isn't it?" She raised it, clenched and unclenched the fist, and wiggled the fingers.

"I got it from the future. I can even read Braille with the fingers, should the need arise. Anyway, I didn't get a chance to thank you for what you did. Given the state I was in, I never allowed myself to hope. Not really. I tried to hum 'Give Me The Moonlight' as a clue but it just came out as retarded noises." She was smiling as she said it but a look of remembered horror appeared fleetingly on her face.

"So all's well in the Common Land and everyone's happy?"

"Not everyone. I ran into Tobias Quinn yesterday and he said if I saw you I was to tell you you still owe him, and he's coming to collect."

"Really," I said. "Should I be worried?"

"I wouldn't lose any sleep over it." It was an old joke but I chuckled politely.

We found a bench and sat, letting the night pass around us. Some of the time we talked; more often we remained in a comfortable silence, listening to the nocturnal sounds around us. She was pleasant, easy-going, entirely unlike her other half now that her ordeal was over. She had a sense of humour, and an infectious, dirty laugh which came easily. We spoke mainly about our families, and our lives before we ever learned about strange doorways.

But we also spoke about the current situation in the Common Land. As it turned out, the power vacuum had already been filled.

"There's a new King of Dreams," Laura told me.

"Worse than Lamb?"

"Not worse, exactly. Different."

"Does the situation affect us directly? I mean, do we have to *do* anything?"

If she'd worn glasses she would have looked over them at me. Like Miss Havers used to. "What do you think?"

I nodded. For over a year I had made only occasional visits to the Common Land, mainly to stave off my need for sleep. Even then I kept to the outskirts, the places close to home, while I concentrated on my new career. It had been a kind of holiday. A good holiday.

"So the holiday's over now?"

"Soon," she said. "When the sun rises. But for now, let's just continue to enjoy the night."

The End

* 9 7 8 1 7 3 9 3 4 9 3 1 8 *
BV - #0127 - 130224 - C0 - 229/152/30 - CC - 9781739349318 - Gloss Lamination